FOR OUR SINS

FOR OUR SINS

James Oswald

WILDFIRE

First published in 2024 by
WILDFIRE
an imprint of HEADLINE PUBLISHING GROUP

1

Cataloguing in Publication Data is available from the British Library

Hardback ISBN 978 1 4722 9883 6
Trade paperback ISBN 978 1 4722 9884 3

Typeset in 12.76/16.24pt Aldine401 BT by Jouve (UK), Milton Keynes

Printed and bound in Great Britain by Clays Ltd, Elcograf S.p.A.

HEADLINE PUBLISHING GROUP
an Hachette UK Company
Carmelite House
50 Victoria Embankment
London EC4Y 0DZ

www.headline.co.uk
www.hachette.co.uk

This one's for the booksellers,
who don't get nearly enough praise.

1

January 8th 1983 – Saturday

He can still feel the heat of the priest's breath on his face, smell the stink of whisky, hear the harshly whispered words echo in his head.

'Stay there and don't make a sound. You know what will happen if you do.'

It's dark here in the closet, warm as he is surrounded by the cassocks so recently removed by the other altar boys. He still wears his. Knows it will be worse for him if he takes it off before he's told to. It will be worse for him whatever he does. The interruption feels like a small blessing. But soon enough the distraction will be done, the special ministrations begin.

God's love, visited through him. That's what Father O'Connell says, and isn't he God's voice? What he says, what he does, can't be wrong. A priest cannot sin. Can he?

Footsteps on the stone floor, and he shrinks back into the closet, wraps the cassocks around himself, breath stopped, eyes squeezed tight. He does not want him to come back, even as he knows it is a sin to refuse God's grace.

A noise of the closet door being yanked open. He can only hold still as a growing warmth spreads from his crotch and down his leg. Fear smells like piss.

An eternity passes as he waits for the hand to reach in and grab him. And then the closet door slams. He trembles with relief as he hears new noises. The clink and thud of silver against silver. Another crash, the familiar sound of the vestry door as it slams shut. And then a silence falls so total he wonders if he has gone deaf. Only his heart, and the soft bubbling of snot from his nose reassure him he has not.

How long does he wait there, unable to move? An hour? Five minutes? He cannot say. And then another sound, low like the sad keening of an injured beast. It rises and falls until he can't know whether it is real or his imagination. He reaches for the door, black in front of him. Father O'Connell had latched it closed, but now it swings open to his touch. Slowly, wincing at the dampness in his trousers, he steps out of the closet.

Across the small vestry, the door to the outside hangs ajar. The censer, chalice and candlesticks are gone from where they had been left for him to polish for Sunday mass. Chairs lie on the floor, hymnals scattered and ripped. The priest is nowhere to be seen.

He should flee, he knows. Run all the way home. But he knows, too, the hell that awaits those who disobey God's will. And who knows God's will better than a priest? Slowly, reluctantly, he walks a squelching path to the other door and the nave beyond.

'Father?'

His voice trembles and squeaks, he knows it will annoy the priest. But there is no answer from the gloom. No light from the dirty, stained-glass windows. Only fat candles on the altar to cast any illumination.

'Father?'

He takes the two stone steps down, passes the pews and into the aisle. A nod of the head, the instinctive sign of the cross as he turns to face the altar. And that's when he sees.

Father O'Connell lies on his front, arms wide as if he's genuflecting. But he is still, so still. No sound of murmured prayer. A step towards the altar, uncertain. Then another, and a third. He cannot see the priest's face, his lank black hair splayed out around his head like a fan. Longer than it should be, it spreads past his shoulders, down the steps to the chancel.

Not hair. Blood.

He crouches by the still form, unsure what to do. There is so much blood. Is the priest dead? Before the thought has faded, a hand reaches out and grabs his wrist. That same hand that has touched him too many times before, administered God's special grace. He tries to pull away, but the grip is too strong, the weight of it heavy as the priest pulls himself slowly around. Bloodshot eyes, crazy and wide with something that looks like fear. Flecks of bloody spittle cover his lips, spot the rough stubble on his chin as the priest croaks in a voice laced with panic and despair and utter, utter terror.

'Help. Me.'

2

She'd seen the church before, too many times to recall. If she thought about it, Detective Sergeant Janie Harrison could probably remember a time when it was still being used, but she'd be hard pushed to say exactly when the windows had been boarded up, and the graffiti had started climbing the old sandstone walls like colourful mould. It was all but impossible to tell how long ago, what with the pandemic losing everyone a couple of years, but a while back the scaffolding had gone up at one end. Not building work, so much as an effort to stop the whole place from falling down. It hadn't worked; a section of roof caving in after the heavy winter snow. And now that spring was on the way, and the weather was improving, someone had finally signed off on a proper demolition.

'Sad when these old buildings are left to rot.'

Beside her in the driving seat, Detective Constable Cass Mitchell guided their pool car slowly under the police cordon tape hastily strung across the road and lifted up for them by a bored uniform. Janie thought she might have recognised him from her old station, before she moved into plain clothes and one of the city's Major Incident Teams, but before she could get a proper look, Mitchell had moved on towards a suitable parking space.

'I guess there's not enough people believe in God these days. All too busy worshipping in the St James Quarter of a Sunday.'

Mitchell glanced across at Janie as she switched off the engine, an expression of mock horror on her face. 'That's a bit cynical for this time of the morning.'

'Well, it's true isn't it, Cass. No congregation means no collection.' Janie climbed out of the car and felt the cool morning air on her face, the slight scent of the Forth on the air all but obliterated by the exhaust fumes spilling over from nearby Ferry Road. She waved a hand at the derelict church. 'Place like this would cost a fortune to heat, and that's even before fuel prices went mental. I'm surprised it's taken them this long to turn it into flats.'

'Not exactly the best part of town for a trendy church conversion though, is it?' Mitchell gestured at the drab grey housing that made up most of the street. They weren't all that far from Trinity, with its large mansion houses and posh boutique shops, but that was the way of it with Edinburgh. A few hundred yards could be the difference between old-moneyed affluence and grinding poverty. 'Place could use a youth centre or some kind of community hub. Guess there's never enough money to go around.'

'Aye, well. Let's go see what all the fuss is about.' Janie scanned the cars already parked, noting the battered forensics van alongside a mud-spattered old Land Rover she recognised. The pathologist was already here, then. And probably Janie's flatmate too.

Half of the street had already been fenced off, a Portakabin and some heavy demolition machinery squeezed into too small a space alongside what must have been the kirk's rear entrance. Had there been a manse here once? If so, Janie could see no sign of it any more among the ranks of council semis.

'Detective Sergeant Harrison?' The uniform officer who'd let them in approached with a weary tread, no doubt at the end of his shift and wondering when his relief would arrive.

'That's me.' Janie almost pulled out her warrant card, but instead nodded towards her colleague. 'DC Mitchell.'

'Aye, Cass'n me go back a-ways.' The young officer grinned for a moment, then stopped himself. 'You'll be wanting to see the body then.'

Janie looked up at the kirk, its roofline jagged where rafters had given way and slates had fallen through. 'It safe in there?'

'All shored up proper, like. Least that's what the building site manager tells us.'

'Where's the CSM? We'd better sign in and grab some overalls before we do anything else.'

The constable directed them to the Portakabin, his step lighter as he moved away from the building and out into the street. It didn't fill Janie with much confidence, and neither did the addition of hard hats to their white paper overalls. Forensics had already laid out a clear path to the body though, which made her hope they'd at least checked out enough of the area.

'You want me to wait outside?' Mitchell asked as they approached the open door. 'Might be a bit crowded in there.'

Janie peered into the gloom, making out a fairly intact space. If there had been pews, they were long gone, and the wooden floorboards looked suspiciously rotten in places.

'Aye, OK. Go speak to the builders or whatever. Find out who found the body and how. Pathologist's already here so the duty doctor must have been and gone. We'll need to know who had access, when it was last checked over before today, what their schedule is, and who actually owns the place.' Janie stopped talking as she could see from Mitchell's face the detective constable already knew all this. Unlike Janie, she hadn't put her hard hat on, and was twirling it nervously between her hands. Not a fan of enclosed spaces, Janie remembered.

'Meet you back at the car when we're done,' Mitchell said, then flicked her gaze upwards to take in the kirk and its perilous roof. 'Be careful in there, aye?'

'Always.' Janie turned away, took a deep breath, and stepped inside.

Across the threshold it was as if she had entered another world. The dull roar of the Ferry Road and the lower rumble of the city were both muted to almost nothing, despite the gaping hole in the roof. Janie stopped for a moment, taking in the whole scene before she had to focus on the particular. As she'd seen from outside, the interior had been stripped bare already. No pews lined up for the faithful to rest their arses upon, no pulpit or lectern for the priest to admonish them from. Even the few memorials that must have adorned the walls had been ripped away, the gaps in the plaster too regular to be collapsed from mould.

Most of the roof looked to be in reasonable condition, with only the altar end rotted and fallen in, and that only on one side. The light flooding through the gap had a grey quality, like used bathwater, illuminating a tumble of broken rafters and cracked slates piled up against the end wall. That was where the support scaffolding had been erected on the outside, and Janie could see the cracks and bowing where the whole altar end threatened to fall down. More light filtered in from the corner, a tumble of collapsed masonry and plaster reaching to a point in front of the altar where a small group of people clustered around something.

She approached the scene with care, sticking to the marked path, both because she didn't want to be shouted at by any of the forensics technicians and because the floor looked like it might collapse at any moment. There might not be anything underneath but hard-packed dirt, of course, but Janie didn't want to chance her luck with there being an extensive and deep crypt of some form. As she neared the group, she began to make out the body, thinking at first that it seemed rather short. At the same time as she realised why it was short, one of the forensic technicians noticed her. Manda Parsons gave her a wicked grin.

'Ah, Janie. You're here. Glad they sent you and not Sandy. She's awfy squeamish when it comes to this sort of thing.'

Janie had last seen Manda only a few hours earlier as they both ate a swift breakfast in the kitchen of the flat they shared across the city, in Bruntsfield. She'd not expected to see her again until late evening when she'd been hoping they might share a bottle of wine and a pizza while desperately trying not to talk shop. But wasn't that supposed to be the joy of the job? That you never knew what each new day would throw at you?

Squeamish, though. It was true that Detective Sergeant Sandy Gregg didn't have the strongest of stomachs. She was the best when it came to organising an investigation, not so good when it got dirty. Or bloody. Janie inched her way into the circle of people, looked down and understood what her flatmate meant.

It was a man's body. She could tell that much from the clothes, the overall build, the heavy scuffed leather boots and most of all the hands. They lay at his sides, clenched into loose fists that showed off the badly-done tattoos across his fingers. His stomach strained against his jacket, and he'd probably complain that his trousers had shrunk in the wash if he weren't dead. And if he had a mouth to speak with.

The best she could tell, he had been lying on the floor in front of the altar when the wall had fallen in from outside. The rubble had engulfed his head and shoulders, crushing them entirely if the pooled blood and flecks of brain matter were any indication. Not much blood though, Janie saw. Chances were he'd been dead beforehand.

'Did nobody check the place was empty before they started?' She looked from person to person, but aside from Manda there was only another forensic technician, the pathologist and his assistant. None of them were likely to know.

'Sorry. Stupid question.' Janie turned her attention to the only man in the group, apart from the deceased. 'What can you tell me, Tom?'

The pathologist crouched down beside the body and shone a hand torch over the more gruesome bits. Tom MacPhail had been taking on a more leading role of late, as Angus Cadwallader eased himself into a long-overdue retirement. Janie missed the old man, but Tom was a good second choice. He knew his job and didn't let himself get too annoyed at her sometimes inane questions.

'Not a lot here, I'm afraid. You can see as well as I can that his head's been stoved in, but the lack of blood suggests he was dead before that happened. Core temperature's close enough to ambient that he must have died late last night or very early this morning. Long before the workmen started at least.'

'Did he die here?'

MacPhail raised a greying eyebrow. 'Strange you should ask that first. Most people want to know what the victim died of. Except Tony, of course. He always wants a time of death even though he knows we can't give anything accurate. I think it's his little joke, you know?'

Janie did. She also noted the pathologist still referred to retired Detective Inspector McLean in the present tense, as if not yet accepting that the man would never grace a crime scene again. She hoped that too, but wasn't going to hold her breath waiting. It had been months since McLean had handed in his resignation, after all.

'But it's a good question all the same.' MacPhail eased himself upright with a minimum of groaning and not a click from either of his knees to be heard. 'If he hadn't been so badly damaged, I'd have been able to say with certainty one way or the other. As it is, the area's too badly contaminated to be sure. We'll have to get him out of here and back to the mortuary before I can give you any more detail. On that or what killed him.'

9

Janie stared down at the corpse, her thoughts branching out in swift possibilities until, with a conscious effort, she reeled them all back in again. 'Do we have any idea who he is?'

'That I can help you with.' Manda Parsons crouched down beside the body and came back up clutching a clear plastic evidence bag. Unlike the pathologist, her knees made a horrible popping noise that echoed in the empty church, and she gave a little grimace of pain.

'This was in his jacket pocket.' She held out the bag to reveal a wallet inside. Old leather, shiny in places, scuffed in others. 'Might not be his, of course. Might be planted to throw you off the scent. But if it is his, then he's Kenneth Morgan. Lives up Granton way. Not far. And by the look of his boots, he's not afraid of walking.'

The name meant nothing to Janie, but it was somewhere to start. She opened her mouth to speak, but was interrupted by an ominous creaking groan. Not from her flatmate this time. By the way all heads turned towards the back wall, it was clear she'd not imagined it either.

'Bodybag. I think we need to get him moved now.' MacPhail spoke to Manda Parsons, but it was the other forensic technician who knelt down and rolled out the black plastic. Janie stepped back to give everyone room to work, letting those that knew what they were doing get on with their jobs as swiftly as they could. As the bag was zipped up, another groan issued from the back wall, followed by a crack like thunder as something important gave way.

10

3

'Everybody out. Now.' Janie backed away towards the door, fully expecting them to leave the body behind. It wasn't like the man was going to get any more dead. To her frustration, MacPhail shoved his case at his assistant and then stooped to pick up the bodybag at one end. He almost dropped it as another thunderous crack boomed in the nave. A beam of dusty light speared through a new split in the altar wall. Everyone else had already scarpered, and he looked up at her with a mixture of fear and confusion on his face.

'Oh for God's sake.' She hurried back, grabbed the other end of the bag. The body was surprisingly light, or was it fear that lent her strength? Janie shook the thought away as together they man-handled their prize along the marked path and out the door, a lot less carefully than when she had entered the building.

As they crossed the threshold, a deep rumble erupted from the rear of the building, like some mythical beast awakening. Over the pathologist's shoulder, Janie saw the wall cave in on itself, the area where the body had been lying mere moments earlier engulfed in a landslide of rocks and plaster dust. The already weak roof collapsed in on top of it, taking out the last of the forensic tech's lights. A blast of air exploded through the doorway, as if someone had thrown a grenade into the kirk. Stumbling down the steps towards the pavement and the road beyond, the two of them lost their footing and fell in a heap along with the body.

'Well, that was a bit bloody stupid.' Janie struggled out from under the mess, her fear escaping from her as anger. The rage died as quickly as it had come when she saw the looks on the faces of everyone else. Wide-eyed, dazed, shocked. She knew how they all felt.

'Anybody hurt?' she asked as she climbed to her feet before helping MacPhail up, too. That nobody answered seemed indication enough, but a quick head count assured her everyone had escaped the collapse with nothing more than bruised egos and scuffed trousers. The forensic technician stared open-mouthed at the doorway, still spilling out fine plaster dust, no doubt mourning the loss of her lights and clear path markers. The site manager, who'd assured them the building was safe enough for now, was nowhere to be seen.

'Right then. I guess we'd better be getting this poor fellow to the mortuary.' MacPhail bent down and gently eased the body-bag into something less crumpled than it had been. His assistant looked from the church to her boss and then to Janie, raised a single eyebrow. She swept off her plastic hard hat and tugged the hood of her paper overalls down to reveal spiky dyed red hair. In the gloom of the church, Janie had thought she was the pathologist's usual assistant, but she didn't recognise this woman at all.

'I don't suppose we'll be needing all this protective clothing any more,' she said in an accent that was unmistakably Welsh. 'Not going to get much in the way of forensics from in there now, are we.'

As if to emphasise her point, another low rumble and clatter of rocks signalled yet further collapse of the building. A single round stone rolled slowly out through the open door and came to a halt right on the edge of the first step.

'Please tell me we at least got some photographs.' Janie pulled her own hard hat off and loosened the neck of her boiler suit as she spoke.

'Not as many as I'd like, but it's better than nothing.' Manda Parsons held up a digital camera that hung from a strap around her neck. 'Shame about the lights, mind you. That's going to come out of someone's budget, and I don't think it should be mine.'

Janie heard the fear in her friend's voice, and the anger. Same as she felt herself. They were all on the edge of shock, which was understandable. She looked around to see where DC Mitchell had got to, saw her standing a good bit further from the unstable building than the rest of them. Halfway across the road, to be precise.

'Perhaps we should all move, aye? Don't much fancy my chances if any more of that wall comes down.'

She stooped to pick up the feet end of the bodybag, but the pathologist's assistant stepped in. 'Here, let me. Not sure it's either of our jobs, really. But needs must, eh?'

'Cheers. I'm Detective Sergeant Harrison by the way. Janie. Don't think we've met before.'

'Cerys. Cerys Powell. And no, we've not. Tom's told me a bit about you, though.'

Janie glanced at the man, but all she could see was the top of his head, a small bald spot beginning to form in the middle of his unruly greying black hair.

She was about to ask what exactly the pathologist had said, but he glanced up then, gaze fixed on his assistant. 'OK, Cerys. Let's get him into the van, shall we. On three. Two three.'

Janie stepped aside as the two of them lifted the bodybag and carried it carefully out to the pavement where a mortuary van waited, wheeled gurney pulled out from its open rear doors. Manda and her assistant were busy putting their remaining equipment into the boxes they'd sensibly left outside. She'd catch up with them later, she decided. Time to see what Cass Mitchell had found out. Maybe track down the site manager and give him a piece of her mind too.

'Glad I didn't go in there with you,' the detective constable said as Janie approached her, jutting her chin out in the direction of the kirk as if there was any doubt as to what she had meant by 'in there'.

'Aye. Don't know how everyone else is feeling, but I nearly shat myself.' Janie held up one hand, unsurprised to see it still shaking slightly. Maybe not a good time to chew off the site manager's ear after all. 'Think I need a sit down and a coffee.'

'Sweet tea's meant to be better for shock,' Mitchell said without a hint of irony.

'I'm no . . .' Janie started to protest, then stopped herself. 'Aye, you're probably right enough.'

'There's a kettle in the Portakabin there. Sure they'll have tea-bags on a building site.'

Janie followed Mitchell's gaze in the direction of the site office. The glass of its single window reflected too much of the sky to see anything inside, but she couldn't help thinking it was closer to the decidedly unsafe building than she wanted to get right now. Judging by the way all of the uniform officers had retreated to their squad cars across the road, they didn't want to be too near the kirk either. She found herself unable to blame them, and in much of the same mind.

'Let's see if we can't find a nice, safe cafe nearby. Something that's not likely to collapse on us when we're no' looking. Then you can tell me what you found out while I was almost crushed to death.'

They ended up in the corner of a rather weary-looking self-service cafe in the nearby supermarket. Despite Mitchell's advice, Janie went for a large latte, dispensed from a machine that whirred and hummed but didn't seem to make any grinding noises. In deference to her colleague, she poured rather more sachets of sugar into it than were healthy, then regretted it when she tasted the result.

'According to the site manager, the place was locked up tight last night. No sign of forced entry when he arrived at six this morning.' Mitchell sipped at her paper cup of suspiciously green fizzy pop and made a face.

'Six? Seems a bit early, doesn't it?'

'He wouldn't have been there at all if someone hadn't called in about the wall collapsing.' Mitchell pulled out her notebook and flipped pages until she found what she was looking for. 'Irene Canter. Lives up the road a bit. Works nights. Apparently, she heard a ruckus about half four and went to see what it was all about. There's a number on the side of the Portakabin for the contractors, so she gave it a call.'

'We got her details? Probably ought to have a wee chat to confirm it all.'

Mitchell nodded, flipped another page. 'Bernie. That's the site manager. He came over soon as he heard. They've monitors on the walls to detect movement apparently. Something to do with how they plan on demolishing it safely. But they're all on the back, not the corner where it caved in. He was a bit evasive about that, but I think it's just professional embarrassment, you know? He was checking the sensors when he spotted the body. Called it in straight away.'

Janie took another sip of her coffee. It wasn't so bad once your tastebuds had been battered into submission by the sweetness, and she needed the caffeine to sharpen up her brain after the shock.

'Did he go in?'

Mitchell shook her head. 'Said he wanted to do a full visual check on the outside before declaring it safe enough. By the time he'd done that our lot had turned up.'

'And he was sure it was safe for us to go in?'

'That's what he said. Showed me the computer readout and everything. You going to lodge a complaint?'

'No, no. That's not it. I know builders. One of my brothers works in the trade. I know what folk say about cutting corners and all, but they really don't when safety's at stake. It's just no' worth the risk.'

'Well, he got it wrong this time, didn't he.' Mitchell spoke as if it had been her nearly crushed by a collapsing church wall. Janie gripped both sides of her mug, suppressed the shudder that ran through her at the memory. Had they really been in danger? They'd moved out swiftly enough after the first crack. Well, apart from bloody Tom MacPhail. In the end, nobody had been hurt, and chances were they'd not need much in the way of forensics from the scene anyway. Probably the old man had wandered in for one last look at his local kirk before it was demolished, had a heart attack and . . .

'How do you suppose he got in there?' The thought that had been niggling away at the back of her mind worked its way through the jumble that Janie knew was delayed shock. 'I mean, the place was locked, wasn't it? All the windows were boarded up too.'

'I asked him that.' Mitchell took another sip of her drink, did another grimace. 'He said the only ways in were the door you all used and the big doors at the front. Main doors were locked, but the side door wasn't.'

'Someone forgot to check when they left last night?'

'Seems likely. I've asked for a list of everyone working there, in case we need to talk to them all. D'you think that'll be necessary, though? We don't even know if the death's suspicious.'

Janie took another sip of oversweet coffee, the taste of powdered milk made even worse by too much sugar. Why had she come here rather than heading straight back to the station? Even the canteen coffee was better than this.

'You're right, Cass. We're overthinking this. There's no point worrying about anything until Tom's given us a cause of death. We've a name and address for the old boy. Might as well stop by on the way back to the station, see if there's anyone home. Speak to the neighbours if not.'

Mitchell raised a razor thin eyebrow, her smooth-shaved dark skin wrinkling over the top of her head. 'You have a name?'

'Did I not say?' Without thinking, Janie reached into her coat pocket and pulled out the evidence bag with the contents of the dead man's pockets still inside. Her hand had known it was there, even though she had only a vague memory of scooping it up off the ground before she'd grabbed the bodybag and helped Tom MacPhail to haul it out of the collapsing kirk. Technically, it should have been logged. It was a serious breach of protocol to take evidence away without telling the crime scene manager. 'Shit. I knew I was shaken up. Didn't think it was that bad. Ah well. I'll have a word. Make sure it's sorted.'

'So who is he then?' Mitchell asked, clearly less concerned about chain of evidence.

'Kenneth Morgan, apparently.' Janie eased the wallet out of the bag and opened it up. Inside were a couple of twenty pound notes, some old receipts and a pair of bank cards. Shoved in a side pocket, a photo ID driver's licence showed a gruff-looking man, jowly where the fat of middle age had melted away and left the skin behind. There was no way to tell if this was the man they had found, since his head had been crushed by falling masonry. Nevertheless, it was a fair assumption.

'Lives up on the Granton Road. One of the old tenements, by the look of the address.' Janie slipped the licence back where it had come from and returned the wallet to the evidence bag. She looked at her latte, still only half drunk. Decided she didn't need any more caffeine, certainly no more sugar. 'Shall we go have a look?'

4

As suspected, the address was one of a short row of stone tenements at the eastern end of Lower Granton Road. A line of three-storey buildings in dirty sandstone, their windows grimed with salt spray from the Firth of Forth. Janie didn't know the area well, but the view across the water to Fife must have been spectacular on a good day. Whether that was enough to make up for the rain and wind she had no idea. Both were making life miserable by the time they arrived. Heavy squalls fizzed the choppy water before spattering against the road, the cars and then the stonework.

'Always wondered what it would be like to live out this way,' Mitchell said as she guided the pool car into a space somewhat further away from the door they wanted than Janie would have liked.

'Wet.'

'Aye, I get that, now.'

They waited for a gap in the showers, as a break in the clouds let sunlight briefly turn the scene into glittering diamonds. Janie hadn't thought it that cold at the kirk, but here on the very edge of the firth the wind cut them like a knife as they hurried along the narrow pavement to the tenement door. An ancient electronic entry phone system suggested six flats, although none of the names read Morgan. Janie was reaching for one at random when Mitchell pushed the door with her foot, neither of them particularly sur-prised to see it swing open.

Inside, a narrow passage led to the back of the tenement and a stone stair poorly illuminated by grubby windows at the upper landings. Doors for the ground-floor flats led off to either side. The address in Morgan's wallet had been 2Fl, top floor, although which side of the building that meant was anyone's guess. As Janie was lifting her foot to the first stone step, the door to one of the ground-floor flats opened a crack, and an eye stared out at them. In the gloom of the unlit passageway, at first she thought it was a child, but as her vision adjusted so Janie saw the eye belonged to an elderly woman perhaps no more than four feet tall.

'Who're youse?' The voice cracked with suspicion and fear.

'Sorry to disturb you, ma'am.' Janie pulled out her warrant card and held it up, aware that it would be all but impossible to see in the semi-darkness. 'I'm Detective Sergeant Harrison. This is my colleague Detective Constable Mitchell. We're looking for a Mr Kenneth Morgan?'

'He's no' here.'

'Do you know him, Ms . . .?' Janie left an opening for the woman to introduce herself, which was ignored.

'Went oot last night. Never came back.'

Well, at least they were at the right address.

'Do you know him well?'

'Youse sure you're polis?' A pause, and Janie saw the old woman's gaze flick past her to where Mitchell stood. 'Youse don't look like polis.'

Janie heard Mitchell's weary sigh, knowing she probably suf-fered this kind of thoughtless racism every day. She took a step closer to the door, held out her card. 'That's my ID, ma'am. I'm a detective with Police Scotland, as is my colleague here. We're investigating an incident at St Andrew's church. Do you know if he might have gone there last night?'

19

'St Andrew's? Auld Kenny?' The woman's laugh sounded like the waking cough of a forty a day smoker. For a moment Janie thought she might actually be having a fit, but then she stopped as suddenly as she had begun. 'Aye, right enough. He's away to mass every Sunday. But no' St Andrew's. That's the wrong team, ken? An' anyway it's all boarded up, is it no?'

'So you do know Mr Morgan, then. Have you known him long?'

The door closed on Janie's question, and she wondered if she'd said something wrong. A rattle of the chain being unhitched assured her otherwise. A bare bulb clicked on, low-wattage and yellow through the fanlight. Then the door swung open again. Any thought she might have had about being invited in for a wee chat and maybe a cup of tea died in the instant Janie saw the tiny woman fully. She might have been small, but she somehow managed to fill the entrance all the same. The arms crossed tightly over her chest only served to emphasise the lack of welcome. A quick glance into the dim and slightly musty hall behind her convinced Janie this was no great loss.

'Mr Morgan, you've known him long?' she asked again.

'No' well, y'ken. He's lived here, what? Must be ten year now, easy. My Jack helped him move his stuff up there, an' he passed six years back now.'

'And you said he went out last night. Mr Morgan, that is. Do you know what time that might have been?'

'Would have been half ten, mebbe? Eleven o'clock.'

'You saw him?'

A scowl flitted across the old woman's face at Janie's question, her whole body tensing for a moment. 'Naw, heard him go, didn't I? He was muttering something. Couldnae make oot what. Did that a lot, mind. Talkin' tae hisself.'

Janie stifled the sigh she wanted to let out. Nothing was ever easy. Sometimes people fell over themselves to be helpful, giving way too much information and clouding the picture she needed to paint of what had happened. Other times you got tiny old women who were both nosey and suspicious to their core. This one would need a proper interview, and Janie really didn't look forward to doing that. For now, she'd got as much as she could expect. And there was always the hope that this would turn out to be an accidental but unsuspicious death requiring no further investigation. Aye, chance would be a fine thing.

She shoved a hand in her coat pocket, felt the plastic evidence bag in there alongside the bundle of business cards she kept for occasions such as these.

'Well, thank you for your help, Mrs . . .' She presented a card to the old woman. 'I'm sorry, I never did catch your name.'

'Forbes.' The old woman took the card but didn't look at it.

'Thank you, Mrs Forbes. That's got my contact details on it. Give us a call if you remember anything else about Mr Morgan.'

Mrs Forbes glared at Janie in a manner that reminded the detective sergeant of her maternal grandmother. They'd likely be of an age, the two of them. Different as chalk and cheese though. With a shrug and a smile, she turned to walk away.

'He's deid, in't he?' the old woman said.

'We don't know that yet. But it's possible, yes.'

'Bloody typical. Bugger owes me money.'

Janie couldn't stop herself from smiling at that. The idea that a man might seek death rather than repay this woman a debt. 'Does he have any family? Is there anyone else living in his flat?'

'Naw. Just him. Crabbit auld bastard. You'll be wanting in to have a nosey I take it?' Mrs Forbes leaned to one side, stretching for something Janie could probably have picked up without reaching. When she stood up straight again, she clutched a single key in her small hand.

Rain spattered against the skylight as they reached the top of the stairs and the narrow landing that separated the doors to the two flats. It had taken all of Janie's considerable powers of persuasion to stop Mrs Forbes from coming with them, the old woman only reluctantly handing over the spare key her tenement neighbour had entrusted her with once she'd had time to thoroughly inspect the detective sergeant's warrant card. It helped that Mitchell had backed away down the front passage and out of sight. One less thing for the tiny woman to be suspicious about.

'Left or right?' the detective constable asked. Neither door had any kind of name plate, although one of them had a polished brass bell pull beside it. The space in the ornate door frame where the other one would have been had been crudely infilled with a square block of wood and painted over in heavy gloss.

'Left.' Janie pointed at the bad repair. 'Least that's what Mrs Forbes said. Sorry you had to put up with her, by the way.'

Mitchell shrugged as if dealing with that kind of attitude was just part of the job. 'I've had worse. Football matches were always fun. One of the reasons I moved to Specialist Crime.'

'Still not nice though. I'll get Jessica to come with me next time. Or maybe Jay.'

'You think we'll need to talk to her again?'

'Maybe. Let's see what the post mortem says. I'm getting a nasty feeling in my gut about all this though.'

Mitchell raised an eyebrow but said nothing more. Janie knocked on the door, listened for movement inside. After a few moments of silence, she slipped the key into the lock and turned. It was a little stiff, but gave with a bit of effort, and the door swung open onto a small hallway.

'Hello? Mr Morgan? Anyone home?'

Again, Janie waited for a response, even though she was certain none would be coming. More rain rattled on the window briefly, she heard the rumble of a lorry in the road outside, and then the silence descended once more.

'Guess we go and have a look, then.'

The first thing she noticed as she stepped over the threshold was the smell. Janie was once again reminded of her grandmother and the tiny little council flat she had lived in until they'd finally persuaded her to move into a care home. A strange mixture of medicated soap, dust and mildew that said 'old person' to her before her eyes had managed to take in much. To one side of the door, a narrow table held a phone and a small bowl with a few sweets, an old biro and a couple of keys in it. Above, hanging from the wall, was a wooden cross, complete with dying thorn-crowned Jesus. Well, Mrs Forbes had said St Andrew's was the wrong team, which meant Morgan had to be Catholic, and reasonably devout about it, too.

'Are we looking for anything in particular?' Mitchell stood in the doorway, hesitant.

'Not really. Maybe confirmation he's the man we found in the kirk. Might be a photograph or something.' Janie recalled the body, the crude tattoos on its hands. 'It's going to be tricky without a face to match. See if we can't find an address book or something. We'll have to track down a next of kin, if it is him.'

Mitchell nodded, squeezed past and on through to the living room. Janie took a deep breath and pushed open what she assumed was Kenneth Morgan's bedroom door.

The smell of old person intensified; a mixture of mothballs and Brylcreem, talcum powder and something slightly rotten she couldn't immediately identify. Nor particularly wanted to. The curtains were closed, leaving the room in gloom, but enough light filtered around the edges and through the thin material to reveal a queen size bed, neatly made. A cheap flat-pack wardrobe stood in one far corner, chest of drawers in the other. There was only one bedside table, which had been obscured by the open door until Janie stepped inside. An old-fashioned alarm clock with bell and hammer on top ticked far too loudly to make sleeping easy. Beside the clock, a pair of reading glasses had been neatly folded on top of an old paperback book. A small lamp and empty glass were the only other items.

Picking up the glass, Janie held it to her nose and caught a scent not of water but whisky. The book had come from the local library, judging by the label stuck to its spine. A much-borrowed copy of *The Wasp Factory* by Iain Banks. She flicked through the pages until she reached the bookmark, which turned out to be a folded printout from the chemist, detailing a list of prescription medicines that made her raise an eyebrow. Kenneth Morgan was certainly getting his money's worth from NHS Scotland, but if that was his body in the kirk, he wasn't going to find out how the story ended. A shame, really. Janie had enjoyed the book herself.

A quick glance at the walls revealed no photographs, only a couple of cheap prints in cheaper frames that might well have been in the flat when Morgan moved in and another wooden cross, although this one was unoccupied. Janie opened the wardrobe to reveal an unremarkable selection of jackets, trousers and shirts, all neatly pressed and hung. Beneath them, a couple of pairs of well-polished brogues lined up with a more scuffed pair of walking boots. They looked to be the same size as the ones on the corpse, and were the same brand. She'd need to get that checked. Probably.

The chest of drawers held no more surprises than the wardrobe; this was a place an old man lived on his own. Or had lived. In the left-hand top drawer, nestling among folded handkerchiefs, Janie found a small leather box filled with a random assortment of cufflinks, tie pins and a few rings. Nothing struck her as particularly valuable or even remarkable. Instinct told her that this was almost certainly the home of the man they had found dead not a mile from here, which only left the question of what he had been doing in the old church in the first place.

'You find anything interesting?' Mitchell asked from the doorway. Janie shrugged, shook her head and pushed the drawer closed. Fixed to the wall above the unit, a tarnished mirror reflected back at her. Beneath it, strands of greying hair tangled around the heads of a pair of brushes.

'Pretty sure he's our man. Might have to confirm it with DNA, though.' Janie rummaged in her pocket for an evidence bag, turned it inside out and then wrapped it around one of the brushes. If she was wrong, and Kenny Morgan had merely gone away for a couple of days, she'd apologise and give it back.

5

Janie let Mitchell drive again. It seemed only right, since the detective constable was a good head taller than her and much longer in the leg. Resetting the seat and mirrors would have been far too much effort, although it might have wasted a little time. The rain squalls from earlier had merged into something lighter but more persistent, and the quiet swish-squeak of the windscreen wipers dragged at her thoughts as she tried to concentrate. The morning hadn't started well, but at least it had been dry.

'You want to swing past the church on the way, aye?' Janie stared at the line of traffic ahead, two buses holding everyone up as they competed with each other in the world's slowest race.

'Sure,' Mitchell said. 'Anything in particular you wanted to see there?'

Janie shrugged, for all that Mitchell wouldn't be able to see her do it, concentrating as she was on the road. 'Not sure, really. Just thought there might have been something I'd forgotten. Not noticed in all the excitement, you know?'

'So it wouldn't be anything to do with trying to avoid the station for as long as possible then.'

'Am I that obvious?'

Janie didn't turn to face Mitchell, but through the corner of her

26

eye she could see the detective constable waggle her head in a manner that suggested she probably was.

'This morning, right? Soon as this call came in you were off. Grab the nearest constable and go. You could have just sent me and Jessica. No real need for a sergeant to do all this legwork.'

'I know. An' it's not like I don't trust you all to do a good job. It's just . . .' Janie let the reason hang in the air. Either because she didn't really know what it was, or didn't want to admit that she did. Truth was, the dynamic in the station had changed over the past few months, and not just because DI McLean had left so abruptly.

She'd hoped he would come back, turn his resignation into extended leave due to injuries. When Chief Superintendent Elmwood had taken early retirement, Janie had been sure McLean would relent. But now the chief super had been gone over a month, and he was still holed up in his mansion house.

'You know if you keep mooning after him, the whole station will keep on believing the two of you were having an affair.'

Mitchell's words brought Janie's thoughts to a shuddering halt. The laugh that escaped her sounded perhaps a little too hysterical in the confines of the pool car.

'God's sake. There's nothing like a copper for idle gossip is there. You know I—'

'I know it's nonsense. Everyone who knows you knows it's nonsense. Doesn't stop folk from talking nonsense though.'

Mitchell indicated, checked her mirror, pulled in to the side of the road. For a moment Janie thought she was going to get a serious talking to, but then she realised they'd arrived back at the church. In their absence, two scaffold trucks had arrived, one loaded with tall metal security fencing.

'It's not To—DI McLean anyway. Sure, I'd like to see him back. Reckon most of us would. I'd far rather that than we get some new DI parachuted in from God knows where.'

Mitchell undid her seat belt, but didn't move to open her door.

Given the rain, it was probably a wise move. She said nothing for a while, then slowly nodded her head. 'Ah. I see. Detective Superintendent Nelson. Aye, that makes sense.'

'Is it just me he's got a problem with?' Janie was glad she didn't have to say who, embarrassed that it seemed everyone else already knew. Mitchell nodded her head again, once, then turned to face her.

'It's not that he's got a problem with you, Janie. Quite the opposite.'

'I . . . What?'

'Please tell me you'd figured that out. Smart cookie like you. I'd have thought it was obvious. But then again, I'm not the one he's picking on all the time.'

Janie felt her ears warm, knew that a blush was creeping up her neck and over her cheeks. Not in embarrassment now so much as outrage. If she was being honest with herself, she had known from his first approach that their newly arrived detective superintendent had taken more than a professional interest in her. What she couldn't understand was why.

'But he's, what? Forty-five or something? And not exactly god's gift, if you know what I mean.'

It was Mitchell's turn to laugh, a joyful bark of a thing that was a little too loud to be polite. 'You're not wrong there. Maybe when he was thirty? The DCI says he was quite the ladies' man when she knew him back in her Aberdeen days. Still. Eww. No thanks.'

Janie stared out the windscreen as a gang of men in fluorescent jackets and waterproof trousers hauled scaffold posts and security gates off the trucks and began the job of making the church both safe from falling down and near enough impossible to enter. There was no good reason to be here at all, she simply didn't want to have to talk to her boss. And the longer she left it, the greater the chance he'd be away to some strategy meeting or another. But how childish was that? Not the behaviour of a seasoned detective sergeant.

'OK, Cass. Point taken. Let's just get it over with then.'

The Edinburgh Major Investigation Team office – or CID room, as Inspector McLean had always insisted on calling it – was on the second floor of the station, close to the back stairs. Janie had sent Mitchell down to the canteen in search of a half-decent cup of coffee for them both, hoping she would find some of the other detective constables and set them to finding out about Kenneth Morgan before anyone more senior noticed she was back. No such luck.

'Ah, Janie. There you are. Little birdy tells me there was some trouble at the kirk.'

Detective Superintendent Peter Nelson half sat on the edge of one of the empty desks. He'd been talking to Detective Constable Lofty Blane, but looked up as soon as he saw the door open. A man of averages, he was average height, average build, his face . . . average. The only thing about him above the median line was his ego, as far as Janie could tell. He'd arrived a few weeks ago, transferred down from Aberdeen to fill the space left by Jayne McIntyre, who had finally risen to the rank of chief superintendent when Gail Elmwood had retired due to ill health. Or been forced to retire depending on which of the station's gossips you listened to. While Janie was pleased for McIntyre, she had serious reservations about her replacement.

'There was a wee bit of a collapse, sir, aye. But we saw the body in situ and got it out before the wall caved in. Doctor MacPhail will let me know when he's ready to do the PM.'

'That must have been terrifying.' Nelson pushed himself upright and crossed the room to where Janie stood. Before she could move, he had grabbed both her arms around the bicep. Not hard, but an oddly possessive gesture and as inappropriate as it was unwelcome. 'You're sure you're OK? Do you need some time off to settle your nerves?'

Janie shrugged his grip away as best she could, ignoring the patronising tone in the detective superintendent's voice. The carefully constructed look of concern on his face momentarily darkened towards anger, but he managed to control himself.

'I'm fine, sir. Just need to run the name and address we got from the dead man's wallet.' She almost put her hand in her pocket to fetch it out, but managed to stop herself. Nelson didn't need to know about her lapse in protocol.

'You should really be delegating that kind of work to the detective constables, you know, Janie.' The patronising tone was back again, and the man stood far too close for comfort. Did he do that with the other detectives? Or was it just her?

'That's exactly what I came in here to do, sir.' She looked past him towards Lofty, whose expression was a mixture of fear and sympathy.

'Excellent.' The detective superintendent patted her on the arm this time, which was better than being grabbed, but still one touch too many. Utterly oblivious both to her boundaries and discomfort, he checked his watch, grimaced. 'Got to run. I've a meeting over at HQ. Get this all squared away, and we can go over it at the evening briefing, OK?'

Before Janie could answer, Nelson had given her another gentle pat on the arm and fled the room. She found she could forgive him the first because of the second, but she was more unsettled by the brief encounter than she had been when an entire church wall had almost crushed her to death. DC Mitchell's words in the car afterwards still echoed in her mind, bringing with them an involuntary shudder.

'I ran the name already. You're going to want to see this.' DC Blane's gentle voice was a welcome relief. Janie navigated a path through the many empty desks until she could look over his shoulder at the screen he'd been working from. He spoke the words out loud, even though she could read them fine herself.

'Kenneth John Morgan. Born fifth March, 1952, so he's seventy-one years old. Was, I should say. Grew up in Broxburn. That's your old stomping ground, isn't it?' Lofty scrolled down a detailed list of records. 'Seems he was in and out of social care until he turned sixteen and graduated to adult crime. Reckon he's spent more of his life behind bars than out.'

Janie scanned the list of records. No need to dig deep into the details, the sheer volume spoke of a life of crime. That would explain the poor-quality tattoos on his hands. Prison tatts. 'When did he get out from his last stretch?'

DC Blane scrolled down to the very bottom of the page, clicked the highlighted link. 'Ten years ago. Released early for good behaviour, two years into a five-year sentence for hamesucken. Not often you see that on a charge sheet, right enough. Seems he turned over a new leaf in the end. Either that or he was getting too old for it.'

Janie peered over the big detective's shoulder, scanning the few details entered into the system. She could pull out the full records if she wanted, but it was probably unnecessary. At the top of the screen, a set of mugshots leered out at her. A younger man than the driver's licence image, and leaner than the body they had found, but then they'd been taken twelve years ago, when she'd have still been in school.

'This is a complication we could really do without.' She put her hand into her pocket and pulled out the wallet in its evidence bag. If the body was Morgan, and Morgan had a lot of form, then his death moved a notch or two up the suspicious list. No longer just an old man wandering into a derelict church and having a heart attack.

'You want me to pull together a list of known associates?'

'Please. Let's hope we don't need it, but better to be prepared.'

Janie reached past Lofty and guided the mouse so that she could scroll to the bottom of the page, unsure why she wanted to know until she saw the name of the arresting officer. Detective Sergeant Anthony McLean.

'Well, there's a thing. Think I might have to give the old boss a call.'

6

March 6th 1982 – Saturday

C hoir practice today. First time with the new priest. Didn't know what to expect, but he's OK, I guess. He looks scary, but he didn't shout at us like Father McCormack used to. Said I had an angel's voice and made me practise the descant while he tutored Callum in the vestry. Not sure what they did, but Cal was very quiet walking home. When I asked him what it was, he just said it was God's special secret.

Mum bought me 2000AD and two Commandos I've not read yet. Brilliant. Just need to get maths homework done and I can read them. Judge Dredd is the best.

7

Despite all the building work that had gone on around it for several years, the brutal concrete monolith that was the John Lewis department store had remained largely unchanged since its construction, even more so in the cafe on its top floor. Tall windows gave a view out over Leith Walk and the rooftops of the northern half of Edinburgh, to the Firth of Forth beyond. Or at least they would if it hadn't been raining quite hard now. Even so, it was a pleasant enough spot for a cup of coffee and a slice of cake. And it was neutral ground where retired Detective Inspector Tony McLean could meet up with his old nemesis, the reporter Jo Dalgliesh.

Time was he'd have crossed the street to avoid her, gone out of his way to make her life difficult, but that was then, and this was now. She had been underhand, bribing junior officers for information, blackmailing them if necessary. She'd written a book many years ago that said unforgivable things about his long-dead fiancée. At least, he'd considered them unforgivable at the time, and for years afterwards. But now he struggled even to remember what they were. Same as sometimes he struggled to remember Kirsty Summers' face, seeing instead Emma's as she crumpled to the library floor. And at the end of the day, the reporter had saved his life from a homicidal maniac one time, and been a useful source of information on occasion. McLean had few close friends, but these days, he and Dalgliesh had enough history to get halfway there.

Which was perhaps why they'd started meeting up on a semi-regular basis. No longer police, he didn't have to worry so much about letting slip confidential information. And the fact that she now used him as a sounding board for some of her trickier investigative stories gave his mind the mental exercise it otherwise lacked. That was perhaps the biggest downside of his having walked from the job, the lack of intellectual stimulus. Looking after Emma as she recovered from her stroke was at times physically demanding, and it brought its own kind of satisfaction when he was able to help, but it didn't exactly stretch the mind.

Coffee and cake on a tray, McLean looked around the busy cafe to see if he could spot the reporter. Sometimes he arrived first, sometimes she'd been there for hours, her chosen table a mess of empty cups and strewn papers. This time he almost missed her and went to find a table of his own. Not because she wasn't easily recognisable, but because she wasn't alone. Sitting opposite her – a more refined and elegant form to Dalgliesh's scruffy hair and lined face – was retired Detective Chief Superintendent Grace Ramsay. She looked up at him with what might have been a glint of mischief in her eye.

'Grace. This is a surprise. You're looking well.'

'I am well, Tony. Good to see you too. I'd say retirement suits you, but . . .' Ramsay cocked her head to one side, taking in the reporter and the cafe with the most minimal of gestures.

McLean placed his tray on the table. Dalgliesh had her laptop open, but snapped it closed before he could see what was on it, shoved it in her bag and grabbed the plate of cake.

'Was beginning to think you'd stood me up,' she said.

'Bus got held up on the Lothian Road.' McLean shrugged off his coat, then settled himself into his seat and wrapped cold hands around the mug.

'Bus?' Dalgliesh tilted her head like a confused puppy. 'Thought you liked tootling around in that wee electric car of yours.'

'It's Em's actually. And parking's a pain round here.'

'Aye, you're not wrong. Guess they want us to take trams everywhere. Got to pay for it all some way or another. How is she? Emma, I mean?'

'Getting better bit by bit. It's slow going, and she gets frustrated she still can't walk properly. And sometimes her speech is a little slurred. If she's tired. But all things considered . . .' McLean paused to take a sip of coffee, turned his attention back to Ramsay as Dalgliesh shovelled cake into her face.

'Should I have bought two slices?' he asked.

'It's OK. I'm on a diet. Sharing an office with Dagwood and Grumpy Bob isn't good for the figure, you know. The number of biscuits those two consume in the average day.'

A half-forgotten conversation filtered through McLean's mind. 'Of course. You're consulting with the Cold Case Unit. All those missing women.'

'That, and a few other cases from my time at Lothian and Borders.' Ramsay nodded towards Dalgliesh. 'Hence this meeting. Although Jo's being a bit coy. Said it would be worth my while coming here, but not much more.'

'Was waiting for Tony to get here so's I didn't have to say it twice.' The reporter spoke through a mouthful of cake, then wiped a smear of it across her cheek with a paper napkin before carrying on. 'Have you heard the name Robert Murphy?'

McLean hadn't, and hoped that his silence was answer enough.

Beside him, Ramsay shifted in her chair as if she'd been prodded with a stick. 'Robert Murphy? Now there's a name I've not heard in a very long time. The wee lad whose parents tried to sue the Catholic Church for covering up the abuse he suffered as an altar boy back in the early eighties, that Robert Murphy?'

Dalgliesh grinned wide, her teeth stained with chocolate. 'The same. I knew it was worth giving you a call.'

'What of him?' Ramsay asked. 'I thought he ended up in a loony bin. After the case fell to pieces. But that was, what? Forty years ago?'

'Aye. Eighty-three when it all kicked off. And you're right, shrinks said paranoid schizophrenia with dissociative identity disorder, probably brought on by the abuse he suffered and the way it ended. He was in secure care for the best part of thirty years, but some new drug treatment sorted him out, apparently. He's doing OK now, and he's wanting to tell the world his story. Part of his therapy, I guess. Asked me if I'd help.'

'And what do you want from us, exactly?' McLean was fairly sure he knew already, but he wanted to hear Dalgliesh say it all the same.

'Well, there's a few things he's mentioned that might throw light on some cold cases.'

'Such as?'

'Oh, you're no fun, Tony. Can I no' just tempt you with hints?' McLean shook his head.

'Fine. Murphy says the priest who abused him was Father Eric O'Connell. Remember him?'

That name did ring a bell, but again it was Ramsay who had the case at her fingertips. Not bad for a woman in her eighties.

'St Aloysius Church.' She waved a hand at the window. 'Over Craiglockhart way, I think? Burglar broke in and stole the church silver, if memory serves. O'Connell disturbed him, ended up with his head bashed in. Never recovered from his injuries. Wasn't my case though. Don't think they ever found out who did it.'

'No, they never did.' Dalgliesh took a swig of coffee and swilled it around her mouth, swallowing it down before letting out a belch that momentarily silenced the chatter in the busy cafe. 'But Murphy says he was there when it happened.'

★ ★ ★

37

The rain had eased off by the time McLean bid Ramsay and Dalgliesh farewell, so instead of waiting at the bus stop he carried on walking. The crowds at the end of Princes Street did their best to get in his way, and road works on North Bridge meant more jostling than he was used to. The going only became easier once he turned off South Bridge and onto Chambers Street, resisting the urge to turn the other way and walk to the police station where he no longer worked.

How were they getting on there without him? Just fine, he was sure, although he knew they'd not yet managed to find a new DI for the team. That was a post that should have been filled swiftly, really. Cheaper than finding a new super, for sure, and there were plenty of detective sergeants in Edinburgh who would have been fine for the position. Harrison could have applied, although it would probably have been more politic to give the post to Sandy Gregg. Except that McLean recalled the struggles she'd had with her sergeant's exams, so perhaps she was happy where she was. Either way, it would have made sense to shuffle the whole team upwards and steal some of the more promising young constables for plain clothes duties.

But it wasn't his problem, even if he suspected that he *was* the problem. He'd taken enough calls from Jayne McIntyre, Kirsty Ritchie, and even one awkward conversation with an unwell-sounding Gail Elmwood a week before she left, all suggesting he might want to change his mind. Maybe consider turning his resignation into a leave of absence. A year's sabbatical, perhaps. Nine months even. Six. He'd turned them all down, of course. Emma's needs had to come first, and while he might miss the intellectual challenge of police work, the politics and paperwork held no appeal.

The rain came back on as he was strolling across the Meadows. Surprised that he'd managed to walk so far without realising it, McLean turned up the collar on his coat and hunched himself in against the chill. Spring was on the way but it was taking its own sweet time coming, every short warm spell followed by a blast of arctic cold.

Something niggled in the back of his mind as he approached Melville Drive and stopped at the crossing to Bruntsfield Links. It took him a while to realise that the tree at the end of Jawbone Walk had been felled. Looking up got him a faceful of sleety rain and a clear view of the sky. No Wych Elm spearing bare branch fingers into the sky, no naked body mysteriously caught at the very top.

That had been Janie Harrison's first case in plain clothes, hadn't it? She'd come with him when he'd gone to interview the wee kid who'd sworn blind he'd seen a dragon flying overhead. It hadn't been that many years ago, really. She'd come a long way since then, grown into an excellent detective. But maybe she needed a little longer before stepping into his shoes. Or maybe he wasn't quite yet ready to shuck them off completely.

Shaking the thought away, he hurried across the road and on up towards Bruntsfield. With luck he might find a taxi there or in Morningside. If not, he could find a cafe and wait for one. Or more likely carry on walking until he got home, soaked to the skin and freezing. All his career, McLean had preferred to walk wherever he could. His brief time on the beat had introduced him to the habit, before the fast track had seen him transfer to Lothian and Borders CID, as it had been back then. The rhythm of his feet on the pavement helped settle his mind, let him concentrate on whatever puzzle was bothering him at the time. And yet now there was no puzzle, or at least not one that was his to solve. He'd speak to this man, Murphy. He'd agreed that much with Dalgliesh. But any information would be for Ramsay and the CCU to deal with, not him.

A gentle vibration in his coat pocket coincided with an unfamiliar ring tone. McLean almost ignored it, not someone he needed to speak to with any great urgency. If it was important, they'd leave a message, and he could deal with it once he got home. Something about the electronic trill tugged at him, though, and he fished out the phone. The number wasn't one in his contact list, although neither was it hidden.

Rain dotted the screen. Without thinking he wiped it away, accepting the call in the process. Oh, well. It wasn't as if he was busy.

He lifted the handset to his ear. 'Hello?'

A slight pause, and then a gruff voice asked 'McLean? Detective Inspector McLean?'

'Who is this?'

'Aye. Where's my manners, eh? Should have introduced myself first. Name's Seagram. Archie Seagram. Reckon youse may have heard of me?'

McLean pulled the phone from his ear and stared at the screen again, as if there were answers to be found on it. All he saw was the number, and a ticking timer to show how long one of the city's most notorious crime bosses was being left waiting for an answer. He put the phone back to his ear.

'I don't know how you got this number, Mr Seagram, but it's a private phone. And no, I'm not Detective Inspector McLean any more. It's just Mr McLean.'

'Aye, I heard that too. Still, once a copper always a copper, right?'

The accusation mirrored McLean's earlier thoughts so closely he was momentarily lost for words. He'd stopped walking, and now looked around as if expecting to see someone watching him, reading his mind and reporting it back.

'What is it you want?' he asked rather more brusquely than he'd intended. But then again, he owed this man nothing. Not even his time.

'Friend of mine died yesterday. You may have heard. Kenny Morgan.'

McLean had heard, a brief conversation with Janie Harrison to let him know the man he'd put away over a decade earlier and who'd apparently lived a sin-free life ever since had been found dead in a disused church. Possibly suspicious, but probably not. Was it worth lying? He considered it, but his chance to just hang up and ignore the man had already passed. Anything he did now would be seen as a reaction.

'St Andrew's Church, off the Ferry Road. What of it?'

'So you do keep up with your old friends? Good.'

'I'm in no position to discuss the matter, Mr Seagram. And even if I was, I wouldn't do so. I'm not sure this conversation can really go anywhere.'

'No, I've heard that about you, McLean. Straight as a die they say. And you've a bob or two, so probably couldn't be bought. Don't worry, I'd not insult you by making an offer like that. I was reaching out for a different reason.'

'Go on.'

'I spoke to Kenny just the other day. We'd usually meet up for a drink every couple of weeks, but I'd not seen him in a month, so I gave him a call. He didn't want to speak to me at first. I could tell he was unhappy about something.' Seagram paused for a while, almost long enough for McLean to check whether the call had been cut off. 'I'd say he was scared, but Kenny doesn't do scared. Didn't do scared, I should say. Scaring other folk, aye. But nothin' bothered him.'

'Someone threatening him?'

'Someone, maybe. Or some thing.' Seagram separated the two words quite deliberately. 'Last thing he said to me was "it's gonnae kill me, Arch. It's gonnae kill me an' I'm going tae hell." Those were his exact words.'

'Mr Seagram, if you think your friend was murdered, you should take that to the police. I can't do anything with this information, even if I wanted to.'

'Aye, I thought you'd say that. No reason why you'd lift a finger to help the likes of me, and don't worry, I'd no' expect it. Time was I had contacts I could tap. But they're mostly all retired now. Or deid.'

'So why the call, then?' McLean started walking again as the rain grew heavier. He'd have been in a nice warm dry cafe by now if not for this man.

'Like I said, the polis won't listen to the likes of me. Probably wouldn't even make a note of the conversation. Way I hear it, you're no' like the others though. So I'm telling you what I know, and if anything happens . . . well, maybe you'll persuade someone to look into it.'

'I think you're mistaking me for someone who cares, Mr Seagram. Please don't call me again.' McLean took the phone from his ear, tapped the screen to end the call. He considered blocking the number, but the rain made it hard to see, harder still to do anything. Slipping the phone away, he hunched his shoulders, rued his lack of hat as he hurried towards Bruntsfield and shelter.

'Look at you, Tony. You're soaked.'

Emma sat in her wheelchair, elbows planted firmly on the kitchen table and a mug of tea held between both hands. Not for the warmth, McLean knew, but because she struggled to hold it up with only one. That she was in her wheelchair suggested today wasn't going well for her. Sometimes she didn't need it at all.

'Thought walking home was a good idea. Seems I was wrong.'

He had already peeled off his coat and hung it to drip on the hard floor of the utility room. It had kept him mostly dry, but not so much below his knees. He'd need a change of trousers at the very least, and his shoes would want some newspaper crumpled up into them, a few hours on the back of the Aga and a good bit of polish. First though, he needed to find a towel for his drenched hair.

Emma smiled, a little lopsided, and carefully put down her mug. 'Admitting your error? Who are you, and what have you done with Tony McLean?'

He smiled at the joke, pulled the hand towel from the rail at the front of the Aga and used it to dry himself at least a little.

'Ah, there he is.' Emma took up her mug again, then put it down heavily when it slipped in her failing grip. McLean hurried over, mopped up the spilt tea with the towel and received an angry look for his pains.

'Bad day?' he asked.

'Just tired.' Emma held up her hands, one seemingly normal, the other half clenched and claw-like. 'And weak. And pissed off.'

There were many things he could say, McLean knew. He could tell her how much her speech had improved, how well she was doing with Madame Rose and their therapy sessions. He could give her all manner of encouragement. And he would in due course. But he sensed that right now Emma needed to rail against the world, and if that meant him getting shouted at then so be it.

'Pissed off's good. You need energy to be angry. Strength.' He went to the Aga once more and hefted the kettle. There wasn't much water in it; Emma couldn't easily lift that much weight. He'd bought a small electric one that should have been easier, but she never used it.

'Easy for you to say, Mr walks wherever he pleases. I'm stuck here in this chair, this room, this fucking house.' Emma banged her hands against the table, and even that was a weak effort. McLean put the kettle back down, three steps to cross the room and then he knelt and did his best to hug her. Awkward, with the chair and the table. She thumped his back with toddler's fists and then burst into tears. He held her until the sobs began to subside, until she unwrapped her arms from around him and pushed him away. Except that she hadn't put the brakes on her wheelchair, so it was her who moved rather than him.

'You smell like wet dog.' She sniffed, wiped her nose on the back of her hand like a teenager. McLean twisted his arm up to his nose and had to agree she had a point. Tweed suits were all good and well, but they gave off a distinctive aroma when damp, even more so when warm and damp.

'I'll go and change.' He made towards the open door through to the front of the house, but she reached her clawed hand to stop him.'

'It's OK. Have some tea first. Tell me what was so interesting you couldn't remember to come in from the rain for it.'

McLean stared at her for a moment. Was he so obvious? Or had she simply known him so long now that she could read him as well as he thought he could read her?

He filled the kettle and slid it onto the hotplate, set about rinsing the pot and filling it with fresh tea leaves.

'I met up with Jo Dalgliesh, you know that much.' He'd not tried to hide their meetings, quite the opposite. 'She's working on a story from way back. Early eighties, long before my time. Wants me to help her talk to someone who might be an overlooked witness. It's intriguing, but she's got Grace Ramsay helping too, so I'm not sure I'm really needed.'

Emma raised a weak eyebrow at the name. 'Intriguing enough for you to get soaked thinking about it.'

'No, that was something else. I had a call while I was walking back here.' The kettle had reached the boil and McLean took a moment to fill the pot before explaining about Archibald Seagram and his strange request. Emma's face went from dark to angry as he spoke.

'Why can't they leave you alone? You retired months ago.'

'And I fully intend staying that way, Em. If he calls again, I'll make a formal complaint. No idea how he got my number in the first place.' Although McLean wasn't all that surprised. He knew enough about Archibald Seagram to understand that getting hold

44

of the private phone number of a senior police officer, serving or retired, would not have been much of a stretch. He fetched milk from the fridge, poured himself a mug of tea. When he offered to top up Emma's, she waved the pot away.

'You're intrigued by it all though, aren't you? I can tell. And not just by the way you walked all the way home in the rain.'

McLean pulled out a chair and sat down. He took a sip of his tea and felt the hot liquid begin to warm him almost instantly. For a while he studied the milky surface, his hands, the tabletop. Anything except look at Emma. Finally he faced her, and saw that weary, patient look in her eyes.

'It's a puzzle, for sure. And you know me and puzzles.' He reached out and laid a hand on Emma's, felt the warmth in it and wondered how cold he must be. 'But I'm not going back, Em. I made you a promise, and I aim to keep it.'

8

'Subject is male, Caucasian, approximately sixty-five to seventy years of age. Height estimated at one metre fifty-five centimetres, weight approximately seventy-five kilos. A touch overweight, but not morbidly obese.'

Janie had never been a big fan of the city mortuary, and did her best to avoid attending post mortems whenever possible. Not like Inspector McLean who seemed almost to live in the place sometimes. But then his grandmother had been senior pathologist for a while, so quite likely he had spent more time amongst the dead than was healthy. It would go a long way towards explaining how he turned out the way he did. Or was that being unfair?

'Subject has suffered crushing damage to the head due to falling masonry. Lack of blood at the scene suggests that this happened post mortem, and was not a factor in the subject's death. Little remains of the face, skull or brain matter, which may make cause of death difficult to ascertain with any certainty. It is not possible to ascertain whether damage had occurred to the subject's face or head prior to his discovery.'

She stood a fair distance from the examination table, hidden in the shadows cast by the bright overhead lights that turned the body of Kenneth John Morgan as white as his ghost. At that remove, the smell wasn't too overpowering either, although she still held thumb and forefinger to her nose.

'Pooling of blood within the body would indicate that the subject died lying, or was laid on, his back very shortly after death. There is nothing to indicate that he was moved post mortem, so a reasonable assumption would be that he died where he was found.'

Tom MacPhail had a different style to his post mortem examinations when compared to Angus Cadwallader. The old pathologist had been a touch more flamboyant, and would often try to drag Janie closer into the procedure as if he were a lecturer and she some poor medical student, rather than pathologist and detective. Cadwallader's assistant – and rather more than that if the rumours were to be believed – Doctor Sharp, was a quiet, competent presence at those examinations, never needing to be told what to do, always one step ahead of the man she had worked with for so long. MacPhail's assistant, Cerys, was a little more hesitant, no doubt still learning the ropes. Janie didn't know anything about her, except that with that name and accent she must have come from Wales.

'No sign externally that the subject has been attacked or put up a defence. Extensive tattoos to hands and arms, but they are all old.'

Janie dragged her attention back to the examination as MacPhail inspected one of the dead man's hands. Photographs of the prison tats could be used to help with the identification, although if this really was Morgan then his DNA was already on the system for a match.

'Externally there's nothing to suggest an obvious cause of death, although as I've already noted, the post-mortem damage to the head makes blunt force trauma impossible to rule out. Scalpel please, Cerys. Let's see if there's any knowledge to be gleaned from his insides.'

Janie wasn't particularly squeamish. A few years of working on the beat and now in plain clothes had burned that out of her. Even so, she found the floor and the scuff marks on the toes of her shoes very interesting for a while. MacPhail was swift and precise as he opened up the cadaver and removed various organs for inspection. Cerys seemed to get into the swing of things quickly, too.

'Liver is enlarged and shows signs of cirrhosis. Something of a drinker, I think.'

Janie recalled the glass on the bedside table, the scent of whisky. 'Fair to say he enjoyed a wee dram. If he is who we think he is.'

'Perhaps a bit more than a dram, but then given his age something or other was going to start failing. Yes, lungs look like someone who's smoked a lot until recently. Ah, now, that's interesting.'

Janie risked a glance up from the floor, just in time to see MacPhail reach a hand into the opened chest. For a moment she thought he was going to bring something out and show it to her, but instead he turned his attention to his assistant. 'Can you get a close up of that please, Cerys? Before I disturb the arteries.'

The whole examination was being recorded on video, but now the pathologist's assistant picked up a handheld camera and pointed it where directed. On the screen behind the examination table, an enlarged image of the dead man's innards appeared, surprisingly dull. Janie found that wasn't as unsettling as seeing the real thing, although she wasn't sure what she was looking at.

'See that, Cerys?' MacPhail's finger appeared on the screen, latex glove flecked with dark blood as he pointed at a mess of tubes and squidge. 'Looks like his heart gave out.'

'That was the cause of death?' Janie asked.

MacPhail raised his bloody hand, waggling it to show uncertainty. 'Probably. As to what caused it to give out like that, suddenly and catastrophically? No way to tell. Might just have been his time.'

'So nothing obviously suspicious beyond where he was when it happened.'

'With the caveat of his head being all smashed up? I'd say that's a fair assumption. He was old, not particularly fit, had a bit of a drink habit, used to smoke. Chances are he was going to keel over sooner rather than later.' MacPhail peeled off his latex gloves and headed to the sink. 'You can sew him back up again now, Cerys. Thanks.'

Janie skirted around the examination table to where the pathologist stood washing his hands.

'I've asked for the DNA to be fast tracked so we can positively ID him,' he said. 'Other than that, I don't think there's any need for more detailed tests. I'll get the report all typed up and over to you this afternoon. Well, Cerys will. Credit where it's due.'

Janie glanced back at the assistant, dutifully replacing the dead man's organs in readiness to stitch him back up again. She must have felt her gaze, as she looked up, smiled and winked.

'Guess I'd better get back to work, then. Thanks, Tom. I'll see myself out.'

Janie knew as soon as she buzzed herself in through the back door of the station that something was up. Was it a feeling in the air? A sensation of dread in the pit of her stomach? Or was it the way the few uniform officers mooching around the corridor to the locker rooms all looked at her as if they knew something she didn't?

She checked her phone as she climbed the stairs to the second floor, but there were no messages. Neither a summons, nor a warning to stay away.

The CID room door had been propped open, and a gentle chatter was escaping into the corridor as she approached. Inside, Janie found Detective Constables Stringer, Blane, Mitchell and Bryant all clustered around one of the desks. She didn't have time to hear what they were chatting about, idle gossip or important case details. As soon as they saw her, they fell silent.

'What am I? Teacher or something?' She tried to inject a little levity into the situation, but the looks on their faces weren't encouraging.

'We were just debating whether or not to text.' Jay Stringer had been elected spokesman for the group, it appeared. 'Boss wants to see you soon as you're in.'

Janie cast a reflexive glance over her shoulder. 'Kirsty? I thought she was over at Gartcosh today.'

'Not the DCI. The boss-boss.' Stringer almost winced as he spoke. 'Nelson. He's in his office.'

'Oh. Did he say what it was about?'

From the look on their faces, it would seem that the detective superintendent had indeed said what it was about, probably at great length. The fact that she'd not been there to intervene and shield the junior detectives from something clearly not their fault was probably what Nelson was angry about in the first place. Logic didn't seem to be his strong suit.

'I'll go see him now.' Janie turned to leave, then stopped. 'Is Jayne McIntyre in this morning?'

'Gone with the DCI to Gartcosh.' Stringer gave her a rueful smile. 'Think that might be what set him off.'

It made sense, Janie supposed, as she climbed up to the third floor. Nelson was Kirsty Ritchie's superior, and by rights should have been more involved with the NCA liaison work. But Ritchie had been doing it for a couple of years now. She'd built up a good relationship with the feds; one that had paid off many times. Nelson was untried, hardly known outside Aberdeen. Janie paused outside the door to DI McLean's now empty office. They'd find someone to take his place soon, she hoped. They had to, surely? And meantime she was left to pick up the slack. She should ask for a raise.

The thought put a smile on her face, which was unfortunate as Detective Superintendent Nelson picked that exact moment to step out of his office. Janie tried to adopt a suitably sombre expression, but she could see by Nelson's scowl that she'd not been quick enough.

'Ah. There you are, Harrison. And about bloody time.'

'Sir?'

'My office, Detective Sergeant. Now.'

Janie did as she was told, slipping past Nelson as he stood in the doorway. Unlike McLean, he closed the door firmly behind her, stalked around his desk and sat down. She stood on the other side, not quite at attention, and waited. The detective superintendent said nothing for a while, probably in an attempt to make her even more uneasy than she already was. Finally, he glanced at his watch with an unnecessary flick of his wrist.

'You seem to have a very casual attitude to core working hours. Day shift starts at eight. Where have you been?'

Janie had taken the precaution of hiding her hands behind her back, which meant that she could flex them into fists without her accuser noticing.

'I was in at seven, sir. I spent an hour checking the rosters and going through the overtime sheets for the DCs and admin staff. We had a team meeting at half eight, and then I got a call from the mortuary about the post mortem examination on Kenneth Morgan.'

Nelson stared at her as if this was some kind of competition. Janie fought the urge to look away, not for the first time seeing how bland his features were. Grey had begun to win the battle with his dark hair, and he'd cut it short to try and hide that. It hadn't worked, only made the patches where it was thinning to nothing more apparent. His nose was too small, his eyes set slightly too closely together. It gave him a look of permanent mild confusion. When he wasn't scowling in anger.

'Morgan? Oh yes. Your heart attack victim in the church. Was that such a suspicious death it required the presence of a detective sergeant to witness proceedings?' The detective superintendent left a short pause after his question, but Janie wasn't stupid enough to try and answer.

'At best you should have sent a constable. Even that would have been a questionable use of valuable resources. We're short enough staffed as it is without you gallivanting off all over the city on a whim.'

All the while, Nelson had been staring straight at her, but now he broke eye contact. A report folder lay on the desk in front of him. He snatched it up, flipped it open and placed it back down again. Janie risked a glance, but from her vantage point she couldn't really see what it said.

'I understand you called Detective Inspector McLean yesterday regarding this man Morgan. You do realise McLean's retired, don't you? And in questionable circumstances. Way I hear it if he hadn't jumped he'd have been frogmarched out.'

Janie opened her mouth, then closed it again. She clenched her fists tight, released them, clenched again. Luckily for her, Nelson was still staring at his report form, but whatever answers he was looking for they clearly weren't there. He flicked it shut so violently it slid across the desk and almost toppled off onto the floor.

'I also hear that you took evidence from the crime scene without properly logging it first.' He locked his gaze on her again, an expression of malicious and triumphant glee on it as if she had been caught in a lie and his own brilliance had unmasked her.

'It's true,' Janie admitted. Now that she knew exactly what Nelson was angry about, she could deal with it. 'When the church wall started to collapse, we all grabbed what we could and made a swift exit. I had the dead man's wallet in my hand, but the pathologist was trying to move the body. I shoved the wallet in my pocket and helped him. Everything happened so quickly it wasn't until later I remembered the wallet. As you're no doubt aware, I logged it as soon as I could. As it happens, I don't think it matters this time since Tom – the pathologist – reckons Morgan died of a heart attack. There's a question as to what he was doing in the church in the first place, but the site manager admitted the back door hadn't been properly secured. Beyond that, I don't think his death warrants much further investigation.'

Nelson narrowed his eyes at her, pursed his lips. Janie tried to keep her expression as bland and unthreatening as possible, counting down the seconds until the man either exploded or deflated.

'Too bloody right it doesn't. There's a mountain of casework needs reviewing, personal appraisals for all the DCs are weeks overdue. I've cut you some slack because I know how short-staffed we are here. But newsflash, Janie. Everyone's short staffed. We were short staffed in Aberdeen, Tayside's running just to stand still. Don't get me started on Fife. Seems the only folk with decent staffing and budgets these days are the NCA, and even then, they spend half their time stealing our people.'

So that was the problem; the root of Detective Superintendent Nelson's general surliness and bad temper. Janie hadn't heard much about his transfer down to Edinburgh, and she didn't have any useful contacts in Aberdeen to ask. DCI Ritchie would have though. What was the gambling Nelson had been trying to get a transfer to the National Crime Agency for a while now and this posting was a poor second best? She wasn't one for betting, but Janie would still have put good odds on it.

'I will try to manage our resources better, sir.' She offered the olive branch even though what she really wanted to do was shout back at him just how unreasonable he was being. Picking on her in particular – here, alone in his office – was borderline at best. If she mentioned it to the union rep there'd be hell to pay. There really should have been at least one other senior officer present, after all. If this was a proper disciplinary.

As if he'd read her thoughts, Nelson sank back into his chair, gaze darting to the door with a nervous flick of the eyes. 'Good. Be sure you do. We need to work smarter here if we're going to cope.

No cutting corners, and no wandering off pursuing hunches that won't play out. Understand?'

Janie nodded once, then added, 'Is that all, sir?' in her most innocent voice.

'For now, yes.' Nelson waved her away with one hand. 'But I want the report into your man Morgan's death on my desk by shift end. Let's get this all wrapped up and move on, eh?'

9

McLean had mixed feelings about the new St James Quarter, especially the hotel that formed its central core. He was not alone in thinking the copper-clad walnut whip of a roof looked like the unfortunate mess left behind by some enormous metal dog. It didn't help that the upturned spike of it – the last squeeze, as it were – could be seen from almost anywhere in the New Town. Turn a corner and there it was, waiting for a monstrous hand wrapped in an inside out plastic bag to pluck it up and then hang the lot on a nearby fence for someone else to deal with.

No, he was not a fan. But this was where Jo Dalgliesh had told him they were going to meet the man who, forty years ago, had been an altar boy in the church in which Father Eric O'Connell had been murdered. Robert Murphy had insisted he wanted to speak to a detective as well as the reporter, and they had all decided that Grace Ramsay looked too much like someone's grandmother to pass muster. McLean still wasn't entirely sure why he'd agreed to go along with the meeting, but the alternatives had been working in a cold, muddy garden or sitting in the kitchen while Emma and Madame Rose talked about him.

So here he was under the giant metal dog turd.

'Ah, there you are Tony. Was beginning to think you weren't coming.' Dalgliesh appeared from nowhere as McLean entered the busy hotel reception area. Before he even had time to take off his coat, she guided him away to a small space to one side artfully strewn with comfortable chairs. He'd read somewhere the top floor was mostly given over to food and drink, with presumably some spectacular views of the city, the Forth and even Fife beyond, in better weather. All the same, he was glad that he didn't have to venture so deep into the belly of the beast.

'Detective Inspector McLean, this is Robert Murphy.'

They had reached a small table with three high-backed chairs arranged around it. Two were empty, although one had Dalgliesh's infamous leather coat draped over its arm. A man sat in the third, although McLean's first thought was that he didn't so much sit in as was contained by the chair. Robert Murphy was a small man who nevertheless managed to make himself look smaller still. Dressed in drab beige and brown, he wore a fleece jacket over a T-shirt, cargo pants with bulging pockets. His unkempt hair might once have been brown, but was now streaked mostly grey. It was his eyes though that caught McLean's attention. Constantly moving, scanning the room for any possible threat. Scared. Paranoid. They only came to a halt – and even then, only momentarily – when he held out his hand. Fixing on that rather than McLean's face.

'Pleased to meet you, Mr Murphy.'

Hearing his name spoken out loud sent a shudder through the man. He stood up swiftly, not adding much to his height in the process, then stared at McLean's outstretched hand as if it were a gun, or a poisonous snake. Slowly, as if only now remembering how to function in a social situation, his gaze lifted until he took in McLean's face, flinched.

'You . . . you're police?' were his first words.

'Sort of.' McLean retrieved his unshaken hand, waggled it in the air to express the complex nature of the situation.

'Sort of?' Murphy's voice parroted his own, but an octave higher now in surprise. He turned to Dalgliesh, who had been watching everything with the faintest of smiles on her weathered old face. 'You said I'd meet the police. Not the "sort of" police. What is this?'

'Calm down, Murph. Tony's police. And he's one of the good guys, trust me. It's just, he sort of resigned about six months ago and hasn't made up his mind to go back again yet.'

The small man stared at Dalgliesh with an expression on his face McLean couldn't quite read. Was it anger? Hate? Or perhaps he was just a little constipated.

'Shall we all sit down?' McLean gestured to two of the seats and then took the third. Dalgliesh dropped into hers with all the grace of a sack of potatoes. Murphy stood for a few moments longer before taking his own seat, no doubt realising how much more attention he drew standing.

An uncomfortable silence settled over them for a while. McLean was about to speak, when Murphy's gaze flicked from him to a point directly behind his head. Turning, he saw a young man in the livery of the hotel, some kind of smartphone or tablet clutched in one hand.

'Good morning, gentlemen.' He spotted Dalgliesh and with commendable swiftness added 'Lady' with a small nod of the head in her direction. 'Can I get you anything to drink? To eat?'

McLean glanced around, saw no menu of any kind. Across their short table, Murphy looked like he was having a panic attack.

'A coffee for me, please,' McLean said. 'Cappuccino, and maybe a small slice of cake if you've got it.'

'Aye, same for me, ta.' Dalgliesh chipped in. 'How's about you, Murph? It's Tony's shout.'

The man's eyes widened at hearing his name spoken so publicly, and for a moment McLean thought he might run screaming from the room. With a visible effort, he began to pull himself together, clasping one hand with the other to stop them from shaking.

'A beer. Lager. Peroni. Please.' He looked at McLean rather than the waiter, as if asking for permission.

'Two cappuccinos, two slices of cake, a Peroni. Anything else?' The waiter paused for a microsecond before accepting that there wouldn't be. A moment later he had turned and left without any indication as to how long they might have to wait for his return. McLean followed his progress away from them by the shift of Murphy's gaze.

'So, Mr Murphy,' he said once the man had regained some small measure of composure. 'I know a little of your story, although I'll admit it all happened long before I joined the force. Why don't you go over it in a bit more detail for me.'

With hindsight, they probably should have arranged to meet somewhere a touch less busy, although at least the hubbub and chatter meant there was little chance of being overheard. Murphy – Murph to his friends, of whom McLean suspected he had precious few – loosened up the more he talked. The beer helped, when it arrived. Not so much because of the alcohol, but that it gave him something to do with his hands.

'I was eight when he started,' he said after the waiter had brought everything and satisfied himself that they didn't need anything more just now. 'I'm fifty, now, and I can still remember every single detail.'

'"He" would be Father O'Connell, I take it?' McLean said into the pause that Murphy left. A nervous nod confirmed it.

'I wasn't the only one he . . . did stuff to, right? There were others. Ask around. I don't know what happened to them, but there was Ali Daniels, George Watson, Callum Gilhooly.' Murphy started counting off on his fingers as he recited the names, as if it was a mantra he had created to protect himself from the bogeyman.

'It's OK, Murph. I've got a note of them all. We'll talk to them right enough.' Dalgliesh reached out and gently touched his arm.

McLean couldn't decide whether the gesture was genuine or calculated. Knowing the reporter, it was likely a bit of both.

'I know this must be difficult to talk about, Mr Murphy,' he said. 'You don't need to go into any detail about the abuse. I'm not doubting it happened, not at all. But you were there that night, right? When he was attacked and left for dead?'

Murphy visibly shuddered. A little beer slopped over the side of his glass and onto his shaking hands. 'Aye, I was there. We'd had choir practice that evening. I didn't want to go, but my folks insisted. It was always the same, every week. He'd pick on one of us, make like we weren't singing in tune or find something else. We all knew what was going on. He'd make whoever it was stay behind after for some "special practice".' Murphy raised his hands and bracketed the words with his fingers, like rabbit ears.

'And he picked on you that night?'

'Aye, he did. An' I hated the others for leaving me there, you know? They all knew what was going on. It'd happened to them too. If we'd just all stood together, maybe we'd have been able to stop him, but . . .' Murphy fell silent again, his gaze focused on past injustices. McLean had considerable sympathy for him. From his own experience not so much of abuse as abandonment at too young an age. The damage done in those early years left scars that lasted a lifetime.

'Tell me what happened that night?' he asked after a suitable pause. 'Not what the priest did to you, but when he was interrupted.'

Murphy's eyes took a long time to regain their focus, his gaze rising from his lap until he finally looked straight at McLean.

'We were in the vestry, right? Off to the side of the altar. Father O'Connell always left the door slightly open just in case . . . I don't know, really? Maybe my folks might come by to pick me up and discover what he was doing? But they never did. I always walked there and back. We all did then. I'd say the world was a safer place, but . . . no.' He shook his head slowly again.

'Anyways. He'd hardly got started, so I guess whoever came in I should thank them. We both heard the noise, they weren't being subtle or anything. Father O'Connell shoved me into a wee cupboard where all the cassocks and stuff are stored, latched it shut wi' me inside. Guess he didn't want anyone to know he had me there all alone.'

'Did you tell the police about this?' McLean asked. 'At the time, I mean?'

'Aye, I did. No' that they were all that interested in anything I had to say.'

'I'm sorry about that. They should have been. So why don't you tell me now? If you can bear to go over it again.'

Murphy gave McLean an oddly quizzical look, his head tilted slightly to one side like a confused puppy. There was a lot of the confused puppy about the man, despite his being fifty years old. He sipped at his beer, considered for a moment before ever-so-slightly nodding his head.

'Aye, well. Like I said. I was locked in the wee closet most of the time, so all I could do was listen. At first Father O'Connell was angry. He shouted, I don't know, "Get out of God's House" or something like that.' Murphy's raised voice as he mimicked the priest momentarily silenced the buzz of conversation all around them, and he shrank into the high-backed chair as if he'd been slapped.

'It's OK, Murph. No one's going to get you here.' Dalgliesh reached out to the man again, but didn't touch him.

For a moment, McLean thought they might have lost Murphy, but he leaned forward again after a few long seconds. 'They was arguing about something, but I couldn't make it all out, you know? And Father O'Connell, he just kept going on about it being God's house and whoever it was shouldn't steal from Him. I got the impression he maybe owed them money? But I'm no' sure. I was just tryin' to keep quiet in case anyone found me.'

'Can you remember what time this was?' McLean asked. 'Evening, I presume . . . but was it late?'

'No' that late.' Murphy shook his head. 'Half seven. Maybe eight. You think there might have been folk about, but it was winter, January. Dark before I even got to the church, ken?'

McLean nodded his understanding, but said no more, leaving the space for Murphy to go on.

'There was this weird noise, ken? Like someone was clapping? Only different. It was only when I heard Father O'Connell scream that I worked it out. They was giving him a beating. An' then it all went silent for a moment an' I knew somethin' had gone wrong. Heard that voice mutter under his breath. I couldnae hear what. Then someone came into the vestry.'

'Wait. They came into the room where the priest had left you?'

'Aye. I was still shut up in the closet. No' sure why they didn't see me, but it's just as well they didn't. Sounded like they was searching the place, only throwing stuff around, right? I knew any minute I'd be found. But then there was a clattering, see? They'd found the candlesticks and the communion silver, I guess. Nabbed that an' then they left.'

Exhausted by the tale, Murphy's shoulders slumped. He let out a long breath, then took up his glass and swallowed down a third.

'How did you get out?' Dalgliesh asked.

'I must've waited half an hour, mebbe? Listening out for any sounds. But it was quiet as the grave. An' when I went to rattle the door it just popped open. The vestry was a mess from where they'd shoved everything on the floor to get at the silver. An' when I went out to the altar, well, there he was.'

'Father O'Connell?' McLean prompted.

'Aye, he was lying on his side. One arm stretched out like he was trying to reach Christ, ken? And there was blood all about his head. I thought he was deid. Didnae want to go anywhere near him. But then he like, groaned. Only it was this weird animal sound. I went to him then, saw the side of his head was this big bloody mess, and there was blood on the edge of the altar too. He must have fallen, smacked himself. Or been pushed, ken?'

'So you called an ambulance?'

Murphy didn't answer straight away, and McLean could see it as clearly as if he'd been there himself. The young, abused boy seeing his abuser lying there. Not dead, but probably dying. The urge to help warring with the desire to see the priest gone, the abuse over. How easy it would have been to just walk away and leave him there.

'Aye, I did.' Murphy's head drooped as he said the words, as if it was something he'd regretted doing ever since. 'Should've just left him to die, the evil paedo bastard.'

'That seems a little harsh,' McLean said, before adding, 'if understandable,' before Murphy could get too defensive about it. 'After all, he never recovered from the head wound, did he?'

Murphy fixed him with an odd expression then. The puppy still confused, but angry now too. 'That's what they told me. What youse lot all said. He died, aye? An' there was a funeral an' everything. So's they could cover up what he'd done.'

It was McLean's turn to be baffled, as much by Murphy's words as his sudden change in demeanour. 'What do you mean? He did die. Never regained consciousness. That's one of the main reasons why nobody was ever charged for his murder. Far as we knew there were no witnesses.'

'I was a witness. And nobody listened to me when I told them what he'd done.' Murphy's eyes shone with barely held back tears and he thumped at his chest with one weak hand as he spoke. 'And if he died, then how come I saw him on the street just a few weeks ago?'

10

'You got a minute, Janie?'

DS Harrison looked up from her desk, momentarily confused by an unfamiliar voice. Detective Chief Inspector Jo Dexter stood half in, half out of the CID room, leaning her spare frame against the doorway.

'Of course. Anything in particular you needed?' Janie made to stand up, but the DCI waved her to stay put and walked across the room to join her.

'The body in the church. They confirmed it was Kenny Morgan, right?'

'Aye. DNA came through. Positive match with the criminal records database. We'd pretty much confirmed it from his tattoos before then, but you know how the PF likes things neat and tidy.'

Without really thinking, Janie had grabbed the computer mouse and brought up the relevant screen, her report for the Procurator Fiscal into the unexpected death of one Kenneth John Morgan.

'Has his body been released then?'

'Think so.' Janie clicked through multiple screens as she spoke, finally coming up with the information she'd been looking for. 'Aye, body's gone to McCreedie and Sons undertakers. He'd no next of kin, so I'm not sure who's paying for it all.'

'That'll be Archie Seagram, at a guess.' DCI Dexter shuffled around the desk until she could see the screen too. 'Need to find out when the funeral's going to be. And where.'

'You want me to call them? McCreedie and Sons?' Janie reached for her phone.

'More than that, I was wondering if you'd go along to the funeral in person. Since you were the officer in charge of preparing the report and all.'

Janie didn't know Dexter well, but the DCI had a good reputation in the station. She ran the sexual crimes unit, universally known as Vice, but had no problem spreading her wings further than that when necessary. No problem poaching officers from other teams either.

'You want me to be seen so they don't see you.'

Dexter smiled. 'I'd like a team monitoring the event. Archie knows me too well from old. Seeing my soor puss would put everyone on edge.'

'Why'd you think he'll be there at all?'

'Seagram and Morgan go way back. Grew up together in Broxburn in the fifties and sixties. He'll want to give his old friend a proper sending off. I'd very much like to know who else turns up to say their last goodbyes. Find out when and where, and we can set up discreet surveillance. You can be the diversion.'

'You think it's wise for any of us to show our faces? If it's a gangland funeral . . .?'

'It'll be noticed if there's no one from the police there. They'll be just as suspicious that way. If it's your team asking questions and attending, chances are they'll not worry so much.'

Janie wasn't so sure, but neither was she going to argue the point with Dexter. There was one possible problem with the plan though.

'I'll need to run it past Kirsty, since we've no DI on the team yet. She's away at the moment, though. No' sure when she'll be back. I could ask Nelson, but . . .' She let the sentence hang unfinished.

'Problems with our new boss?' Dexter asked, her tone dripping with sarcasm. She left an uncomfortable silence that Janie really didn't want to fill, but after a few awkward moments, she had no choice but to relent. 'Aye, I know what he's like. Finding his feet's one thing, but I've seen the way he picks on certain officers. You know you can go to Jayne if you've a problem, right?'

'A DS making a formal complaint against a super? Not sure how well that would look on my record.' Janie reached for the mouse again, then took her hand away, flexed her fingers as if they ached. Not quite sure why this conversation was making her uncomfortable. 'And it's no' all the time either. Sometimes he's right in my face about stuff. Next day he's all praise and encouragement. Never know where I stand.'

Dexter patted Janie on the shoulder in an oddly motherly gesture. 'He's testing you, Janie. Seeing how you react under pressure. Don't let him get to you, and he'll ease off in a month or so.'

Janie didn't believe that for a minute. It felt far more personal. Although maybe that was the point.

'You hear anything from Tony recently?' Dexter's tone was so perfectly pitched, Janie almost thought that it had been an afterthought rather than more likely the main reason for this visit.

'Spoke to him on the phone the day we found the body. I thought he might have more info on Morgan, since he was the one arrested him. He said I should speak to Grumpy Bob.'

'And did you?'

'Wasn't necessary in the end. We had enough to be going on with, and Nelson pretty much said to wrap the investigation up quickly. Waste of our overstretched resources seeing as how Morgan had a heart attack. Not sure Kirsty would have agreed. I know McLean wouldn't have. But she's hardly ever here, and he's . . . well . . . And Nelson's the senior officer anyway, so . . .'

65

Dexter made a face that Janie couldn't immediately interpret, although she took it for scepticism. That was her own attitude to the detective superintendent's dismissal, after all. Perhaps she should go and have a chat with Grumpy Bob anyway. Never hurt to know a little bit more about someone, especially if you were about to attend their funeral.

'Have you considered applying for it yourself?'

It took Janie a moment to make the connection, coming as it did almost completely out of context.

'Me? The DI post?' She almost said, 'Tony's job,' but managed to stop herself. She shook her head. 'Haven't passed my Inspector's exam yet. Way things are going I don't think I'll ever find the time to study for it either.'

'You'd have no problems there, Janie. You've been doing a DI's job for months now.' Dexter gave a little shrug and headed for the door. 'Let me know when the funeral's happening. I'll go square it with the boss.'

She hadn't been down to the basement in a while. Not since they'd moved the bulk of the evidence store to a secure facility on the outskirts of town. Janie rarely ventured into the long room with its low vaulted brick ceiling that made up the offices of the Cold Case Unit. Something about the older, below-ground levels of the station gave her the creeps, if she was being honest. It wasn't that she believed the stories about ghosts from the Victorian precursor to this more modern building; poor unfortunates who had died in custody, in lightless cells. It was more the airlessness of the place and the flat light from the fluorescent tubes that leached the colour out of everything. The slightly damp and musty smell that clung to your clothes even after you'd left. At least the CCU room had a window, albeit one that looked out onto a rubbish-strewn light well at the back of the station car park, and was more often than not blocked almost entirely by armoured transit vans.

'Detective Sergeant Harrison. Janie, isn't it?'

The voice that answered Janie's knock on the door wasn't either of the ones she had been expecting. It was female for a start, although cracked with age and maybe cigarettes. There were three desks in the room, clustered close to the entrance as if retreating further into the gloom might come with the risk of never seeing the light again. Two of these desks were unattended, but a small figure sat at the third. It took Janie a moment to recognise former Detective Chief Superintendent Grace Ramsay. Not because the woman had aged since they had last met, but quite the opposite.

'Ma'am. Sorry. I didn't know you were working cold cases now.'

'A consulting role is how Charles sold it. I was bored and he needs all the help he can get.' Ramsay stood up with remarkable litheness for a woman of her age. The last time Janie had seen her, she'd been using two walking sticks and occasionally a wheelchair. She'd been hidden away in a nursing home, counting the days until the end.

'You look . . . well.' She couldn't help saying it.

'I feel well. Thank you. All that nonsense with Anya gave me a renewed sense of purpose. I never was much of a one for knitting or whatever it is octogenarians are supposed to do these days, so I'm putting my skills to more practical use.'

Janie was about to ask how Ramsay's daughter was doing, but then she recalled how the former support officer had almost died at the hands of a cult engaged in some weird cannibalistic ritual. Perhaps slightly more embarrassing, she remembered what it was Anya had been doing before she had fallen into their hands.

'Who was it you were looking for?' Ramsay asked, seeming to sense Janie's unease. 'Perhaps I can help.'

'I . . . Ah. I was hoping to speak to Bob. About a couple of old school gang types. Kenneth Morgan and Archibald Seagram.'

Despite her age, Ramsay held herself remarkably upright. At the sound of the two names, she straightened even more. Janie could have sworn that a light went on behind her eyes, such was the intensity with which they twinkled.

'Archie Seagram and Kenny Morgan. There's two names to conjure with right enough. What did you want to know about them?'

'You know them?'

'After a fashion. I heard Morgan died, right enough. Put him away at least once. Spent a good chunk of my career trying to do the same to Seagram. Unsuccessfully, I'm sad to say.'

'You heard we found Morgan's body in a church up Granton way? Pathologist reckons he had a heart attack. No suspicious circumstances.'

Ramsay leaned against her desk, arms crossed, head tilted slightly as if one ear didn't work as well as the other. 'But you don't believe that, right?'

'It's weird how he was in the church in the first place. Should've been locked tight. But that's no' why I wanted to know about him. His funeral's next week, and Seagram's paying for it all.'

'Aye, that sounds like Archie to me. Rewards those who stay loyal to him, even if they're dead. And there wasn't anyone more loyal than wee Kenny.'

'How so?' Janie realised that she'd crossed her own arms, not so much defensively as because she couldn't think of anything else to do with them. She still stood little more than a pace in from the doorway.

'That's quite a story.' Ramsay stood up, reached over the desk and plucked a jacket from where it hung on the back of her chair. 'Let's the two of us go and grab a coffee and I'll fill you in.'

Janie had thought they would go to the staff canteen on the ground floor of the station, but Ramsay dismissed that with a curt, 'had quite enough of that place, thank you', and they walked to a rather less institutional cafe on Nicolson Street.

Two cappuccinos, a chocolate chip cookie and a poppy seed

muffin lighter of wallet, she sat opposite the old DCS and waited to be enlightened. Away from the fake basement light, Ramsay's improved health was even more marked. Where her face had been sunken and lined, now it had filled, her wrinkles easing. Her short-cropped hair was still as white as fresh snow on the Pentland Hills, but it seemed thicker now, less scalp showing through. Her eyes had always been sharp and piercing, so no change there. When she lifted up her cup, there wasn't a tremor in her grip.

'Archie Seagram grew up in Broxburn,' Ramsay said after she'd placed her cup back down again. 'That's your neck of the woods, isn't it?'

Janie was surprised that the old woman would know that, but nodded anyway, her mouth full of cookie.

'He started off with petty burglary, boosting cars, that sort of thing. We did him and his mates a couple of times, but they were young, came from broken homes, care system, all the sorts of things a sharp defence lawyer might use to sway a judge towards leniency.'

Ramsay paused to take an indelicate bite out of her muffin, and washed it down with another sip of coffee.

'Archie always managed to work the system to his advantage. Quick learner, I guess. Certainly, after we'd felt his collar a couple of times he got wise to us. Last time he came anywhere close to being arrested must be, what? Couple of decades ago? No, more. Late nineties maybe. Kenny wasn't quite so smart, and I reckon Archie used that to his advantage. Kept him close enough to feel important, but far enough removed that nothing he did could blow back, if you get my meaning.'

'The last thing Morgan did time for was a hamesucken charge. Tony – DI McLean – was the one put him away for it.'

'Hamesucken. Ah me. There's a word you don't hear much these days. Breaking into a person's house and beating them up.

69

Breaking in for the intention of causing bodily harm, rather than just burglary gone wrong. Who was the victim?'

Janie racked her brain. She'd made notes from Morgan's arrest file, but somehow taking out her notebook felt like an admission of defeat. 'Drug dealer called Igor something, I think. Russian.'

'Igor Sokolov?' Ramsay made a huffing noise, shook her head once. 'Well, Kenny never was the sharpest pencil in the box.'

'You know him?'

'Knew him. He's dead. Heard he went home to Moscow for a visit and fell out of a tenth-storey window. Seems to happen a lot over there these days.'

'Why did Morgan beat him up then?' Janie asked through a half-chewed mouthful. Then added a quick, 'sorry,' as she remembered her manners too late.

'Well, if I remember right, Sokolov was the drug dealer of choice for the Eastern European community in the city. The Polish plumbers and Romanian farm labourers. Russians, Ukrainians, when they were still speaking to each other. Either he got over ambitious and started moving onto Archie Seagram's turf, or Archie fancied a cut of that market for himself. I expect he made an offer first, then sent Kenny in when that offer was refused.'

'Conjecture?' Janie made sure she'd finished chewing this time.

'Aye, well. Here's the thing about Archie Seagram. You'll struggle to pin anything on him. I'd have heard it if he'd been taken down, so Kenny must have kept his mouth shut about why he had it in for Sokolov. Or spun a reasonably plausible lie.

'He got sent down for it. Served two years of a five-year sentence. Been out for ten years and kept his nose clean since. Nothing on our records, least ways.'

Ramsay picked up her mug, held it in both hands, elbows resting on the table as she stared across the surface of her coffee straight at Janie. 'So, why are you really interested in Kenny Morgan and Archie Seagram?'

'Two reasons, if I'm being honest. First is that DCI Dexter is planning on running a surveillance operation at Morgan's funeral. She wants to see who turns up, who talks to who, who's not talking to who. That sort of stuff. She asked me to go as a distraction. Since I'm the detective nominally in charge of the investigation into Morgan's death, and I've no connections to drugs or Vice, it makes a kind of sense. There needs to be at least some police presence there, and if they're all worrying about me then they'll maybe not notice anyone else.'

Ramsay continued to stare across her cappuccino, her focus drifting as she parsed the information. After a while she gave a slight nod. 'Makes sense. Although it puts a perfectly good officer in the spotlight. The kind of people who'll be there will do their best to find out everything they can about you. Still, I can see why Jo thought of it. And the other reason?'

It was Janie's turn to pause before answering. She had been expecting to talk to Grumpy Bob, who was a known quantity and someone she'd worked with in the past. Ramsay's reputation preceded her; the few officers still at the station who'd been there before she retired all noted her obsessiveness, perfectionism and terrifying rudeness. She didn't suffer fools at all, let alone gladly. And yet Janie found herself warming to the old woman.

'I don't think his death was natural. Morgan, that is.'

Ramsay arched the pale ghost of an eyebrow. 'Go on.'

'I don't know. Maybe I worked with DI McLean too long, but the whole thing felt off from the start. Nobody's asking why Morgan was in the church in the first place, what was he doing there.'

'He had a heart attack, though. No evidence of foul play.'

'Aye, he had a heart attack, sure. I went to the post mortem, and I trust the pathologist to get that right. But there's many reasons why someone's heart might give out. His head was pretty badly bashed in, although that was an accident happened after he died.

71

But I don't know. Someone might have done that to hide something? Or am I overthinking things?'

Ramsay took a long draught of her coffee, savoured it for a moment before swallowing. She didn't speak until she'd put the mug back down on its saucer and clasped her hands together in front of her.

'It's easy to overthink things, especially in our line of work. I should know, I spent an entire career being told to stop trying to tie a whole load of missing persons cases together. I was the laughing stock of Lothian and Borders CID for many years.'

'But . . . You were right.'

The old woman smiled, crow's feet crinkling out around her eyes. 'And I've you to thank for proving it. You and Tony McLean. Learn to trust your instincts, Janie. But don't be a slave to them. Go to this funeral, speak to people, listen to what they say.'

'You think they'll talk? To me?'

'Oh, not about the things Jo Dexter wants to know. Not about their drugs, the people trafficking, sex slavery and all that other misery. I doubt you'll find out much about that at all. And maybe they won't even talk to you about why Kenny died. But they'll talk, and you'll learn as much from what they don't say as what they do.'

11

L ow cloud scudded across a sky the colour of bruised slate as Janie climbed out of the car and huddled into her coat. What her mother had always called a lazy wind blew in off the Firth of Forth, going straight through her rather than making the effort to pass around. A hundred metres or so up the road, the gates to Mount Vernon cemetery stood open, a small cluster of people hanging around as if unsure whether they dared enter. Or perhaps they were simply waiting for the star of the show to arrive.

The hearse rumbled slowly past her as she walked towards the gates. Janie waited for it to slide through, followed by the bulk of the people, before going in herself. She kept back from the mourners, walking a roundabout way to Kenneth Morgan's last resting place that took her around the edges of the cemetery and through areas less well cared for. A few graves showed signs of regular visits from the bereaved, but most were overgrown, unloved, forgotten. Headstones leaned like rotting teeth, one or two collapsed entirely.

Perhaps twenty metres ahead of her, she saw a lone figure. He stood regarding a particularly ragged grave site overgrown with brambles, a weed elder all but obscuring a headstone cracked in two.

As she neared, he turned, and Janie was surprised to see that the figure was a priest. Dressed in black robes, his face was gaunt, framed by lank black hair tumbling close to his sloping shoulders. He stared at her with eyes so black they might have been portals to the void, his expression unfriendly enough that she glanced away, hoping to see if there was a different route she could take to rejoin the funeral party. But there was nothing obvious that wouldn't involve walking on the dead. Janie shook her head at her foolishness, turned back to where the priest stood.

Except that he was gone.

The smallest tremor of unease ran through her as she carried on along the path, mitigated somewhat by the knowledge that she'd not now have to confront the man. Janie paused at the grave he'd been beside just long enough to peer at the headstone, but the missing half made it impossible to read anything other than the year of death. 1983 wasn't so long in the scheme of these things, although more than a decade before she'd been born. Another shudder as the cold wind picked at her coat, looking for a way in. She stepped away from the anonymous grave and went in search of the more recently deceased.

A surprisingly large crowd had gathered to witness Kenneth Morgan being committed to the earth, or whatever the phrase was. Janie kept herself to the back, catching only occasional words from the priest at the centre of it all, the bulk of his litany carried away on the breeze.

Not being the tallest of people, Janie struggled to see over the heads and shoulders of the closest mourners, but she managed to identify Archibald Seagram after a few moments. Six foot if he hadn't been slightly stooped with age, his white hair thinning over a well-tanned scalp, framing a crumpled, leathery old face. The wind whipped tears from his eyes, but Janie was fairly sure they weren't shed in mourning. He hadn't carried his old friend's coffin, she noticed. That task had been left to a group of younger men.

Strapping lads who strained their dark suits at the bicep, chest and shoulder, unlike Seagram's old man gut.

As she watched, the crowd of mourners began to arrange themselves, shuffling towards the grave like some bizarre zombie apocalypse in reverse. After a moment's confusion, Janie understood. Each was taking a small handful of dirt from a wooden box and sprinkling it over the coffin deep in the ground. Some crossed themselves, some bowed their heads, most moved as quickly as they could to complete this one last act of remembrance. Across the open grave from the line, Seagram observed it all with narrowed eyes. Occasionally he would give a nod to someone he recognised, and every once in a while he tapped the side of his nose as if he was having trouble with his nostrils.

'Not joining the line?'

A voice beside her startled Janie. She looked around to see a woman in her late sixties or early seventies, dressed in a heavy black coat against the cold, her short-cropped grey-white hair almost hidden under a stylish black hat with a minimalist netting veil. More fashion statement than mourning garb.

'I . . . I don't think it would be appropriate.'

'No?' The woman gave Janie an appraising stare. 'Not family, I see. Kenneth didn't have much of that anyway, and all of them are long dead. One of Archie's lot, perhaps? A wife dragged along to keep up appearances?'

Janie struggled for an excuse, then remembered that the whole reason for her being there was that she be recognised for who she was. She held out a hand to the woman. 'Detective Sergeant Harrison, Police Scotland Specialist Crime Division. I was the officer charged with investigating Mr Morgan's death.'

The woman looked at the proffered hand for a few seconds, then took it. She wore black leather gloves, her grip firm but not uncomfortably so.

'Come to make sure he's properly dead then?' She smiled at her little joke. 'Anna Machin. Anna Morgan as was, but that was a very long time ago.'

'You were his wife?' It felt like a stupid question to ask, given that was what the woman had just said.

'Briefly, aye. And as I said, a very long time ago. The madness of youth, I suppose. Kenneth swore he'd mend his ways, get a proper job, we'd raise a family together and everything. Then not six months after the wedding he gets himself arrested for armed burglary. Twelve years the judge gave him. Well, I wasn't going to wait for him, was I? Even if he did only serve six.'

Janie knew most of the details already from reading Morgan's file. His wife's maiden name had been Roberts, though, so she must have remarried at some point.

'I'm surprised you came, if it's been that long.'

Machin half smiled half grimaced. 'I had a call from one of Archie's men. Said it would be poor form if I didn't come and see Kenneth off. I figured it'd be easier to waste a morning and be done with it than have them pester me for months.'

Janie looked back at the graveside, where the crowd had all but finished throwing dirt on the deceased. Seagram took that moment to look up, his gaze falling on the two of them. He stared for a moment, then called one of his men over. Heads together as words were exchanged; it was inevitable that the younger man would soon be heading their way.

'Mr Seagram wonders if either of you two ladies would care to pay your last respects to Mr Morgan. Before the grave is filled in.'

It was voiced as a polite enquiry, but Janie knew a command when she heard one. She was about to politely decline when the old woman reached out and touched her gently on the elbow. In a voice loud enough to be heard on Arthur's Seat, she said, 'Why don't we both do that, Detective Sergeant. See the old boy off on his final trip.'

★ ★ ★

The route to the burial took them past a number of much older graves, their occupants remembered in ornate stone. Janie did her best not to tread on anyone, but it was hard to tell where bodies lay and where was path. Given the age of the cemetery, it was probably bodies all the way down. How many of them had died from natural causes? How many of them were victims of men like Archibald Seagram? Only the poor unfortunates who crossed his path more often ended up in the foundations of some new building or fed to the pigs on one of the big factory farms outside Broxburn, if half of the station gossip was to be believed.

By the time they reached the graveside, most of the mourners had dispersed. Groups clustered together as they wandered back towards the gates, their waiting cars, and a wake in one of the city's better hotels. Seagram stood with a couple of other old men, the six young lads who had carried Morgan's coffin now a few paces back and spread out as if expecting trouble to appear at any moment. There was a distinct Spaghetti Western feel to the scene, which helped to relieve the tension a little in Janie's mind. What could have been terrifying instead turned faintly ridiculous.

'Anna, I'm so glad you came.' Seagram took a couple of steps forward, clasped Machin's hand in both of his and kissed her on the cheeks, French style. Janie studied the other two old men while this was going on, trying to put names to the faces and failing. It didn't matter, really. Jo Dexter's people would have photographed everyone in attendance, and they had far more sophisticated ways of identifying suspects.

'And you must be the unlucky police officer who drew the short straw?' Seagram released Machin's hand and turned to Janie. His entire posture changed, the warmth he showed to the older woman now replaced with a cold hardness.

'Detective Sergeant Harrison.' She offered her hand to be shaken, but he didn't take it. 'I put together the report into Mr Morgan's unfortunate death. I'm sorry for your loss.'

'Are you?' Seagram cocked his head towards the nearest of the other two men. 'You hear that, Billy? She's sorry for our loss. And here's me thinking Lothian and Borders would be glad to see the back of us all. One less thing to worry about.'

'We're Police Scotland now, Mr Seagram. All one happy family from coast to coast.'

The old man stared at her, his face dark. Janie knew he could be dangerous, but not here, not now. She'd met plenty of men like him in her time. Used to getting their own way, to pushing people around. He was an old school gangster, not far off his own end if she was any judge. Was that why he'd paid for his friend's funeral? Or was there more to it than that? A debt that needed to be settled, an obligation he couldn't deny.

'All one happy family.' He parroted her words, face breaking into an approximation of a smile as he nudged the other old man with him. 'Hear that, Ray? Oh, I think I like her.'

He turned back to face her. 'What was your name again, sweetheart? Harrison, wasn't it? I'll keep an eye out for you.'

'I'm sure I could say the same, Mr Seagram.' Janie smiled, then let her gaze slide past his head and over to the housing blocks that lined the road beyond the cemetery wall. As expected, he turned and looked in the same direction. Not that there was anything to see, but it was always good to encourage a little paranoia in the criminal classes.

'But I've taken up enough of your time. I'll let you get on to the wake. Out of this wind.' She shoved her hands in her pockets and turned away, giving the old woman a polite nod.

She was twenty metres or more towards the gates, her shoes crunching on the gravel pathway, when she heard the sounds of someone approaching from behind. Not the heavy tread of one of Seagram's goons, but a quicker, lighter step. Janie wasn't at all surprised when she slowed down to find Machin fall into step beside her.

'Not going to drink with the boys?' she asked, receiving a well-deserved withering stare in return.

'To think I once fancied Archie Seagram. But then I fell for Kenneth's charms, too. More fool me.'

'Different times, I guess. When did you get married?'

'Nineteen Seventy-Six. Summer we had that big drought. I was eighteen years old, Kenneth was twenty-four. You're right. Different times.'

Janie did the maths in her head. Almost two decades before she was even born. 'You got out, though. Away from them.'

'Well, I'm here now, aren't I. You never really get away from people like Archie. They're always somewhere in the background, keeping an eye on you, manipulating you. Don't be surprised if he starts digging around in your background now.'

'Doubt he'll find much of interest there,' Janie said, although her breezy dismissal didn't match the feeling of unease that had only grown with the distance between her and Seagram. The man might be old enough to be her grandfather, but he'd grown up in Broxburn, same as she had. Same as her father and uncle had.

'Why do you suppose he's paying for all this?' she asked in a bid to make the uncomfortable thoughts go away. 'Plots here aren't cheap, and the wake's going to cost a fortune.'

Machin laughed, a high-pitched and desperate trill like a caged bird. 'Archie's minted. He won't even notice the money. It's about loyalty for him. Loyalty and reward. Ken was always loyal. Took a lot of punishment for it, too. Physical and years served in jail. He could have given your lot enough information to put Archie away for the rest of his life, but he kept his mouth shut. Archie always respected that about Ken. I suppose this is his way of saying thanks. And letting his other men know how they'll be treated if they give him the same respect.'

It made a kind of sense, Janie had to admit. She couldn't help thinking there was more to it than that, though. An obligation of some kind.

'Those other two men with him. You know them?' she asked.

'Am I being interrogated, Detective Sergeant Harrison?'

'A bit, maybe. Force of habit. Sorry.'

'Well, I suppose it's only natural.' They had reached the gates now, and Machin stopped. She had a slim black bag hanging from one elbow, fished around in it until she found a heavy car key fob. When she pressed the button, a nearby BMW flashed its lights and unfolded its wing mirrors.

'That's me. It was nice talking to you.' She started walking towards the car, then stopped, turned. 'Thin one's Billy Creegan, the other's Ray McAllister. Surprised you didn't know that.'

12

A week had passed since the funeral, and Janie still couldn't stop her mind from wandering back to the case when she should have been concentrating on other things. Duty rosters and overtime allocation and the thousand and one jobs that should have been the work of their team's detective inspector. If only their team actually had one.

She called it a case, but it wasn't one. Not really. The investigation had been completed and no further action was necessary. Everybody else seemed happy to draw a line underneath it, and it wasn't as if she didn't have more than enough to deal with already. And yet she just couldn't leave it alone.

She'd spoken briefly to Jo Dexter. Not so much an official debrief as a casual conversation while the detective chief inspector smoked a cigarette in the glass shelter at the back of the building. Apparently, nobody unexpected or unusual had turned up either to the funeral or the burial afterwards. A couple of notable names had been at the wake, but they were known associates of Seagram who might well have been simply paying their respects while enjoying some free hospitality. Janie had earned herself some Brownie points with Dexter, and she'd been able to keep out of Nelson's reach for the best part of a day, but other than that it had been a bit of a waste of time.

She couldn't stop coming back to that one simple question though. What was he doing in that church? Kenneth Morgan had been a regular at Sunday mass and laid to rest in the city's Catholic cemetery. So why go into an Anglican church? One that had been deconsecrated and was scheduled for demolition, too.

'Coming to the briefing?'

Janie looked up from her desk, startled by the voice. Detective Constable Jessica Bryant smiled at her with a smattering of worried frown thrown into the mix.

'You OK, Janie?' Bryant said. 'Only you seem a little preoccupied.'

'Ach, I'm fine. Just tired is all. No' sleeping well. Too much on my mind.' She gathered up the few folders that had been lying ignored on her desk, hooked her jacket over her shoulder. 'Come on then. Let's go listen to the boss's latest pep talk.'

When she followed Bryant, Cass Mitchell and the other detective constables into the smaller incident room, Janie was surprised to find DCI Ritchie standing by the whiteboard-covered far wall, head bent close as she listened to something Detective Superintendent Nelson was saying. She couldn't remember the last time Ritchie had been at a briefing; all too often the DCI was away at Gartcosh these days, liaising with the NCA. Janie had a horrible feeling Ritchie might jump ship to the agency soon, leaving them even shorter handed than they already were.

'OK everyone, let's get this started.' Nelson broke away from his conversation, turned to address the collection of detectives. The hubbub of conversation faded to nothing, all eyes turning to the man in charge.

'Right then. I'll start with the bad news. I've just had word from Strathclyde that Detective Inspector Cummings, who was supposed to be joining the team, will not now be doing so.'

A collective groan ran through the room, although secretly Janie felt a mixture of relief in with the frustration. As soon as the name had been first mentioned, she'd asked around about DI Steve Cummings and nothing she'd heard about the man had been encouraging. The day he'd been announced as DI McLean's replacement he'd suffered a suspected minor heart attack and gone on long term sick. That was one of the reasons they were still a DI short, and she was doing the work of two officers.

'A bit more sympathy please, people. Steve was a fine officer and would have been a great fit here. Sadly, his condition has worsened and he's being pensioned off.'

From what Janie had heard, he would have been a very bad fit indeed. And as for being pensioned off, well he'd only a couple of years left to go anyway. Then the team would be right back where it was.

'We've a couple of possible new transfer candidates. Should have some news for you by the end of the week. In the meantime, thank you for all your hard work. Keep it up. And now I'll hand you over to DCI Ritchie.'

Nelson made a theatrical flourish of both his hands as if the DCI was walking on stage rather than already standing beside him. Ritchie looked suitably mortified, and also as tired as Janie felt. At least she only had a single sheet of paper in hand, so her talk would be short. Small mercies.

'Thank you, Peter.' She glanced briefly at Nelson, an expression on her face that reminded Janie the two of them had considerable history from their years working together in Aberdeen. He didn't seem to notice, his own gaze passing over the pathetically small collection of detectives that was their team. Janie looked away before he saw her, focusing once more on the DCI.

'Morning, everyone. And once again sorry about my lack of presence here these past months. As some of you will know, I've been main liaison between Edinburgh Specialist Crime and our friends at the NCA, particularly with regards to Operation Train Car. I'm happy to say that thanks to your hard work, the operation has been a complete success. We've made multiple arrests, seized enough cocaine to satisfy a cabinet minister's appetite, and shut down one of the largest drug smuggling gangs in the country.'

A smatter of laughter at the cabinet minister jibe rippled around the room, but it was subdued. None of this was news, particularly. Most of the detectives present had worked on the operation, one way or another, and the big bust over on the west coast had been the talk of the station all week.

'Now that's done and it's just the paperwork to contend with, you'll be seeing a lot more of me.' Ritchie caught Janie's eye and gave her a small nod. 'Hopefully that'll mean I can pick up some of the slack until our new DI arrives.'

Janie had hoped to escape unnoticed at the end of the briefing, make her way back to the CID room and crack on with the extra paperwork their lack of a new detective inspector had landed her with. Not that she was the only one dealing with it, of course. Sandy Gregg had taken on a lot of the overtime processing and shift allocation. They'd need to get together somewhere quiet soon to thrash out a new plan, given the confirmation about DI Cummings, but by the way DCI Ritchie flagged her down as she headed for the door, it was yet another thing that would have to wait.

'Janie? A moment before you run off, if you don't mind.'

She put on her best tired smile and let the last of the constables past her before crossing the room to where Ritchie and Nelson still stood.

'Sir. Ma'am. Is there anything I can help you with?'

'Don't you "ma'am" me, Janie.' Ritchie's chide was meant to be humorous, but then the DCI looked at her boss and her tone changed. 'Never mind. I was just catching up on all that's been going on. Gather you did a little bit of work for Jo Dexter.'

It wasn't a criticism. Janie had known Ritchie long enough to read her tone. Nelson on the other hand looked very unhappy, even though he was the one who had authorised it in the first place.

'Kenneth Morgan's funeral, aye. Well, burial, I should say. Jo wanted me to be the Police Scotland visible presence so her team could watch things without being noticed.'

'Morgan?' Ritchie's eyebrows furrowed together, or at least they would have done if she'd had any. 'Oh yes, the body in the church. That was just a heart attack though. Nothing unusual.'

'Apart from the question of why he was in the church in the first place, no.' Janie knew as soon as she mentioned it that she was treading on dangerous ground. Not with Ritchie, but Detective Superintendent Nelson physically twitched. She could almost read the thoughts moving across his high forehead like teletype. Case closed. Leave it alone. No unnecessary expense. Leave it alone. We haven't the manpower. Leave it alone.

'I understand it was about to be knocked down. Couldn't he have just been giving it a last look over? For old times' sake?'

'Well, he could have.' Janie rushed her words out before Nelson could interrupt. 'But St Andrew's is Episcopalian, and Morgan was a devout Catholic. All his life, apparently.'

'It's all academic.' The detective superintendent finally managed to get a word in. 'Your report's already gone to the PF. No more action necessary. And frankly, Detective Sergeant, it's not as if you need to go looking for more work, is it?'

He sounded reasonable at that moment, but Janie wasn't so easily fooled. She'd seen Nelson's reasonable side turn swiftly before, and this time he'd used her rank rather than name, which was always a warning sign. At least here she had Ritchie's support, or her witness.

'I certainly don't need to do that, no sir. It's just . . .' How to phrase this? 'Just that apparently Archibald Seagram made a request for the death of his friend to be thoroughly investigated.

He had some information about a recent contact and the state of Morgan's mind, or so I'm told. Only, nobody passed any of that on to me. There's no' even a record of his call. Odd, given it was my task to prepare the report into the incident.'

Nelson twitched again, as if someone had a tiny taser and was prodding him with it in the back of his neck. 'Nonsense. Why would a man like Seagram ask anything of us? He's a drug dealer, a violent thug. Oh, I know we've never managed to pin anything on him, but we all know it's true. If he suspected foul play, he'd get his own goons to investigate it, not come begging to the police. And even if he did ask, why would we do anything for the likes of him?'

Janie wanted to say, 'a man's dead, for God's sake', but managed to stop herself. There was nothing to be gained here but grief.

'I quite understand, sir. I'm not suggesting we reopen the case or anything. Like the pathologist said, Morgan was old, unfit. By all accounts he drank whisky like it was about to run out. Hardly surprising he died the way he did. I know we've neither the resources or inclination to look into it any further, but that doesn't stop me wondering.'

'Well do it on your own time, aye?' Nelson glowered at her, turned his attention to Ritchie. 'Talk some sense into her, will you, Kirsty?' he said, then turned and stomped out of the room.

'You're walking on thin ice you know, Janie,' Ritchie said after a long enough pause for the door to have swung closed behind their boss. 'And Archie Seagram? Contacting us? Who on earth put that idea in your head?'

'DI Mc—Tony, actually. Seagram called him first. He'd have to be pretty desperate to do that, don't you think?'

'Tony?' Ritchie did the thing with her non-existent eyebrows again. Hadn't she lost them pulling McLean out of a fire and they'd never grown back? That was the story Janie had heard.

'I spoke to him about Morgan, seeing as he was the one put

him behind bars the last time. He said Seagram contacted him and he told him to call us.'

Ritchie crossed her arms like a schoolteacher admonishing a slow pupil. 'So you don't actually know whether Seagram phoned the station at all? Just that he spoke to Tony?'

'I know, I know. Chances are he didn't once Tony gave him the brush off. It's just . . . this whole thing feels off, and I know if I don't do something, it's all going to come back and bite us in the arse.'

'You sound just like him, you know? Tony, that is.' Ritchie rubbed a weary hand against her forehead. 'And we don't have the time or people to go looking into something the PF's already closed down. Sorry, Janie, but you'll just have to let this one go.'

Janie knew the DCI was right, even if the jibe about her being like McLean stung a little. She was about to say as much, but the door to the incident room banged open. A flustered DC Mitchell bustled in, holding a single sheet of paper that she proffered to the two of them.

'Janie. Ma'am. This has just come in from control. Old boarded up church in Gorgie. They've found a body.'

13

Tucked away in between two rows of grimy tenements on a steep street leading up from the Gorgie Road, St Mark's church might have been mistaken for a meeting hall or even a masonic lodge. Its stone front consisted of two narrow windows, blackened with age and soot. They flanked an arched entrance at the top of a small series of worn stone steps. A little bit of flair had gone into the design, but time and weather had worn most of it away. What might once have been elegant, fluted columns were slicked with green from leaking gutters, their details smoothed off so that they now appeared like a much-used bar of soap. Scraggly vegetation poked from gaps in the mortar, and a sizeable sapling was growing from one of the cracked, cast-iron downpipes.

Janie approached from the far side of the road, as that was where they had managed to find a parking space. The climb up the hill made her wheeze a little, a reminder of how unfit she had become in her increasingly sedentary, paperwork-driven life. Beside her, DC Mitchell strode effortlessly, her long legs making easy work of the gradient.

A small cordon had been set up around the front of the church, two uniform constables in attendance. Janie presented her warrant card even though one of the constables seemed to recognise her. It was something of an embarrassment that she couldn't immediately place him, certainly couldn't recall his name.

'CSM's set up just inside,' he said, pointing up the steps to where one half of a pair of solid wooden doors stood open. Janie noticed that a heavy hasp and padlock had been fitted, in addition to the overlarge keyhole. This wasn't the best part of town, so it made sense to try and keep an empty old building secure. Was there another way in? She'd have to find out.

'Hey, J. Thought it'd be you turning up.' Manda Parsons stood in a small lobby area directly inside the front door, pulling on white paper overalls. Police Sergeant Kenneth Stephen seemed to be the man in charge.

'Hey, Manda.' Janie nodded to her flatmate then turned her attention to Stephen. 'What's the story, Sarge?'

'Best see for yourself, although you'll need to get kitted up first.'

'Suspicious?' Janie looked around for a spare set of overalls, to find Parsons already holding one out for her.

'I'd say. Again, easier seen than described.'

Intrigued, Janie tore open the plastic wrapping and set about hauling on a pair of overalls designed to fit all sizes except hers. Overboots, gloves and hood pulled tight, she went towards the door that she assumed would open onto the nave, then paused, directed a question at her flatmate.

'This one's not going to fall down on us, is it?'

Parsons smiled, then tucked a stray curl of hair back under the hood of her own pair of overalls. They fitted her much better than Janie's did.

'No. Building's sound enough. A bit of damp in the corners, but otherwise fine.'

'OK. Lead on.'

The door did indeed open on to the nave, a narrow gap between rows of dark wooden benches that speared towards the not-too-distant altar. Some light filtered in through the high windows above, revealing a small group of people clustered at the front. As she approached, Janie recognised Tom MacPhail and his assistant Cerys. A crime scene photographer, almost impossible to identify in their full overalls, clicked away, the flash making little electronic pop sounds, its light bouncing around the walls. The noise, or perhaps the body, was too distracting for any of them to notice until she and Amanda were almost upon them.

'You going to give that a rest, Bobby?' Parsons said to the photographer. The white-suited figure looked up, still not readily identifiable, snapped a picture of Janie and her flatmate that would inevitably wind up in some end of year presentation or staff calendar. Janie ignored it, her attention focused entirely on the reason why she was here.

A man of somewhere between sixty-five and seventy years, he lay on his back, arms crossed over his chest as if someone had carefully placed him at the foot of the altar. He wore a dark suit, well enough tailored to have been made for him rather than pulled from a rack in M&S. His black polished shoes had worn almost to nothing at the sole, but were otherwise tidy, as was his neatly trimmed grey-white hair. Death had drained the blood from his face, but his pale skin was cleanly shaved. His mouth hung slack and slightly open, cheeks sagging slightly under gravity's pull.

Two things struck Janie almost immediately as she took in the details of that face. First was the livid black and red mark of a cross that appeared to have been burned into his forehead, something that confirmed what everyone had told her about this being a suspicious death. The other was the flash of recognition as she pushed the brand from her mind and took in the face as a whole. She knew this man, had seen him alive somewhere quite recently. A funeral. No, a burial.

'Oh crap.' Her voice echoed in the cavernous space of the church. 'This is William Creegan. He's one of Archie Seagram's men.'

★ ★ ★

90

'We really could have done without this just now, you know, Janie?'

It felt like almost no time at all since she had last stood in this office, in front of this desk, being admonished by this man. From the way he spoke, it was almost as if the detective superintendent thought she was solely responsible for the body of William Creegan being found in St Mark's church. Janie tried to let it wash over her, but it hurt all the same. She held back the urge to ask Nelson if he'd rather she shut down the investigation and pretend it had never happened. Sarcasm didn't go down well with the man.

'You've confirmed the identity, I take it? It's definitely Creegan?'

'Aye, sir. We've enough mug shots of him to be sure, and I saw him myself not that long ago. At Kenneth Morgan's funeral. He had his wallet on him, too. Cards and stuff in his name.'

'Next of kin been to see the body?' Nelson sounded like he was clutching at straws, although how being uncertain of the dead man's identity made things any easier, Janie couldn't say.

'He didn't have any, sir. Never married, no siblings, parents long dead. I thought we could maybe ask Archibald Seagram to confirm it's his old friend.'

She wasn't serious about the suggestion, but it was interesting to see the effect it had on Nelson. His face froze like the wind had changed, a look of almost terror in his eyes. It lasted only a moment before a strange kind of shudder ran through him.

'Don't make jokes about this sort of thing, Detective Sergeant.' Nelson grabbed up the stack of printed sheets that made up Creegan's extensive arrest record. If Janie didn't know better, she'd have thought he was using it as a shield.

'Sandy . . . DS Gregg is setting up an incident room. Post mortem's scheduled for tomorrow morning. I'd like to have a look around Creegan's house, get hold of his phone records, start tracking his movements before he died. Build up a picture of his life as best we can.' Janie paused before adding the last item on her list, knowing how well it would go down. 'We will have to talk to Seagram at some point, sir.'

Again, that rabbit in the headlights stare. Although only for an instant this time, as if Nelson was conditioned to react to the name, like one of Pavlov's dogs. It was strange. From what Janie knew about Seagram's criminal empire, it was mostly central belt. Nelson's entire career, until now, had been in Aberdeen. It wasn't so unusual that the detective superintendent would have heard of Seagram, but why have this more visceral reaction simply to hearing his name?

'You're doing good work, Janie, but I think that's possibly above your pay grade. I'll have a word with Jo Dexter. See if we can't poach one of her DIs for this. She's been tracking Creegan and his operation for years now.'

'Happy to give them the whole investigation, if you want me to, sir.' Well, it was worth a shot. For a moment Janie thought Nelson was seriously considering it, too. But he shook his head slowly, placed the sheaf of papers back down on his desk.

'No. This death is clearly suspicious, and it falls under the Major Investigation Team's remit. Liaise with Vice, of course, but this is an MIT investigation.' He let out a long sigh, rubbed at his eyes with the heels of his hands and then stared up at her with an attempt at a smile. 'I know it's unconventional, but until we can get a temporary DI in place, you're in charge, Janie. Don't let me down, eh?'

And there was the switch again, from bad cop to good. Only that wasn't how it was supposed to work, was it?

'I won't, sir. And thank you.' She turned to leave, but was stopped by Nelson raising his arm.

'Just one thing though. Stay clear of Seagram, OK? We'll get to him in time, but let's not rock that particular boat until we have to.'

Janie said nothing, not trusting herself to be tactful. Instead, she simply nodded her head once and then fled the room as swiftly as she could without it seeming too obvious.

Outside, the corridor was quiet, the reception area at the far end where Chief Superintendent McIntyre's secretary would normally be working empty. That meant McIntyre herself was most likely away at headquarters. DCI Ritchie's office door was open, but she was not inside either, and the next office along was McLean's. Empty now, awaiting its new occupant.

Not quite sure why she was doing so, Janie pushed open the door and stepped inside. Nothing much was changed about the room save for the lack of a detective inspector sitting at the desk. The furniture was still the same, with a small conference table in one corner, a couple of comfortable chairs and a shelving unit in the other. Like all the rooms on this floor, the outer wall was entirely glass, currently smeared with spring rain that blurred the view across the street to the shop fronts and tenement floors opposite. The desk was clear save for the phone handset.

'Eyeing it up for moving in?'

Janie almost jumped out of her skin. She had only taken one step into the room, but it was enough to miss the sound of someone approaching up the corridor. Either that or she'd been so lost in her thoughts she'd blanked it out. She turned to see DCI Dexter standing in the doorway, her eyes wrinkled in amusement.

'Oh. Sorry, no. Just . . .'

'Don't worry. I won't tell if you don't.' Dexter leaned against the door jamb, crossed her arms. 'You should consider it, though. Reckon you're as ready as anyone to move up the ladder.'

Janie shook her head, but couldn't bring herself to voice her disagreement.

'Well don't leave it too late. Be a shame to have you stuck as a sergeant forever.' Dexter stood straight again, stepped out into the corridor. 'Now if you'll excuse me, his nibs wants a word.'

14

April 1st 1982 – Thursday

April Fool. Managed not to get caught by anyone till late and choir. George got me and all the others good though. Special tutoring with the new priest today. I don't like him. Don't like the way he touches me, even if it is what God says we must do. I want to ask George and Ali if they know God's special secret too, but what if they don't? Will I go to hell for telling them?

Rogue Trooper killed all the Norts in 2000AD this week. I wish I had Gunnar and Bagman to help me. Helm would know what to do.

15

The call had interrupted him as he'd been leaving the house; DS Harrison breaking protocol and any number of regulations to let him know the latest news. So it only came as a small surprise to McLean when he arrived at the cafe on the Royal Mile to find Jo Dalgliesh already knew about Billy Creegan's death.

'Heard they found him in an abandoned church. Sound familiar to you?' she said around a mouthful of cake McLean had just paid for. He'd barely had time to bring the plate to the table before she'd swooped on it, as if she'd not eaten a thing since their last meeting.

'I only got the basic details, Jo. Chances are you know more than I do.' McLean settled into a seat that was a lot less comfortable than it looked, picked up his mug and took a sip of coffee.

'Aye, you're probably right. Still, makes you think, doesn't it? Like someone's out for Archie Seagram? I know youse lot never managed to pin anything on him down the years, but we both know he's behind most of the loan sharks in the city, a good chunk of the drugs and prostitution too. Fingers in all the pies, that one.'

'You writing a piece on it? Might want to tread carefully there.'

'Oh, aye. Careful's my middle name. I'm no stupid enough to mess wi' the likes of Archie Seagram. Just wondering, y'know. What if someone's making a move on his operation?'

'You reckon that's what this is about? A turf war?' McLean shook his head slowly. It didn't sit with the telephone call Seagram had made to him, although Creegan's death gave a little more credence to the claims the old gangster had made about Morgan.

'You think it's something else?' Dalgliesh rubbed a thumb along the edge of her lips, then stuck it in her mouth.

'I don't know. Don't much care, really. But if I was making a move on Seagram's criminal empire, I'd not start by knocking off a couple of old boys like Morgan and Creegan.'

'No' even to send a message?'

'Well, aye. I suppose. But what kind of message? It's personal, not business, isn't it? Taking out two of the man's oldest friends?'

Dalgliesh eyed him suspiciously, and it occurred to McLean he'd not told her about the phone call. 'You know something about this I don't, Tony? Only don't hold back, aye?'

'How's Murphy?' he asked in a not particularly subtle attempt to change the topic.

'Murph's fine,' Dalgliesh said through another mouthful of cake. 'Well, as fine as he ever is. Poor wee sod's had a life, you know? In an' out of care. He's stable now, but that's the meds as much as anything. An' all because some shite of a priest took a fancy to him when he was a bairn. Folk like that deserve to rot in hell, far as I'm concerned.'

'That the angle you're taking on the story, then? Another nail in the coffin of the Catholic Church?'

'Mebbe. It all happened a long time ago, mind. Need to find a way of making it relevant, see? Strange they never managed to catch who did for the priest though. That's the angle I'll probably take. Who was in charge of the investigation? Did the church put pressure on them to make the whole thing go away? That sort of thing.'

'Why would they do that?'

'Well think about it, Tony. A full investigation into O'Connell's death would've opened up a nasty can of worms. Probably why nobody paid any attention to poor wee Murph back then. That an' he was only nine. It didn't all come out until much later, when he was in a psychiatric hospital and his folks tried to sue.' Dalgliesh picked up her mug and took an unladylike slurp of coffee. 'Still, enough about him. What do you know about Seagram an' his pals that you're no' telling me?'

'Nothing, really. I mean, apart from what I've picked up over the years. You've probably heard more rumours than I have about the stuff he's done. Half the gangland disappearances in the city over the past four decades are supposed to be down to him, and yet somehow no one's managed to pin anything on him since he was a teenager. Don't think I'd ever spoken to the man until he phoned me with some nonsense when Morgan died.'

Dalgliesh's eyes widened, the fork with its last piece of cake paused halfway between plate and mouth quivering slightly as she stared at him. 'Archie Seagram phoned you? Archie "Mad Bastard" Seagram? The man youse lot have been trying to pin at least a dozen murders on over the past three decades, an' that's just the ones where they found the bodies? That Archie Seagram? Phoned you?'

'It's not a big deal, Jo. I'm not in his pocket or anything. Told him to take it to the police.'

'And you've the nerve to tell me to tread carefully?' Dalgliesh remembered her cake, shoved it swiftly into her mouth. 'But why you?'

'Probably because I'm retired? Far as I know, he never did phone the police with his concerns. You can imagine how that conversation would have gone anyway. He didn't think Morgan's death was natural causes though. Given what's happened to Creegan, maybe he was right. I'll not lose any sleep over it either way.'

'Jesus, Tony.' Dalgliesh shook her head. 'You actually said no to Archie Seagram.'

'What's he going to do? Break my legs? Burn my house down?'

'Aye, both of those things, an' worse.' Dalgliesh snatched up a paper napkin and used it to smear chocolate around her face. 'You be careful around Seagram. He might be old, an' he might put on airs an' graces, but he's a vicious wee thug underneath it all.'

He was so wrapped up in his thoughts as he walked south from the Old Town that at first McLean didn't notice the car following him. Only when it slowed to a crawl and then gently tooted a horn did he stop and turn to see what the fuss was about.

A long, black Mercedes. One of those new electric ones if he wasn't mistaken. It had a personalised number plate and dark tinted windows at the rear. He could still see the driver, though; a young man who looked more like a nightclub bouncer than a chauffeur. When the rear window slid silently down, it all suddenly clicked in McLean's head. Of course this would be happening now, after the conversation he'd just had with Dalgliesh.

'Can I give you a lift anywhere, Inspector?'

Archibald Seagram looked up from what was undoubtedly a very comfortable seat. He was alone apart from the driver, and a quick glance around showed no other cars obviously part of his retinue.

'You have me mistaken for someone else, Mr Seagram. I'm no inspector. Not anymore.'

'Force of habit, Mr McLean. Is that better?' The car had stopped on a double yellow line. A taxi held up behind it pulled out with an angry clatter of its diesel engine and loud parp of its horn, tyres squealing for grip as it tried to get past before the oncoming traffic closed the gap up once more.

'You'd better move on before you cause too much of an obstruction,' McLean said.

'Just five minutes of your time, eh? I'm not going to try and corrupt you, Insp—McLean. I've no money to offer you or threats to your loved ones. Five minutes'll save you twenty walking, and you might be interested to hear what I've got to say.'

McLean glanced around the street. Short of stepping into a shop or an office, there was no easy way to lose Seagram. And chances were that he would only persist. Dalgliesh's words of warning hung in the air, too. The man was being reasonable now, but what if he decided to force the issue? It was true the police had never been able to pin anything serious on him, but they all knew the violent punishments that had been done in Seagram's name. How many times had he wielded the knife himself? And here he was offering to talk, one to one, about . . . What?

In the end a sudden shower of cold rain made the decision for him. McLean shivered as water ran down his neck. He pulled open the door, forcing Seagram to shuffle across to the other side, and settled in.

'Where you headed, sir?' the driver asked.

'Morningside.' McLean decided that was close enough to home, even though he had no doubts Seagram knew exactly where he lived. A barely perceptible nod from the old man, and the car pulled silently into the road.

McLean made a show of taking in his surroundings. 'They always said crime pays. I'd no idea it was quite so lucrative.'

'It's a laugh-a-minute with you, isn't it, McLean?' Seagram dug a hand into his jacket pocket and came out with a hip flask. He unscrewed the lid before offering it over.

'Bit early for me, thanks. You said you wanted a chat, not a drink.'

'Suit yourself. That's a fine seventy-year-old Teanninich, though. Not easy to come by.' Seagram took a swig, let it swirl around his mouth before swallowing. He seemed to savour the taste for a while before letting out a satisfied 'ahh', and with it a scent of sherried oak.

'I take it this is about your friends, Kenny and Billy?' McLean watched the old man's face as he spoke, not surprised to see it darken into a frown.

'Aye, it is. An' it's a bad business that. See if you'd had a word wi' that young detective lassie like I asked, Billy might still be with us. What was her name? Harrison, wasn't it? I know her uncle. Runs a big garage out at Broxburn. I've put business his way over the years.'

As threats went, it was reasonably subtle. Seagram showing off the breadth of his knowledge and the length of his reach. McLean had met Harrison's uncle, too, and he had a fairly good idea how the man would respond to the sort of threats Seagram might bring to him or his niece.

'I'd tread carefully where Detective Sergeant Harrison is concerned. Friendly warning and all. You underestimate her at your peril.'

'Duly noted.' Seagram wiped at his upper lip with one scarred knuckle, sniffed as if there was snuff spread on it, or something stronger. He said nothing more, leaving a gap for McLean to fill.

'So, Kenneth Morgan and William Creegan. My lot – that's to say the police and the pathologist – didn't think there was anything suspicious about Kenny other than where he was found. Seemed a fair enough conclusion at the time. Now, Billy dying so soon after? That makes me wonder if someone's not trying to put a move on your operations, Mr Seagram.'

McLean had already discounted that explanation, but he put it to Seagram anyway, hoping for some reaction. He wasn't disappointed. The old man's shoulders slumped, not so much a sign of annoyance as the defeated shrug of someone who had hoped for better and now realised he was going to have to spell it out in big letters and short words.

'Let me get something straight here, Ins—Mr McLean. I'm not about to confess to any of the things your lot have accused me of down the years. Not now, not to you, not to anyone. But I can tell you this. There is no turf war in this, no new player trying to muscle in on some hypothetical market in illicit goods and services. This isn't gang on gang violence. Kenny was seventy-one years old. He retired after he served his time on that assault charge you put him away for.'

'Hamesucken.' McLean couldn't stop himself. 'Or was it Stouthrief?'

'Whatever.' Seagram waved it away with an angry hand, rubbed that knuckle against his upper lip again. 'Point is he was an old man doing no harm to anybody. Same wi' Billy. An' the way I hear it youse lot are taking his death a lot more seriously, aye?'

'I can't comment on any ongoing investigation, Mr Seagram. You know that. Even if I did know, which I don't.' A half-lie, but what the hell.

'It's not important. I know what I know. Someone murdered Billy. Murdered Kenny too. They were my friends, so I know how that's going to look to the polis. What I'm telling youse, because I know nobody in a uniform will listen to me, is that it's no' what it looks like. It's no' gangs an' it's no' business. I've my own people looking into it. Probably more effort than youse lot, too. And they've got nothing. You go looking down that avenue an' I guarantee you'll no' find anything either. It's a waste of time when there's precious little of it to spare. This . . .' Seagram reached into his pocket for his hip flask again, and when he pulled it out, McLean could see the old man's hand was shaking. 'This feels personal.'

McLean stared out the windscreen, surprised to find they were already at Tolcross. The rain was coming down steadily now, too. There was something off about Seagram's claims, something the old man wasn't saying. But it was clear he genuinely believed that part of it he had said out loud. And it was true that any investigation by the police into the deaths of two noted Edinburgh gangsters, however old and allegedly retired they might claim to be, would consider a turf war to be the primary motiva-tion. If it wasn't, then what the hell was it?

'When you phoned me, the day after Morgan died. You said he'd called you not long beforehand. Said he was frightened by something.'

'No' frightened, McLean. Kenny was never frightened. He was fuckin' terrified was what he was.'

'And you're worried whoever came for him will come for you.'

Again, Seagram said nothing for a while, his eyes taking on that glazed thousand-yard stare as if he were considering his next words carefully. Finally, he turned and spoke. 'You a religious man, McLean?'

The question brought McLean up short, not because it was unexpected so much as it showed a glaring hole in Seagram's knowledge about him. Unless that was the whole point, of course. To make McLean think the old man didn't have a clue who he was dealing with.

'Not exactly, no. Yourself?'

Seagram rubbed his hands together as if his joints pained him. 'Used to be. A long time ago. I was raised a good Catholic, but the shine went off it when I hit my teens. All that talk of goodness and godliness, and it was all a lie. Just another way of controlling the little people, relieving them of their cash.'

'But you paid for Kenny's funeral?'

That got McLean an appraising look. 'Someone knows more than they're letting on. But aye, I did. Least I could do for an old friend. Kenny still believed, see. Still went to mass every week.'

'Worried for his soul.'

Another strange look, Seagram narrowed his eyes. Not angry, but wary. A nerve struck.

'What I mean, McLean, is that it's no accident he was found in a church. Billy too. An' I know they're neither of them Catholic churches, but that's no matter. It's the link between the two of them an' their deaths. Religion, not some kind of drug war. That's what you need to be looking into, believe me.'

McLean glanced out the window, saw that they were approaching the lights at Holy Corner, appropriately enough. He had a book on order at the Edinburgh Bookshop. Might as well pop in and see if they'd got it.

'You can let me off here,' McLean said to the driver as he unclipped his seatbelt. Then he turned his attention back to Seagram. 'I'll pass your message on to the team investigating Billy Creegan's death, Mr Seagram. Not much more I can do, but for what it's worth I believe you when you say this isn't about your business. Your alleged business if you prefer.'

The car came to a halt, as much because the lights were red as because he'd asked the driver to stop. Never one to pass up an opportunity, McLean opened the door and climbed out as red flicked to green again. 'Thanks for the lift,' he said, then left Seagram and his driver to their fates.

16

Janie stood in the examination theatre in the city mortuary, staring at a naked body laid out on the table. What had gone so wrong in her life that this was preferable to being a few hundred metres up the road in the police station, doing her job? Well, technically this was a part of her job, but a part few detectives bothered with anymore. She had some inkling of why DI McLean had liked to escape here, though. For all the smell and the deeply unsettling sights, it was quiet and strangely peaceful.

'You sure you don't want to come a little closer, Detective Sergeant? We've not opened him up yet.' Cerys, the pathologist's assistant, waved Janie over, and she found herself approaching the table even before she'd thought through the implications.

Laid out in much the same position as they had found him, William Creegan nevertheless looked very different under the cold bright light. He was naked for one thing, his skin almost white. Janie couldn't help but notice how thin he was, too. His arms and legs were like sticks, his stomach flat, and his ribs prominent in his chest. He had large, narrow feet with unnaturally long toes. His hands were large and long-fingered too, as if he weren't quite human. Some alien attempt at mixing in, or perhaps a throwback to a jungle-dwelling hairless ape.

Such was the oddness of those hands and feet, it took Janie a while to understand what else about the body was unusual. Once she'd seen it, of course, she couldn't understand how she could have missed it in the first place. Apart from the neatly trimmed grey on top of Creegan's head, he was as smooth as a new born baby. No hair on his chest, nor his arms or legs. Even the triangle beneath his navel appeared to have been shaved, his shrunken member looking like one of those Australian grubs that Janie had seen in a documentary.

'Not often you see a man his age keep himself trim like that.' Cerys caught Janie's eye, winked. 'Looks like he's waxed it all, too.'

Too much information. Or was it? The whole reason for being here was to build up a picture of the man William Creegan had been, after all. The fact that he shaved his whole body was worth noting, even if the pathologist's assistant seemed to find it amusing.

'When you're done admiring his topiary skills, perhaps we could focus our attention a little north?'

Janie felt the blush in her cheeks as the pathologist reminded them of the business at hand. She moved a little further away from the body, taking in his neatly shaved face, trimmed eyebrows and that ugly welt of a cross branded into his forehead. MacPhail bent low, flipped a set of magnifying lenses strapped to his head so that he could get a better look at the mess.

'Judging by the charring of the skin, and the puckering at the edge of the wound, this was done before he died. Not easy to be certain, but I've seen branding used as a form of torture before and this bears all the hallmarks. A red-hot piece of metal – iron probably – in the shape we see here. Pressed firmly against the forehead to make this mark. Not a straight piece used twice, one at right angles to the other. This is a mark made with a cross.'

'Any idea how long it was done before he died?' Janie asked.

MacPhail looked up at her, his eyes weirdly distorted through the magnifying lenses until he swung them out of the way. 'Not long. There's little sign of the wound weeping. It wouldn't bleed, of course. The heat has cauterised all the blood vessels. But given time it would inflame and then start to ooze. It's possible the shock of it caused his heart to fail. We'll have to open him up to check that. Otherwise, there's nothing obvious externally to suggest how he died. Except the brand.'

Janie took the opportunity to step back, putting enough distance between herself and the cadaver that she didn't have to witness it being cut open. She hardly watched as MacPhail and his assistant went about their work with swift efficiency, let her mind wander instead to what kind of a man Creegan must have been.

She'd seen him once before he had died, standing at the graveside of Kenneth Morgan, along with Archibald Seagram and one other man. What had his name been? Ray McAllister, that was it. Another of Seagram's old guard.

From his arrest record, Janie knew that Creegan was seventy years old, although seeing his body laid out there she'd have knocked ten off that easy. He was in good shape for his age. Well, apart from the whole being dead thing. Perhaps his health was a result of a rather ascetic lifestyle. He didn't seem to be a man overfond of food, unlike Morgan. There were none of the signs of excessive drinking she might have expected either, so his tastes must have been directed elsewhere. Drugs? She'd have to find out.

'Ah, yes. That would probably do it.'

Dr MacPhail's words broke through Janie's thoughts, and she looked up, wishing almost immediately that she hadn't. He held a glistening lump of muscle and connective tissue in a blood-smeared latex-gloved hand, peering closely at it with those magnifying lenses of his as he turned it this way and that.

'Heart attack?' she asked, her own rising up in her gorge.

MacPhail's shoulders slumped in disappointment, and he almost seemed to forget what he was holding for a moment, until Cerys took it from him with gentle hands.

'That's such an imprecise term, Janie. You really should know better.' He looked back to his bloodstained fingers, momentarily surprised to see the organ no longer there. 'But essentially yes. A very similar myocardial infarction to the fellow we found in the other church. He'd have felt a little chest pain probably, shortness of breath, but it would have been very quick.'

'Could the shock of being branded have done it? Brought on the infarction?' Janie asked.

'It could certainly have been a trigger, yes. Although I suspect it was a ticking time bomb just waiting to pop.'

'You think something similar might have happened to Morgan's face?' Janie pointed at the cross seared into Creegan's forehead. 'Maybe that's what made his ticker give out, too?'

MacPhail fixed her with a stare that, while not unfriendly, wasn't exactly warm. 'You do remember the state that body was in when we pulled it out of that falling building, don't you? There wasn't enough of his face left to identify anything, and I think I said as much in my report.'

'Sorry. Just a thought.'

'No, you're right. If we'd known we were looking for something like this, it might have been possible to analyse skin fragments for signs of burning. As it is . . .'

We could always exhume the body. The thought rose unbidden in Janie's mind, followed immediately by a dozen reasons why they really couldn't. Not least of them Detective Superintendent Peter Nelson.

'I'll have a look at the photographs once we're done with this fellow, OK?' The pathologist gave her an apologetic smile. 'Best I can do, Janie.'

★ ★ ★

'You are absolutely not going to exhume Kenneth Morgan's body. He's barely been in the ground a week.'

Standing in her usual spot in the detective superintendent's office, Janie couldn't help thinking that Morgan's relative freshness was actually an argument in favour of digging him up, rather than against. The longer they left him in the ground, the less chance there was of any useful information being garnered from a second post mortem examination. And a week in, the soil over the coffin would have hardly settled, so the digging would be easy. It was a moot point anyway, as she hadn't suggested exhumation in the first place.

'I really don't want to, sir. I know how much paperwork it involves, let alone the trouble we'd be in if the press got hold of the story. Or Seagram, for that matter.'

Mentioning that name was perhaps not wise, but Janie had found she couldn't help herself. Ever since she'd first noticed the way Nelson flinched when he heard it, she'd been dropping it into their discussions. It was childish, she knew, but given how uncomfortable the man made her, she'd take small victories where she found them.

'What's the state of the investigation anyway? Twenty-four hours since we discovered the body. Have you found out how he got into the church yet?'

'The main entrance was locked, but there's a back door you can access from the communal garden behind the tenements. It's not very secure, just a latch and a couple of bolts on the inside. They weren't closed, so someone could've gone out that way.'

'Anyone see anything?'

'DC Stringer's finishing up door to doors with some uniform officers right now.' Janie glanced at her watch. 'I was going to head over there and see how that's coming along.'

'Who looks after the church?'

'There's a caretaker goes in once a week to check the place over. He's the one who found the body and called us.'

'Once a week?' Nelson's voice rose an octave. 'How long was Creegan's body in there?'

'Tom . . . Dr MacPhail reckons he died about twelve hours before we found him, so late night, early morning of the day before yesterday. Lucky for us that was just before the caretaker was due his weekly visit, otherwise we'd likely not have found the body yet.'

Nelson leaned back in his chair, brought his hands up to his face and laced his fingers together as if praying. When he spoke, his voice was muffled for a moment until he moved them out of the way again. 'What's your plan then?'

Janie wanted to say that she'd hand it all over to the nearest detective inspector and do what they told her to, but of course there was no one available. 'You still want me to lead on this, sir?' she asked instead.

'Is there anyone else?' It wasn't a question that demanded an answer.

'I'd remind you this is a murder investigation, sir. With possible links to organised criminal activity. It should really be a DCI in charge. Probably a superintendent. I'm just a sergeant.'

Nelson's expression was almost sympathetic. 'I know, Janie. But we work with what we've got. You'll have to take the lead, at least for now. Kirsty's due back from Gartcosh this evening and she'll be SIO, at least in name. Meantime, I've every faith in you.'

Janie didn't know whether to laugh or cry at that, settled for a nod to show she understood. 'What about overtime, sir? And we'll need to poach a few constables from uniform, just to cover all the bases.'

Nelson grimaced, but she could tell it was just for show. 'Well, we've no DI's salary coming out of the budget just yet, so I guess that eases up the spending a bit. Don't go mad though, and I'll need to see the daily rosters. If you can get this wrapped up quickly, so much the better.'

Janie nodded once – not trusting herself to speak lest she say something regrettable – and left the detective superintendent's office in silence. Everything about this case screamed complicated to her, and she could see it drawing out into the future with no obvious resolution. Add to that pressure from Seagram, who seemed to have far too much influence over both senior police officers and politicians, and it was hard not to see the poison bubbling away in the chalice she'd been handed.

17

As it happened, the book he was waiting for hadn't come in, but McLean bought a couple of paperbacks he'd had his eye on and tucked them into the inside pocket of his coat against the rain. It was easing off anyway as he stepped back out onto Bruntsfield Place and set off on the now not so long walk home.

The two conversations he'd been part of earlier that day tumbled around in his thoughts as he measured a steady pace along Morningside Road. Despite having retired, and throwing himself wholeheartedly into Emma's rehabilitation, McLean couldn't deny that he missed a great part of the detective work that had been his career for well over two decades. Not the admin, for sure. And certainly not the endless politicking and backstabbing that went on the higher you rose through the ranks. That was likely the same in any organisation, of course. What he missed was the puzzle, the pattern matching, the uncovering of mysteries. And here was something that had all the hallmarks of the kind of case he'd never been able to ignore.

Archibald Seagram was not a difficult man to read. He was of a type that McLean had encountered all too often down the years. Happy to dole out pain to others, but quick to cry foul when it was done to him. He'd been a brutal, violent man in his youth and middle years, if the stories were to be believed. You couldn't build a criminal empire the size of his without being brutal and violent, so they were probably true. How many of the city's recent buildings had more than concrete in their foundations courtesy of Seagram and his minions? Too many, for sure.

And yet for all that, McLean had believed the old man when he said that the killings of Morgan and Creegan were not the opening shots in a new turf war. Apart from the fact that Jo Dexter would know if someone was trying to move in on Seagram's territory – probably even before the old man himself – there was no good reason for him to have lied about it. Seagram wanted these deaths investigated properly, and he didn't want them slowed down by the inevitable attempts to work out who might have been looking to make a move. That was how the investigation was going to play out regardless, even if McLean spoke to his old colleagues on Seagram's behalf.

But why would he consider doing that? He owed the man nothing, less than nothing. No, he'd pass on the message as asked, something he needed to do soon anyway if only to avoid suspicion he was somehow in Seagram's pocket. And then he'd put it all behind him and get on with more important things.

Aye, right.

At least the other conversation was easier to ignore. Jo Dalgliesh would have her reasons for chasing the dead priest story, but it was a very cold case. Much more Ramsay's thing, although the retired detective chief superintendent probably shouldn't be helping. Not given her security clearance and access to old case files. McLean trusted that she'd keep to the right side of the line, even if she came very close to it, but again it wasn't his problem. He had plenty else to be getting on with.

And yet as his feet stomped out their rhythm on the damp paving slabs, he couldn't help seeing links where there should be none. Someone had killed a priest, in a church, after all. And now two men were dead, laid out in churches, at least one with a cross burned into his forehead. And Seagram was convinced the reli-gious angle was what the police should be looking at, rather than anything gang-related. That might have been misdirection, of course. Or something else entirely.

Glancing up for a moment, McLean saw that he was just pass-ing what he thought of as his church, even though he had rarely set foot inside it, and never as a part of a congregation. He paused at the gate to the vicarage next door. He could see if Mary Currie was in, but what would he ask her? She was Anglican, not Cath-olic. Doubtful she'd know much about Father Eric O'Connell, dead these past forty years, although she might be able to tell him about St Andrew's and St Mark's.

A flurry of wind swept the rain from the trees, their branches just beginning to bud at the tips. The chill reminded McLean that he was cold and wet, and would almost certainly be told off by Emma when he got home. There was no need to talk to the priest about any of it, since he wasn't a detective any more. Time to go home and warm up a bit.

He knew that something was up even before he reached the back door. An unfamiliar car stood on the gravel circle in front of the house. Unfamiliar it might have been, but McLean knew that it was a police pool car without having to look too closely. As he pushed open the back door and stepped into the utility room, he heard the low mutter of conversation. Emma and someone else, judging by the tone, although he couldn't make out any actual words. Retrieving his books from the inside pocket, he hung his coat from an empty hook to dry, then carried on through into the kitchen.

'Ah, Tony. You're back.' Emma looked up from the far end of the table, where she'd wheeled herself. Beside her, in the chair McLean usually had for himself, sat Detective Chief Inspector Jo Dexter.

★ ★ ★

'Seems you've been getting mighty pally with old Archie Seagram lately. You want to tell me what that's all about?'

McLean stood in the half-open doorway to the coach house, damp coat back on, hands deep in his pockets. He'd brought Jo Dexter out here not so much because he worried about Emma hearing their conversation, but because the detective chief inspector had been fiddling with her cigarette packet and was clearly in need of her regular nicotine fix. She stood under the overhang of the roof close by the old stone mounting block, fag in hand. She took a deep drag, held it in for a moment, and then blew pungent smoke out through mouth and nose.

'Funny you should mention Seagram,' McLean said. 'He gave me a lift halfway home today. If you'd not been here already, I'd have phoned and told you all about it. Soon as I'd made myself a cup of tea.'

'Let me guess. He's trying to persuade you his two closest mates winding up dead is not some kind of turf war?'

'Exactly that. Told him I couldn't care less, but he won't listen. Thing is though, I think he might be telling the truth.'

'First time for everything.' Dexter dropped the almost-dead cigarette onto the ground and killed it with her boot. 'And between you and me, there's been nothing in the wind lately. One of the reasons why I'm happy enough to let wee Janie look into it all. I don't think this is gang-related, which puts it in your team's remit. Your old team, I should say. None of us have staff to spare, mind. And we're not exactly shedding any tears over the loss of Kenny Morgan and Billy Creegan.'

'But much as we'd like to ignore it, we can't not investigate.'

'We?' Dexter arched a greying eyebrow at him.

'Force of habit. Figure of speech. Whatever. I'm doing my best to keep my nose out of it. But Seagram seems dead set on my being involved.'

'He threatened you?'

'Not yet.' McLean recalled his earlier conversation, and the veiled hints Seagram had dropped about DS Harrison. 'Think he might have Janie in his sights though. She's from Broxburn, has family there. That's Seagram's stronghold, is it not?'

Dexter kicked at the brick pavers, then took a step back as a gust of wind brought more rain in under the overhang. 'That's my fault, probably. I asked her to go to Morgan's funeral.'

'Aye, I know. But she's smart. She can look after herself. I might ask around a bit, see if anyone knows anything about Seagram's old gang. There was another one at the funeral, I understand. Ray McAllister. Might be worth finding out a bit more about him.'

'Ray? Jesus, Tony. I'd steer clear of him. Mad as a badger that one. And mean with it. Seagram's an evil bastard, but at least he's more or less predictable. McAllister's . . .' Dexter shook her head without saying what McAllister was.

'Don't worry. I've no intention of talking to him. And I'm not doing anything to help Seagram either. Easy enough to see why he's trying to pull our strings, after all.'

'Oh aye?' Dexter cocked her head to one side, pulled out her cigarette packet and then put it away again.

'Well think about it, Jo. He's pushing us away from the turf war angle because he's certain that's not what's going on here and we're wasting time digging into it. The way I see it, he knows perfectly well why Morgan and Creegan were killed, but he can't tell us without implicating himself in something. And for whatever reason, he can't do anything about it himself.'

'How d'you figure that?'

'I've seen the man. He's genuinely scared. He'd have to be to reach out to us like he has. But see if we do find out who's behind these killings? I'd not put much money on them staying alive long enough to stand trial.'

Dexter considered this while she took the packet out again and this time slid a cigarette from it, tapped the end against the cardboard in the way smokers do that McLean had never understood.

'Makes sense, I guess. Use us to do the legwork, then exact his revenge before whatever he doesn't want known comes out.'

'Or at least silence someone who presumably has a lot of dirt on him. The whole thing stinks.'

'Aye, you're not wrong there.' The detective chief inspector lit up, huddled close to the door, back to the wind as it continued to whip the rain at them both. 'What you got tucked away in this place anyways? Coach and four, is it?'

McLean stepped aside, gestured for her to go in. For a moment he wondered whether it was wise, given the cigarette, but the only thing flammable was in a sealed metal can, petrol for the ancient lawnmower. On the far side of the space, by the large wooden garage doors, sat the twisted remains of his old Alfa Romeo. His father's car before him, it had survived forty years unscathed. Mostly because it had been parked up unused in this very coach house. Getting it running and using it himself had not been quite such a good idea.

'Wondered what happened to the old jalopy.' Dexter stuck her cigarette between her lips as she wandered over to the car and tugged at the tarpaulin draped over its battered roof. 'That'd polish out no trouble.'

'I did think about getting it restored. That would be the second time, though, since I put it back on the road.'

'Aye, I remember the first time it got smashed up.'

Hardly surprising, given that it was one of Dexter's junior officers whose body falling from a third-storey balcony had smashed in the roof.

'There's a place I read about that takes the old engines out and puts in electric ones. Thought about doing that, but then I was told how much it would cost.' McLean glanced through the open door to where Emma's little Renault sat, plugged into its charging point.

'Might just stick to modern cars for now. Don't think I'd dare take the Alfa out if it was fixed.'

'Ach, you'd be fine. Not as if you're going to be using it for work.' Dexter pinched out the cigarette and stuck it behind her ear. 'Unless you're actually thinking of coming back, of course.'

'I don't think so, Jo. Can't say there aren't things I miss about it, but I need to be here.' McLean stared out past the parked Renault towards the back door to the house.

'Aye, for now. But Em's getting better every day. There'll come a point where she'll no' want you crowding her all the time. Might need to find yourself a hobby.'

Was this the real reason Dexter had come out to his house for a chat, rather than simply phoning? McLean had heard about his replacement as DI falling through, but if they were that desperate, he'd expect Jayne McIntyre to be the one who paid a visit. No, he was just being paranoid.

'Anyways. I need to get some kind of official statement from you about your interaction with Seagram. Interactions plural, I should say now.' Dexter retrieved the cigarette from behind her ear and carefully slid it back into the packet. 'You mentioned something about a cup of tea?'

18

Janie sat at her desk and stared at her computer, trying to ignore the flicker and buzz of a dying fluorescent tube in the light fitting overhead. It didn't help that she had a dull pain behind her eyes that, for once, wasn't the fault of her flatmate and an ill-advised bottle of Chardonnay. She and Manda had both cut down their drinking considerably in the past couple of months, mostly because they were so overworked there was hardly time for any kind of social life.

'You're in early, J.'

She looked up to see the bright smile and perfectly made-up features of DC Bryant. Always fresh and enthusiastic, as if she'd had a full night's deep sleep and plenty of time between waking and heading out to work. Everything appeared effortless to Jessica, but in that moment, Janie couldn't even muster the energy to hate her for it.

'Thinking of setting up a bed in the empty office at the back of the station. I don't imagine anyone would notice, and it would save a fortune in bus fares.' She yawned, picked up her coffee mug and stared at its emptiness for far too long before understanding what that meant.

'You want a refill?' Bryant reached for the mug, but Janie shook her head, stood up.

'It's OK. I'll get it. Need to stretch my legs anyway.' She wandered over to the far side of the room where a filter coffee machine was still half full. One benefit of coming in first thing; the coffee was always fresh and hot if you made it yourself, and there was even a chance the milk might not have run out.

'So, what you been up to?' Bryant asked as she helped herself to the last mugful.

'Reading up on William Creegan. There's a background folder on him thick as my wrist. Led a colourful life, probably as much of it behind bars as not. He last got out about five years ago though. Kept himself on the straight and narrow since. Or at least hasn't come across our radar.'

'What was he in for?'

'Serious assault, apparently. He beat the shit out of some pimp in Sighthill. Broke the man's jaw and both of his wrists. You'll never guess who put him away for it, too.'

'Who?'

'To—Detective Inspector McLean. One of his last collars as a DS. I think it's probably what got him promoted.'

'Huh. So he was the one who arrested both Morgan and Creegan last. I'd call that something worth actioning, if I was running this investigation.'

Janie couldn't quite tell whether Bryant was joking or not. The detective constable had a dry wit at the best of times, and before she could be pressed on it, the door to the CID room banged open. DS Stringer came in first, closely followed by Cass Mitchell and Sandy Gregg, a couple of lost looking uniform constables in their wake.

'No Lofty today?' Janie couldn't recall the roster sheets and who was on the day shift this week, too much else cluttering up her brain, too little sleep.

'On his way up,' Gregg said. 'Kirsty's in, too, at least for the next hour. Think we can move the briefing forward a bit?'

Janie glanced at her desk, the cluttered screen of information and the heaps of folders. So much paperwork for one dead man. 'Aye. Sooner we get started the better. Incident room in half an hour?'

It was a pathetically small team to be conducting a murder investigation. Two detective sergeants, four detective constables, an absentee detective chief inspector overseeing it all. At least they had a decent roster of uniforms to help with the grunt work, and Sandy Gregg always managed to poach the best admins. Janie looked out over a desperately quiet and empty incident room, checked the clock that hung above the door at the back. No need to clear her throat or call for attention; hardly anyone was chatting at all.

'OK, team. Thanks for coming in early. We've a lot of ground to cover, and few enough of us to cover it, so let's get cracking. You'll all be aware that the body of one William Creegan was found in St Mark's church in Gorgie the night before last. He'd been branded on the forehead with a cross . . . or something intended to form the shape of a cross. The post mortem reckons he died of a heart attack, but the branding was done just before he died. Can't rule out the shock of it caused his ticker to give out. Either way, it's a very suspicious death, so we're treating it as murder.'

Normally Janie would have expected some comment from the crowd at this point, a muttered insult or sotto voce criticism. Instead, all eyes remained on her, their attention total. It was enough to give her stage fright.

'Door to door in the tenements either side of the church has turned up nothing of substance, although Creegan and whoever attacked him must have entered via the back door accessed through the communal gardens. St Mark's hasn't been used in years and is only checked once a week. Word is it was being considered for deconsecration and sale, but no decision has been made on that yet. We're waiting on a list of all the people who had access to the place.'

A noise at the door broke the searchlight attention on her. Heads turned as DCI Ritchie stepped into the room. Janie's heart sank when she saw that Detective Superintendent Nelson was following her. This briefing would have been swifter, easier and much more effective without his input, she was sure.

'Carry on, Janie,' Ritchie said as the two senior officers shuffled into the ample space behind the rest of the team.

'William Creegan is a known associate of Archibald Seagram. He is – was – a career criminal. It would appear that he's been keeping on the right side of the law since his release from Saughton five years ago, but I'd take that with a pinch of salt. We've never managed to pin anything on Seagram, so chances are his old mate's just been careful.'

'Not careful enough, aye?'

Janie recognised the voice and suppressed the smile it provoked. DC Stringer could always be relied upon to lighten the tone.

'We need to establish Creegan's whereabouts in the hours leading up to his death. We have his phone, so IT will do their best to get the GPS data off it, but that might take a while. Meantime we'll be talking to his known associates, neighbours, anyone who might have seen him. Forensics are as certain as they can be that he died in that church sometime in the early hours of Wednesday morning, so why did he go there? Was he meeting someone? If so, who?'

'This have anything to do with the other dead man in a church from a couple of weeks back?'

Janie didn't recognise this voice, but by the way everyone else in the room turned their heads, she saw that it had come from one of the uniform constables. A lad so young he couldn't have long been out of school, his pale face mottled into freckles as he blushed at the attention. He'd cut his ginger hair short, presumably to avoid being the brunt of too much locker room humour, but all that did was emphasise how much his ears stuck out. Poor sod.

'Kenneth Morgan's death was not thought to be suspicious. But in the light of this new case, and the fact he and Creegan were friends, we can't rule anything out at this point.' Janie glanced across at the detective superintendent as she spoke, saw his face turn thunderous. 'We'll be concentrating our resources on Creegan for the now, though. Only go back over Morgan's case if something new comes up,' she added. Nelson's nod of approval at her words were hardly any consolation.

'DS Gregg will be handing out assignments as soon as we're done here.' Janie directed her voice to the back of the room. 'Sir? Ma'am? Anything you'd like to add?'

Ritchie started to shake her head, but Nelson pushed through the small crowd and came to stand by Janie's side.

'Good work, Detective Sergeant,' he said quietly to her, before turning to the audience.

'Right, team. I know we've a lot of ground to cover and not much in the way of manpower, but I also know you're up to the challenge. Chances are this is someone with a grudge against a man known to be violent in the past. Motive and opportunity, aye? Find out who's got both and you're done, so let's get this all wrapped up quickly, eh?' He paused a moment as if expecting some response before going on. 'And I know there's a tendency to hold back a bit when the victim's a man like Creegan. Long term criminal; probably deserved what he got. Why bother looking for the killer? They did us a favour. I've heard it all before and I don't want to hear it again. A man's dead and someone out there killed him. Let's find out who and put him away before he does it to someone else.'

The silence continued for an awkward moment, and then the

crowd began muttering. Janie risked a quick glance at Nelson to see how well he was taking it. Not well, if the reddening of his cheeks was any indication.

'OK people,' she said. 'No time for chattering. We've got plenty of work to do so get stuck in. We'll have a catch-up session this evening and I want to see solid progress by then.'

19

Janie watched as Nelson moved among the detectives; a word here, a pat on the shoulder there. As if he were a general among his troops on the eve of an assault in which he had no intention of taking part. He'd given her a slight nod once she'd wound up the briefing, the closest to a thanks for curtailing his embarrassment as she could expect. She wished he'd just go away, if she was being honest with herself. Having him watching over her – over everything – was a distraction she could do without.

'Stuff just in from forensics. Where d'you want it?'

Janie turned to see one of the admin support staff with a cardboard box, on top of which balanced a clipboard.

'Here's fine.' She gestured to the table behind her, then grabbed the clipboard and signed the relevant sheets. Technically she should have gone through all the individual items first, checking nothing had gone missing on its journey from crime scene to forensic labs and then on to here. Life was too short sometimes.

Inside the box were the personal effects of William Creegan at the time of his death. Or more accurately the time of his being found dead, as there was no way to know whether his killer might have made off with some crucial piece of evidence. The only thing missing from the box was his phone, which had already been sent down to the tech labs in the basement. She'd pay a visit to Mike Simpson later in the day and see what he'd managed to come up with.

'Anything interesting?'

DC Mitchell wandered up to peer into the box as Janie took the items out and placed them on the table. Creegan's clothes had all been neatly folded and individually bagged. Janie doubted there was much to be gleaned from them, but they'd be held in evidence until the case was closed. The contents of his pockets were nothing unexpected. Some change, a clean handkerchief, a blister pack of generic painkiller tablets, only two of the twelve remaining.

One bag held a thick wallet; old leather, cracked and fading at the crease. Janie counted out nine hundred and fifty pounds in a mix of ten, twenty and fifty pound notes, placing them on the table alongside a couple of debit cards, a credit card and a bus pass. This last had a photograph that was readily identifiable as the man whose body they had found, and was issued in the name of William B Creegan.

'That's a lot of cash for an old man,' Mitchell said as she looked over Janie's shoulder. 'Guess it rules out robbery as a motive though.'

Janie nodded, her attention mostly absorbed by the wallet for a moment as she checked all the little slots and pockets. Satisfied it was empty, she placed it down alongside the cards and then picked up the final bag. This contained a set of keys on a keyring. Two different latch keys and a slender mortice key, along with a couple that looked like they might be for padlocks. No car keys, but then neither had there been a driver's licence.

'We got an address for him?'

Mitchell reached out and picked up the bus pass, peered at it a moment, then held it up for Janie to see. Tiny writing identified a street in Stockbridge. A bit more upmarket than she'd been expecting, but then looking at the bagged clothes she could see Creegan had dressed well.

'Check that with records can you, Cass?' Janie carefully placed the wallet and its contents back into the bag, sealed it shut. 'Then I think you and me should go pay Mr Creegan's home a visit.'

William Creegan lived in rather grander circumstances than his old friend Kenneth Morgan: a mid-terrace townhouse in Cumberland Street that had to be worth at least a million these days. Given his age, he might have bought it decades ago, of course, but it was still more than your average criminal would likely be able to afford.

'How the other half live, eh?' DC Mitchell raised one perfect eyebrow as she looked up at the building's facade. Three storeys and a basement, with a pair of tall, narrow windows either side of the large front door that was accessed at the top of a short flight of stone steps. It might have been split into flats like many of the other houses along the street, except that there was no multiple button entryphone system, and Creegan had been listed as the only occupant.

'Bit big for one man, too.' Janie selected what looked like the right key from the bunch that had come back from forensics. When that didn't work, she tried the next one, then the next. Of course, it was the last one that worked. With the lightest of clicks, the door swung open. Now would be the time to discover that he had an alarm fitted.

Stepping into a neat hall, Janie looked around and listened for the telltale beeps. A car rattled along the street outside, but otherwise there was no noise at all. Strange how a man so deeply embedded in the Edinburgh criminal underworld would not bother with securing his own home, but then maybe he felt his reputation as a hard man, second in command to someone like Archibald Seagram, was enough to prevent anyone even thinking of burglary.

'No alarm?' Mitchell asked as she followed Janie inside and

closed the door behind her. She turned and studied the door frame, looking for sensors, finding none. 'Huh.'

'Lucky for us. It's always a pain having to call that in, and the noise drives me up the wall.' Janie pulled on a pair of latex gloves, just in case they found anything suspicious. 'Come on. Better not waste too much time or the boss will be bending my ear again.'

Doors either side of the hall led to a large sitting room and a similarly sized dining room. As Janie stepped into the first, looking around at neatly presented furniture, a few so-so paintings on the wall, bookshelves lined with old leather-bound books and an open fireplace, clean and empty, Janie was struck by how much it looked like a photograph from some kind of House and Home magazine. An interior designer's idea of how an Edinburgh town house should look rather than something that was lived in. The air had a stale quality to it that spoke of little use, too.

Across the hall, the dining room was the same. More pictures that might have been picked up in any antique warehouse in the city looked down on a large mahogany dining table with twelve matching chairs. The fireplace in this room had been boarded up, a long, bow-legged sideboard shoved a little incongruously into the corner. As if the designer had got their measurements wrong. Beside it, another door led through a butler's pantry into a kitchen, and here a little more sign of life being lived was evident. Only a mug placed upside down on the drainer beside the sink, but it was something.

'It's all very . . . clean.' Mitchell ran a gloved finger over the surface of the kitchen table, leaving the barest mark behind, a perfect line in a thin covering of fine dust.

'Place this big? One old man? He'd have to keep it clean, or it'd overwhelm him. Probably has someone come in regularly anyway. We'll have to check that, track them down.'

'You don't think it's more than that?'

Janie looked around the spotless room, the gleaming cooker,

the shiny cupboard doors and perfect tile splashbacks. It was very clean indeed. Far cleaner than the chaos she and Manda shared, even though both of them were reasonably fastidious when it came to tidying. Where were the inevitable fat spots on the cooker back? The water stains around the sink? Even the bare wood surface of the kitchen table bore no marks, as if it had only recently come from the workshop that made it.

'Let's have a look on the other floors before we jump to any conclusions, shall we?' She headed out of the kitchen door, back to the hall and the grand staircase leading to the upper storeys. A smaller set of stone stairs led down to the basement. Why on earth would a single man need such a large house?

'You want to split up?' Mitchell waved a hand towards the down stairs.

'Sure. It'll be quicker that way. Shout if you find anything interesting.'

On the first floor, Janie found four bedrooms, all with ensuite bathrooms, none of which looked like they'd been used in months. The beds were made, but the wardrobes were empty save for a few coat hangers. Each of the bathrooms had towels and toiletries laid out as if this was some kind of boutique hotel, not someone's home. A narrower flight of stairs took her to a dark wood panelled landing, off which were a half dozen smaller bedrooms, a single bathroom shared between them. Again, the beds were made, but the cupboards empty; nothing personal to be seen. It was as if William Creegan didn't actually live here at all.

As she stepped out of the bathroom and took one more look around before heading downstairs to see what Mitchell had found, Janie noticed a part of the panelling that was slightly out of alignment with the rest. A hidden stair to the attic above, no doubt. These old houses rambled on forever.

Finding the latch, she pulled open the panel to reveal a steep, narrow set of steps. The attic stretched the whole length of the building, from party wall to party wall, the large space made larger still by a pair of dormer windows looking out the back. As she stepped onto the bare wood floorboards, Janie caught a slight scent she couldn't immediately place. Her attention was more on the utter lack of anything to be seen in the space. She had never seen an attic so bare.

The view from the windows showed a small garden that opened onto a narrow mews lane. Beyond it the backs of the tenements on the next street, and – further still – the rooftops of the north city stretching away towards Newhaven and Granton. How far was it from here to St Andrew's church, to the much smaller and far more lived in flat where Kenneth Morgan had spent his declining years?

'Bloody hell. This room's bigger than my whole place.'

Janie turned swiftly to see Mitchell emerge from the narrow stairwell, eyes wide.

'Mine, too. And a lot cleaner.' She caught that scent again, and finally realised what it was. 'Too clean. It's been professionally scrubbed.'

'What, since Creegan died? But that was only a couple of days ago.'

'No. A while back. Maybe a week or two?' Janie crouched down and touched the floorboards by her feet. In any normal house they would be dusty at the very least, but the white latex of her gloves came away clean. Not spotless, but still far less grubby than they had any right to be. 'There's dust, just hardly any. And there's a smell of disinfectant. Very faint, but I keep catching it now and again.

'Why would they . . .?'

'No idea, but I think it's fair to say Creegan didn't actually live here. You find anything interesting in the basement?'

Mitchell shook her head. 'Couple of rooms that could be used for anything. Lots of power sockets in the walls, not much furniture. No sign anyone's been here recently except for that one mug in the kitchen. Can't have been used for anything except a drink of water as there's no food in the place. Not even a jar of instant coffee or some teabags.'

Janie checked her watch, aware that they'd probably spent more time on this part of the investigation than they should have. It was a puzzle, for sure, but it didn't really help with tracing Creegan's last movements before his death.

'OK. We'd better head back to the station. See how the rest of the team's getting on. If Creegan wasn't living here, where the hell was he staying?'

20

The incident room was uncomfortably empty when Janie returned, with Cass Mitchell close behind her. A couple of admin staff were muttering into phones, presumably trying to track down the last of the residents in the neighbourhood of St Mark's. Sandy Gregg stared motionless at an all-too empty whiteboard, a marker pen clutched in one hand. Only Lofty Blane looked like he was actually doing something, sat in front of a large computer screen in that hunched up position he always adopted. Like an adult using a child's furniture. He glanced up as they came in, a moment's furrowed brow as if he couldn't quite remember who they were.

'You get anywhere with Creegan's house?' Gregg asked Janie before she could say anything. There was an edge of desperate hope in the detective sergeant's voice, and it wasn't hard to understand why. Too much time had already passed since the body had been found. The trail Creegan might have left before he arrived at St Mark's was already going cold.

Janie shook her head, explained what they'd found. Or not found. 'Don't think anyone's lived there for at least a fortnight, maybe more. Perhaps he was going to sell it. Who knows?'

'I can have someone phone around the local estate agents. Maybe talk to the ESPC, see if there was a listing being prepared.' Gregg made a note on her pad. More data to put into the HOLMES II computer, even though Janie reckoned it was something of a red herring.

'How are you getting on with the list of potential suspects?' she asked instead.

'Slowly.' Gregg indicated the empty whiteboard. 'We've started pulling out names from Creegan's arrest record, folk he's beaten up in the past. So far, they're all dead already or serving time themselves. And that's just the ones we have on record.'

'Have you spoken to Vice?'

'Aye, they're asking around, too. Should get a list of names from them in the next day or two. Might not be much use, mind, since Creegan's been off everyone's radar for the last five years.'

'Or it might be as long as my arm, given he's been cracking heads for half a century and more. Could really do with a break here, Sandy. Every question we come up with has no answer, and just begs a dozen more.'

'We've got some partial GPS data back from the phone.'

Both Gregg and Janie turned to where Lofty sat. Despite the large size of his computer monitor, he could still look easily over the top of it, even while sitting.

'Partial?' Janie crossed the room and peered at the screen, currently displaying what looked like a spreadsheet.

'Aye. Said something about the data being scrubbed recently. There's only about twenty-four hours before we found the body.'

'Better than nothing. You got it there?' Janie pointed at the screen.

'That's it, aye. Raw data anyway. They're trying to get it sorted into a map right now.'

Janie glanced around the sleepy incident room once again, checked her watch. 'OK. Thanks, Lofty. Think I'm maybe due a visit down to the basement anyway. I'll go have a chat with the IT boys in person.'

★ ★ ★

Janie considered herself reasonably smart when it came to computers. She was young enough to have grown up with the internet, more or less, and the same analytical skills she had developed as a detective served her well when it came to dealing with the latest technology. Even so, the labs she entered were a mystery to her. Tucked away in a series of interconnected rooms in the basement at the front of the station, the IT department was one of the few forensic teams still working in house. That the team kept the building's network running might have had something to do with that, but Janie was grateful she didn't have to traipse across town, or deal with the complex budgeting requirements of outsourcing. Mike Simpson, who ran the lab like it was his own fiefdom, was a jovial fellow too.

'Hey, Janie. You got the message about the phone data then?' He greeted her with a smile as she peered around the half-opened door.

'Yeah. Lofty said you'd only managed a day's worth?'

The smile faltered. 'Sorry I couldn't do better, but whoever set up the phone in the first place really knew what they were doing. All location data's set to self-delete after twenty-four hours. It was lucky I noticed when I did, otherwise we'd have nothing.'

'That's . . . paranoid?'

'And then some. I don't think I've ever seen anyone do that before. I mean, you can turn off the GPS altogether, then nobody can track you. But your maps won't work either. So I guess maybe your man needed them but didn't want anyone to know where he'd been. And was clever enough to know how to set it up that way.'

Creegan had not long turned seventy at the time of his death. Would he have been that *au fait* with the technology? Janie wasn't even half his age, and she didn't have a clue. Hadn't even known it was possible until this conversation.

'Either that or he had someone set it up for him. Anything else of note on his phone we should know about? It looked like a fairly new one.'

Simpson reached across his workbench and fetched a clear plastic evidence bag to him. Inside, a large slab of glass and darkened aluminium.

'Top of the line. Not more than a year old, but then some people change their phones every six months. This is fairly rare, though. It's not an iPhone. Android based, but there's some military grade security features built on top of that. They're popular with wealthy businessmen and celebrities. People who don't want to be hacked.'

'I take it that wasn't a problem for you, though?'

'That depends on what you mean by problem. It wasn't easy, but luckily enough I had to break something very similar a couple of months back. Made all my mistakes on that one. And we had his fingerprints too. I wouldn't have fancied taking it down to the mortuary to unlock it with face recognition. That doesn't always work with dead bodies anyway.'

Janie recalled the cadaver, shaved smooth like some septuagenarian infant. What were they dealing with here? 'So, what can you tell me about where he was before he died?'

Simpson spun around on his chair to face a pair of large screens. He brought both to life with a click of a mouse, one showing much the same spreadsheet as Janie had seen on Lofty Blane's computer, the other a mess of spindly green lines it took her a while to recognise as a street map of Edinburgh. Not something normal folk used, this looked more like something from a pre-internet era games console.

'This is the cell tower network,' Simpson said as he tapped and clicked and moved the lines around. 'A lot of the time phones aren't using actual GPS. Not actual satellite signals, but triangulation from transmitter masts and very sensitive dead reckoning from the built in accelerometers.'

'I'll take your word for it.' Janie stared harder at the screens, trying to work out exactly where in the city the map was centred. Before she could get her head around it all, Simpson clicked on one of the first entries in the spreadsheet and a green dot flared on the map.

'This is the earliest data we've got for him. About twenty-four hours before we accessed the phone. Timestamp there shows it was 10:21 on Tuesday morning.' He pointed to the spreadsheet where, now it had been drawn to her attention, Janie could see a string of numbers representing date and time.

'And that's where, exactly?' she asked.

'Cumberland Street.' Simpson scrolled the wheel on his mouse down the spreadsheet column. 'Stays there until about half eleven.'

'That'll be the house we have listed as his address, but it's not been lived in for a while. If he was there for an hour or more, he could be – what? – picking up mail?'

'That's more your department than mine. I can tell you where he went and how long he spent there, but what he was doing?' Simpson made a gesture.

'So what time did he get to the church, then?'

It took a while for Simpson to scroll all the way down the spreadsheet, but when he clicked on the final entry the wavy green lines of the map spun and twisted until the green dot appeared in the middle of a different configuration. Janie would have been hard put to say it was Gorgie, but she was prepared to take that on faith for now. Scrolling backwards through the data entries, the dot stayed motionless for what felt like hours before it finally moved, jumping in an instant to a point a half a mile away.

'Arrived in the vicinity between half eleven and midnight. We've not got the granularity to track exact movements, but he's certainly in the church by twelve and doesn't come out again. Well, the phone does, but that was it being brought to us here.' Simpson swivelled round again and picked up the evidence bag, holding it out for Janie to take. Once she had, he searched around on his desk until he found the paperwork for her to sign. Chain of evidence must be maintained at all times.

As she scrawled her signature in the allotted space, added date and exact time, Janie winced at the memory of shoving Kenneth Morgan's effects in her pocket without a thought. But then they had been fleeing from a collapsing building.

'I've taken the security settings off that now, so you can get in and have a look at contacts and suchlike. It's all backed up too, just in case. I'll put everything onto a tablet so you can follow the route on a decent map. Should have something for you by lunchtime. That OK?'

'Perfect, Mike. Thanks.' Janie weighed the phone in her hand, wondering what secrets it might contain. Too much to hope Creegan had taken a photo of his attacker. Life just didn't work that way.

'Ah, Janie. There you are. Got a minute, have you?'

It was one of those questions that wasn't really a question at all, she knew. Janie had been about to walk the short distance down the corridor to the incident room, hand over the phone to one of the detective constables to get started on, and then grab herself a much-needed coffee. Detective Superintendent Nelson stood halfway up the stair to the third floor, presumably having been on his way to find her. Although why he couldn't have called down, she wasn't sure.

'Of course, sir.' She began to climb the stairs, hoping he would carry on ahead. Instead, he waited for her to reach him before falling into step alongside.

'I've just had the GPS details back on Creegan's phone, sir. Mike Simpson down in IT forensics has managed to track its movements over the twenty-four hours before he died.'

Nelson didn't tell her not to speak, but neither did he reply.

Instead, he increased his pace so that she had to skip a couple of steps to keep up. The secretary's desk outside the office was unoccupied again, Janie saw, and as soon as she was past it and inside the room, Nelson swept the door closed. Something was off, although Christ only knew what. The detective superintendent's moods were a mystery.

'I understand you and Detective Constable Mitchell went to Mr Creegan's house this morning?'

'That's correct, sir. We're trying to track his movements prior to his death, like I outlined at the briefing. Only, there's a bit of a problem. It doesn't look like –'

Janie stopped as Nelson held up a hand, palm out, to silence her.

'Put it in the report. I'm not here for that kind of detail just now.'

'I . . . OK.' Then what are you here for? What am I here for? Janie kept the questions to herself, let the silence grow.

'Was it really necessary for you to accompany DC Mitchell to the house? Would it not have been more cost effective just to send her and another detective constable? Maybe even a uniform officer?'

For a moment, Janie didn't know how to answer. It wasn't that the question had thrown her; the detective superintendent seemed to be determined she never set a foot outside the station, after all. But that wasn't how she was used to doing things, and neither was it the best way to get them done. Especially not when they were so understaffed and overworked.

'You think I should be here, sir. Directing the investigation from the incident room.' Janie deliberately didn't make it a question, and also didn't add the 'like a DI' that she wanted to.

Nelson gave her a smile that was both patronising and unsettling. 'Exactly so, Janie. I know it's unorthodox, but the situation demands you step up and take on the senior investigating officer role in this case. If not in name, then certainly in responsibility. Your job is to oversee, theorise, strategise and delegate. As you say, you should be running the incident room, and the detective constables doing all the legwork. That's something you need to properly understand if you're ever going to make inspector.'

'Of course, sir. I do understand. Only, sometimes it's quicker if I do the job myself. More efficient.'

The smile slid from Nelson's face. Somehow without her realising, the two of them had taken up the familiar headmaster and unruly pupil positions. Now the detective superintendent leaned forward, elbows on his desk, fingers steepled together under his chin as he looked up at Janie.

'You worked . . .' He tried to speak, realised his hands were in the way and sat up straight again. 'You worked closely with Detective Inspector McLean. He . . . mentored you, I think it would be fair to say.'

Janie disagreed, but kept the thought to herself.

'I've spoken to plenty of officers – plain clothes and uniform – since coming to this station. They tell me McLean plucked you from the ranks himself. Co-opted you into Specialist Crime Division, as it were. I've heard a few other tales too, about the detective inspector and you, but I don't put much credence in them. Nothing but gossip, and mean-spirited gossip at that. But . . .'

Nelson paused, as if looking for the right words. Janie knew it was an act. He'd made his feelings about McLean clear in the past. Dropping disapproving hints like this was nothing new. She didn't believe the detective superintendent's dismissal of idle gossip either. He was a no smoke without fire kind of person, the sort of policeman who liked to come to a conclusion first and then go out looking for evidence to support it. She almost opened her mouth to challenge him, instead falling back on a trick McLean had taught her as she clenched her fists tight behind her back and counted slowly to ten.

'But the fact is, Janie, you do appear to have picked up some of his worst habits, swanning off and leaving the incident room without anyone in charge. Delegation is the key to successful management. You can't do everything yourself.'

The most frustrating thing about this was that nothing Nelson said was untrue. Janie knew that the step up from sergeant to inspector brought with it much more managerial responsibilities and far fewer opportunities to get out there among the people. The criminals and the victims both. And yet, hadn't she joined up in the first place to help the public? To protect and serve, if you liked? It was something McLean railed against, she knew. He'd hated being bounced up to chief inspector, and had breathed a huge sigh of relief when circumstances knocked him back down again. But then, he was wealthy enough that he didn't have to worry about his salary. And she had to admit for all her protestations, the thought of a detective inspector's pay packet was enticing. Much as she liked Manda, she didn't fancy sharing a rented tenement flat for the rest of her life.

'I understand, sir.' She released the tension in her fists, willing her annoyance away with it. 'I'll try to do better.'

Nelson fixed her with that patronising smile again. Or was he trying for something else? The man wasn't easy to read at all. 'You do that, Janie. And remember. If you ever need any advice, my door's always open.'

21

'Where to first, boss?'

Sat in the passenger seat of the Nissan Leaf pool car, Janie stared at the screen of the electronic tablet Mike Simpson in the IT forensics department had given her, with strict instructions not to lose it, and then give it back as soon as she was done. The hard to read mapping from the data on Creegan's phone had been overlaid on something that looked a lot more like Google Maps. A pale coloured line linked a series of waypoints where the dead man had stopped for fifteen minutes or longer. DC Bryant was at the wheel, and Janie glanced briefly up at the rear flank of the police station as it overlooked the car park. Daft to think that Detective Superintendent Nelson might be at one of those windows staring down on her, since she had already seen him leave for some important meeting on the other side of the country, but she could feel his disapproval all the same. Damned if she was going to sit in the incident room and stew though.

'Not much point going to Cumberland Street again, so I guess we head to the next stop. Looks like he went directly from the house to an address in Piershill. Just off Moira Terrace. Must have been driven given the timestamps.'

'You want to head over there for a look?'

'Aye, might as well.'

Janie checked her phone as the car pulled away, but there was no text from Nelson. With luck, he'd never know she was gone. And if he got back before she did . . . well, DS Gregg was always on hand.

Through Holyrood Park and down to Jock's Lodge, the two of them rode in comfortable silence, helped by the quiet of the electric car. It was only as they reached the Portobello Road that Bryant spoke up.

'Still getting grief from the detective superintendent?' It was voiced as a question, but only just.

Janie let out a weary sigh. 'Aye, you could say that. One minute he's chewing my ear off, the next it's all praise and shouldn't I be applying for the DI job. Can't get a handle on him at all.'

'Cass reckons he's got the hots for you.' Bryant said it without a hint of judgement in her voice, but it stung all the same. Was the whole station gossiping about her? Again? Bad enough when it had been McLean they all thought she was shagging.

'Well if he has, he can keep it in his pants. Christ, I could do without all this endless tattle.'

'Aye, well. You know what coppers are like. Nothing beats a good chewy piece of gossip, and don't let facts get in the way of it either.' Bryant paused as she negotiated a short set of roadworks. 'Still, would probably help your case if you had a boyfriend, y'know. Or even a girlfriend.'

'When's there even time for relationships, Jessica?' Janie looked down at the tablet again, noting their position against the mark on the map. 'Just here, if you can find somewhere to park.'

Bryant pulled into a space in front of a small line of shops and tapped the button that switched off the car. Janie still found it strange how there was no drop in noise from a killed engine anymore, but on balance it was most certainly an improvement from the clattery diesel motors of old.

'The cafe, you reckon?' Bryant leaned forward, peering through the windscreen. Janie followed her gaze, recognising the place from a case the previous year. She'd met the sister of a young man who'd died of a drug overdose here, what was her name? Maggie Devlin, that was it. What were the chances? And what was she up to now?

'You think he came all the way over here for breakfast?'

Bryant shrugged. 'Everyone's got to eat, right?'

'Is that your subtle way of saying you want a coffee?' Janie reached for the handle, popped open the door and stepped out into the chill, damp air.

'Well now you mention it. Maybe a bacon roll, too, since it's past lunchtime.' Bryant climbed out her side and the two of them crossed the pavement to the cafe door. They were almost at it when Janie noticed the sign two shops down.

'Hang on a minute.' She set off towards the shop front, then stopped outside. Following her, Bryant read the sign on a stand at the entrance, unable to keep the laughter from her voice.

'Male waxing. Face, chest, back. Intimate areas too. Ask inside about a full Hollywood. Janie, I had no idea. Or was it something for the detective superintendent?'

'That's quite enough of that, Detective Constable.' Janie looked at her tablet, zoomed in to see how long Creegan had been at this spot. Or at least his phone had. 'Creegan was here for a little over an hour. Could have been taking his time over coffee, true. Or he could have been getting himself all neat for some special occasion.'

'Why would you say . . .' Bryant looked at the sign again, then to the obscured glass windows of the shop front. 'Oh.'

'So you did read the pathology report. Good. Creegan was bald as a newborn everywhere except his head. He couldn't have done that at home. Least, not on his own.'

'But why here?' Bryant asked. Before she could answer, Janie saw movement behind the frosted glass. Either they'd been spotted, or someone was coming out.

'Let's get that coffee.' She grabbed Bryant's arm and directed the detective constable back the way they'd come. As they entered the cafe, a hunched figure left the waxing salon. Was there something familiar about him? Janie tried to get a better look without being seen herself, but he turned the other way, pulled out his phone and walked off before she could see his face.

Inside the cafe, they took a table by the window and ordered coffee and bacon rolls when the old lady in the stained apron wandered up to ask what they wanted. While they waited, Janie scanned through her contacts until she found the number she was looking for and dialled. A moment later the wrong voice answered.

'Tom MacPhail's phone. That you, Janie?'

'I . . .' It took her a moment to parse the Welsh accent and realise who was on the other end of the line. 'Cerys? Sorry. I was expecting Tom.'

'Figured. He's up to his elbows in someone right now. Anything I can help you with?'

Janie tried to rid her mind of the image, not quite succeeding. 'The body in the church. The second one. You remember he was neatly trimmed?'

'Waxed, I'd say. Yes, I remember. Why?'

'Any idea how recent that might have been done? Like, could it have been the same day he died? Would you be able to tell that?'

A muffled sound as the mortuary assistant put her hand over the receiver and spoke something, presumably relaying Janie's question to the pathologist himself.

'Tom says he'll have another look once he's finished with his current patient. Between you and me, I don't think the prognosis is good, mind.'

'What, the waxing . . .? Oh.' Janie understood Cerys' joke a second too late. To be fair, she wasn't used to that kind of humour from the pathology team. Angus Cadwallader's wit was as dry as a towel, and his assistant Dr Sharp never joked about anything.

'If you asked me, I'd say it's very possible he was done that same day. I don't remember any sign of regrowth, so it would have been recent, for sure. I'll give you a bell soon as we've had another look, that OK?'

'Brilliant, thanks.' Janie hung up just as the coffees and bacon rolls arrived.

'What was that about?' Bryant asked before she could take a bite.

'A hunch? I don't know.' Janie was about to go on, but movement outside dragged her attention away. The man who had come out of the waxing parlour, or at least someone wearing very similar clothes, had come back the other way. He held his phone in front of him, mouth moving as if he was talking at it, and stopped briefly outside the cafe to gesticulate with his free hand. He didn't look inside, but in the brief moment before he moved away, Janie remembered where she had seen him. At Kenneth Morgan's burial, standing a few paces back from Seagram, Creegan and the other old man.

'Wait here, Jessica. Something I need to do.'

Before the detective constable could react, Janie stood up and hurried to the door. She slipped out of the cafe, her own phone in hand as if she were reading a text. Through the window, Bryant raised an eyebrow, her questioning words lost against the sound of traffic on the main road.

A chill wind played with the rubbish strewn across the pavement, the threat of rain in the air as Janie pulled up the collar of her coat and tried not to shiver.

The young man she'd seen come out of the waxing parlour had his hands shoved deep into his pockets now, as he walked along the street about twenty-five metres ahead of her. She knew it was foolish, following him like this. A dozen different reasons for leaving well alone played through her mind while she casually made her way toward the bus stop as if that had been her plan all along. He might have an entirely innocent reason for being here, just another customer in for the full Hawaiian. He might be under surveillance by another branch – even the NCA, given who he worked for – and even now Janie was being watched from an unmarked vehicle. He might have spotted her with Bryant earlier and be leading her on deliberately, either to take her away from something she wasn't supposed to see, or to lure her into a trap.

All of these possibilities and more held her back as she watched him reach the point where a side street cut through the pavement, but he didn't even look around before he took the turning. She caught the white flash of earbuds in his ears before he disappeared from view, oblivious to the world around him.

Janie waited a few seconds before setting off after him. When she reached the side street, she carried on across it rather than follow him along the route he had taken. It was a residential street, small semi-detached dormers set far enough back from the road to have front gardens. Although most of these had been paved over for parking. The young man had reached another, smaller, road now and was heading deeper into the housing estate. Still he didn't look around, and as he disappeared behind a rough harled garden wall, Janie noticed the upper storey and dark slate roof of a much larger house tucked away behind the bungalows. No doubt this whole area had once been a wealthy merchant's estate, its gardens slowly eaten away by the unstoppable expansion of the city until all that remained was the mansion. Was that where Seagram's man was going?

She was about to set off after him when the sound of an approaching vehicle drew her attention. A high-sided Transit van, it slowed on the main road before turning down the side street. Janie watched as it slowed again, then turned into the smaller lane. A delivery perhaps? Or was it taking things away?

Still aware that she was chancing her luck, she set off along the side street to see if she could get a better look. A couple of estate agent signs had been attached to the railings of the bungalow just beyond the turning, so she could always pretend she was out house hunting if anyone asked. Not that a detective sergeant's salary would get anywhere close to the cost of a house in this part of town. On a whim, she pulled out her phone and made a quick search to see, winced at the figure that came up.

'You the two o'clock?'

The voice made her jump, almost drop her phone, but when she looked to see who had spoken, Janie saw an old woman standing at the open front door to the house for sale.

'I'm sorry?'

'The two o'clock viewing? Mrs Patterson, right? You're early, but no bother there.'

Janie glanced down the narrow lane towards the large house. She could just about make out an ornate entrance gate, a couple of trees and beyond it the bulk of a house not much smaller than DI McLean's. To either side of the gate, a wall encircled the much smaller garden than the property would originally have had, and part of that wall formed the boundary at the rear of the property she now stood outside. The property whose owner thought she had come to view. Well, why not?

'Aye, that's me.' She smiled brightly at the old woman and pushed through the metal gate to the front garden.

22

It would have made a nice home, if she was earning banker's money. The old lady's name was Eleanor Brodie. 'Not Jean, although I was a teacher for forty years you know,' she insisted as she gave Janie the tour. The selling solicitors had thoughtfully provided a stack of particulars for viewers to help themselves to, which described in rather gushing prose how delightful the neighbourhood was and what a prime purchasing opportunity this would be for an elegant home for the young professional couple starting a family.

'Do you have children?' Mrs Brodie asked after they had seen the living room, large kitchen-diner, front and rear bedrooms and bathroom. She was leading Janie up a narrow and steep flight of stairs into what would once have been an attic, but which had now been converted into more accommodation.

'No,' Janie answered perhaps a bit too decisively. Then added, 'At least, not yet,' as that seemed to be what the old lady wanted to hear.

'Plenty of room for them when they come, dear.'

The upstairs area was on a smaller scale, with lower ceilings, but to the rear of the building a large dormer window made for what would be a fine master bedroom. It overlooked a small, neat garden, at the end of which was the wall and then the mansion house beyond.

'That's Reid Manor.' Mrs Brodie correctly guessed at Janie's question before she could ask it. 'Andrew Reid was a Leith merchant, sometime in the mid nineteenth century. I've a book about the period somewhere downstairs. Goes into quite some detail about him. He built that house, but died before he had a chance to live in it much, poor fellow.'

'Who lives there now?'

'Worried about the neighbours, are you?' Mrs Brodie smiled. 'You needn't be. Think it belongs to some foreign family. There's a few folk coming and going, but they're very quiet. Helps that everything's double glazed, of course.' She tapped on the window to emphasise her point.

After the tour, Mrs Brodie retired to the front room and told Janie to have a wander on her own. She checked the time, aware that it was quite a while now since she'd left Bryant at the cafe up the road. The real viewer might turn up at any time too, which would be awkward. Janie dashed out a quick explanatory text as she went through to the kitchen. Beyond it, she found a small laundry and utility room and the door to the back garden. A spatter of rain fell as she stepped outside, and she could see without going any further that the wall was too high for her to get a view from this level.

'They have parties in the summer, sometimes. You can hear the music when you're in the garden. But it's not loud or anything.'

Janie whirled around again, once more taken by surprise. Mrs Brodie had somehow snuck through the kitchen and now stood directly behind her.

'Thank you.' She pretended to inspect the small drying green and storage shed from the relative shelter of the doorway. To one side, a narrow gate gave access to the lane, presumably so the owner could put their bins out. 'Might I have another quick look upstairs?'

'Of course, dear. Of course.' Mrs Brodie stepped aside. Janie made a show of wiping her feet on the mat before heading once more to the large room at the back. Peering out she stared at the van, its back doors open so that they almost touched the house. Something was being moved in, or out, but she couldn't quite make out what it was. And then the young man she'd followed here – Seagram's man – was there. He smacked his hand hard against the metal of the van, the noise muted by the distance and what was clearly top quality double glazing. Once, twice, three times in quick succession, as if chivvying someone along.

And then, as the young man slammed the van door closed, Janie saw a small group of people clustered in the open doorway to the house. It was only an instant, but it was long enough for her to make out young women and men, scruffy clothes, faces thin and haunted. A moment later Seagram's man had ushered them all inside and out of sight. A puff of black diesel smoke from the van, and it pulled away towards the gates, even now opening themselves. Janie made a note of the registration plate and then headed back downstairs.

She found Mrs Brodie waiting in the hall, and darted past the startled old woman in her rush to get to the door. 'It's lovely,' she said over her shoulder. 'Can't wait to tell my husband about it. Thanks for showing me around.'

Back in the cafe, Janie found a worried-looking DC Bryant sitting in front of an empty plate and mug. Janie's own bacon roll and coffee were untouched and cold, but she tucked into them anyway, relating what she'd seen between mouthfuls, in what her mother would have called a most un-ladylike manner. It had been a long day already, and she was hungrier than she realised, eyeing up the menu board above the counter as she wiped congealed bacon fat from her lips with a paper napkin. Could she justify a second one?

'So, what's the score then?' Bryant asked once the tale was told. Janie paused a while before answering, trying to get her thoughts into some semblance of logical order. They were all over the place with the rush of having stumbled upon something so unexpectedly.

'It's what's been bothering me about the house in Cumberland Street. It was cleaned down professionally and then dressed for a sale or something.'

'Aye, I remember that. I put young Connor – you know, PC Fairley – onto ringing round the local estate agents and the ESPC.' Bryant checked her watch. 'Should have something for us by the time we get back to the station.'

'But what if that wasn't it at all? What if it was cleaned down because there was something going on there and whoever was doing it didn't want it found out?'

'Is that not a bit of a leap? And why now? You said it looked like it had been done a couple of weeks back. Creegan only died on Wednesday.'

'Aye, but Kenneth Morgan died a fortnight ago. He and Creegan were mates. Both of them worked for Archie Seagram back in the day. Seagram doesn't just deal in dodgy loans and drugs, right? He's behind a lot of the trafficked sex workers in the city. At least, that's what everyone says even if nobody's managed to pin anything on him.'

Bryant narrowed her eyes, her expression still sceptical. 'You think the house in Cumberland Street was some kind of, what? Brothel?'

'Stranger things have happened. And what if Creegan was running it? He'd have known his mate's death would bring too much attention for a while, so he shut down the operation and cleaned up the house.'

'And you think they've moved the whole shebang over to . . .' Bryant waved in the direction of the housing estate. 'No one can move a whole organisation that quickly. Can they?'

The same point had bothered Janie as she'd been walking back to the cafe, but hearing the detective constable voice it brought a possible explanation to mind.

'The old lady selling her house told me they sometimes had parties there, in the summer, but mostly the house stood empty. She thought maybe it belonged to some rich foreigner or something. But what if it's just one of several sites Creegan was operating, moving around them every few weeks or months to avoid drawing the wrong kind of attention? That'd explain Cumberland Street, too. Could have been Morgan's death that prompted them to move, or it might just have been part of the schedule. Houses like those . . . we're not talking some kind of cheap massage parlour operation. This is high end.' Janie saw the naked cadaver in her mind again, skin as smooth as a baby's. 'Maybe catering to customers with unusual tastes.'

Bryant stared at her, mouth slightly open, one eyebrow arched. 'All that from the fact he liked a back, sack and crack wax?'

'It's a wee bit more than that, Jessica. But I know it's a stretch too. The waxing might be nothing. Maybe he had a skin complaint and that was the only way to deal with it. But with Seagram's man and that van?' Janie pulled out her phone, tapped through to the contact list again. 'I think we need to give Jo Dexter a call.'

23

'This the fellow? Or was it this one?'

Janie stood in the main incident room for the Sexual Crimes Unit – also known among the ranks as Vice – and stared at a series of grainy images on a large computer screen. She'd gone straight to DCI Dexter as soon as she had arrived back at the station, sending DC Bryant off to begin writing up the day's activities. On the plus side this meant she avoided a chance encounter with Detective Superintendent Nelson and the inevitable dressing down that would ensue. On the minus side, it meant she was only putting off the inevitable until later.

'That one, I think. Can you blow it up a bit?' She pointed at one head shot, cropped from having been taken out of doors. When the detective constable operating the machine clicked on it, the image widened out to show parts of the cemetery where Kenneth Morgan had been buried. The quality of the picture suggested it had been taken with a long lens, probably from one of the blocks of flats that surrounded the site. Was she also in some of these photographs, too? Janie wouldn't have put it past the Vice team.

'Aye, that's him. Sure of it.'

'Seamus Donald. Nasty wee scrote.' DCI Dexter leaned in over Janie's shoulder, bringing with her a stench of cigarettes so powerful it was a wonder she didn't set the smoke alarms off.

152

'You know him?'

'Oh, I know him. Man has form. Spent a lot of time in youth custody. Petty thieving, drug dealing, breaking heads. Quite the temper on him, but he seems to have found a steadying influence in Archie Seagram. Hasn't done anything we can pin on him in a few years now. Not that we're no' looking.'

Janie stared at the photograph, matching it against her memory from earlier in the day and from the funeral. 'Definitely him. And I don't think he's up to any good in that house. You might want to look at the waxing parlour, too. He was coming out of there when I first saw him.'

'Waxing parlour?' Dexter raised a greying eyebrow. 'Why don't you go over it all from the start.'

Janie reached into her jacket pocket and pulled out both her phone and notebook. She passed the one to the detective constable to download the photos she had taken, leafed through the pages of the other until she found her notes. It took almost as long to tell the story as it had to view the dormer bungalow, the particulars for which were tucked in the pages of her notebook as well. By the time she'd finished, the whole Vice incident room had fallen silent, the collected detectives her rapt audience.

'Ever fancy a transfer from Major Investigations?' Dexter asked.

'Don't tempt me.' Janie tried not to grimace. 'Still have to answer to the big boss though.'

'Nelson?' Dexter's question held genuine surprise in it for a moment, and then something of a realisation dawned across her face.

'Aye. He'll not be happy I've been out all day instead of standing around in the incident room. Gave me a telling off once today already. Sooner we get a new DI the better.' She glanced at her watch. Where had the day gone? 'Talking of which, I'd better get a shift on. Evening briefing's going to start soon.'

'If he gives you any grief about this, let me know, aye?' Dexter took Janie's phone from the detective constable and handed it back to her. 'Truth be told I think he's a bit feart of me.'

Janie nodded her thanks. 'You going to raid the place?'

'Need to get a wee bit more information about their operation first. Just knowing that van's registration helps. We can track it round the city if they don't ditch it straight away. We'll get some surveillance on the house, too. Run background on who owns it, see who comes and goes over the next week or so. But aye, we'll be raiding the place soon enough.' Dexter brought her hand up to her face as if smoking a cigarette, then dropped it down again when she realised what she was doing. 'And don't worry, Janie. We'll keep you in the loop on this one.'

Whether it was luck, Janie couldn't know, but she managed to make it all the way from the Vice team up to her own incident room without being accosted by Detective Superintendent Nelson. Nor was the man waiting for her when she arrived. Maybe he wasn't back from his meetings yet. That was a relief for now, but he'd find out what she'd been up to soon enough.

She walked in on a scene of quiet busyness that nevertheless had a feel of great effort for little reward about it. The whiteboard was too clean, the desks only half manned, the conversation muted almost to silence by her appearance. DC Bryant was over in one corner, hunched at a desk and typing furiously with two fingers, so it wasn't as if they didn't know she was back.

'Got something you might want to look at, boss.'

Janie scowled at the title Cass Mitchell had given her, and which everyone else was using now, but went over to where the detective constable sat in front of a pair of large screens all the same. As she approached, she could see CCTV footage; a dozen grainy thumbnails to each screen.

'That's dedication, Cass,' she said as she leaned in for a better

look. Even just a glance made her eyes ache. The thought of staring at those images for hours on end made her shudder.

'Helps that Doc MacPhail gave us a fairly narrow time of death
for both victims. And the phone data's useful for Creegan.'

'Both?' For a split-second Janie's blood ran cold. Realisation
was a mixture of blessed relief and despair at how much more
work there was still to do. 'You're looking at Morgan as well as
Creegan, then?'

'Aye. And it's not easy either. There's no cameras anywhere
near the churches, but we've got some half decent footage from
Granton Road, Ferry Road and Gorgie Road. Think I might have
managed to spot something. See?'

Mitchell reached for the mouse and began clicking away. On
the left-hand screen, one of the thumbnails expanded to full size
and started playing. Janie took a moment to realise she was looking at a view of Gorgie Road.

'This is close by the railway bridge, looking east. There was a
match at Tynecastle that evening, so quite a few folk wandering
around earlier on. By the time this comes up, it's quietened down
a lot.'

The image zoomed forward like a time machine as Mitchell
sped up the video, buses and cars almost blurring, people dancing
in strange, jerky patterns without any sign of movement from
their legs. As the numbers approached 23:35 another tap brought
it down to normal speed and a much emptier view. Janie watched
as a car pulled in to the side of the road and someone got out. The
resolution wasn't the highest quality, but it was enough to recognise William Creegan, if that was who you were expecting to see.
He was dressed as they had found him the next morning, and, as
the car peeled away into traffic, he appeared to be reading something on his phone. After a frustratingly short distance he
disappeared from the camera's field of vision.

'Tell me we got the licence plate of that car,' Janie said at exactly the same time as Mitchell tapped her mouse and brought it up on the screen. A blurred mess of pixels, squinting at it only made her head hurt.

'None of us can make it out, but I've asked IT if they can maybe enhance the image. Sandy—DS Gregg's already got the admins calling round the city taxi firms to see if anyone had a driver in the area then. Long shot, I know, and it's slow going. Might be worth getting in touch with the local Uber guys too. They'll know exactly where all of their drivers were if we give them that timeframe.'

'Probably want a warrant to release the information though. I'll have a word about getting something sorted.' Janie waved at the still image on the screen again. 'We any idea what Creegan was looking at on his phone?'

'I've asked Mike Simpson to look into it. We know the exact time, but he deleted a bunch of messages not long before he got to the church. Did it properly, too. Apparently, there's no way of getting them back.'

'Of course not.' Janie tried not to let the frustration show in her voice. 'Anything else interesting?'

Mitchell moved her focus to the second screen, clicked another thumbnail to make it bigger.

'This is Granton Road, the night Morgan died. Half eleven at night.'

The street was even quieter than Gorgie Road at that time, but then there wasn't a large football stadium nearby, or anything like as many pubs. Janie watched a hunched figure walk towards the camera, face lit by the glow from the phone he was carrying. As he came closer, Janie realised that she'd never actually seen Morgan's face in the flesh so to speak. His head had been crushed by falling masonry as the church collapsed. Even so, it was clear enough to see that it was him.

'Whatever happened to his phone?' she asked, but she already knew the answer. It would have been bagged up with the rest of his possessions and handed over to his next of kin once his death had been found unsuspicious.

Except that he had no next of kin. Mitchell's face suggested that she had no idea, so Janie turned to the nearest person she could find. So close that she almost bumped into him, the young uniform constable with the sticky-out ears and short-cropped ginger hair took an involuntary step back. What was his name? PC Fairley, that was it. Conor. Eyes wide with surprise, he clutched a piece of paper between nervous fingers.

'Is that for me?' Janie asked.

'I . . . Err. Yes, ma'am. I mean, no. It's nothing.' He held up what looked like an email printed out. So much for saving the planet.

'Nothing?'

'The house in Cumberland Street, ma'am. It's not listed with any estate agents or solicitors in the city. Not even being prepared for sale.'

Given the sheer number of calls it must have taken him to find that out, Janie didn't have the heart to chide the young man. And it was a result, after all. 'Good work, Conor. Thanks. Now I need you to track down what happened to Kenneth Morgan's personal effects. His phone, wallet, keys. You can do that, aye?'

The constable nodded, almost tripping over his own feet in his haste to attend to this new task. Had she ever been that young and naive? Janie almost laughed at the thought. It wasn't as if she was even thirty yet, for god's sake.

'There's something else I think you should look at,' DC Mitchell said before they could be interrupted again. Janie turned to the screens, seeing that the detective constable had changed the views. One still showed the image from Gorgie Road, but the other one looked out over a bus stop and in the background a familiar supermarket.

'Ferry Road?' she asked and received a nod by way of confirmation.

'Closest bus stop to the church. Thought I'd run through it just in case anything stuck out.'

Janie didn't need to look around the quiet incident room to understand the subtext; that there was so little else to go on this was what the investigation was left with. 'Something did, I take it? Stuck out?'

'Oh, aye.' Mitchell tapped at the mouse and pointed at the Ferry Road screen as it started up. There weren't many people around. But then, it was late, and this not exactly a part of the city where people walked much. Judging by the heavy traffic, the car was still king here.

After maybe a minute of nothing, a figure shuffled along the pavement, head down and hands in pockets, aimlessly wandering until he was almost in the centre of the camera's view. Then he stopped dead in his tracks, staring at something on the far side of the road. The image resolution wasn't good, but Janie could have sworn he looked like he'd seen a ghost. He stood there, transfixed, for a full two minutes on the timestamp clock, and then a bus pulled in, blocking the view. At that, he seemed to come to his senses, hurried onto the bus and was gone.

'Well, that was weird,' Janie said.

'It gets better. See.' Mitchell clicked the mouse again and the other screen started moving. More people milling about, including a small gang of football fans, obviously the worse for wear. She was concentrating on them so much, she didn't at first notice the middle-aged man trying his best to avoid being seen and accosted by them.

'Is that?' She leaned in close, as if it was distance from the subject making it hard to see details, not the lack of resolution in the city's CCTV systems.

'I think it is.' Mitchell tapped a few more buttons, bringing up screen grabs of the man from both cameras side by side. Blown up, the resolution was even worse, the images grainy and indistinct, but they certainly looked very much like the same person.

'There you are, Harrison. Where the fuck have you been all day?'

Both Janie and Mitchell spun around at the words, although it was no surprise who had shouted them. Detective Superintendent Nelson stood in the doorway to the incident room, his face red as if he had sprinted there from his meeting on the other side of the country. He took in the whole room with a series of jerky head movements that made him look like some kind of automaton, then stalked towards them. Janie had been leaning down, the better to see the screens, but now she stood slowly, the most reasonable smile she could muster plastered on her face.

'Ah, sir. I was just coming to find you.'

Nelson's eyes narrowed in suspicion. 'Why? Have you arrested someone?'

'Not yet sir, no. But I think DC Mitchell has just found us a suspect.'

24

She really should have gone home, Janie knew. The detective superintendent might have left her in charge of what was looking suspiciously like a double murder investigation, but she was still only a sergeant. Shift end had come and gone, and now the incident room had taken on the quiet calm of the late team. Not much to do but work through the actions thrown up by the computer and make a few follow-up calls from DC Stringer's door to door team. Even Mitchell had left, having printed out the blown-up images from the CCTV and pinned them to the whiteboard. A potential suspect? Or an electronic glitch that made two separate innocent people look slightly similar? The more she stared at them, the more Janie leaned towards the latter. Either way, they'd have to try and identify the man. Both of them.

'Err . . . Ma'am?'

The voice was so quiet, the title so unexpected, Janie almost didn't realise it was directed at her. For perhaps a little longer than was polite, she carried on staring at the words on her screen, the report she'd been trying to read. Then it dawned on her that some-one was trying to get her attention. She turned to see the young uniform constable with the sticky-out ears and close-cropped ginger hair standing just a little too close behind her again. He stepped back in alarm, freckles darkening across his cheeks. What on earth had persuaded him to become a police officer?

'It's Conor, isn't it?' Janie tried her best to put the young lad at ease, but judging by the colour blooming at the tips of his ears that wasn't working. 'PC Fairley,' she added.

'Aye, ma'am.' He nodded his head so vigorously it might have fallen off, but said nothing more.

'Well?' Janie asked. There had to be a reason why he'd approached her, after all.

'I . . . You asked me to track down the phone, aye?'

For a moment she couldn't understand what he was talking about, but then it clicked. 'Kenneth Morgan. The dead man in the church up Granton way. You found it?'

PC Fairley's shoulders slumped in relief. 'Aye, ma'am. I mean, sort of. It was with all his stuff when the mortuary released the body for burial.'

'So where is it now?'

'Oh, aye. Right. That was in his will, see? He left everything to some woman by the name of Machin. Anna Machin. I've got her address.'

'His ex-wife? Why would he . . .?' Janie started to ask the question, then waved it away. 'It's no matter. Where does she live?'

'Blackford Road. That's Grange, isn't it? Posh part of town.'

Janie couldn't quite place the constable's accent. West Coast perhaps, but he was well enough spoken. Diligent, too, to have tracked down Morgan's belongings so late in the day. She wasn't sure how he'd ended up on her team, found that she knew very little about him at all, which wasn't good. If she wanted to rise further up the ladder, she'd need to get better at all the little details of managing people. If she wanted to, of course. That was the eternal question.

'You want me to give her a call, ma'am?' the constable asked. 'I can sort a car to go and fetch the phone if she's happy to hand it over.'

Janie realised she'd been staring at nothing, the ghost of an idiot grin on her face as her mind wandered. Was she that tired? Almost certainly.

'Sorry. Long day. That the details there? I've met her before, so probably best I call her myself.' She held out her hand for the piece of paper the constable was holding. Grange wasn't far from the station, and it was also on the way home if she chose to walk. A bit of fresh air and exercise would do her a power of good. As would getting out of the station and away from the job for a few hours. It wasn't as if it wouldn't all still be waiting for her tomorrow.

Sat in the nice, warm and dry incident room, Janie had imagined it a short walk to the house on Blackford Road, and in truth it hadn't been all that far. What she hadn't reckoned on was the cold wind that dropped off the Pentland Hills a few minutes after she set out. Nor the short, sharp rain showers that fizzed against the pavement for a moment and were gone. By the time she reached her destination she was regretting the decision to walk, and rather more damp than she would have liked.

Anna Machin had done well for herself to be living in this part of the city. Writer's Block, some wags had christened it, after the higher than average concentration of bestselling authors who lived in the area. Grange was mostly noted for its air of gentility and quiet, old wealth. Not quite in the same league as DI McLean's neighbourhood, but perhaps knocking at its door. It certainly wasn't the sort of place you might expect to find a Broxburn-born gangster's ex-wife living, and yet here she was.

'Detective Sergeant Harrison. Did you walk here?' Machin stood in her open doorway and glanced past Janie at the night outside. The rain chose that moment to come hammering down again, but the ample porch that jutted out from the front of the faux-baronial pile did a good job of keeping the worst of it off.

162

'Thought it wasn't quite so far. I should probably have checked the weather before setting off, too.'

'You look soaked through. Come in. Come in.'

Janie left her coat and boots in the lobby, squeezed the worst of the damp from her short fringe and wiped her face dry with her hands. Machin led her through a wide hall, past a grand staircase and on into a kitchen at the back of the house that was probably the same size as Janie's entire shared flat.

'Can I get you a drink? Wine perhaps? Or would you prefer something more warming?'

'It's a cliché I know, but I'd love a cup of tea.' Janie rubbed warmth into her hands she hadn't realised was missing until now. The kitchen was modern, but neatly packaged into an old, high-ceilinged room. Beyond a wide, granite-topped island, part of the wall had been taken down and opened up into a conservatory. Between the two, a large oak dining table held a cardboard box of the size and shape used for archiving files. Its lid lay upside down beside it, along with a few clear plastic bags, their contents still untouched by the look of things. A half-filled wine glass suggested Machin had been about to start going through her ex- husband's effects when Janie had rung the doorbell.

'Milk's in the bottle there, sugar's in the bowl.'

She turned to see a mug on the island, teabag already steeping in the hot water, steam rising from the surface. Surprised she hadn't heard the noise of a kettle boiling, it took Janie a moment to understand the kitchen had one of those newfangled instant taps. Not one to complain, she mashed the bag a couple of times, then put it on the saucer Machin had thoughtfully provided. A splash of milk and she was good to go.

'You've been through it all then?' she asked after thanking the old woman for the tea.

'Hardly. I shoved the box in the cupboard under the stairs as soon as it arrived. Only took it out again after your call. Can you believe we'd been divorced forty years and Kenneth still left every-thing to me?' Machin walked over to the table and picked up her wine, took a sip.

'And yet you went to his funeral.'

That got Janie a raised eyebrow. 'As, I recall, did you. And like I said at the time, that was only because Archie Seagram made it known I was expected there. Came as quite the surprise when I found out I was lumbered with being Ken's sole beneficiary. But then I don't suppose he had anyone else.'

Machin reached for the nearest bag as she spoke, picked up a neatly folded shirt. She placed one hand briefly on the front, as if feeling for the pulse of the dead man who had been wearing it, then put it back down again and picked up another bag. This time it was Morgan's watch, the face cracked, hands stopped at what probably wasn't the moment of his death but felt like it should be.

'Do you think this is valuable?' She held it up for Janie to see. No expert, Janie could do nothing but shake her head.

'You're probably right,' Machin said. 'Kenneth never was any good at holding onto money. Even his flat was rented, so it'll be down to me to clear it out. Probably end up costing me more than he owned.' She put the watch down, reached into the box for more things. 'I, on the other hand . . .'

Janie wasn't sure whether it was meant to be a reference to the fine house. The difference could not be more marked between here and the slightly shabby tenement flat where Kenneth Morgan had lived. She recalled Machin's expensive car, too. Not short of cash then. And yet there didn't appear to be a Mr Machin around. It seemed indelicate to ask, and frankly not all that relevant. She'd only come here for Morgan's phone, after all.

'Ah, now this I do remember.' The woman had reached almost to the bottom of the box, and this time came out clutching a bag in which had been placed a small silver cross on a chain. Where she had been content to leave everything else in their individual bags, this one she pulled out and held up so it could twist in the light. A tiny figure of Jesus writhed in agony, arms wide, head crowned with thorns.

'I heard he was quite religious, Mr Morgan. Went to mass every Sunday.'

Machin gave Janie an appraising look, then offered the cross to her. 'It's true. One of the stranger things about him, really. He didn't strike me as the religious type when we first met. Quite the opposite. Oh, he was raised a good Catholic, that's true. His parents were very strict about that. They gave him this cross when he was a boy. But Kenny was a rebel when I knew him. At least for a while.'

Janie took the cross, surprised at quite how intricately wrought it was. The chain on which it hung was slender, but with a weight and strength to it. Dark tarnish marked the silver, worn shiny in places where a thumb might rub while clasping the tortured Christ in prayer. It was a strangely personal thing, quite out of keeping with the man she had never known but had read enough about to think she might have understood.

'You can have it if you like it so much.' Machin's words cut through Janie's thoughts, and she realised she'd been staring blankly at the cross, her own thumb gently rubbing at the silver in mimicry of how Morgan must have caressed it. Embarrassed, she put it down on the table.

'Actually, I really only wanted to get hold of his phone.'

Machin was no fool, it was clear. She arched that grey-white eyebrow again, then dug into the box until she found the slim device. 'Something come up, has it? Or were you hoping to get information about Archie Seagram from this?' She handed the phone to Janie. 'If so, good luck with that.'

For a moment, Janie thought the woman was being flippant. But her tone was all wrong. She truly did wish them luck in taking down Seagram.

'Does he know?' she asked. 'That you've got all this?'

Machin took a little while to answer. 'I suspect not. Otherwise I'm sure one of his goons would have been round asking for it. He'll find out sooner or later, I've no doubt. If he does, I'll just tell him that you lot have still got everything.'

As if that had made her mind up, the old woman began putting everything back in the box. When she had finished, she placed the lid on top carefully, then picked up her wine glass and took a long draught.

'There you go. It's all your problem, now.'

Janie looked from the box to the window onto darkness outside. It wasn't heavy to carry, but it would be awkward. As potential evidence, it would probably be OK for her to call in a passing squad car to pick it up. Or she could call a cab. There was another reason why she had come here herself though. She took a sip of tea, trying to work out a subtle way to introduce the subject. Then decided it was probably best to jump right in.

'How well did you know William Creegan?'

'Billy?' Machin raised that eyebrow again. 'Why?'

'You asked me if something had come up.' In for a penny, in for a pound. 'Well, it has. Creegan's dead.'

The old woman pulled out a chair and sat down, indicated for Janie to do the same.

'Not peacefully in his sleep, I take it?'

Janie had a momentary vision of the man laid out in front of the altar. He had looked almost as if he might have been sleeping when it happened, apart from the brand on his forehead. 'Not exactly, no. His body was found in an old church in Gorgie. We're treating it as suspicious and having another look at Morgan's death too.'

Machin took another drink, more of a gulp than a sip this time. She twiddled the glass around in her fingers for a moment before speaking again.

'Hence the need for his phone. Are you planning on digging him up again? Only, I'd rather not be involved in any of that.'

166

Janie wasn't sure if it was meant to be a joke until she looked the old woman directly in the face. The wrinkles around her eyes were laughter as much as age, and once she had Janie's gaze she broke into a grin.

'Poor taste?'

'Not really. I don't think so, anyway. And I hope it doesn't come to that. Exhumation is so much paperwork. But either way I – we – need to put together a better picture of Mr Morgan's life leading up to his death. Hopefully we'll find something on his phone.'

'Well, I wish I could help, but I moved away from that crowd a very long time ago. Should really never have got myself involved, but Ken, well he was a charming man when he was young.' Machin stared into the past for a while before fixing her gaze on Janie again. 'Billy, on the other hand, was a grade A piece of shit. Never understood why the others put up with him.'

Janie drank some more of her tea, let a little silence build for Machin to fill.

'There was something about the way he looked at women, you know? It wasn't lustful, quite the opposite. Almost a revulsion. As if he hated having to share the same space as us. Thought we should all be away in the kitchen getting his tea. He was always more happy with the boys. I'd have pegged him as gay, but if he was, he kept it suppressed. Archie would never have stood for that. Not sure Ken would, either. Very old fashioned, those two, especially when it came to that sort of thing.'

That didn't square with what Janie knew of Seagram's business interests, the trafficking of women and men to work in the sex trade, the drug dealing, the loan sharking. She kept that to herself though. 'I don't suppose you've had much contact with any of them in recent times.'

'Me? Heavens, no. I'd not spoken to Ken in, what? Ten years? That'd be about right. He called me not long after he got out of

Saughton the last time. Said he was too old for that. Going to put the life of crime behind him.'

'And you believed him?'

'Not for a moment.' Machin drained the last of her wine, stood up and went to the fridge. One of those enormous stainless steel American things, when she opened its twin doors Janie saw that one side was neatly shelved and filled with wine bottles. The old lady pulled out one and brought it back to the table, talking all the while. 'Men like him don't change. Well, not the way you'd want them to. They get better at not being caught, I suppose. Better at persuading younger fools to do the dirty work for them. But they're still a bunch of crooks underneath.'

'You got out, though. Away from all that. Made something for yourself.' Janie waved a hand in no particular direction, indicating the whole house.

'Let's just say I learned my lesson. Married better the second time around. And before you ask, my husband died five years ago, rest his soul. He was a hedge fund manager, which is what I'd call legalised banditry, so maybe I didn't learn my lesson after all.' Machin squeaked out the cork and poured herself a healthy measure before offering the bottle to Janie. 'Sure I can't tempt you with something a little stronger? You must be off duty by now.'

Janie couldn't help herself warming to the old woman. From what little she had seen of the house it was well-furnished, expensive, but sterile. It didn't feel particularly lived in. There were no photographs of children, or even the long-departed Mr Machin. No evidence of any hobbies or pastimes, with the possible exception of the well-stocked wine fridge. It occurred to Janie that Anna Machin was lonely. Why else invite a detective less than half her age to share a bottle of wine and a chat? She looked at her half-finished mug of tea, glanced briefly at the clock on the wall, took in the label on the bottle. It was past her shift end, why shouldn't she have a drink?

'Perhaps just a small glass,' she said.

25

August 25th 1982 – Wednesday

Dad's birthday. We went to a restrant for tea and I had a burger and a milkshake and some fries. Asked if I could miss choir practice on Saturday, but they said no, I have to go for my soul. Told dad Callum stopped coming, but he won't listen. I don't want to go any more, but I don't want to be punished.

If I had a time bomb like Johnny Alpha, I'd send myself back to before he came to the church and stop Father McCormack from leaving. He was mean, but he didn't make us keep God's secrets.

26

He felt much fitter than he had in a while, McLean had to admit that much. True, his hip still ached when the weather was changing, and now he had a similar twinge in his arm where it had been broken too. Six months of the best physiotherapy money could buy had worked wonders all the same, and the diet he'd been doing his best to stick to had helped. Like Merlin, he'd taken to walking everywhere. That was something he'd missed as the demands of the job had grown ever more onerous. Now, without needing to be across town in minutes, he was rediscovering the city on foot, come wind or rain.

Today's walk into town had been, somewhat ironically, in search of a new pair of boots. The outer edges of the heels on his current pair were so worn that they almost fell over when he sat them on the floor after taking them off, and both his physiotherapist and the bright-eyed and impossibly young woman who came three times a week to help Emma with her slow recovery had been nagging him to get a new pair for the best part of a month.

Boots were, McLean had discovered, surprisingly expensive. They now came in a bewildering array of different styles, and for different activities, too. It had taken far longer than he would have liked to settle on a pair that were comfortable and lightweight and not garishly coloured. The walk back home, however, had taken considerably less time than the walk out, and the absence of any complaint from his hip reassured him that he'd made the right purchase. Just as well, since he'd splashed out on two pairs.

He saw the taxi turning out of his gateway as he approached from the other side of the road. The lack of any passenger in the back seat was ample forewarning, so that when he shucked off his coat and trod his new boots into the kitchen, it was no great surprise to see Madame Rose standing at the Aga.

'Tony. How good to see you. And perfect timing, too. I've just put the kettle on.'

The fact that it was his house and his kettle didn't seem to bother the medium. She moved about the kitchen with the ease of someone who has done it many times before. McLean found it comforting rather than annoying, and he wasn't going to complain if someone else made his tea for him. He was about to ask if there might be cake to go with it, when Emma wheeled herself in through the propped-open door to the front of the house.

'Oh, hey Tony. You're back. Wasn't sure how long you'd be.' She slid her wheelchair to its place at the head of the table and clicked on the brakes. 'Successful trip?'

McLean lifted one foot to show off his recent purchase. The bag with his old boots and the second new pair was still in the utility room. 'After a fashion.'

The pun elicited the response it deserved, which was to say it was ignored. McLean let Rose busy herself with tea making and pulled out a chair to sit.

'Is it Em's therapy again?' he asked as the medium placed a large tin he knew wasn't his on the table. 'Only, I thought that was yesterday.'

Madame Rose prised open the lid to reveal a sponge cake slathered in thick buttercream icing. So much for the diet, although given the distance he'd walked McLean felt he might have earned it.

'Actually, it was you I came to see, Tony. I called, but Em said you were out and to come over anyway.'

'Oh, yes?' McLean felt a current of unease. A chilling in the pit of his stomach that might have been worry, or simply anticipation of the coming feast. Probably the first though; Rose rarely sought him out with good news.

'Have we known each other seven years yet?'

Thrown by the question, it took McLean a while to work out the answer. 'I think so, yes. More. Why?'

'Bad luck to pour tea in the house of someone you've not known that long.' Rose picked up the teapot and began filling mugs.

'That's not what you came to talk to me about though, is it.' McLean accepted his, along with a slice of cake thick enough to feed a family. Madame Rose cut a smaller slice for Emma, but took a sizeable chunk for herself. She forked in a mouthful, savoured it and washed it down with some tea before answering.

'You've got itchy feet, Tony.' Rose waited a moment for him to make the obvious joke, but McLean was wise to that.

'I know several of your former colleagues have paid you a visit, suggesting you might want to go back to work.'

'Been talking to Jayne again?'

'Aye, but I have other sources.' Rose glanced down at the rug in front of the Aga, where Mrs McCutcheon's cat had resumed her place now that the potentially hazardous business of kettles had been dealt with. 'It's not important. The question is, how seriously are you contemplating it?'

All this while, Emma had said nothing. Now McLean looked at her, expecting a suspicious narrowing of the eyes, or perhaps an expression of hurt. Instead, she smiled at him as if in encouragement. It was quite unsettling.

'I . . .' he began, then stopped.

'It's only natural,' Rose said. 'You've been a detective for most of your adult life. It's what you do best and you're very good at it.

Why else would you be helping Jo Dalgliesh? Time was you couldn't bear to be in the same room as her. And I hear you've been contacted by one of the city's less pleasant characters, too. Someone who sees you as a middleman between their problems and the authorities.'

'You're talking about Archie Seagram, I take it.' McLean didn't bother asking how Madame Rose knew of that. He'd not hidden any of it from Emma, so there was every chance she had passed the information on as part of their endless conversations while Rose helped her with her speech. Or maybe the damned cat had told the whole story as part of its weekly reports. That made almost as much sense.

'He's lost a couple of old friends in unusual circumstances recently, I hear,' Rose continued. 'Takes a lot to scare a man like him, but that's got him very worried.'

'Well, I told him to speak to someone at the station. Only, unless he goes there and confesses to running half of the city's loan shark operations and several other criminal enterprises as well, then I don't think anyone's going to take him all that seriously.' McLean cut a slice of his cake with the side of his fork and shoved it in his mouth before realising it was larger than he'd thought. Tasty, though.

'And that's the problem.' Madame Rose leaned her elbows on the table, mug held in both hands. 'Nobody in the police will go out of their way for a man like Seagram, and that's quite understandable. Likewise, they'll probably not give the investigation into William Creegan's death the full scrutiny it requires. And I hear Kenneth Morgan's end is being considered natural causes.'

'And you think it isn't?' McLean managed to say without spitting out too many crumbs.

'I am not sure. The cards are hazy on this one. I do know that there's one detective working in Edinburgh who wouldn't let the victims' criminal past get in the way of doing the best job he could of investigating their deaths. And I think it's very important those deaths are investigated properly.'

'Two detectives, actually. Even if one of them has retired.' McLean met Rose's gaze as he spoke.

'Ah yes. Janie. She's not one to cut corners, it's true. But she's also too junior to disobey orders. Or even just ignore them too often. Especially when they're coming from the very top. You put a heavy weight on that one's shoulders when you left, Tony.'

McLean wanted to shout that he'd left precisely so that Harrison and the rest of his team would still have a job that could weigh on them at all, but instead he took a sip of his tea and tried to calm himself.

'You don't have to stay here for me, Tony.' Emma reached out a hand and placed it on his forearm. 'It would probably do you good to do more, even if it wasn't full time. The garden would certainly be better for it.'

For a moment he thought she wanted him to spend more time with the weeds, but then he caught the ghost of a smile on one side of her face and understood what she had really meant.

'Am I that bad a gardener?' He put on a tone of hurt, of pride wounded.

'Not so much bad as overzealous, I think. The fruit trees will recover from your pruning, but we might not get many apples this year.'

McLean glanced at the kitchen window and the garden beyond. He'd tried to impose some order on the place once his arm was healed enough, but he'd be the first to admit it wasn't something he knew much about. And it was true he'd been spending more time with Grumpy Bob of late. Jo Dalgliesh too, and even Grace Ramsay. They all brought him problems, and while none of them had specifically asked for his help in solving them, he knew that was where his true skills lay. Where he found the greatest sense of fulfilment.

'I could speak to Jayne, I suppose. See about taking on a consultant role, maybe. They always need help in the Cold Case Unit.'

Even as he said it, McLean felt a weight lift off his shoulders. Had he been so wound up by not working? Looking across the table at Madame Rose, to Emma as well, he saw similar relief in their faces. As if this was what they really wanted. It wouldn't have surprised him if they hadn't planned this whole episode. They had to be talking about something during those endless speech therapy sessions.

'That's sorted then,' Emma said, her words hardly slurred at all now. 'You can give them a call in the morning.'

27

Police Sergeant Don Gatford was on the desk when Janie pushed through the front door of the station. She would normally go in the back entrance, but she'd overslept and had to take a different bus, which meant this was the better option. He gave her an expression that was half 'and what time do you call this to be showing up?' and half something else she couldn't put her finger on.

She managed a quick, 'Morning, Sarge,' as she passed, got a, 'Morning, Janie,' in return as he buzzed her through, picking up the desk phone at the same time. Not like Don to pass up the chance for a blether, but Janie was glad all the same. She couldn't muster the energy for one of his famous long chats. Her arms ached from lugging the box Anna Machin had given her, with all of Kenneth Morgan's personal belongings in it. Her head ached too, from the bottle and some of very fine Chardonnay the two of them had drunk together. Machin had told some hair-raising tales from her youth, painting a picture of Broxburn in the sixties and seventies that was a completely different place to one Janie had grown up in three decades later.

She wasn't much of one for mid-week drinking, especially not on an empty stomach, which was another reason why she was in a rush to get to the incident room. Late for the shift to start, she was in danger of missing her own morning briefing if she didn't get a move on. And she needed to take Morgan's phone down to IT for Mike Simpson to work his magic on first.

As she stepped into the incident room fifteen minutes later, Janie felt a buzz about the place quite out of keeping with the lack of progress before she had left. For a moment she wondered if something had come up. Had they managed to identify the man in the CCTV footage? Had someone handed themselves in and given a full confession? But no, she knew it couldn't be anything like that. Her phone would have been buzzing with messages, and probably someone would even have called to let her know.

'What's up?' she asked the first familiar face she saw. The young uniform constable, PC Fairley, flushed at being singled out, the freckles on the tops of his cheeks darkening into an almost warpaint band.

'I . . . Ma'am . . . It's the Vice team,' he managed to stammer out before losing the ability to speak. It was enough to give Janie some small idea of what was going on.

'They raided the house already?' She put down the box and dug out her phone, but there were no texts from DCI Dexter or any of the other detectives from the Sexual Crimes Unit. She felt a slight disappointment at not having been kept in the loop. But then again, she hadn't expected there to be any movement on the information she'd passed on to them for days yet. Planning a raid took time, as did securing a warrant.

'Aye. Went in just before dawn, so I heard.' DC Stringer approached from the far corner of the room, scratching at his cheek where he must have missed a bit shaving. 'Sounds like it's some kind of high-class knocking shop or something. DCI Dexter was in here maybe half an hour ago? Think she was looking to tell you the good news herself.'

Janie scanned the room, checked her watch. She should really be rallying everyone, setting them their tasks for the day and doing whatever she could to stop them all chattering about this admittedly good news. On the other hand, apart from trying to pin an identity on the man from the CCTV footage, there wasn't a lot that they could be doing right now. And if the house in Craigentinny had anything to do with Billy Creegan, then her murder investigation was going to collide with Jo Dexter's Vice operation anyway.

'I'll go see if I can find her. Tell everyone we'll have the morning briefing in half an hour will you, Jay?'

DC Stringer began to speak, but closed his mouth as the incident room door clicked open again and DCI Dexter stuck her head through the gap.

When she saw Janie, she committed fully, pushed the door wide and strode in. 'There she is. My favourite detective sergeant. I was beginning to worry you'd booked the day off.'

'In the middle of a murder investigation?' Janie shrugged.

'Fair point. Still, sorry we didn't let you know in advance, but we had to move quickly. Looks like they were about to pull out and clean the place down, so your timing was impeccable.'

'Glad to be of help. You'll let us know if anything comes up about Creegan, aye?'

Dexter looked at her as if she was mad, and for a moment Janie thought she'd said something wrong.

'I'll do better than that.' The DCI grabbed Janie by the arm and pulled her towards the door. 'Just heading back there myself. You can come with me and see what we've found.'

It was both completely changed from her previous visit, and very much the same. Janie noticed as they passed it that the waxing parlour was closed, a pair of uniform constables loitering by the front door. Before she'd had time to mention it to Dexter, their car had made the turn into the side street and then down the narrow lane to Reid Manor. She caught a brief glimpse of the dormer bungalow, its flat-roofed window jutting out from the rear, and then they were passing through a police cordon into an area of organised chaos.

The big house had no doubt once been surrounded by landscaped gardens and probably a larger farm estate when first it had been built. Now the city had engulfed it like a grey concrete flood, leaving a building in mock baronial style, with a large garage block that reminded Janie of DI McLean's coach house, and a small garden dotted with spindly trees. The whole site was surrounded by a wall, the slate roofs and dormer extensions of the nearby bungalows poking over the top of it. Beyond them rose the tower blocks of Restalrig, and in the opposite direction the rising back of Arthur's Seat.

'Forensics are still going over the place, so we'd better suit up. Wouldn't want to get shouted at by your flatmate.' Dexter popped open the car door and climbed out. Janie watched through the windscreen for a moment as a stream of white boiler suit-clad police and forensics technicians trooped in and out of the front door. Another team was making a start on the coach house, while a third had fanned out into a line that inched slowly across the garden. The sheer numbers almost made her weep when she thought about how few officers she'd been able to gather together for her own investigation.

It took a while among all the bustle to find a set of overalls. Longer still to clamber into them. One size might fit all, but it did so badly as far as she was concerned. Walking like a toddler who's wet herself, Janie followed DCI Dexter into the house, through a sizeable atrium and into a grand central hall. A round cupola spilled light into the space, revealing first and second-floor landings reached by an elegant, curved staircase.

'We hit them just before dawn, when pretty much everyone was sleeping.' Dexter led Janie to the foot of the stairs, but instead of going up they took a narrower flight of steps down into a basement.

'Most of the upstairs rooms were unoccupied, sadly. They were gearing up to move everything out, so business was closed. The residents, however . . .' The detective chief inspector let her words tail off as she indicated a narrow corridor leading from the bottom of the stairs. Doors opened on both sides at regular intervals, a final one at the far end. The walls here were stone, the ceiling vaulted and low enough that Lofty Blane would have struggled to fit. Modern light blocks provided harsh white illumination. Janie looked through the nearest open door onto what might originally have been a wine cellar, or something similar. Now it was kitted out as a very basic bedroom. Two narrow beds shoved up against the walls left barely enough space between them to reach the far end. Each had only a thin pillow and thinner blanket.

'There's no ventilation. Just a grille in the door. No natural light. Can't begin to imagine what it must be like sleeping down here.'

Janie had noticed the smell as they reached the bottom of the stairs, a musty odour mixed with something she hadn't been able to place until seeing the tiny room. Now she looked to the end of the corridor and the single door there.

'Shared toilet,' Dexter confirmed, wrinkling her nose even though Janie wouldn't have thought the heavy smoker had much of a sense of smell. 'There's no plumbing, so it's pretty crude. We found sixteen people locked up in these rooms. We're still processing them, but my guess is they're all Eastern European. Not much English between them. Trafficked, of course. And put to work upstairs.'

'Doing what, exactly?' Janie thought she knew but asked the question anyway.

'Well, perhaps you'd like to have a look at some of the other bedrooms now. They're a bit different to these.'

The clean air in the hall only served to emphasise how rank the atmosphere had been in the basement. Janie paused a moment to try and clear her head of the fug before climbing to the first floor. Here there were six rooms accessed from the landing, and she followed the detective chief inspector into the nearest. It was smaller than she had expected, one tall window looking out over the back of the property. Strangely, there were three dressing tables arranged along the wall opposite a single bed, and to the side of the doorway, a long, wheeled rack of the kind you might find in a discount clothes store. Janie thought that the faint smell of latex must have come from the fitted plastic sheet covering it, or perhaps the forensic technician dusting the middle dressing table for prints. But when she lifted a corner, she saw a collection of fetish clothing that brought her an unexpected flush of embarrassment.

'Quite the sight, is it not? Haven't seen that many gimp masks in one place since me and Tony raided that place in the New Town.' Dexter frowned, cocked her head to one side as if shaking loose some memory. 'That'd be before your time, of course.'

'Of course.' Janie tried to ignore the squeak in her voice as she dropped the cover back down. Another door led through to a well-appointed bathroom with modern fittings. A second forensic technician crouched in the shower, inspecting the drain hole with a handheld UV light. Another had opened a deep cupboard, stacked with towels and linen.

'This is where they washed and prepared. Or I should probably say were washed and prepared.' Dexter stood half in, half out of the bathroom while Janie peered around. 'There's a couple of large reception rooms downstairs, one with a well-stocked bar. The back of the house is mostly admin, I think. That and a good-sized catering kitchen. If it weren't for the basement and who we found in it, and for those . . .' Dexter waved her hand at the hidden costumes '. . . you might think this was just another boutique hotel.'

'It's not though, is it.' Janie brushed past the detective chief inspector on her way out of the bathroom. There was more to see, but right now she wasn't sure she wanted to see it.

'Indeed not. From the equipment we've found, the layout of the other rooms, and those poor unfortunates down in the basement, I'd say this is most certainly a brothel catering to extreme tastes. Wish we'd known about it sooner, really. That way we might have been able to catch a few more of its clients. Amazing the information you can get out of a man who's been caught with his trousers down and a butt plug up his arse.'

Dexter was clearly in her element, and rightly enjoying the rush of having busted open an operation such as this one. Janie sympathised with her; you had to make the most of the victories when they came, it wasn't often. But she also had her own investigation ongoing and few leads at all.

'You mentioned Creegan,' she said. 'When we were back at the station.'

Dexter said nothing, but she strode across the room to the door, hooking a finger for Janie to follow. Upstairs to the second floor, and still she was silent. The landing was narrower here, the ceiling lower. A short corridor ran from the top of the stairs to a window at the back of the house, a single door on either side. One stood open, and Dexter motioned for Janie to go in.

'I think this is probably what you've been looking for,' she said.

Even though she was short, and the door was a standard height, Janie still found herself ducking slightly as she stepped through. Built into the eaves, it would probably have been a store, or perhaps a servant's quarters, when the house was of less ill repute. Now it had been pressed into service as a bedroom, and it didn't take her long to work out who had been sleeping here.

William Creegan had been fastidiously clean in his person, almost to the point of fetish. Or indeed, all the way to the point of fetish and beyond given what appeared to be going on under his roof. His bedroom showed that same meticulous tidiness. Nothing was out of place, the bed itself neatly made, not a speck of dust to be seen. An antique desk had been placed in front of a dormer window with a view across rooftops to Arthur's Seat. Arranged neatly in the centre of it, waiting to be dealt with on his return, was a stack of envelopes with the address in Cumberland Street.

As she scanned the room, she saw other indications of the man she'd last seen laid out on the mortuary slab. In the wardrobe, a half dozen identical suits hung neatly alongside a similar number of ironed shirts. They were all the same as the clothes Creegan had been wearing when he had gone to St Mark's for his appointment with his killer. Clearly he was a man who didn't like having to choose what to wear of a morning.

On the wall beside the wardrobe, an old, framed photograph had been hung where it would be seen whenever the room's occupant got dressed. Somewhat incongruously, it appeared to have replaced a larger picture, the darker shade of the surrounding wallpaper indicating where the light had not reached until recently. Then again, if Creegan really had been living in Cumberland Street, running something similar to this place until his old friend Kenneth Morgan's death had made a move necessary, then he'd likely only been using this room for a week or so before his own untimely end.

Squinting at the picture, Janie saw it was a group photograph. Four men in their late twenties or early thirties. She was no expert, but the style of their clothes suggested it had been taken sometime during the eighties. She recognised Creegan quickly enough, and was fairly sure two of the others were Kenneth Morgan and Archie Seagram. The last man was vaguely familiar, so probably the other mourner she'd seen at Morgan's burial: Raymond McAllister. In the background the old Forth Rail Bridge rose into a pale blue sky, although the colours of the photograph were so faded it might have been slate grey cloud originally.

'They've dusted for prints in here. Plenty of good ones.' Dexter stepped into the room, immediately making it feel crowded. It reminded Janie a bit of her first flat when she'd been at college, only a lot tidier.

'No doubt this was where Creegan was living.' She flicked through the envelopes, finding a couple addressed to Reid Manor in with the rest. 'Begs the question what he was doing over the other side of town the night he died.'

'Also what his role here was. Can't imagine he was living above a brothel for the ambience. Our best intel was that he'd retired. Seems we were ill informed on that score.' Dexter crossed to the window and peered out at the garden beyond, where a group of uniform constables was still scouring the grounds for evidence. Quite why they needed any more than they already had, Janie wasn't sure.

'He had a laptop, which we've already parcelled off to Mike Simpson in forensic IT. We'll share anything we find, of course. Chances are though whoever killed him was linked to what he was doing here. There's sixteen people we found in the basement who've plenty motive to brand a cross into his forehead. Who's to say how many more he's run through places like this down the years?'

Janie doubted it was as simple as that, although she couldn't immediately say why. Nor was she about to turn down help from the Vice team, which was considerably better resourced than her own. 'Thanks. What about the . . .' she struggled for the right word for a moment. 'What about those people in the basement?'

Dexter turned back from the window to face her, the smile on her face weary. No doubt she'd been up all night planning the raid, and now had a mountain of time-sensitive work to get through before she could have a break. Still, the euphoria from such a significant bust would keep her going for a while yet. That and the cigarettes.

'We'll be starting the interviews soon as we can get translators sorted. After lunch, I'd guess, if you want to watch.'

28

Back at the station, Janie checked in with the team to see if any-thing had happened while she'd been away. From the atmosphere in the incident room, it seemed unlikely. The poor-quality images taken from the CCTV footage still stared down from the whiteboard. A pair of scrawled black question marks beside them spoke eloquently to how far that line of investigation had progressed. They'd need to get an artist's impression out to the press if they were to have a hope of identifying the man, although she knew such a course of action would also lead to the crazies all phoning in, convinced it was their weird uncle or simply someone who'd annoyed them. Such was ever the way with stalled investigations.

'Those the best we could manage?' she asked DC Bryant, who had made the mistake of coming up to see if anything needed doing.

'IT are working on an enhancement, but that's pretty much it. I've been going through some of the other footage to try and get something better. Still waiting to hear back from the bus company too. They've got cameras, so we might get lucky with the Ferry Road sighting.'

Janie nodded absentmindedly. Talk of IT reminded her that she'd dropped Kenneth Morgan's phone in on them that morning.

Should she pay Mike a visit and see if he'd got anywhere yet? Or was it best to leave him to get on with it? He'd text her the moment they had anything, surely. And he'd be busy with William Creegan's laptop too.

'You OK, Janie?' Bryant asked.

'What . . .? Oh. Sorry. A lot on my mind and I didn't sleep all that well last night.'

She was halfway through explaining all about her meeting with Anna Machin when a ping on her phone interrupted the story. Thinking it would be IT, she was surprised to find a message from Jo Dexter. It was all very nice the DCI keeping her in the loop on Reid Manor, but Janie couldn't help thinking it was only adding to her workload. Still, Dexter was her superior officer, so she couldn't exactly ignore her. She tapped the screen to see what it was all about.

Interviews with trafficked workers ongoing, if you'd like to observe. Might be interesting.

'What is it?' Bryant asked, but Janie was already heading for the door.

'Keep on the photo for now, can you? And check with Mike in IT how he's getting on with Morgan's phone. I'll be down in the observation room if anyone needs me.'

The young man in interview room three had a cadaverous look, his bones prominent beneath skin tinged an unhealthy yellow. From her position in the observation room, Janie couldn't tell whether he was ill, or his colouring was due to his ethnicity. Probably a bit of both, as he certainly didn't look well. If she had to guess, she'd have put him in his early twenties, but there were flecks of grey in his spiky, long hair that spoke of far more trauma than two score years of life should have inflicted upon anyone. He sat on one side of a wide table, flanked by an interpreter and a solicitor, although as far as she was aware he hadn't been charged with anything. On the other side of the table, Jo Dexter was asking questions, Detective Constable Sean Wyse taking notes. Janie was surprised to see Wyse working in Vice. She'd known him back in her uniform days but hadn't felt any great need to keep in touch.

'My English not good,' the young man said in what was far better English than Janie often heard on the city streets at chucking out time. 'You are police, no? I am arrested?'

Dexter gave the solicitor a look that suggested he might want to explain, then did so herself. 'No, Mr Shahid, you're not under arrest. Not yet at least. We have reason to believe you are in this country without the correct paperwork, however. And you know where we found you. You will be given an opportunity to claim asylum in due course, but you've got yourself tied up in some very shady business. We need to know how you came to be locked in the basement of that house. As I understand it, you're from Syria originally?'

'Is correct,' the young man answered before his interpreter had a chance to say anything. 'I come from Idlib, in the north. Much war there, and then new government with very strict rules. Sharia. People like me. We not allowed to exist. Put to death if found out. So I flee.'

Dexter said nothing for a moment, simply watching the young man as if appraising him. He was doing his best to hold it together, Janie could see. But he was also exhausted, frightened and abused. It took her a moment to work out what he had meant when he'd said, 'people like me', but the penny dropped around about the same time it must have done for the detective chief inspector. She gave a very slight nod of her head before continuing.

'How is it that you ended up in Edinburgh? Did you want to come here? To the UK?'

'I . . . My English not good, but is better than my French. I have number of people to contact in London. That is where I was told I would be taken. I should know better, but I am desperate, no?'

'Is there a reason to this interview, Detective Chief Inspector?' the solicitor asked out of nowhere. 'Mr Shahid is a victim of a serious crime here. He's not a criminal. He should be treated as an asylum seeker.'

From where she stood, Janie couldn't see Dexter's expression. By the set of the DCI's shoulders, and the way the solicitor flinched back into his chair, his eyes widening, she could imagine what it looked like. That the young man barely moved showed exactly how far gone he was. Too tired to care any more. Too brutalised.

'I am aware of your client's status,' Dexter said. 'It was my team that raided the house where Mr Shahid was being held captive and, I believe, forced into sex work.' She turned her attention back to the young man. 'Am I right in thinking that was the case?'

An emotion crept over the young man's face that Janie took a while to recognise. He seemed to fold in on himself without actually moving. After a few excruciating seconds he turned to the interpreter and said something in a fluid, rhythmic tongue. Her eyes widened almost as much as the solicitor's, before her expression hardened into one of anger. She opened her mouth to speak, but the young man reached out and put a hand on her arm to stop her. He had very long fingers, Janie noticed. Except for one that ended at the first joint, the skin at the end of it smooth and pink.

'I do not think "work" is right word. For work you are paid, no?' Shahid cocked his head to one side, but didn't wait for an answer. 'They use us for their sex, yes? They are sick, but they are strong. They have guns, knives. They lock us up in dark places, starve us, beat us if we do not do as they say. Cut us.' He held up his hand and waggled the missing finger. Where before he had been almost motionless with fatigue, now some last reserve of energy animated him. In his halting English, with occasional help from an increasingly horrified interpreter, he painted a detailed

188

picture of the horrors that had gone on in that house and others before it, for so long he had lost count of the days.

Janie wanted to leave, to slip out of the observation booth and creep back up to the incident room. She had heard stories of the work Vice did, of how it corroded even the hardest of souls. How had Dexter managed to stay sane leading the team for as long as she had done? Well, maybe sane was pushing it a bit, the detective chief inspector had some strange idiosyncrasies. Still, she forced herself to stay and listen as the young man's story of his time in Edinburgh unfolded. She owed him that much.

'And do you know who ran the place? Who organised it all?' Dexter was asking as Janie turned her attention back to the interview. The young man glanced up at the observation window, almost as if he could see her watching him, even though it was a mirror on his side. Or maybe he was seeing himself now, what had become of him.

'The old man. They call him "sir". Or "Mr Creegan".' The young man pronounced the name as if it were two separate words, and for a moment Janie thought he was going to spit at the taste of them. 'They fear him. We all do. He is worse than those I fled Syria to escape. He did this to me.' He held up his hand again, the half finger easier to see now. The wound where it had been cut was swollen, but it had all but healed. Months old, not weeks. 'And he did much worse.'

Janie was still standing in the observation room, staring through the glass at the empty space beyond, when DCI Dexter came in to join her some long minutes later. For a moment the detective chief inspector stood silently beside her, both of them processing the horrors they had heard.

'How do you cope with it?'

'Badly.' Dexter shoved hands deep into her jacket pockets, brought them out again with a packet of cigarettes and a lighter.

'These help. And shouting at the sky. Mostly you keep on so that poor sods like Mr Shahid there might get the future they deserve rather than the shit that's been heaped on them.'

Janie suspected there was more to it than that, but didn't press the point. She'd seen enough cruelty and death to last her a lifetime, and she was only at the start of her chosen career. Dexter was twenty-five years her senior, maybe more. Was that all she had to look forward to? A terminal cigarette habit and shouting at the sky?

'Look at it this way,' the DCI continued as if she had read Janie's thoughts. 'You saved that man's life. Saved the lives of all the other poor bastards we found in the cellar of that house. On top of that, we now know Billy Creegan's behind it all. He's operated out of Reid Manor and that house in Cumberland Street. Probably a half dozen other places too. Forensics are going over it in much finer detail now, but better than that we can trace him back to those other properties, more of their sick little sex clubs or whatever the fuck it was they were running. And who knows? Maybe we even get to tie him to Archie Seagram. Someone has to be the money behind it all, wouldn't you say?'

Janie still couldn't bring herself to say anything.

'Creegan's dead. He can't hurt anyone any more. If it wasn't for your quick wits, Janie, then his operation would have just moved on elsewhere. You should be pleased with yourself. I'm certainly pleased, and so are the high heidyins. You did good.'

'But that's the thing though, isn't it?' Janie finally found her voice, the words for what she was feeling. 'I was lucky, not skilled. It was pure chance I found that house for you. Don't get me wrong, I'm glad it's shut down. I hope everyone involved gets locked up for a very long time. But I still have to find whoever it was murdered Creegan. I still have to arrest them. Even though right now I'd like nothing more than to shake their hand and buy them a drink.'

Dexter reached up and laid a hand gently on Janie's shoulder, an oddly reassuring gesture. 'You can buy someone a drink and then arrest them after, you know?'

'Aye, I guess. Got to find them first, mind. Don't think Mr Shahid there's going to be much help.' Janie nodded at the glass even though the young man was long gone. 'What'll happen to him, anyway?'

'A problem for immigration services, I think. Given what he's been through and what would happen if he was sent home, I'd be surprised if he was denied asylum. Mind you, I'm too often surprised these days.'

'Know what you mean.' Janie finally turned to face Dexter. 'Well, I guess I'd better get back to finding whoever it is I owe a drink. Thanks for letting me see that interview. I think.'

'No bother. Seeing as how Creegan seems to have been running that place, looks like our two teams are going to be working together for a while anyway.'

'True.' Janie wasn't sure about the idea of it being 'her' team, even if she was nominally in charge of the current investigation. She was still only a detective sergeant, after all. Dexter was a DCI.

'Good. You can start by joining us all in the pub at shift end.' The detective chief inspector gave Janie's shoulder a quick pat. 'We've something to celebrate for a change.'

29

Janie couldn't remember the last time she'd been out to the pub to celebrate a successful conclusion to an investigation. Time was the whole team would troop down to the local and DI McLean or DCI Ritchie would stick a couple of hundred quid behind the bar for them all to have a drink, blow off steam, let go after days, weeks, sometimes months of high stress and higher stakes.

Of course, this wasn't one of her investigations being celebrated, even if she'd had a fairly pivotal role in cracking the case. Her involvement had been by accident more than design, but who was complaining? Well, to be fair, there were a few sour faces among the Vice team, but not their leader.

'There she is: the woman of the hour.' DCI Dexter spotted Janie as she stepped into the crowded pub, gestured her and DC Bryant over. The waves didn't quite part to grant them access, but enough of a path cleared that they could make it to the bar.

'What's your poison?' Dexter shouted over the hubbub. Janie settled on a glass of wine, Bryant a rum and coke.

'Couple of your team already here.' Dexter nodded towards the tables in the far corner as she handed over the drinks. Janie caught sight of DCs Stringer and Mitchell deep in conversation. Was their relationship on again? She thought it had come to nothing, which had been a relief at the time as she hadn't wanted the hassle of reassigning one of them to another team. She was surprised to see another figure sitting next to them. Cerys Powell, the mortuary assistant, appeared to be laughing at some joke Stringer had just made. Then again, the mortuary was as close to this pub as the police station, so it made sense she might pop in here for a drink after work.

'I'm away for a fag,' Dexter said, her cigarette packet already in hand. 'Don't either of you run off, now. I've a speech prepared and everything.'

Janie winced. She wasn't one to crave the limelight, and while it was nice to be valued and praised, she'd have been as happy heading home for a pizza and a glass of slightly better wine than the one she'd been given. On the other hand, this was team building, wasn't it. All part of the job.

'Let's go see what Jay and Cass are up to,' she said to Bryant as the gap Dexter had left at the bar was immediately filled by another body. Bryant gave her a thumbs up, mouth too busy with the straw in her drink to say anything. She set off in the direction of the tables, and Janie followed, letting the taller woman forge the path through the throng.

She was almost there when a hand landed on her shoulder, firm grip turning her around so swiftly she spilled her wine. An instant of anger was washed away when she saw who had dared to accost her. Detective Superintendent Pete Nelson's face was flushed, as if he'd been at the bar far longer than anyone else. Or maybe he just drank quicker.

'Sir, I . . . Sorry.' Janie looked down at Nelson's shoes, now gently spattered with cheap Chardonnay. 'I wasn't expecting to see you here.'

'None of this sir nonsense, Janie. We're celebrating here.' Nelson raised a tumbler filled with amber liquid and ice cubes. As if the man couldn't go down in her estimation much more.

'Aye, I know.' Janie took a sip of her wine, reckoned she'd not missed anything by spilling half of it. 'But we've not caught who- ever it was killed Creegan yet. Seems a bit . . . I don't know. I should be collating the evidence we've got so far, sorting through the actions for tomorrow's shift.'

Nelson reached out with his free hand and clasped Janie's shoulder again. 'Tomorrow's soon enough. If half the things I've heard about Creegan are true, then whoever branded him in that church did us all a favour.'

She resisted the urge to grab his wrist and put him in an arm lock. Clearly the detective superintendent was in his cups, as Janie's mum was fond of saying. That didn't excuse the over- familiarity. Even less so when he pulled her toward him so that someone else could get behind them and to the bar. It was uncom- fortably close, the stench of body odour mingling with the whisky on his breath strong enough to make her stomach churn.

'If you don't mind, sir. I need to have a word with someone.' Janie dragged her shoulder from his grip, a feat that required far more strength and persistence than it should have done. His face was all too readable as he stared at her, and there was no doubt in her mind what he was thinking. With a final wrench, she broke free and turned away, elbowing through the crowd until she reached the table where the detective constables all sat.

'Budge up, will you, Jay?' she said to Stringer, who lounged on the bench that ran most of the length of the wall. Instead of doing so, he slid out from behind the table and stood up.

'Call of nature,' he said by way of explanation, then disappeared into the throng. Janie put her glass down and sat, finding herself alongside Cerys Powell from the mortuary.

'I'd heard about coppers having a knees-up. Thought it was all exaggeration, but they never told me the half of it.'

Janie took another sip of her wine, grimaced, then swallowed a larger gulp. Perhaps it would get better the less she was able to taste it.

'It's been a while since we last had anything to celebrate, so I guess they're all making up for lost time.' She wiped her mouth with the back of her hand. 'Surprised to see you here.'

'Usually pop in after work, see?' Cerys had a pint of Guinness, which she held up without drinking. 'Takes away the taste of the mortuary. Lets me settle my head before going home.'

Janie was about to ask where home was, but a clanging sound of someone hitting the side of a glass echoed through the pub and slowly silenced the crowd. Looking past the collected bodies, she saw DCI Dexter standing on a rung of a bar stool to give herself a bit of height. Time for that speech she'd promised.

'Oh god. Here we go.' She threw back the rest of her wine, and knew it wouldn't be enough.

'OK you lot. Pipe down for a bit, will you? I've something important to say for a change.'

DCI Dexter's shout silenced the last few voices muttering in the corners of the pub and all eyes turned to her.

'It's not often we have something to celebrate these days. Too much work, not enough detectives, isn't that so?'

A half-hearted grumble of yeses and ayes and too fucking rights rose up in answer.

'And even when we do succeed, it's usually only temporary. Close down a knocking shop here and before the day's gone another's popped up somewhere else.'

More muttering of general agreement; Dexter was playing to an easy crowd here. Janie fingered the stem of her wine glass, both wishing she hadn't finished it and not wanting any more. She had a horrible feeling she was about to be the centre of attention, and there were few things she liked less.

'So, when a result like today's comes along, well . . . I'm not going to lie . . . I feel like we should make the most of it.'

Dexter paused to take a drink, raised her glass in a little salute, then before anyone could start applauding, she started off again. 'Of course, it's a little bittersweet when the result comes not from our own hard work but that of another team. Still, I'm not going to complain. We did the groundwork, and that was what allowed us to run with the information when we got it. To recognise it as important information in the first place.'

A few muttered grumbles in the crowd at that, most likely from those who'd finished their drinks and wanted at the bar for refills. Preferably before the DCI's generosity ran out.

'But credit where credit's due.' Dexter raised her voice to still the unruly crowd, and Janie couldn't help but be impressed at how well she kept them in line.

'We're here this evening because of the keen eye and quick wits of one officer. So, I think it's only fair we give her a proper Vice team thank you. Detective Sergeant Harrison? Janie? You want to come up here?'

It sounded like a question, but Janie knew it wasn't. She could no more refuse than she could if Dexter had issued her with an order. Even so, she found herself hesitating, reluctant to get involved. What she wouldn't have given for a quiet night in. Telly, pizza, wine. Drinkable wine.

'You'll be fine, Janie.' The quiet voice of Cerys in her ear was accompanied by a gentle squeeze to her arm as the mortuary assistant leaned in to reassure her. Janie caught the faint whiff of formaldehyde or whatever it was they used to preserve organs for later study, but far from it being an upsetting reminder of the woman's profession, she found it strangely reassuring. Too much time spent working with DI McLean, no doubt. The thought of him gave her a little courage, too. What would he have made of all this?

'Thanks,' she whispered, then reluctantly got to her feet. The crowd parted to let her through to where Dexter stood, Detective Superintendent Nelson by her side. It was almost as bad as school, being called up at assembly for something. Not helped by the way the detective superintendent looked at her, something beyond a drunken leer in his eyes. Janie refused to meet his gaze, focusing on Dexter instead. Normally the DCI was the most observant of people, but for some reason she didn't seem to notice her superior officer at all. Perhaps, like Janie herself, she was doing her best to ignore him.

She opened her mouth to speak, but before any words could make their way out, Nelson pushed himself upright and bellowed into the crowd. 'I've not been here long, as you all know. Thought I was getting away from the funding cuts and understaffing when I left Aberdeen, but it's been just as bad here. Having said which, I've been very impressed with the way you all continue to work in such difficult circumstances.'

Janie looked at Dexter with what she hoped was a quizzical expression. The DCI's simple shrug suggested this hadn't been part of the plan. Neither of them were going to interrupt the boss, though.

'All of you do a good job, at least most of the time. I know senior management don't acknowledge that often, so I'll say it myself here, and thank you all for it. There's a little something behind the bar for you all too, in case you think I'm just full of shite.'

That got a laugh from most of the audience, but then anyone paying for a round was a copper's friend. Janie wished the detective superintendent would get to whatever point it was he wanted to make. The sooner this was over, the sooner she could flee. Back to the table in the corner, or back home, either was better than here in the spotlight.

'But every now and then an officer goes above and beyond the call of duty. And one such officer is our own, dear Janie Harrison here.' Nelson almost fell off the bar rail as he waved erratically in Janie's direction, his foot coming to rest on the edge of the nearby stool more by luck than design.

'Not content with running her own investigation, she's single-handedly cracked open a case that the Vice team have been working on for years.'

Janie felt the atmosphere chill at this last claim, the good-natured hubbub disappear.

Nelson, oblivious to it all, carried on. 'And only a detective sergeant, can you believe it? Filling in until we can find someone to replace poor old Detective Inspector Cummings. God rest his soul.'

Had the man died? Janie exchanged another quizzical look with Dexter, but neither of them had heard anything about it.

'Well, I think we have a replacement now,' Nelson said, and as he did Janie felt a horrible sensation in the pit of her stomach. He wasn't going to . . .

'Step up, won't you, Acting Detective Inspector Janie Harrison.'

The sky had darkened by the time Janie managed to extricate herself from the pub, and into streetlights that shone hazy in the damp, heavy air. It would rain soon, she was fairly sure. Hopefully not before she managed to walk to the bus stop. Or should she splash out and call a cab? She had something to celebrate, after all. Even if, somehow, she didn't feel much like it.

'They told me you were one to watch out for when I took up the job.'

She whirled around at the voice, although even as she did so Janie knew who it was who had spoken. Detective Superintendent Nelson leaned against the pub wall, past the window where he might have been seen from inside. Close to the narrow alleyway she knew led round the back, and the blocks of flats beyond. It was a shortcut she'd taken to the station from South Bridge on many an occasion, but in this light and with this company it didn't seem quite so appealing any more.

'Sir?' She didn't approach him, but he kicked away from the wall like some teenage Romeo, hands shoved in his pockets.

'Shift's over, Janie. You don't have to call me "sir", now.' He slurred his words slightly, and his exaggerated movements were a puppet show she had seen repeated a thousand times every Saturday night when she'd been a beat officer. The stiff-legged, narrow focused walk of the drunk man intent on getting home, or to the nearest kebab shop.

'I need to catch my bus.' Even as the words came out, she knew that it was the wrong thing to say.

'Bus?' Nelson straightened so swiftly he almost fell over, his head snapping upwards in theatrical indignation. 'Acting detective inspectors don't take the bus, Janie. Here. Let me call you a cab.'

The detective superintendent pulled his phone out of his pocket, almost dropped it, then tapped at the screen to bring it to life. It took him far too long to realise it was upside down. Even longer to turn it the right way and bring it to life.

'It's fine, sir. I'm used to it. There's one goes right past my flat anyway.'

Nelson gave up with his phone, although it took a couple of attempts to get it back in his pocket. 'In that case, let me walk you to the bus stop. Streets aren't safe these days, you know.'

'It's really not necessary, sir.' Janie took a step away from him, but he lurched forward to close the gap again. One hand out as if trying to balance, he tripped and fell towards her. She should perhaps have let him fall, but some deep-seated instinct kicked in and she reached out to catch him.

'Steady there, sir. Oh—' Her words were cut off as he pushed her towards the shadows by the narrow alley, hands all over her, face suddenly too close as he leaned in and tried to kiss her. He stank of whisky and something rotten, and for all his drunkenness, he was stronger than she had expected. Another instinct kicked in, one even deeper-rooted than the last. Twisting around, hands ready to push him away, she brought her knee up sharp into his groin.

'Oof!' The air exploded out of him in a rush, and Janie felt the splatter of saliva on her face before he doubled up, wheezing. She shoved him hard, sent him toppling backwards just as another figure came running towards her. Adrenaline high, she whirled around, fists ready to punch the next man who tried it on.

'Whoa, steady there, tiger!' Cerys skidded to a halt, both hands up in surrender. 'Thought you might need some help, but I see you've got it all under control.'

Nelson groaned an oddly high-pitched whimper. Before Janie could intervene, Cerys took a step past her and kicked him in the ribs.

'That'll teach you, you pervert. I've half a mind to call out some of the fine upstanding officers of the law drinking in that pub there.'

'Cerys.' Janie reached out and took hold of the mortuary assistant's arm, tugged her gently away. 'He's police.'

'Is he?'

'Aye, he is. My boss. Well, technically my boss's boss. I think.' Adrenaline rush ebbing away, she started to shiver as the shock of what had just happened overtook her.

'Well, I saw him trying it on. Saw you trying to get away from him too. Wouldn't matter if he was the chief constable himself, he can't go doing that.'

'I . . .' Janie started to speak, but words wouldn't come. She didn't know what to say. All she could do was stare down at the miserable form of the detective superintendent, curled up in the foetal position with his hands shoved into his crotch. Had she caused him lasting damage? Should she call an ambulance? He was drunk, how much would he remember come the morning? All her years of training, experience on the job, the far too many women she had helped when they were in positions much worse than this one, and she couldn't think what to do.

'You're in shock, Petal.' Janie felt a gentle touch on her

shoulder, then a warm embrace as Cerys steered her away from Nelson. 'Here. Let's get back inside and make sure everybody knows what's just happened. Who's at fault here.'

Janie looked at the pub door, half expecting it to burst open and a dozen burly members of the Vice team to come charging out.

'No.' She pushed back against the fuzziness edging her thoughts, did her best to pull herself together. 'No. Thank you, Cerys, but I don't think I want to be surrounded by police just at the moment. Think I'll just call a cab and get myself home.'

She cast a quick glance back at the detective superintendent. He was rocking gently back and forth as he lay on his side, still alive, still drunk. Someone would find him soon. She really didn't want to be here when they did.

'Fair enough.' Cerys took her arm from Janie's shoulder. 'Walk you to Nicholson Square? There's a taxi rank there, isn't there?'

'Aye, there is.' Janie stepped around the still-moaning detective superintendent and set off up the hill towards the main road. Cerys fell into step beside her, a comforting presence even though in truth Janie hardly knew the woman. They'd gone maybe fifty feet when something occurred to her.

'Here. Did you call me "Petal" back there?'

30

She'd hardly had anything to drink at the pub, and hadn't felt like starting once she'd finally made it home, so Janie couldn't help thinking it unfair that she woke the next morning with a hangover. Not one of those Saturday-morning-after-a-difficult-week heads she knew all too well, the mirror of which she often saw on her flatmate's face as they ate silent breakfast together. This was more of a dull headache from midweek drinking kind of hangover, which suggested the wine in the pub had been even worse than she'd thought.

The pub. That was another reason for the hangover, but nothing to do with alcohol either. Janie lay in her warm bed, the grey dawn light filtering in through the curtains, and stared at the ceiling as the events played themselves over and over again in her mind. The packed front bar, all faces on her. Some envious, angry even. Most congratulating her, offering to buy her drinks which she deftly declined. Vice might be celebrating a notable victory, but her own team still had very little to show for the days they'd been trying to find out who had branded William Creegan with a cross on his forehead in a disused church. No idea even why.

And there had been the promotion, too. She should have been pleased, delighted even. OK, so it was only Acting DI, but that was a step in the right direction, and it came with a substantial increase in pay. A substantial increase in responsibilities too, except that she'd been basically doing the job since McLean had left. She deserved the recognition, so why was she not happy to have received it?

Perhaps it was the way it had been announced. Sprung on her, even. She'd never been a fan of those public marriage requests men – and it was always men – liked to spring upon their surprised partners. This must be what it felt like for the poor, unsuspecting bride to be. All but impossible to say no in front of a crowd all giddy with vicarious expectations. Maybe she should have refused.

Janie squirmed under her duvet as the later events of the evening replayed themselves in all-too-graphic detail. Detective Superintendent Nelson outside the pub. She knew he must have planned it. Hadn't he just announced there was money behind the bar and not to drink it all at once? He'd known that would keep all the Vice team inside for another half hour at least. Most of her team had already gone, which meant he only had to wait for her to walk out on her own.

But why? Why had he done that? Forced himself on her? He must have known she wasn't interested. Must have known it was entirely inappropriate. To put it mildly. No good could have come of his actions, and yet he'd done it anyway. Her last vision was of him lying there on the unswept pavement, down among the discarded chip pokes and spat-out chewing gum, cradling his manhood and groaning in agony. She'd done that to him, and while she had no regrets on that score, he was her superior officer, and he would almost certainly make her pay for it.

'You up, J?'

Manda's voice filtered through the door. Her flatmate hadn't been in when she'd made it home the night before, another reason why the bottle of wine was still in the fridge. Janie rubbed at her face, eyes gritty, then levered herself out of bed.

'I'm up, aye.' She padded across the floor to the door, opened it as if she somehow needed to prove that she wasn't lying. Manda was already fully dressed and ready to leave, although the dark bags under her eyes suggested she'd not had much sleep.

'You OK?' they both asked at the same time. The smile that brought to Manda's face helped Janie feel a little better.

'Late night,' Manda yawned into the back of her hand. 'Probs going to be another long day today too. You?'

'Got promoted. Sort of. Not sure if it'll stick though.'

'Wait. What?' Manda checked her watch, eyes going wide. She grabbed Janie into a quick hug. 'That's brilliant. You can tell me all about it tonight, aye? Gotta go now, but seriously, J. About bloody time.' And before Janie could say anything, she had crossed the narrow hall, opened the front door and left.

Janie stared at the empty space for long moments. Then the insistent beeping of her alarm broke through the stupor, and she padded back into her bedroom to switch it off. Shower, coffee and toast made her feel a little more human, but the lingering horror at what might await her at work still sat in the back of her mind, keeping company with the headache. Ah well, there was no point in putting it off.

Her phone beeped as she was locking the front door. A quick glance at the screen as she hurried down the stairs showed a message from Cass Mitchell, but it wasn't until she stepped out onto the street that she managed to read and take in the full text. Against all the laws of nature, the bus that would take her to work stood waiting at the bus stop, not more than twenty paces away. Enough people queued outside to get on that she didn't even need to run to catch it. Instead, she stared at the message again, her breakfast turned sour in the pit of her stomach as she drew a mental map of the city. The bus rattled away in a cloud of black diesel smoke as she tapped out a quick reply. Then she shouldered her bag and set off in the opposite direction.

★ ★ ★

She'd thought it would take ten minutes, but it was actually a quarter of an hour later that Janie rounded the end of the street and saw the all too familiar sight of squad cars, forensics vans and uniform officers keeping the public at bay. This was a quiet part of town, so they didn't have all that much to do. By the time she reached the blue and white tape, DC Mitchell had spotted her and strode over. She'd already donned white overalls, wearing them like a catwalk model.

'Hey, Cass. What's the story here, then?' Janie looked up at the dark grey stone of the church tower, and for a moment it felt like the world was spinning as the clouds scudded past overhead.

'A lot like the last one.' Mitchell lifted the tape for her, waving off a PC who had come up to see what was happening. 'Old lady across the road noticed the door was slightly open, went over to have a look and got the fright of her life. Jessica's with her at the moment.'

Janie looked briefly at the neat row of semi-detached stone houses that lined the other side of the street. Not big, at least not by DI McLean's standards, but it was an affluent enough area.

'She called it in, I take it?'

'Aye, she did. Said nobody else had come past before the first uniforms arrived. They secured the scene and set everything in motion.'

'I guess we'll need to talk to all of them then. First, I'd better get an idea of what we're dealing with.'

Mitchell led her to a parked incident van, where Janie signed in to the crime scene and nabbed a set of overalls. Forensics were already hard at work, a clear path from the pavement to the church door marked out. At the iron railings, a faded and paint-peeled board identified the building as St Michael's, Church of Scotland.

'The last one was Church of Scotland too, wasn't it? William Creegan?'

Mitchell's focus shifted as she considered the question for a moment. 'Yes, it was. And the one that nearly fell down on you was Anglican. You think it means anything?'

'No idea what anything means any more, Cass.' Janie carried on down the marked path, one last look back along the street before she stepped into the dank interior. She passed through a small antechamber, marks on the stone walls where fittings had been removed, and on into the main space.

Janie had never been much of a one for religion, something she had in common with DI McLean. All the same, she could appreciate the effort that went into building these places of worship. St Michael's wasn't a large church, but its interior had once been grand. The high vaulted ceiling had been painted with frescoes between the dark wooden beams, themselves ornately carved. Niches in the walls might once have held statues of saints or similar, although now they stood empty. Most of the pews had gone, a few stacked up at the back, but an elegant stained-glass window towered over the heavy stone altar in three narrow sections. It cast coloured light on a small cluster of people at the end of the nave. She recognised two of them straight away, although the relief at seeing the pathologist's assistant was mixed with a twist in her gut at the memory of when they had parted the night before; the reckoning she knew awaited her at the station. Beyond them a crime scene photographer was busy recording everything, and in the centre of it all lay the body.

'Well now. If it isn't Detective Inspector Harrison,' Cerys said, her emphasis on the rank Janie wasn't sure she'd have for very much longer. At her words, her boss looked around and nodded.

'Janie. I hear congratulations are in order.'

'Maybe. Let's see.' Janie glanced across at Cerys. It would seem only some of last night's events had been shared with her boss. 'What's the story then?'

'I hesitate to jump to conclusions, but this looks very much like the work of the same person who did for the previous victim. See?'

206

The pathologist had been crouched beside the body, partially obscuring it. Now he stood and carefully stepped to one side so that Janie could get a better look.

The man was fully clothed, heavy overcoat over jacket, shirt and tie. His arms were folded neatly over his chest as if he had lain down at the head of the nave for a snooze. Eyes closed, he might almost have seemed peaceful were it not for the livid cross that puckered his forehead. Even with it, Janie recognised him. The last time she'd seen him he'd been standing beside the grave of Kenneth Morgan along with Archibald Seagram. And William Creegan.

'Oh crap. That's Ray McAllister.' She shuffled around the body until she was standing at his feet, squinting to get a better look, but she was sure it was the same man. Glancing away for a moment, her gaze fell on the figure in the middle section of the window. Christ hanging from his cross. If only he'd been real, perhaps he'd have been able to tell her what had happened here in his church, but Janie didn't hold out much hope for answers from that direction.

'You know him?' Cerys asked.

'Not exactly. I know of him, though. And if this is what it looks like, then things are about to get very complicated indeed.'

31

Half an hour later, Janie was glad to be out of the church, gladder still to be out of the white paper overalls. Her head still hurt from troubled sleep, that one glass of unpleasant white wine, the worry over what manner of trouble awaited her at the station. Maybe all three. Or maybe she was coming down with something. That would be just her luck.

Shoving the used overalls into the communal bin bag, she looked around for directions to the lady who had called in the discovery of the body and found herself shortly afterwards ringing the doorbell of the neat bungalow directly across the road. DC Bryant answered the door.

'Oh, hey, Janie. Hoped it would be you.' The detective constable stepped aside to let her in. 'Or should I call you "ma'am", now?'

'Don't start, Jessica. Not in the mood.'

Bryant shrugged an apology, then led Janie through to the front room, where an elderly lady sat in studied silence. She had a small black terrier on her knees, but it jumped off as soon as it saw there was new company and wandered over to say hello. Janie wasn't much of a fan of dogs, but this one seemed amiable enough. It sniffed her proffered hand, then ambled to the fireplace and lay down, letting out a deep sigh and an audible fart as it curled into a tight ball. The old lady watched all this with a slight smile on her face before returning her gaze to the two detectives.

'Don't mind Roger. He's harmless.'

'Mrs McDaid?' Bryant raised her voice as she spoke. 'This is Detective Serg—Inspector Harrison. My boss.'

'Oh, hello dear. I must say, you look awfully young for an inspector.'

Mrs McDaid spoke with a broad Morningside accent, which was fair enough since they were on the edge of that part of the city anyway. She indicated for Janie to take a seat on the settee, close by her, then turned her attention to Bryant.

'Jessica, dear? Would you be so good as to make us both a cup of tea?'

Janie did her best not to laugh as the detective constable forced a smile onto her face, nodded once and then left.

'Lovely girl, that one. She must have the boys eating out of her hand.'

On balance, Janie thought it best not to point out that DC Bryant's affections lay elsewhere. 'I'm sure she does,' she said. 'And she's a very good detective too. I understand you're the person who called us in this morning.'

'That I did, Inspector. Terrible business. Of course, it's not the first body I've seen. I was a nurse for forty years, you know. But it was a shock all the same. What with his . . .' Mrs McDaid clutched her hands together at the memory, her fingers swollen with arthritis, her skin blotched, crackly and wafer thin.

'I can arrange for a doctor to call,' Janie said. 'If you feel that would help.'

'That's very kind of you, but no.' Mrs McDaid reached across and patted Janie's knee. 'I'm a little deaf, but I'm still robust. Now, I expect you have all manner of tedious question you need to ask.'

'I do. I'm sorry. I'll try not to take up too much of your time. Perhaps you could start by telling me what you remember.'

'Well, now. Where to begin?' Mrs McDaid clasped her hands together again, stared at the mantelpiece for long enough that Janie began to wonder if she wasn't quite as robust as she claimed to be. Following the old lady's gaze, she saw a photograph mounted in a silver frame. A man and a woman, both in their early twenties, bride and groom. Next to it another frame, another photograph, this time a man's portrait. The same man from the first one, but many years later, his hair all gone save for a droopy moustache. There had been no mention of a Mr McDaid, so presumably he was no longer around.

'I was up at about half past five.' Mrs McDaid's voice was so sudden, so loud, Janie almost jumped. 'I seem not to need as much sleep as I used to, and it's nice to see the dawn rise. The sun always catches the church tower. Makes it look like a painting. It's grey now, but first thing it was a lovely pink. Of course, that's never a good omen, is it? Red sky in the morning, sailor's warning, don't they say? Still, it was beautiful for a while. And then I noticed that the vestry door wasn't closed properly.'

Janie glanced over at the window. She couldn't see much, what with the net curtains and the full police presence parked in the road beyond the bungalow's short front garden. Behind it all the church was a solid presence, nonetheless. If it was a view you were used to looking at regularly, then something not quite right would doubtless stick out a mile.

'It's not in use anymore, the church,' she said. 'Did you attend it when it was?'

Mrs McDaid shook her head. 'No. Well, not really. St Michael's is Church of Scotland and I'm a Methodist. Still, it's been used as a meeting hall on occasion, and there used to be carols at Christmas.'

Janie could feel the conversation drifting off track, tried to bring it back. 'So, you saw the door was open and thought you'd go and have a look?'

'That's right. I was going out for my morning constitutional anyway, so it was easy enough to check. They've been clearing a lot of stuff out in the past few months too. I thought maybe one of the workmen had forgotten to lock up when they left, but then I remembered they've not been for over a week. And I'd have noticed if the door was open all that time.'

'Workmen?' Janie recalled the inside of the church, stripped of almost everything, the empty niches in the walls.

'Oh yes, dear. They've been gutting the place this past month and more. It's quite exciting. No idea what they're going to turn it into.'

Janie already had her notebook out, and scribbled a note to find out more about the church.

'Was there anyone else about when you went for your walk?' she asked. 'Anyone in the street?'

'Not that I saw, no. It's usually very quiet here at that time of the morning. We're not much of a rat run for cars, thankfully. I think Mr Nesbitt at number five was up. His kitchen light was on, anyway. But no, I didn't see anyone out on the street.'

'How about last night?'

Mrs McDaid tilted her head slightly at the question, her wire-thin hair catching the light from the window almost like a halo.

'I don't spend my whole time staring out at the street, you know? I've curtains drawn after dark.'

'Of course, Mrs McDaid. I only—'

'Having said which, there was the car that sat idling for a long while about half past eleven. Right outside my house, too. I was in bed reading or I might have gone out and given him a piece of my mind.'

'Him?' Janie asked.

'Well, I don't suppose a woman would have been so inconsiderate. I'd even got myself up to go out anyway, but then I heard its door slam shut and it drove off. Some people have no consideration at all.'

'Did you look to see who it might have been?'

Mrs McDaid narrowed her eyes at that question, although Janie could see it was only for show. The old lady clearly loved to talk, and an inconsiderate driver was probably the most exciting thing that had happened to her for years. Until this morning, that was.

'As it happens, I did. Came through here for a better view, but all I could see was the car lights as it turned at the end of the street. Roger was whining to be let out by then, poor wee mite. He's fine if he's asleep, but soon as something wakes him, he needs to go out.'

Janie looked at the terrier, curled up in front of the unlit gas fire. As if sensing he was being observed, or perhaps hearing his name, he looked up, farted, and wagged his tail.

'I was wide awake by then, of course. So I put on my coat and took him out into the front garden. Normally I'd have just let him out the back, but, well, the car and everything. Can't say I wasn't a little bit curious.'

'And did you see anything? Hear something?' Janie had her pen poised over the page, ready to write down the clue that cracked the case wide open. Not that it ever worked that way.

'Not a thing, sorry. Roger had his pee, sniffed around a bit and then we both went to bed.'

Back outside, Janie stood at the bungalow gate and stared across the road at the church for a while. Apart from being able to put some kind of timeframe on the proceedings, Mrs McDaid had not been as much help as she might have hoped. True, there was the car idling outside her window for a while the night before, but given the suburban nature of the area, it was unlikely there'd be much in the way of CCTV footage to scour for clues. Most likely the car was a taxi bringing Ray McAllister to his appointment with doom, much the same as the one that had ferried Billy

Creegan across town from Craigentinny to Gorgie, which reminded her she needed to see how the team were getting on with that investigation.

Which meant going in to the station, of course. For an hour or so she had been able to forget all about that, absorbed by the immediate demands of the crime scene. If they hadn't already, then soon enough they'd be bringing the body out. Forensics would take the time they needed to process the scene, and Cass Mitchell had the uniforms knocking on doors up and down the street. There really wasn't much she could do that wouldn't be getting in the way.

It was then that she remembered she'd walked here from her flat. There seemed little chance of cadging a lift from a squad car, since all the uniform officers present were busy at their jobs. No option but to walk to Morningside Road and see if she could catch a bus.

Janie found Mitchell three houses along from Mrs McDaid's bungalow. The detective constable was standing at the front door, having just pressed the doorbell, a uniformed constable a couple of steps behind her. It didn't look like there was anyone in, as by the time Janie joined them there had been no answer.

'We'll get as many contact details as we can from the other houses, come back later to catch the rest of them,' she said before Janie could comment.

'No worries. You never get everyone in at the same time anyway. Make a note and move on to the next one, aye?'

Mitchell dipped her head in understanding, but as she made to walk back to the street, Janie noticed something behind her.

'Hang on.' She stepped past Mitchell and approached the front entrance. A couple of steps led up to an old wooden door with two frosted glass panels set into the top half. Fixed somewhat incongruously in between them was one of those modern camera doorbell things. It was this that Mitchell had pressed. Janie pressed it again, listening for any sound from inside. A very faint *ding* might have come from the hall, but she couldn't be sure. There certainly didn't appear to be anyone home.

'What's up?' Mitchell asked as Janie turned her back to the door and then crouched slightly so that her eye was at the same level as the camera. Since the owners had turned the front garden into a paved parking area, it gave a half-decent view of the road.

Standing up again, Janie looked around the front of the house for any other security features. Tucked into the eaves was a dome-covered camera, although she couldn't tell which way it faced. She was about to tell Mitchell to make a note about security cameras in the area when a clunk-clack noise made her spin around. The door opened and a sour-faced man peered myopically out at them.

'You any idea what time it is?'

Janie checked her watch before realising that it was a rhetorical question. The man was wrapped in a long dressing gown, hairy feet shoved into a pair of baffies a size or two too small. His hair awry, he'd clearly just crawled out of bed. Either a night shift worker or a writer then.

'I'm sorry.' Janie pulled out her warrant card and held it up. 'Detective Sergeant Harrison, Police Scotland. There's been an incident over at the church and we need to talk to all the local residents. I take it this is your house, Mr . . .?'

'Bailey. Robert Bailey.' The man rubbed at one eye with the heel of his hand, yawned expansively and scratched at his scalp. 'Aye, this is my house. And I'm awake now so I suppose you'd better come in.'

The difference between Mrs McDaid's neat bungalow and Robert Bailey's untidy, rambling house could not have been more marked. There were boxes everywhere. Stacked against the walls in the hall, set on the steps leading upstairs, tumbled untidily around the kitchen at the back of the house where he led the three of them like some shambling untidy shepherd.

'Coffee?' he asked as he went about filling a glass filter jug and pouring water into an industrial-sized machine. Janie wanted to get on with her questions, but she was aware that they'd woken this man up and, so far, he was being reasonably considerate. She'd never turn down a decent brew either, so she did her best to be patient.

'Grab a chair if you can find one. Sorry about the mess.' Bailey made no attempt to explain his untidiness, nor why he had been asleep when most people were up and about.

'How long have you lived here, Mr Bailey?' Janie asked as she gently manoeuvred a stack of small unopened parcels to one end of the surprisingly large kitchen table. The whole room was bigger than she'd expected, with a view through the window onto a size-able garden. Nice for some.

'Let me see? Ten . . . no, twelve years now.' Bailey tapped the side of the coffee machine as if that might make it work more quickly. It rumbled and gurgled and hissed. 'Always meant to get round to decorating the place, but there never seems to be time.'

'What is it you do?' Mitchell asked.

'Goodness, am I a suspect?' Bailey laughed. 'Don't even know what I'm supposed to have done. An incident at the church, you said?'

'That's right, Mr Bailey. And no, you're not a suspect. We're just talking to everyone who lives on this street in case they saw anything late last night or early this morning.' Janie put on her best reasonable smile. 'I take it you're not a morning person?'

Bailey frowned for a moment, then seemed to remember him-self. He held his arms out from his body, hands splayed to indicate his dressing gown and baffies. 'Oh, this. Aye. Well. Extenuating circumstances. I've been over in LA on business for the past month. Only got in yesterday. Jet lag caught up with me, I'm afraid. I was working up till past four. Finally crashed about . . .' He looked up at a clock hanging on the wall by the door. 'About three hours ago.'

Janie noted that he hadn't said what it was he did for a living, but it wasn't important. Not now, at least. 'I couldn't help noticing the security camera. And the front door, too.'

'That? Aye, well. You'll have noticed I get a lot of post. It's mostly rubbish. Stuff for reviewing or testing or whatever. This is a quiet part of town, not much passing traffic, no reason for people to be walking past. For ages it was fine if the delivery driver just left things by the front door, but a year or so ago stuff started going missing. I had the cameras installed, and the door system's connected to my phone, so I can let people into the front porch, even when I'm in California.' Bailey pulled a shiny tablet phone from his dressing gown pocket and tapped at the screen. When he turned it around for Janie to see, it showed a live feed of the front parking area and the street beyond.

'That doesn't record, does it?' she asked.

'That one doesn't, no. But the camera in the eaves does. It backs up to the cloud. Can't remember the exact details, but I think it records forty-eight hours then overwrites from the start.'

Bailey was about to say more, but the coffee machine started sputtering. This must have been an indication that it was ready. He hauled out the glass jug and poured fine-smelling liquid into mugs. Only once everyone had theirs, milk and sugar as required, and he'd taken a first sip of his own did he speak on the matter again.

'I suppose you'll be wanting a copy of the recording, then?'

32

For once, Detective Chief Inspector Ritchie was in her office when Janie finally made it back to the station. Like DI McLean before he'd left, the DCI kept her door open when not in conference, and it was something of a relief to see it ajar. Janie tapped lightly on the frame to get the DCI's attention and a weary smile.

'Janie. I heard the news.'

The briefest flash of panic ran through her at that. Had Ritchie heard about the previous night's altercation with Detective Superintendent Nelson? Had he spoken to her already? No. That was being stupid. Ritchie meant the body in the church, of course. Didn't she?

'We've a good ID. Need confirmation, but I'm pretty certain it's Raymond McAllister.'

'McAllister?'

'Another one of Archie Seagram's friends. He was at Kenneth Morgan's funeral along with Billy Creegan and Seagram himself. That's how I recognised him.'

Ritchie rubbed at her forehead, finger and thumb massaging her temples as she leaned a heavy head into her hand. 'I suppose a body in a church . . . It was too much to hope it would be unconnected with the other two. Different part of the city though.'

'Aye, over Morningside way. Not so far from Gorgie Road, mind, but a fair distance from the first one.'

'What's the plan, then? I take it forensics are at the scene?'

'Manda reckoned they'd be a while. I doubt they'll find anything though. There wasn't any use at St Mark's. They didn't really have much of a chance to go over the other one.' Janie felt an echo of that panic as they all exited the supposedly safe building at speed.

'Have you spoken to Nelson yet?' Ritchie asked, prolonging Janie's sense of panic.

'No. Is he in?'

'He was, half an hour ago. Let's go break the good news to him now, eh?' Ritchie pushed her seat back and stood up. She was around the desk and halfway to the door before Janie managed to get a grip on herself and follow. This wasn't something that could be put off. Sooner or later, she would have to confront the man, and the distraction of a new murder investigation might make things a little easier to deal with. For now, at least.

Unlike Ritchie's door, Nelson's was firmly closed. The DCI knocked on it and waited until a muted 'come in' filtered through. Janie kept back as the two of them entered the room, although she couldn't exactly hide.

The detective superintendent sat at his desk, a laptop open in front of him and a stack of folders to one side. A casual observer might have assumed he was hard at work, but to Janie it looked staged. None of the folders were open, there was no notepad, no pen. She was reminded of the way her brothers had tried to pretend they weren't playing games on their computer when they were meant to be studying. Or maybe she was just naturally biased.

'Kirsty.' Nelson nodded once at the DCI, then saw she wasn't alone. Janie was sure that the moment he saw her he would react. Scowl maybe, or perhaps flinch before getting himself back under control. It still surprised her that there hadn't been a summons awaiting her arrival at the station. A short, sharp dressing down and removal of her acting DI status. Instead, the detective superintendent acted as if nothing had happened. No mental change of gear, no involuntary shudder. He simply smiled at her. 'And our newest Detective Inspector. A little late in, Janie. Too much celebrating last night?'

For a moment she was too surprised to speak, but only a moment. Janie had three brothers, after all, and they could be just as infuriating. 'Actually, sir, I've been at a crime scene all morning. Another dead man in a disused church. Ray McAllister. Do you know him?'

That last question had been meant as a throwaway, an attempt to sound more glib than she felt. She hadn't expected to see the flinch and shudder that the name provoked, less still the way all the blood drained from Nelson's face.

'McAllister? You sure?'

'I recognised him from the funeral, sir. You remember, DCI Dexter asked me to go along to Kenneth Morgan's burial? I met him there, along with Billy Creegan and Archie Seagram.'

Now that she'd seen it once, Janie couldn't help but notice that each name brought the same involuntary tic to Nelson's face. It wasn't surprising that he knew of these people, they were all of interest to the ongoing investigation into Creegan's murder, even if none of them were particularly suspects. She'd seen him react to any mention of Archibald Seagram too, but this was something different.

'Were you the one to make the identification?' Nelson asked once he'd regained some of his composure. The scowl Janie had been expecting had finally arrived.

'I recognised his face, aye. He had ID on him that confirmed it though. We've yet to speak to next of kin, so formal identification will have to wait. His DNA and prints are on file, though, since he's done time more than once in the last couple of decades. Shouldn't take long.'

Nelson leaned back with a creak of springs and a fart of soft cushioned leather. Elbows on the chair arms, he steepled his fingers and shoved two of them into his philtrum. Once more Janie was struck by how false the gesture seemed, how performative.

'How did he die?' the detective superintendent asked after a brief pause.

'Pathologist is unsure at the moment. He'll get the post mortem exam done as soon as possible, but there weren't any obvious wounds on the body. Apart from the cross on his forehead, that is.'

'A cross?' Nelson asked.

'Same as Creegan, aye.' Janie took out her phone and tapped at the screen until she found a suitable photograph, held it up for Nelson to see. He waved it away without looking.

'You think they're related?'

'I think the chance they're not related is almost impossible, sir. They knew each other. Were friends, even. And they've both died in similar settings and similar manners within weeks of each other. It's very possible this is the third such murder in two months. We just got unlucky with Morgan. If that wall hadn't fallen on him and crushed –'

'That's quite enough Serg—Acting Detective Inspector. I get the point. So, what? You think we've got some serial killer out there with a thing for old gangsters and churches?'

Janie looked to Ritchie for help, saw only an expression of disbelief on her face. Not at the murders so much as the detective superintendent's reaction to them.

'I think it's possibly a bit more focused than that, sir. The victims have too strong a connection for it to be anything else. We really need to talk to Seagram, and soon.'

'You're not suggesting he's behind all this, surely?' Nelson's voice oozed condescension.

'No sir. I'm more worried he might be next.' Janie tried to keep her tone level and reasonable. 'It's only been a few hours since the body was discovered. We've not had a chance to find next of kin yet, let alone inform them. The press are already asking difficult questions about Creegan, so it's only a matter of time before they start putting two and two together and coming up with five. I'd like to be ahead of them before then.'

Nelson leaned forward with another explosion of creaks and farts. He grimaced slightly as he rested his elbows on his desk, although whether that grimace was due to the noises, Janie couldn't be sure.

'You want this investigation, even though you're already running two? Isn't that a bit ambitious for an acting detective inspector on her first day in the new role?'

'I'm happy for you to assign it to someone else, sir. But whoever it is, we'll need to co-ordinate closely. Given the shortage of detectives though . . .' She let the sentence hang, an awkward silence growing between the three of them until Nelson finally broke.

'No, you're right. Get on with it, and if we need to draft in more bodies, you can steal some from Vice. Maybe see if the CCU can't help too, since they've got clearance. Steer clear of Seagram for now though. I'll have a word with Jayne about how best to tackle him.'

'I'll get everything started,' Janie said. Ritchie gave Nelson a curt nod, a barely registered 'Pete', and strode out of the office. Janie made to follow, was almost at the door when the detective superintendent spoke again.

'One other thing, Janie?'

She turned back to face him. Now it would come, for sure. But Nelson's face had that bland, expressionless look on it again.

'This is a big responsibility, you know. I want regular updates, and don't fuck it up.'

'Sir.' She fled the room before he could say anything else, confused and relieved in equal measure. It was only as she reached the stairs at the end of the corridor that she realised Nelson had not stood up for the whole of their meeting, had indeed barely moved at all and grimaced when he did. Her mind went back to the feel of her knee as it connected solidly with his privates, how he'd doubled up and rolled around in the dirt. Had she done lasting damage?

Smiling to herself as she trod swiftly down the stairs, Janie found that she really didn't care.

'OK everyone, listen up.' Janie stood in the incident room, beside a newly printed A4 size photograph of Raymond McAllister. Taken at the crime scene, it showed clearly the burn to his forehead in the shape of a cross. Alongside a similar picture of Billy Creegan, the near-identical nature of the marks was impossible to deny.

'As I've no doubt you're all already aware, we've had another body turn up in a church. Raymond McAllister. He was sixty-eight years old and the address we have for him is in Corstorphine, so a fair distance from where he died. His body was discovered first thing this morning in St Michael's Church in Morningside. PM's not been done yet, but given the state of the victim, I think it's fair to say his death is suspicious. MO seems identical to Creegan's.'

As she looked out across the silent room, Janie could see all eyes fixed on her. The team was still smaller than she would have liked, especially with Bryant and Mitchell both still out at the crime scene helping with the door to doors. They were going to have to work smart to make up for the lack of manpower, but then when had that ever not been the case?

'I've spoken with the detective superintendent, and he's agreed for now that we'll run the two investigations side by side from this incident room.'

'Three?' someone asked from the back. 'Shouldn't that be three investigations?'

Janie glanced over her shoulder at the whiteboard. Kenneth

Morgan's photograph hadn't been added yet, mostly because the post mortem pictures didn't have any identifiable features in them. They should have printed out his mugshot all the same.

'Three, aye. We need to review whatever we've got on Kenneth Morgan too. They all three knew each other, and it looks like they all died in the same way. We need to investigate that link, of course, but don't get fixated on it.'

She paused a moment, half expecting someone to pipe up with some unhelpful comment. The silence grew heavy.

'It's possible we'll have some security cam footage to go over soon. No public CCTV, but a couple of the nearby houses had those wee camera doorbells, and one had a half-decent high-definition camera trained on his front drive. Soon as we've got a timeframe for McAllister's death, we can start piecing together his last movements. Meantime, he should be on the system for his past offences. Let's start building a picture of this man, OK?'

There was no applause, no hand up to ask questions, no heckling from the constables. One by one, they returned to their desks, one more task added to what was already a long list. Janie let her shoulders slump, exhausted by it all. A glance at the wall clock showed that it was barely past noon, still a lot of the day left to get through. Then it occurred to her that she'd only had a slice of toast for breakfast, and it was fast approaching lunch.

'You want me to start setting up the systems for this new one, J?' Detective Sergeant Sandy Gregg approached with her signature clipboard in one hand, pen in the other. 'Oh, and congrats on the promotion, too.'

For a moment Janie couldn't think what she was talking about, and then it came back to her. Of all the officers who could have said something, Gregg was the most awkward. She'd been a DS far longer than Janie, and should really have been a shoe-in for the position. If she harboured any resentment about being passed over, she didn't show it.

'Thanks, Sandy. Aye, if you can get the computers all sorted that'd be great.'

'No bother.' Gregg made to walk away, then changed her mind. 'Oh, and Janie?'

'Aye?'

'I mean it when I say congratulations. No hard feelings, you know? I'm happiest here, sorting through the actions and marshalling the troops. Sergeant's quite enough responsibility for me. You're a much better fit for DI.'

Janie couldn't think of anything to say, but even her nod of acknowledgement was lost on Gregg as she turned away and set to her tasks. The irony of the detective sergeant's words wasn't lost on her though. If anything, the skills she had and her preference for directing operations from the incident room made her far more suitable for the promotion than Janie would ever be.

33

She was about to head into the canteen in search of a sandwich when a strange noise alerted Janie to the approach of Detective Superintendent Nelson. He hadn't seen her, she was fairly sure, concentrating instead on the laborious process of walking down the stairs from the third floor one wincing step at a time. The strange noise was his shoe sliding on the linoleum as he did his best not to lift his leg any higher than necessary. Had she kneed his bollocks that hard? It was very possible. She found however that she really didn't want to know. Any conversation with the detective superintendent was going to be awkward, and if he had to limp towards her first then his injury would be hard to ignore. She ducked past the corridor that led to the locker rooms and the canteen, took the steps down into the basement instead. Lunch would have to wait.

The door to the Cold Case Unit room stood ajar, as it almost always did. Janie had hoped to find Grumpy Bob at his desk; the old sergeant was always a good sounding board. When she rapped a knuckle on the door frame and peered inside though, his and Detective Superintendent Duguid's desks were empty.

'Well, now. If it isn't our newest detective inspector.' Detective Chief Superintendent Grace Ramsay, retired, peered over the top of her spectacles as she looked up from a folder. She was standing behind her desk, almost entirely obscured by a pile of cardboard boxes remarkably similar to the one in which all Kenneth Morgan's personal effects had been stored.

'It's only temporary, I'm sure. I'll be back to plain old Detective Sergeant Harrison soon enough.'

Ramsay raised a thin white eyebrow at that but made no comment. 'If you were looking for Dagwood and Grumpy Bob you're out of luck. They snuck off early yesterday on some errand and haven't been in all day.'

'Actually, I was mostly trying to avoid Detective Superintendent Nelson, but I was also hoping to pick some brains for information.'

Ramsay closed the folder, stepped out from the piles of boxes and took a seat at her desk. 'Nelson is best avoided wherever possible. He still trying it on with you?'

Janie was momentarily taken aback. She'd forgotten how straight to the point the retired detective chief superintendent could be. Utterly unable to beat about the bush. And how much she knew about what was going on in the station to which she had only recently returned, although that much could be down to sharing an office space with Grumpy Bob.

'It's a little more than that, actually.'

'You didn't sleep with him, did you?' Ramsay voiced the question without any inflection, which was probably worse than if she'd been horrified by the idea.

Janie herself was horrified, for sure. 'God, no. Eww. He's older than my dad.'

'I'd hope that wouldn't be the only reason, but it's a start.' Ramsay fixed her with a glare that must have had many a poor constable quaking in their boots. 'So what happened, then? I thought you were his favoured one.'

This hadn't been what Janie had come to the CCU for at all but something about Ramsay's candour made her easy to talk to.

And she was a woman who had succeeded at a time when the police force was far more male dominated than now. She pulled up a chair and sat down, chose her words carefully.

'It was last night, when we all went to the pub to celebrate the bust in Craigentinny.' The day had been so busy, Janie hadn't had the time or mental capacity to fully process the events, but as she recounted them, so the true horror of what had happened began to sink in. For her part, Ramsay simply sat and listened, nodding occasionally to show that she was taking an interest. Right up until Janie told her about putting the knee in, at which point she let out a joyous bark of laughter.

'Oh, God, that's perfect. The number of senior officers I've wanted to do that to over the years. Janie my dear, you're a treasure.'

'I . . . But he can barely walk today. What if he decides to press charges?'

Ramsay's smile was like a shark's. For a woman of her age, she had remarkably straight, and white, teeth. 'And risk it coming out what he tried on with you? I think even he's bright enough to know how that would work out. I don't suppose anyone else saw what happened?'

'Actually, there was one witness. Cerys Powell, from the mortuary. She helped me get a taxi home.'

'Oh, this just gets better and better.' Ramsay clapped her hands together like an excited little girl. 'Do you know why Grampian let Nelson go?'

'Let him go? I thought it was his choice to transfer down here.'

Ramsay smiled again, the wrinkles around her eyes mischievous. 'That's the official story. Peter probably believes it himself. There's maybe even a little truth in it, but only because he'd hit a promotion ceiling. There was no way he was going to get beyond DCI in Aberdeen, not with all the rumours circulating about him.'

'Let me guess. Wandering hands? Inappropriate behaviour with junior officers?'

'His reputation precedes him. You can ask Ritchie if you want details, but I think you already know.'

Janie felt a tension ease out of her shoulders she hadn't known was there. Simply talking about the experience to someone who understood was an enormous relief. It wasn't the end of it, though, only the beginning.

'You think I should make a formal complaint?' she asked. 'Get it all on record?'

Ramsay considered this for a while before answering. 'You've spoken to me, and you say there's a witness, right?'

'Cerys. She's the new pathology assistant. Works with Tom MacPhail.'

'Well if you want to make it formal, that's your right of course. But you might want to pick your moment. Maybe even hold it in reserve, just in case.'

'What do you mean? Wouldn't it be better to report it now? If I'm going to report it at all?'

'In an ideal world, yes. But you need to tread carefully, Janie. As soon as you speak out, you'll be marked. There'll be other officers, men mostly, who'll think you're not to be trusted any more. Not a team player. It could affect your future promotion prospects just like Nelson's behaviour has affected his. This isn't a battle you can really win, I'm sorry to say. But that doesn't mean he can't be made to pay.'

'How? I mean, he's a super and I'm only acting inspector. Soon as they find someone to take on the job, I'll be back to sergeant, I'm sure.'

'Don't be so defeatist, dear. It's unbecoming.' Ramsay leaned forward, elbows on her desk, hands clasped together as she stared at Janie over the top of her spectacles like a headmistress admonishing a promising but hesitant pupil. 'Your best course of action is to do what you're doing right now. You're a good detective. You've got good instincts and a knack for recognising patterns in noisy data. Do the job you've been given. Do it well, and there's no way your promotion won't be made permanent. And as for Nelson? If he's pretending it never happened, then play along. At least for now. You can always bring it up if he starts making life difficult for you, and with any luck he's learned his lesson this time.'

Wherever Detective Superintendent Nelson had been shuffling, he appeared to have left the station by the time Janie climbed the stairs from the basement to the second floor and the incident room. Her chat with Grace Ramsay had left her feeling much better about the situation, but also, if anything, even more angry. She needed something to take her mind off it all. Luckily for her, DS Gregg had the perfect solution.

'Just off the phone with McAllister's parole officer,' she said almost the moment Janie walked into the room.

'He not that long out then? I thought . . .' But Janie realised that she knew very little about McAllister at all. Apart from that he was dead.

'Six months. He was sent down for assault. Served five years of a ten stretch in Saughton.'

Janie did the maths as quickly as she could. 'Five. And six months. So he assaulted someone when he was – what? – sixty-two? Sixty-three? Jesus.'

'It gets worse. He put two lads half his age in the hospital. One of them lost an eye.'

'And they let him out early?'

'Maybe needed the space. And he was a model prisoner by all accounts.'

Janie knew the story all too well. Sometimes she wondered why they bothered catching criminals and locking them up. Those that knew how to play the system were usually out and reoffending in no time, it seemed.

'You sent anyone out to his place to break the news?' she asked.

'Not yet. Seemed little point if he lives alone, which it turns out he does.'

'Still need to get someone over there.' Janie cast an eye over the room, searching for any spare detective constables and finding none. 'Might as well do it myself. Unless you fancy going?'

Gregg shook her head minimally. She'd never been one for legwork. Likewise, DC Blane, who had taken that moment to enter the room clutching a sheaf of freshly printed papers. Lofty was slightly better out in the field, but his height tended to either intimidate or provoke, and never the right way around. Her gaze fell on the short hair and sticky-out ears of PC Fairley, his back turned to the two of them as he stared at a computer screen over the shoulder of one of the admins. Could she take him?

As if in answer to her unspoken prayers, the incident room door banged open and DC Stringer came striding in, a cup of coffee in one hand, what looked suspiciously like a bacon roll in the other. He noticed Janie and DS Gregg staring at him only when he was halfway across the room, heading in the direction of DC Blane's massive computer screen.

'Hope you brought enough for everyone, Jay.' Janie had meant it as a joke, but her stomach chose that moment to let everyone know how poorly she had been treating it all day.

'Still plenty in the canteen, boss. I can run and fetch one if you want.' Stringer waved his bacon roll in the direction of the door, then took a quick bite out of it before anyone could steal it from him.

'Sure, I can get my own. You can sort us out a pool car and meet me downstairs in twenty minutes.'

34

If Kenneth Morgan had lived in a tiny tenement in Granton, and Billy Creegan had moved between terraced houses in upmarket Cumberland Street and Reid Manor in Craigentinny, what manner of gaff would Raymond McAllister live in?

From the address in Corstorphine, Janie had expected something on the grander side. But when DC Stringer pulled the silent Nissan to the kerb on the quiet suburban street, the house that bore the right number was nothing special. A grey-harled bungalow set in its own grounds, it would be expensive to buy now, of course. Nothing in Edinburgh was cheap these days. But it was small compared to the two-storey houses either side.

The gate at the edge of the pavement opened onto a neat front garden, the narrow path spearing straight to the front door with small squares of grass either side. McAllister had clearly not been much of a plantsman, but someone had kept the lawn mowed, and its edges neatly trimmed. Janie rang the doorbell, gratified to hear a deep *bing bong* from inside. There was no other sound, and after an awkward minute she tried again. Not that she was expecting anyone to be home, of course.

'Let's have a wee look round the back before I use this.' She held up the bunch of keys that McAllister had been carrying in his jacket pocket. Properly signed for this time. Stringer nodded once, then set off along the narrow concrete strip of a path that surrounded the entire house.

Around the back, there was a larger garden equally devoid of anything except lawn. A low wall harled in the same grey pebble-dash as the house itself surrounded the space on all sides. This aspect of the bungalow faced south, but the possible view across the west of the city towards the Pentland hills was somewhat ruined by the line of two-storey buildings that formed the next street along. Their upper-floor windows would have a fine view into the narrow conservatory that had been tacked onto the back of the bungalow at some point in the past when uPVC was all the rage.

'Nothing much to see, is there?' Stringer observed as he cupped a hand over his eyes and peered in through double glazing hazed with age.

'Knowing our luck, this is just somewhere for his mail to be delivered.' Janie sorted through the selection of keys until she found one that looked like it matched the back door. First time lucky for a change, it slid in easily, turned as if regularly used and well oiled. She pushed down the handle, listening for any beeping of alarms. 'Here goes nothing.'

Much like Billy Creegan's house on Cumberland Street, Ray McAllister didn't seem to believe in electronic security. Unlike Creegan, McAllister did actually seem to have lived here. The back door opened onto a small laundry room, with an elderly top loader washing machine and a Sheila Maid ceiling mounted drying rack, empty save for a stained hand towel. Beyond it, the kitchen had a single window that looked out onto the neighbouring house and spilled daylight across a cluttered table. A pint glass and plate beside the sink were most likely the last meal of the condemned man. On the stove, a frying pan held three cold sausages and beside it stood a pot of congealed mashed potato, another with some baked beans.

'*Haute cuisine*,' Stringer observed, but Janie had already turned her attention to the kitchen table. A stack of envelopes appeared to be mostly junk mail, flyers from local businesses, and what looked like bank and credit card statements. Everything with an address on it was for Mr R McAllister, so at least they had the right place. Propped up against the salt and pepper and a bulging plastic ketchup bottle, a postcard caught Janie's eye. A garishly coloured photograph of the Kylescue bridge, when she flipped it over, there was only the address and a date scrawled where a message should have been.

'Fourteenth today, isn't it?' she asked.

'Fifteenth,' Stringer corrected without turning around. He was working his way methodically around the kitchen, opening the cupboards and drawers but touching nothing inside for now.

'Right. So this date was two weeks ago?' Janie put the postcard back down. 'No idea what it means, though. Come on. Let's get the rest of the place checked over.'

It wasn't a large house, although the rooms were well proportioned. Two bedrooms, shared bathroom, living room that opened out onto the conservatory at the rear. It was clear that whilst Ray McAllister lived at this address, he didn't spend much time here. There were few pictures, no keepsakes on the mantelpiece, only a few books on the shelves. Even the television was ancient, with a genuine VHS recorder on a stand underneath it. A stack of home-recorded tapes sat beside it, their labels blank. One empty cardboard case sat on top of the machine, the cassette already loaded.

'You know how this thing works?' Janie asked as she fiddled with a pair of remote controls and somehow managed to bring the whole setup to life. The screen flickered grey static until she found the 'play' button and pressed it.

The picture quality was very poor, low resolution grainy and with the colours washed out. A man sat at a table, hands flat on the

233

tabletop in front of him. Janie didn't recognise him, but then she doubted even his mother would have recognised him, such was the damage done to his face. His eyes were swollen almost shut, blood dripped from his nose and mixed with spittle from his mouth, his lips, the twin razor slashes to his cheeks. Without warning, from off camera, some kind of baseball bat smashed into his face, sent him reeling sideways. It sounded like wet meat dropped to the floor, like a cabbage run over by a truck, like nothing Janie had ever heard before. She couldn't understand why the man didn't scream, didn't put his hands up to stave off the blow, except that he probably hadn't been able to see it coming. And as she peered closer at the dreadful image, she could see something holding his hands in place. Were those . . . Nails?

'Jesus Christ.'

Stringer was so close behind her, Janie jumped at his exclamation. And possibly let out a squeak of frightened surprise. She turned and slapped him on the arm, a little harder than she had intended, but he surely deserved it.

'Don't creep up on people like that, Jay. Near jumped out of my skin.'

'What is that?' Stringer made no apology, but by the way he was staring at the still-running torture scene, face white, eyes wide, Janie was prepared to forgive him. As she turned her attention back to the television, the bat hit the man in the side of the head again. Blood and teeth splattered over the table, and he slumped forward, motionless. Quite probably dead.

'Evidence of a crime. We need to call this in.' Janie already had her phone out, shaky fingers poking at the screen. 'Get this house locked down tight before the wrong people find out McAllister's dead.'

It was getting dark by the time Janie made it back to the station. Partly on account of the thick grey clouds that had rolled in from the west, but mostly because the day was sinking into evening and the threat of a long night ahead. Her stomach grumbled at the abuse it was receiving as she bypassed the corridor that would lead to the canteen and food, taking the steps up to the second floor and the incident room instead.

She and Stringer had searched the rest of the bungalow in Corstorphine while waiting for a contingent of uniform officers to arrive from the nearest station. Some poor sods would have to sit in a car and watch the place all night, make sure that nobody tried to get in now the owner was dead. Tomorrow, a forensic team would go over the place properly, take it apart if necessary, and ship anything they thought relevant back to the station. Except for the stack of VHS cassettes. Those Janie had brought with her, including the one in the machine. Now some poor bastard was going to have to watch them all. It was unlikely they'd be holiday videos, given what she'd seen already.

'You want me to get started on those, boss?' Stringer asked as she put the box down on a tiny clear space at the edge of one of the tables. They'd need to be logged into evidence before anyone else touched them.

'You really want to?' Janie shook her head. 'Anyway, your shift's going to be up soon, Jay. Reckon this can wait till tomorrow. It's not like we can charge McAllister with anything.'

'Fair point.' Stringer conceded. 'Not sure I've the stomach for more'n five minutes of that anyway.'

'You and me both.' Janie reached into the box and pulled out a cassette. 'What do you think this is? Some kind of snuff movie collection? These things for sale?'

'Seems a bit low rent, doesn't it? I mean who's got a VHS player these days?'

'Could be he was old and set in his ways.' The problem had been tumbling around in Janie's mind all the way over from the far side of the city, and now that she was back in the incident room, with its familiar bustle and quiet noise, the solution seemed tantalisingly close. 'But what if it was on purpose? What if he deliberately chose these tapes?'

'Why would he do that? *They* do that? Whoever do that?'

'Well, they're hard to trace, aren't they? If that video we saw was online, it'd leave a trail for someone smarter than me to follow back to wherever it was uploaded. Mike Simpson down in IT would probably be able to tell you when and where it had been filmed, too. But an old VHS camcorder and a stack of tapes? That's pretty much untraceable.'

Stringer stared at her as if she'd grown an extra head. 'That's . . . a stretch?'

'Best I can come up with for now. It's been a long day, aye?' Janie put the cassette back with the rest. 'Still, someone's got to know who that poor bastard is getting his head stoved in. We put a name to him, maybe we can work out what's going on.'

'What's going on where?'

Janie's grumbling stomach froze at the all-too recognisable voice behind her. She turned slowly to see Detective Superintendent Nelson standing in the open doorway. By the way he held the handle, she figured he was still needing a little extra support, but he kept his wincing to a minimum as he limped into the room.

'Haven't seen you about all afternoon, Janie. What've you been up to?'

It was impossible to tell whether the question was meant as a criticism or simple curiosity, so Janie went for the latter, bringing the detective superintendent up to speed on their findings as swiftly and succinctly as she could manage. He looked briefly at the box of cassettes, then fixed her with a gaze that was disturbingly bland.

'And what are you planning to do with this new information? McAllister's dead, isn't he? You can't exactly charge him with assault or murder.'

'No sir. I can't. But we are trying to find who killed him. One avenue of investigation is working out why someone killed him, and this looks very much like a possible motive, does it not?'

She knew as soon as she'd said it that she shouldn't have added the question at the end. In her defence, Janie was tired, hungry and not thinking straight. And the detective superintendent was a dick.

'I really couldn't say.' Now Nelson's voice dripped with condescension. 'But I can say that as SIO, you really shouldn't be gallivanting off across the city all the time. Indeed, I seem to recall having already said it multiple times, and yet you continue to ignore basic investigatory procedure. Why couldn't you send a sergeant to check over the house? Why not a constable?'

Janie was about to tell Nelson to look around the room and see who was available, but at that exact moment the door banged open and DCs Bryant and Mitchell tramped in. The Detective Superintendent whirled around at the noise, then let out a high-pitched yelp of pain, swiftly cut off. He grabbed the nearest available support, which happened to be Janie's shoulder. She tensed, unsure whether breaking his fingers in front of the whole team would be good or bad for morale. Or her ongoing employment prospects for that matter.

'You all right, sir?' It was Stringer who asked the question, but the glare by way of an answer was directed entirely at Janie.

'Fine. Old injury. Flared up yesterday.' Nelson pulled his hand away, stood a little more upright, grimaced, and walked gingerly from the room. Only once he'd gone did Janie realise that everyone had fallen silent, all eyes on her.

'What?' she asked, but nobody answered. 'OK, be like that. But you can do it on your own time, aye? We've three dead bodies and no murderer in the cells. Let's find out who this sick bastard is before he gives us a fourth.'

35

January 7th 1983 – Friday

Choir practice tomorrow. Told mum I don't want to go, but she insists. She says Father O'C tells her I am the most promising of all the altar boys. That maybe someday I will be a priest too. He wants me to take extra lessons with him at the church, but I know it will be more of God's special teachings and I don't want to be a priest. Not if they are like him. I want to be like Judge Dredd and kill the bad men. Is it bad to want to kill a priest?

36

He heard the crunch of car tyres on gravel as he sat in the coach house, contemplating the mangled wreckage of his once beloved Alfa Romeo. McLean had been thinking about it on and off ever since DCI Dexter had dropped by for a chat some weeks earlier. He didn't need a car for much, and Emma's little electric Renault Zoe more than sufficed. True, he missed the more modern Alfa that had been stolen from the police station car park and then driven at speed through a plate glass shop window shortly after, but the thrill he'd once taken from skilfully controlling five hundred horses all at once seemed to have dwindled in recent years. Was this what growing old meant? Was he growing old?

A shake of the head to dislodge the thought, he stood and went to the door. Despite all his reservations, he had called a few restoration specialists, asked around, and now he was expecting a visit from a man who might be able to bring this fifty-year-old wreck back to life. For an eye-watering sum of money, of course, but then nothing good in life was free. Only, as he stepped out into the light, McLean saw that it wasn't a transit van and trailer parked up by the house but a squad car. One of the posh ones they used to ferry the top brass around. With a sigh, he checked his phone for any missed texts or calls, found none. What he did find, when he reached the back door, was Chief Superintendent Jayne McIntyre peering in through the glass. She must have caught his movement in the corner of her eye, turned to face him with a worried smile.

'Ah, Tony. You're here. Good.'

'Jayne.' He opened the door and gestured for her to go in. 'I take it this isn't a social visit?'

'Alas, no.' McIntyre checked her watch. 'Although I have maybe got time for a cup of tea.'

In the kitchen, the Aga gurgled contentedly. Both cats were curled in front of it, tight wound coils of black fur separated by a precisely measured gap. It wasn't that cold out, so the fact they were in probably meant a change in the weather soon. Neither of them moved an inch as McLean filled the kettle and slid it onto the hotplate. A change for the worse then.

'Emma doing OK?' McIntyre asked as he set about finding teapot, tea and mugs. There were some biscuits in a cupboard somewhere too, he was sure. Unless Madame Rose had found them the last time she was around. Although to be fair, she usually brought cake, as his expanding waistline could attest.

'I'd say so, though I reckon she'd argue the point. It's very frustrating for her not being able to do the simple things. Being reliant on me must be particularly galling, too. She's off having physical therapy this afternoon. Then Rose is taking her to the hairdressers or something.'

McIntyre pulled out a chair and sat. She was in uniform, McLean noticed. Probably on her way to a meeting over at Police Scotland headquarters. Or on her way back. Something important and official. He'd not seen her in a while, but then truth be told he'd not seen many of his old colleagues since he'd handed in his resignation all those months ago. She looked as old as he felt, her hair more grey than not, worry lines creasing her face.

'I'll not beat about the bush, Tony,' she said as he began to pour tea into two mugs. 'I know it's pointless with you. I need you to come back to work.'

McLean opened his mouth, found he had nothing to say, closed it again.

'It needn't be permanent. Doesn't even have to be full reinstatement. You can be a consultant to the CCU like Grace Ramsay if you want. But I . . . We need you back at least for the duration of this current investigation.'

'What investigation?' McLean asked, because McIntyre hadn't actually mentioned any. He knew the answer of course, but it was always good to check.

'These church murders. There's muttering about a serial killer and you know how much the press love that kind of story.'

'Murders?' McLean emphasised the plural. 'So they've decided Kenny Morgan was killed too?'

McIntyre stared at him like he had two heads. Then slow realisation dawned. 'You've not heard.'

'Not heard what?'

'They found another one this morning. Over at St Michael's in Morningside. Ray McAllister. Same distinctive branding as Billy Creegan.' McIntyre spooned enough sugar into her tea to make any dentist wince. 'Surprised Archie Seagram hasn't been badgering you about it. He was pestering you before, wasn't he?'

'He was. Called me a couple of times and even tried the "we know where you live" routine on me. I told him to speak to the investigation team, but I don't think he ever did.'

'Aye, that's what I thought. We need to speak to him now, though. That's three of his old associates dead in a few weeks. Two of them murdered, probably the third one too. Something's going on and he knows what it is.'

'So bring him in. Have whoever's running the investigation interview him. Under caution if necessary.'

This time McIntyre's expression was more of a mother admonishing her child for saying something particularly stupid.

'First off, Janie's running the investigation. And while I've every hope she'll one day make a very good detective, she's not in Seagram's league. Not yet.'

'So get Kirsty to do it. Or have a crack at him yourself. Jo Dexter would love a chance . . .' McLean stopped as the dots began to connect in his head. 'Ah.'

'Glad we're on the same page. Seagram's old school. As old as it gets. The chances of him speaking to a female detective are slim. And the chances of getting anything useful out of him even if he did are nil. He'll be all lawyered up anyway, especially if we ask him to drop by the station. But you . . .' McIntyre held her mug in both hands and stared at him through the wisps of steam coming off the surface. 'You, he came to of his own volition. Seems to think he can trust you. Anyone else I'd be very suspicious about that, but I'd bet my chief super's pension you're not in his pocket. Not in anyone's pocket.'

McLean gave her a slight nod of the head at that. 'I'm glad to hear it.'

'He's trying to play you though. You know that, right?'

'Oh, don't I know it. First time he approached me it was plain he'd done a lot of background research. Trying to find out what kind of person I was, what my weaknesses might be. How he might exploit them. It's quite impressive, in a way.'

'How so?'

'Well, he's already worked out he can't bribe me, and threats are likely to backfire. So instead, he's appealing to my innate curiosity. He wants Morgan's death investigated, Creegan's too. And I guess McAllister if he's gone the same way. But he's got a lot he doesn't want uncovered, too. We both know that.'

'You think it really is a turf war after all?' McIntyre asked.

'No, this is something different. A settling of very old scores, I reckon. Seagram knows why it's happening, but not who's doing it, and that scares him. He'd no more tell us the reason for it than admit he's behind half of the drug dealers and sex workers in the city, but he wants the killer found. Once we've done that for him, I doubt anything we'd call justice will be given a chance to prevail.'

McIntyre nodded her head slowly as she took in his words, drank her tea, but said nothing more. For a while McLean was happy to let the near silence stretch out. Nothing except the sound of the Aga and the occasional cat snore to break it.

How many of his former team had made this journey, come to drink tea, reminisce about the old times and then suggest he really ought to come back to work now? Harrison had been the first, and had come by a few more times after that, but she didn't really count. Ritchie had been more direct, and the visit from Jo Dexter had been a surprise. Perhaps he was being unfair. All of them had reasons other than persuasion to pay him a visit. Even McIntyre had been prompted by a specific need, not a general desire to have him back. But did he want to return?

'So how about it, then?' The chief superintendent put her mug down and placed her hands flat on the tabletop either side of it as if she were about to perform some kind of magic trick.

'I'll need to double check with Emma. Her needs come first.'

McIntyre's smile was less forced this time, and it wiped years of worry from her face. 'Of course. I understand completely.'

He'd gone back out to the coach house once McIntyre had left, opened the old wooden garage doors to let the light and air in before the rain came on again like the cats had promised it would. When he heard the sound of another vehicle on the drive, McLean assumed that this time it would be the mechanic come to see the car, but again he was disappointed. A shiny black Range Rover. He knew who it was by the familiar face of the driver.

Archie Seagram opened his own door and climbed out, one shiny black-brogued foot reaching for the ground like a timorous snake as he lowered himself from the high up seat to the gravel.

How old was he now? Born in the early fifties if memory served, so he was only just past seventy. Old, for sure, but not as ancient as he looked.

'Nice place you've got here, McLean. Must be worth a bit.'

'Mr Seagram. This is . . . unexpected.'

A little doddery at first, the old man's steps grew stronger and more confident as he approached the coach house. Clearly the Range Rover wasn't as comfortable for him as its price tag would have suggested, sitting had left his joints stiff. He glanced past McLean for a moment, appraising the wreckage.

'1750 GTV? Lovely cars. Used to have one myself, you know. Back in the day it could outrun anything your lot had. Lose them on the twisty roads. Looks like you lost that one yourself, mind.'

McLean wasn't particularly impressed at Seagram's ability to recognise the car from the twisted metal half covered in tarpaulin. It was a nice touch, but no more background research than he'd have done if the situation was reversed. As attempts to build a rapport went it was well-judged though. Another alarm bell to heed, and a reminder that this affable old man was a ruthless and violent gangster at heart.

'Did you speak to the police?' he asked. 'About Morgan and Creegan?' McLean didn't mention McAllister, waiting to see if Seagram already knew about the death of yet another of his old guard.

'I'm speaking to you now, aren't I?'

'But I'm not police am I, Mr Seagram? I retired.'

'Once a copper always a copper, McLean. And I know you've just had a visit from your former boss. She asked you to come back, right.' It wasn't a question this time.

'I've been asked many times since I left. And yet, here I am.' McLean raised both hands to encompass his house and the gardens within which it sat. 'My condolences, by the way.'

A brief flash of something more dangerous than anger marred

Seagram's features, but he suppressed it swiftly. 'You heard about Ray, then? Bad news always travels fastest right enough.'

So he did know. McLean wasn't sure if that made things easier or more difficult. It certainly suggested Seagram still had his informants in CID, or whatever they were calling it these days.

'That was why McIntyre came to see me, actually,' he said. 'And yes, she wants me to come back to work, find out who's behind these deaths. Only why should I, Mr Seagram? Seems like someone's doing the world a favour.'

That look again, only this time it took the old man visible effort to push it away. 'You're talking about my oldest friends, McLean. Some sick fuck's killed them all. Youse lot should be very worried this isn't about to turn into a turf war.'

McLean raised an eyebrow at that. It was the closest he recalled Seagram ever coming to admitting he was involved in anything illegal, and in total contrast to their previous conversation where he'd suggested the precise opposite. The man was rattled, scared, but then that only made him more dangerous.

'As it happens, Mr Seagram, the police are taking a keen interest in these deaths. A major investigation team has been working on the cases since Billy Creegan's body was found in St Mark's church in Gorgie. But I think you know that already. Same as you know what Billy was up to in Craigentinny and on Cumberland Street. Seems he was a man of peculiar tastes. Some might say ungodly.'

'Was being the operative word. He's no' going to harm anybody now. But whoever it was did that to him? Three murders, all the same. That's the work of a serial killer, aye? You happy sitting here in your big hoose wi' your fancy car while the press start winding themselves into a frenzy?'

A prickle of unease slithered down McLean's spine at Seagram's words. Quite likely the old man was feeding information to his friends at the local papers in an attempt to prompt more action from the police. Or to flush out whoever was behind the three deaths.

'The press will print whatever they want, Mr Seagram. I can't stop them, although I suspect you could if you wanted. Same as you've ways of finding out information that I haven't. If your thugs can't get any leads on who's got it in for a bunch of old-time crooks, what makes you think we'll have any better luck playing it by the book?'

That look crept over the old man's face again, as if he wanted to hit something. Or someone. It wasn't McLean, though, and the more he watched Seagram, the more he saw the internal struggle written across his features. There was something else going on here, and it didn't take a genius to work out what. Seagram was a man of action, or at least he had been. He was used to getting his way, by fair means or foul. And now he was being stymied as much by old age as anything. And it was obvious he knew more about the deaths of his friends than he was letting on. But whatever it was, he couldn't share it for fear of implicating himself, even as he knew that doing so might be the only way to stay alive. McLean might have felt sorry for him, had he been any other man. Had he not led with threats and only now come to pleading.

'Why was it you really came here, Mr Seagram? It wasn't to look at my car, and it wasn't to exchange pleasantries. So what do you actually want?'

Seagram pulled himself up straight, or at least as straight as he could manage. His shoulders still slumped with age, his neck bowed as if the memories of all the terrible things he had done in his life were weighing down his head. 'I want you to find out who killed my three friends, McLean. I want you to put a stop to this before they come for me too. Because if I die . . .' He paused a moment, head tilted to one side as if this possibility had never occurred to him before. 'If I die the same way Kenny, Billy and

Ray died. Then all hell will break loose across this city. And don't think your fancy big hoose will protect you from that.'

McLean held the old man's gaze, but it wasn't easy to do. There was a fire in his eyes now, a righteous anger. And the threat was none too subtle either. How long they stood there in silence he couldn't know. Not as long as it felt, for sure.

Finally, the old man sneered, turned away and shuffled back to his car. This time the driver helped him into the back, closed the door carefully and returned to his own seat. McLean watched as the Range Rover backed and turned, then slid silently away. Only then did he let go of the breath he'd not known he was holding.

He'd been putting off going back to work, he knew. Focused solely on being there for Emma at her time of need. But try as he might, the job just kept on coming for him. Harrison, Dexter, and now even Jayne McIntyre all pleading with him. And now the push from the other side, too. There was no getting away from it, he was going to have to go back at least for long enough to sort out this ungodly mess. If it could be sorted. Dammit.

With a shake of his head for no one to see, he trudged back to the house. Emma would be home soon, no doubt with Rose in tow. He hated having to admit that they'd both been right.

37

The reservations he had felt all the way on the drive over evaporated as a uniformed constable lifted the barrier to the station car park and waved him in.

'Morning, Detective Inspector McLean, sir. Kept one of the charging spots clear for you to park in.'

He didn't have the heart to tell the man that the car was fully charged before he left, and would go back and forth between home and work for a fortnight before it needed plugging in again. It was all about the gesture, so he made a show of connecting into the station charge point.

McLean had come in early, partly to avoid being waylaid by too many officers welcoming him back, and partly because there was a mountain of admin to be dealt with before he could officially resume work. He'd agreed with McIntyre only to return on a consulting basis, and only for the duration of the church murders investigation in the first instance. After that, well. It depended on Emma as much as him. She came first, after all, even if she'd as good as ordered him out of the house. As it was, the station was busy despite the hour, but most of the people he saw on the way up to the second floor and the major incident room were too busy to do much more than nod.

'Morning, sir. Heard you were coming back to help us out.'

Detective Sergeant Sandy Gregg met him at the first floor, her arms clutched around a stack of papers as if they were her newborn child. The whiff of ozone from the printers surrounded her like a faint perfume.

'Not sure how one ageing detective can help, but aye. I'll see what I can do. You want a hand with those?'

'It's okay, sir. I can manage. Need to get these up to the incident room sharpish for the morning briefing though. Take it you'll be there?'

'Not much point my being anywhere else.' McLean glanced at his watch. 'It's a bit early yet, isn't it?'

'Aye, I know. But getting everyone in the one place at the right time's like herding cats.' Gregg stepped off the stairs onto the second-floor landing. 'You heading up to your office, sir? Only I'll let Janie know that's where you are. Sure, she'll be wanting a word before we get started.'

McLean paused, unsure for once what he should do. Was it even his office anymore? Surely they would have assigned it to someone else? His replacement, most likely. But then they hadn't managed to replace him yet, had they? That was one of the reasons he was here.

'I'd better go and check in with Jayne first. Pete Nelson too, if he's in. I'll see everyone in the incident room once I've done with that. Then you can bring me up to speed before the briefing.'

The door to his old office hung open, but McLean resisted the urge to poke his head in and see if anything had changed. Truth be told, he'd never really liked the overly large room with the glass window wall that made it too hot in the summer and too cold in the winter. He much preferred the old box room at the back of the station where he'd been put when he first made detective inspector. Perhaps they'd let him have it back.

Chief Superintendent McIntyre's office, larger than the others on this executive floor, was at the end of the corridor. Outside it, the reception area was empty, the secretary's desk unattended. McIntyre's door was closed, voices spilling out through the flimsy wood. Well, one voice. McLean felt like a guilty schoolboy as he stood close and listened in.

'. . . dreadful mistake. She's clearly not suited to the role. Overwhelmed by the responsibility and making far too many stupid decisions. Frankly I'm surprised she's even in plain clothes, let alone a DS.'

McLean didn't know Pete Nelson well, but he'd recognise that nasal whine and Aberdonian accent anywhere. It didn't take a genius to work out who he was talking about either, and the detective superintendent's assessment rang very false indeed.

'I think you're perhaps being a little hasty, Pete. You've not been here long, and don't know how we operate. It's been a blow, losing Steve Cummings before he had a chance to even get here. But I think you'll find Janie Harrison more than capable if you let her do her job. Besides, wasn't it your idea to promote her in the first place?'

'Aye, and I regret that now. Let her do her job? She doesn't know what her job is. No respect for procedure, chain of command. She won't delegate, and it doesn't matter how many times I try to tell her, she just ignores me entirely.'

Noise from the far end of the corridor stopped McLean from eavesdropping any further. He'd heard enough anyway. He tapped on the door, then pushed it open.

'Morning everyone. Hope I'm not disturbing anything.'

Jayne McIntyre sat at her desk, full uniform suggesting her day would mostly be meetings with important people. Standing almost to attention on the other side, Detective Superintendent Nelson looked rather less tidy. His suit was crumpled, as if he had either slept in it or on it, and his thinning hair could have done with a brush. His face was haggard and grey, so maybe he hadn't slept at all, although he must have shaved that morning, as he'd missed a bit round the edge of his jaw.

'McLean,' he said with only slightly less venom than he had been using to put down Detective Sergeant Harrison. No, *Acting Detective Inspector* Harrison. McLean would have to remember that.

'Tony. It's good to have you back.' McIntyre stood, smoothed down the front of her jacket and came round the desk to greet him. Her warmth was in stark contrast to Nelson's frigid hostility. This was going to be fun.

'You ready to jump straight in? I think Sandy Gregg's been preparing some briefing notes. That should get you up to speed. Oh, and you can have your old office back if you want for now. Since nobody else is using it. I've asked IT to sort out your network access, phone, all the usual stuff.' McIntyre turned briefly to Nelson. 'You anything else to add, Pete?'

The detective superintendent opened his mouth, but no words came out, so he closed it again. A moment later McLean caught a whiff of bad breath on the air. Tinged with whisky, if he wasn't mistaken.

'Good. Well. I believe there's a team briefing starting any moment now, so I won't keep you both.' McIntyre reached past McLean to the edge of her desk, where her cap lay upside down. She picked it up, gave it a distasteful look, then shoved it under one arm. 'Duty calls.'

McLean stepped aside to let her leave the room, then made to follow.

'One moment, McLean.' Nelson's voice stopped him in his tracks. He turned slowly, aware that McIntyre wasn't hanging around for the pissing contest, even if it was happening in her office.

'Sir?' he tried.

'You're here to consult, understand? You're not running this investigation. That's Harrison's job. For now.'

Something about those last two words made McLean's skin crawl. Or maybe it was simply that he couldn't stand being in the same room as the detective superintendent.

'I'm sure Janie's got everything under control. She and DS Gregg have made a great team in the past, and the detective constables are shaping up well. At least they were when I last worked with them. I quite understand the situation here. I will help wherever I can, not direct operations.'

Nelson stared at him for too long, eyes narrowed, eyelids puffy. The man wasn't well, and something had clearly happened between him and Harrison. McLean was no fool, and he knew the detective superintendent's reputation, so it wasn't hard to guess what. He knew Janie, too, and could imagine exactly how she would respond. As the thought occurred to him, he had to suppress the smile it wanted to bring to his face. This wasn't the place, nor the time.

'Was there anything else?' he asked as blandly as he could manage. 'Only I've a lot of catching up to do, and the briefing's going to start soon.'

'Go on, then.' Nelson seemed to deflate in front of him, waved a hand to dismiss McLean as if this was his office, not the chief superintendent's. 'God knows we need the manpower. But don't start trying to do your old job. Things have moved on.'

In the end, he only made it as far as the landing before another voice accosted him. More welcome this time, McLean glanced down to see DCI Jo Dexter climbing up the stairs.

'Finally saw sense and came home, did you, Tony?' She wheezed, a little breathless from the exertion as she reached the top.

'Home?' He looked around the familiar surroundings. 'That's an odd way of putting it. And if you're looking for Jayne, I think you just missed her. Nelson's in his office though.'

'Actually it was you I was looking for. Already spoke to Jayne downstairs and she told me you were here. Thought you might like to know we've just arrested Archie Seagram.'

'You have?' McLean pictured the old man in his Range Rover, his thinly veiled threats. 'What for?'

'You mean apart from he's a wee toerag who's been thumbing his nose at us for years?'

'Saughton would be full to bursting if that was all it took.'

'Aye, well. Seagram's a canny wee bugger, but I reckon he'll no' wriggle his way out of this one. You heard about the brothel over Craigentinny way? The one Janie Harrison found?'

'Run by Billy Creegan, I was told. Always thought there was something a bit unsavoury about that one. Too clean.'

Dexter cocked her head at that, with a half-smile at something she kept to herself. 'Clean, aye. You should have a look at the pathologist's report on that. But never mind. That house we raided had only been operating for a couple of weeks. Seems they moved the place around a lot, never staying anywhere for long. Smart, really. Makes it hard for us to catch them.'

'So, you got lucky. Or Harrison did.'

'Never look a gift horse in the mouth, Tony. Or any horse for that matter. Horrible bitey things. Aye we were lucky, but them moving around a lot meant Creegan had all his records on his laptop. The man was some kind of tech security nutter for all his age, but our boys in IT forensics managed to break it open. And now we've got enough to tie Seagram into the whole operation.'

'That's some work, Jo. We've been trying to take him down for years now.'

'Pretty much my whole career, and before I even started. Seagram and his pals have been on the scene since the eighties, but he's the only one of them who's never been put away. We make this stick, that'll be a nice feather in my cap before retirement.'

McLean looked at the detective chief inspector as she leaned on the railing beside him. Dexter was a little older than him, but not much. Then again, hadn't he retired already? And he'd only worked in Vice for a year; she'd somehow managed to stomach it for over a decade now.

'You think there'll be a problem?' he asked. 'Making it stick, that is?'

Dexter checked her watch. 'Who knows? We're waiting for his lawyer to turn up so we can start interviewing him. There's more than enough to press charges already, but I'd like to see what he has to say for himself.'

'Wouldn't mind seeing that myself.'

'Funnily enough, that was why I was looking for you. We'll be starting soon, and I'd like you to observe the interview if you can.'

'You want me to speak to him?'

The detective chief inspector waggled her head as if unsure. 'Maybe once we've done our initial interview, since he came to you first about his mates getting done in. That's Janie's investigation, though, and nothing to do with him being charged. Not directly, at least.'

'I reckon he knows more about their deaths than he's let on so far. Maybe he'll be more inclined to tell us what that's all about, now he's facing a potential prison sentence. I know Janie wanted to talk to him anyways, so perhaps once you're done with him we can have a go too.'

'She'll get her chance. I've asked her to sit in on this one. Should make Seagram sweat if he thinks the two investigations are linked.' Dexter leaned forward and looked down the stairwell to the ground floor far below. 'You going anywhere the now?'

'Well, I was headed to the morning briefing.' McLean checked his watch. 'But I guess that's been postponed if you're doing interview prep with our SIO.'

'Aye, sorry about that.'

38

The observation booth off interview room one wasn't the largest of spaces, even when empty. As McLean gently pushed open the door to step inside, he found that it was already crowded with senior officers. Detective Superintendent Nelson scowled at him, but didn't go as far as to tell him to get out. Chief Superintendent Jayne McIntyre was much more welcoming. He'd thought she'd be halfway across the country, having important meetings with important people, but clearly the chance to see Archie Seagram being questioned was too good to miss.

'Tony. Glad you could make it.' She spoke quietly so as not to be heard in the adjoining room. 'You got Jo's message, then?'

He nodded and took a step closer. Most interview suites had cameras in them now, both for recording the proceedings and so that other officers could observe unseen. Interview room one had been built in a less technological age, and while a feed from the cameras was available, it was also possible to stand in this tiny cubicle and watch through a one-way mirror. McLean was old school; he preferred to see things with his own eyes rather than on a tiny screen. The view they were offered was from the side too, well-suited to spotting any reactions that the interviewing officer might miss.

Not that he expected Detective Chief Inspector Dexter to miss much. He'd known her all of his career, and a better detective he'd be hard pushed to name. She sat on one side of a small table, slouched in her chair as if nothing in the world concerned her. Beside her, DI Harrison had been drafted in to be the silent one, which must have been why Dexter had wanted to talk to her. It was an odd choice on the face of it, but then again Seagram was misogyny writ large. Being questioned by two female officers would put him on edge.

Or at least that might have been the plan. The man himself looked strangely relaxed. That may have had something to do with the solicitor sitting beside him. McLean had encountered Fraser MacFarlane, senior partner of MacFarlane and Dodds, far too many times before. Sharp as they come, he could tear the most well prepared witness to shreds in a courtroom. It was unusual to see him at this stage of the proceedings, though, which went to show how important a client Archie Seagram must be.

'Mr Seagram. You are no doubt aware that we recently raided a house in Craigentinny. Reid Manor. It was being used as a brothel, catering to the more extreme end of the market. Your old friend William Creegan was running the place, with the aid of several men in your employ.'

Seagram leaned forward, peering at Dexter as if his eyes were failing him. Maybe they were. Before he could speak, MacFarlane butted in.

'Would that be the same William Creegan whose body was found in St Mark's Church in Gorgie? Whose murderer you have yet to identify, let alone apprehend?'

Dexter ignored the lawyer, her focus solely on Seagram. The old man still leaned forward, head slightly tilted to catch her words, as if he were hard of hearing as well as partially blind. 'The workers in the brothel were all foreign refugees, trafficked to the city and forced into sexual slavery. They were housed in the basement, in airless cellar rooms, only allowed up into the house when customers arrived.'

'This is all very edifying, Detective Chief Inspector. But I don't see what any of it has to do with my client.' In contrast to Seagram, MacFarlane leaned back in his chair like a Tory politician, one leg crossed over the other, hands loosely clasped. 'Of course he knows William Creegan. Knew, I should say. But are you seriously suggesting my client had anything to do with this alleged brothel of yours?'

'Actually, no.' Dexter smiled like a shark. 'Not the house in Craigentinny, at least. But that had only been operating for a few weeks, according to the refugees we freed from the place. Before that they were in another house, closer to the city centre. They were only there for a fortnight, having been moved from a third property where again they'd only spent a short while. A few had been together in that hellish life for months, but mostly some would be taken away, new ones brought in to replace them. Only the customers remained the same. Mostly the same.'

'Fascinating, I'm sure. I look forward to the court case against Mr Creegan. Ah, only he's dead, isn't he? How unfortunate for you.' MacFarlane abruptly uncrossed his legs put both hands down on the table. It was probably meant to make Dexter flinch, but she ignored it completely. McLean was pleased to see that Harrison didn't fall for the theatrics either. 'Now if you're simply going to throw a load of baseless allegations conjured from supposed association with a man who can no longer answer for himself, then I think it's time the both of us left.'

He made as if to stand, but Seagram remained seated. Again, Dexter didn't move a muscle until finally MacFarlane relented and dropped back into his seat.

'Your client has been arrested and read his rights, Mr MacFarlane. I'm sure you're familiar enough with the law to know that we can hold him for questioning for twenty-four hours should we choose to do so.' Dexter sat up straight now, suddenly all business. 'As to your protestations about Mr Creegan and Mr Seagram being merely acquaintances, I think we both know that's not true.

We have recovered evidence from the house in Craigentinny that links the two of them in a business capacity. We have sworn testimony from one of the men working at that brothel that Mr Seagram was the source of the trafficked refugees. And I also have positive identification from two of those refugees forced to work there. Forced to perform sexual acts on each other while Mr Seagram watched. Because, apparently, that's his thing, you know?'

MacFarlane turned in his seat to look at Seagram, an expression on his face that McLean would enjoy remembering for a long time. It would probably be on video, too, which meant it might well make it to a Christmas party compilation, or perhaps someone's screensaver. Although obviously he couldn't condone such gross misconduct.

'You knew about this?' he whispered to McIntyre, who was watching the interview play out with a mischievous glint in her eye.

'Jo's got more than that. More than enough to send Seagram down for a long time. Janie played an absolute blinder when she uncovered their operation. A couple more days and they'd have cleaned it out, moved on, but Creegan's death so soon after Morgan's took them all by surprise, I think.'

'Morgan was in on this, too?' McLean nodded towards the glass. 'Thought he'd packed all that stuff in?'

'It's quite possible he had, actually. There's nothing yet to link him directly with the rest of them, but his death spooked them all. They had a very slick operation going, but mistakes are always made when people panic.'

McIntyre was about to say more, but they were both distracted by the show in the neighbouring interview room. DCI Dexter read out a long list of charges before informing Seagram that he would be taken to the cells and kept there until he could appear at the next sitting of the Sheriff Court.

'We'll be seeking bail, of course.' MacFarlane reached for his briefcase, ready to leave, but Seagram placed a hand on his arm.

'No, Fraser.' It was the first thing he'd said in the whole interview.

'I . . . Archie?' MacFarlane, the most unflappable barrister in the whole of Scotland, flapped.

'No bail, Fraser. I'll stand trial. Sure, you can get these charges laughed out of court. But I don't want bail.' He looked up at the glass, a mirror on his side but McLean felt sure the old man could see him. 'Reckon I'm safer on the inside right now.'

McLean felt like a third wheel as he wandered the station, not quite sure exactly what he should be doing. His intention had been to get stuck into the triple murder investigation, but everyone had been distracted by Seagram's arrest. By the time the old man had been interviewed, charged and taken to the cells to await transport to the Sheriff Court, much of the useful part of the day had gone. DS – no, DI – Harrison had been busy helping Jo Dexter and working out the best way to co-ordinate what were two only marginally linked investigations, which left McLean surprisingly rudderless.

He was on his way from the canteen and a cup of tea when he met Harrison coming from the direction of the Vice squad offices.

'Not quite the first day back at school I was expecting,' he said as she gave him a weary smile. 'You getting on OK with Dexter?'

'Apart from not having a chance to question Seagram myself before he was charged, aye. Quite wanted to ask him about his old friends in a formal interview setting, but apparently he's off to court soon. Means it'll have to be tomorrow and likely over at Saughton since he's not looking for bail. Seems everyone's in a rush to get him out of here when he's only just arrived.'

'I rather think Nelson wants him out of here and into the hands of the prison service as quickly as possible. Makes a certain sense, given how old he is. Might drop dead at any moment, and that would be very awkward if it happened while he was in our care.'

Harrison had been scuffing her foot on the floor in irritation, but now she looked up at him with a quizzical expression on her face. 'You think that's it? Covering his arse?'

'Partly, yes. More likely he's had a call from someone and is acting on their orders. Question is, were they police?'

'You don't think Nelson . . .?' Harrison trailed off.

'I'm sure I have no idea, Janie. But Seagram's influence reaches far and wide. That's why I'm so surprised he's saying he doesn't want bail. Choosing months on remand rather than an ankle tag is not normal behaviour.'

'So why do it then?'

'Because he's scared. Whoever did for his mates is going to be after him too. He knows it, same as he almost certainly knows why. He doesn't know who, though; he'd have taken steps to deal with them if he did. No. Being inside is a layer of protection, and I don't think he'll be sharing a cell with an unwashed six-foot-five repeat sex offender, if you get my meaning. Seagram has connections everywhere, so he'll have an easy time of it. Relatively speaking.'

'Still would have liked a chance to interview him.'

'Not sure he'd have said any more to you than he did Jo Dexter, though. Not a fan of women in positions of authority, if you know what I mean. Maybe I should have taken him more seriously the first time he approached me.'

'He'd not be here to question at all if you had done though, would he? If you'd been the great detective he was expecting and solved the crime before Morgan's body was even cold, then we'd never have had Creegan's phone to crack. I'd never have stumbled on that house in Craigentinny, and we'd have no reason to arrest anybody.' Harrison looked at her watch, shook her sleeve back down over it and shoved her folder under one arm. 'Anyway. I'd better get back to the incident room and add what Vice gave me to the system. See if any useful actions pop out. Who knows? Maybe they'll have got somewhere with the CCTV footage in my absence.'

39

I t wasn't until she lifted the empty mug to her mouth to take a swig of coffee and realised this wasn't the first time she'd done it, that Janie knew she really should call it a day. Most of the team had knocked off hours earlier, only the night shift manning the phones and working through the desk-based actions. She'd found a spare computer and made a start on reviewing the security camera footage the door-to-door teams had managed to get their hands on.

Even as she stared at the dark and blurry images, she could hear Detective Superintendent Nelson's voice at the back of her mind. 'This is work for a constable, not a detective inspector. Delegate, Janie. Or you'll never make it.' Did she want to make it, though? She wasn't even sure she wanted to be a DI, let alone clamber any further up the greasy pole. Or maybe that was just because she was tired, not thinking straight.

Something changed on the screen, and she tapped at the keyboard to stop, then rewound back a minute or two. Letting her mind wander wasn't the best way to review video footage. She really should have been doing this with another officer. Always better to have two sets of eyes on a job like this.

Backwards at double speed, the movement was no more than a flash, then back to the almost motionless view of the street. She had the footage from Robert Bailey's eaves-mounted camera up at the moment. It showed mostly the empty parking area and a couple of wheelie bins, but the edge of the image strayed out over the pavement and into the road. It wasn't a bad camera, much better than a lot of the council operated CCTV installations in the city centre. Even after dark the image was crisp, if a little monochrome. Far-spaced streetlights threw scant illumination onto the road, but the houses spilled a surprising amount of light into the night. Did nobody have curtains anymore?

Janie slowed the footage, trying to work out what it was that had caught her attention before. A car trundled along the road, headlamps briefly turning the view to colour as it passed. Janie glanced at the timestamp in the corner of the screen to see whether this might have been the vehicle that had disturbed Mrs McDaid and her smelly wee terrier. It could have been, but the angle of the screen made reading the number plate impossible. How had McAllister crossed town to get to that church? How had Creegan, for that matter. Morgan could have walked, but it was too far for the other two, surely? Both of them were old men, after all. So, a taxi, perhaps? A private hire or Uber or something similar? It was a line of enquiry Sandy Gregg had been pursuing, hadn't she? That was right. Exactly the sort of desk-based work she was so good at.

Picking up the coffee mug again, Janie had already lifted it to her lips before remembering it was empty. This was stupid, sitting here in the semi-darkness fighting to stay awake when the sensible thing to do would be to go home and get some sleep. She reached for the keyboard to stop the video, turn everything off, and that's when she saw it.

A lone figure walked across the view of the camera. Head down, hands in the pockets of his dark overcoat, there was never-theless something familiar about the way he moved. Janie found herself willing him to slow, to look up at the camera so that she could see his face. And as if her wish had gone back in time, he did exactly that. It was brief, only a split second before he was head down and marching off screen with a purpose, but it was more than enough. A stab at the keys had him striding backwards, frame by frame, until Janie paused on exactly the right one.

It was far clearer than the other images, and a much better angle. Even so, Janie was as certain as she could be that this was the same man who'd been loitering at that bus stop, and who'd also been on Gorgie Road the night Billy Creegan had died. Now here he was not fifty metres from St Michael's Church. Once was nothing. Twice could just be coincidence, although like McLean, Janie was no great believer in coincidences. But three times? Now that was suspicious indeed. And this time they had the clearest image yet of their only suspect. He stared at her, unmoving, from the frozen screen, thinning hair over a bland, slightly jowly face. Eyes made fire by the reflected glare of the nearest streetlights.

All that remained was to find out who the hell he was.

The discovery had given her a bit of an adrenaline rush, but Janie knew better than to push her luck any further. There was nothing that could be done that night; far better to get some sleep and make sure she was in early in the morning. She bade goodnight to the late shift team, grabbed her jacket and bag, and headed out the door.

'Goodness, Janie, you still in? I'd have thought your shift had ended hours ago?' Chief Superintendent McIntyre had either been waiting for her or just happened to be walking down the corridor at that exact same moment.

'The way I heard it, inspectors don't work shifts.'

McIntyre conceded the point with a gracious nod of the head. 'True, but you should start as you mean to go along, and working all hours until you collapse of exhaustion isn't necessarily the best strategy.'

'Well, I'm headed home now. Get some kip before tomorrow. I reckon it's going to be another very long day.'

'Any progress on the case? I've not had time to read the daily updates yet.'

Janie almost cursed, nearly turned back to the incident room. She knew there was something else she was supposed to have been doing.

'I've just been reviewing the security camera footage we managed to get from the houses around St Michael's.' She told the chief superintendent about the lone figure and how they now had a half decent image of his face. 'Could be nothing, of course. And if we can't identify him soon, we'll have to go to the press. Not sure we can put that off much longer anyway, given the rumours already circulating.'

McIntyre sighed. 'You're more right than you know. I've been fielding calls all day. Maybe a press conference is what's needed. Put a few facts out there before the speculation gets out of control. You've a good enough photo for an appeal to the public?'

Janie considered the split-second image from the camera footage, washed out by a combination of infra-red sensors and the glow of the streetlamps. Someone would be able to spruce it up into something presentable, she was sure. 'Think so. You want me to get started on that now?'

McIntyre's laugh was as tired as Janie felt. 'Heavens no. It can wait for the morning. You'll need to get Sergeant Hwei to organise things, and he's been kind of busy dealing with the fallout from Seagram's arrest.'

'The press must be having a field day. Haven't had a chance to catch up with it yet.'

'Not much to report, really. Half of them are praising us for a job well done. The other half are asking us why it took so long. At least it's distracted them from the church deaths for a little while.'

'How much longer though? What's the betting Seagram starts mouthing off to them now he knows he's safe?'

'He's in remand, Janie. I don't think he'll have much access to the press. And they'll be treading carefully in case they prejudice the trial.'

'Aye, I know that. But I can't help thinking this is all part of some plan of his and we're just doing what's expected of us. There's enough press out there who'll plead public interest and print whatever guff he's fed to them anyway. That's how people like him work, isn't it?'

McIntyre gave Janie an enquiring look. 'I didn't realise you knew him.'

'Me? I don't. Not really. Only spoken to him twice in my life, at Kenneth Morgan's funeral, and then again this afternoon. But I grew up in Broxburn, and he's a bit of a legend in those parts. My uncle used to tell stories about what he was like in the old days.'

'Aye, well. He might be getting on, but he's still sharp. And he's got plenty of young muscle ready to do his bidding.' McIntyre hefted her bag over her shoulder. The weight of all the work following her home made Janie feel guilty at leaving hers in the incident room. 'He's right about one thing, for sure. Alive, even if he's in prison, he can control his little empire. For a while at least. But only if he's alive. If whoever's done for Morgan, Creegan and McAllister brands a cross on Seagram's forehead, then we're in for the mother of all turf wars.'

'That doesn't seem right, really. Having to protect a scunner like him just because if we don't someone worse'll come along.'

McIntyre gave Janie a gentle pat on the shoulder, her touch far less intrusive than Detective Superintendent Nelson's unsubtle mauling. 'Welcome to modern policing, Janie. Welcome to modern policing.'

Her brief encounter with McIntyre had lifted Janie's spirits, despite the chief superintendent's parting words. Perhaps that was why she wasn't thinking too much about any threat as she left the station by the back door and walked out across the car park in search of a bus home. Something must have registered though, as she felt a prickling at the base of her skull, the hairs rising as if a storm was coming, before a sneer of a voice confirmed her worst fears.

'You could have had it all, you know? Nice easy ride up the ladder to the top floor, keys to the executive bathrooms. You could have been a DCI in a couple of years, maybe even Super in ten. Why'd you go and piss that all away, eh?'

Detective Superintendent Nelson seemed to have finally recovered from his bruised bollocks, walking with a slow but steady gait as he emerged from the shadows between two armoured Transit vans. Janie stood her ground, bathed in the glow of the overhead streetlights and, if memory served, within the arc of the CCTV cameras. They'd been upgraded since the embarrassing incident of DI McLean's Alfa Romeo being boosted from a parking space not more than ten paces from where she stood. Nelson would be a fool to try anything on somewhere so well watched. But then again, she knew he was a fool already.

'Is that what you thought you were doing, sir?' she asked, raising her voice a little more than strictly necessary just in case there might be anyone else nearby. 'Helping me up the promotion ladder? And – what? – in return I jump gratefully into your bed?'

'You'd be nothing if it wasn't for me.' Nelson didn't exactly deny Janie's accusation, she noticed.

'Would I not? It was Chief Superintendent Elmwood who promoted me to DS, sir. That was a while ago now, and I've not had a problem getting through any of my performance appraisals since. You might find it hard to believe, but I was happy enough being a sergeant for now. Truth be told I don't think I've the experience to be an inspector just yet. Sandy Gregg would've been a better fit for the job. But then she's married, right enough. Maybe a bit old for your tastes, too.'

Nelson still hugged the edge of the shadows as if he was aware he might be seen at any moment. Janie should have been afraid of him, she knew. He wasn't that much bigger or stronger than her, but he was her superior officer, the head of their team. He could make life impossibly difficult for her if he chose. And yet she had all the cards here. He was the outsider, not her. She'd come up through the ranks in this city, this police region. People knew her. He had only his rank. And she'd bested him once before, even if he had been very drunk at the time.

'I could have you struck back down to constable. Not even plain clothes, just walking the beat and directing traffic. One call. Just like that.' The detective superintendent snapped his fingers, but instead of a nice sharp *click*, they made little sound at all. Hands too sweaty, Janie reckoned.

'And yet you haven't, sir. You've acted like nothing happened at all.'

Nelson took a couple of steps forward, into the light, until he was standing right in front of her. Janie almost retreated, but a small voice in the back of her mind told her to stand her ground, face up to the bully. It sounded a lot like Grace Ramsay.

'Nothing did happen. Did it, Acting Detective Inspector Harrison.' Nelson put heavy emphasis on the 'acting' part. 'Any suggestion to the contrary would be the end of your career, understood?'

'My career . . . Sir?' Janie put her own emphasis on the possessive pronoun, just enough of a pause before the last word to be provocative. Nelson leaned in towards her. The stink of his breath brought a flash of fear with it, an echo of his drunken attack.

'My word against yours. My injury as evidence. No witnesses.' He reached out as if to poke her with a finger as he spoke, then changed his mind. Was that a flash of uncertainty that crossed his face?

'Are we done here, sir? Only I've a bus to catch.' Janie mimed looking at her watch, turned and walked away from him towards the gates. She waited until she was a half dozen paces away before throwing a last word over her shoulder. 'And what makes you think there were no witnesses?'

40

S he hadn't even made it as far as the bus stop before her phone started buzzing in her pocket. Janie ignored the first text, certain it would be something from Nelson demanding to know what she meant. She was going to ignore the second one too, but then the phone began to ring. Fishing it out, the number on the screen wasn't the detective superintendent at all. It was control. She tapped to accept, shoved the handset to her ear.

'DS . . . *DI* Harrison speaking.'

'Sorry to call so late, Detective Inspector. I've got you listed as SIO on the investigation into the death of Raymond McAllister.'

'Aye, that's right. Has something come up?' It was a stupid question and Janie knew it as soon as the words came out. Of course something had come up.

'We've had report of a fire at his address. Multiple units have been dispatched. I've sent you a text with all the details.'

Janie thanked the operator, killed the call and then shouted a very rude curse into the night. Feeling a little better for that, she retraced her steps to the station, entering by the front door this time to avoid any chance of another encounter with Nelson. DC Bryant was on the night shift, looked up from her computer as Janie entered the incident room at speed.

'Thought you'd gone home,' she said through a stifled yawn.

'Aye, me an' all. Someone's tried to torch McAllister's place, though. It not come through here yet?'

As if on cue, Bryant's computer pinged a new message. Nothing like bad news to travel fast.

'How far had we got with searching the place?' Janie asked. She'd been meaning to go back there herself, but Seagram's arrest had put an end to that.

'Don't think anyone's been back there since you and Jay.' Bryant tapped a few keys on her keyboard and brought up the list of actions for the investigation. 'Forensics haven't started yet, but there should have been a couple of uniform constables guarding it.'

'Aye, well. Either they're asleep or someone's decided they're needed elsewhere. See when I find out who . . .' Janie left the threat unsaid, aware that as the most junior detective inspector in the region she was unlikely to be able to do much about it if that was the case.

'You going over there?' Bryant asked.

Janie took out her phone, checked the texts from control. She could try calling the fire service and they might put her through to whoever was in charge at the scene. Chances were they'd be busy right now. Would they be any less busy if she turned up in person and asked? In the back of her mind, she could hear Nelson's wheedling voice telling her to delegate, co-ordinate actions from her command centre here in the incident room. Nothing to be gained from a senior officer traipsing halfway across the city just to look at some pretty flames. Aye, right. As if she'd do anything that wee scrote told her to.

'Grab us a pool car, will you Jessica. I'll meet you at the back in ten minutes. Need to coax some coffee out of the vending machine first.'

They could smell the smoke from miles away, even through the advanced air filtration system of the little electric Nissan pool car.

Janie drove, and she craned her neck to look at the low clouds over Corstorphine Hill as they waited for green at a set of traffic lights past Murrayfield. Was that a subtle, flickering orange and red glow reflected over the spot where Raymond McAllister had lived? Hard to tell against the glare of the city's endless streetlights.

There was no doubting it once they came closer. Flames leapt into the air, topped with thick black smoke that spread out like a dark mist, nudged towards the zoo by the lightest of breezes. The end of the road had been cordoned off, a dozen or more squad cars with their lights lazily flashing. Janie could have wept to see the manpower available for such an emergency. What she couldn't have done with half of them for her investigation.

They parked a distance away and walked to the cordon. Three uniform constables and a sergeant blocked their way until Janie showed her warrant card.

'It's a nightmare up there, ma'am,' the sergeant said. An older man, she recognised his face, but wasn't sure of his name.

'Is the fire bad? There was supposed to be a couple of constables on the house. How'd it get out of control so quickly?'

The sergeant frowned. 'Nobody told me about anyone watching a house up this way. Might have been able to do something about the double-parked cars if they were.'

'Double-parked . . .?' Janie started to ask, then waved the question away. 'Don't worry about it. I'll find out whose heads need to roll and swing the axe myself.'

Further up the street, the problem became more evident. Three fire engines were stopped a full fifty metres from the blaze by an old Volvo estate that didn't appear so much parked as abandoned in the street. The two tyres Janie could see as she approached were both flat, and she would have bet good money the ones on the other side were too. Beyond the burning house, another car blocked the street from the eastern approach. No accident this.

'Doing the best we can,' a fire officer told her once she'd

270

identified herself. They had rolled their hoses as far as they could and were directing water into a building completely engulfed in flame. Janie knew enough about these things to understand that their first priority was to stop the fire spreading to the neighbouring houses. There'd be no concern for preserving forensic evidence, and she wasn't about to ask them to change that.

'Get a note of the licence plates on these cars will you, Jessica?' She indicated the Volvo and its twin up the road. 'My guess is stolen, probably cloned plates too.'

'On it, boss.' Bryant pulled out her phone, took a photo, then set off down the far side of the road until she was close enough to snap the other one. Janie followed her more slowly, the two of them keeping well away from the fire crew and the conflagration. Even so, she could feel the scorching heat of it. By the time those flames were out, she doubted there would be anything left but a shell of brick and broken roof slates.

The detective constable returned a few minutes later, still clutching her phone. 'Volvo Estate's got the plates from a Ford Focus registered in Glasgow. The car at the other end's one of those Mitsubishi people-carrier things, but the plates belong to a Fiat Panda from Newburgh in Fife. They've both had all four tyres slashed to make them harder to move. No way this isn't arson.'

'And pretty obvious why, too. What I want to know is what happened to the constables who were meant to be guarding the place.'

'You want me to give Jay a call? He was the one made the request.'

Janie stared at the flames, crackling away in the night. At least they had the VHS tapes. Raymond McAllister's bungalow wasn't going to be yielding any more clues about him though, least of all who might have killed him.

'It can wait till the morning. There'll be a justifiable excuse, or a cock up we can't prove is corruption. Damage is done already, no point hanging around. Let's get out of here.' Janie pulled the car keys from her pocket and held them up. 'You can drop me home on your way back to the station.'

'Hey there, stranger. I was beginning to think I lived here alone.'

Janie glanced through the open living room door as she hung her coat on the rack in the hallway and shucked off her boots. Bag dumped beside them, she shuffled across the bare wooden floor-boards and stepped into the warmth. Manda Parsons slouched on the sofa in a lurid pink onesie, feet up on the coffee table and watching something on the telly. She had a glass of white wine beside her, condensation glistening on the outside in stark contrast to the lukewarm pish they served in the pub close to the station. Even better, a flat, square box bearing the all-too familiar logo of the local pizzeria lay just far enough from her bare feet.

'Please tell me there's pizza in that box, and wine in that bottle?' Janie slumped into the cushions beside her flatmate and let out a weary sigh. Manda leaned in close, her scent of shampoo and coconut moisturiser a pleasant distraction from Janie's own odour. She sniffed once, then again. Wrinkled her nose.

'What have you been up to, J? You reek like bonfire night.'

Janie hauled herself into more of a sitting position, less of a slouch. 'Aye, fair enough. You know that house up Corstorphine way you were supposed to be giving the once over? Don't bother now. Time you get there tomorrow it'll be nothing but ashes.'

Manda sat up straight too, reached for the remote and muted the television even though it was so quiet Janie had hardly noticed it.

'Thanks for the heads up. That was going to be an early start, but now I get a lie-in.'

'Aye, well. It's an ill wind and all that.'

'Sorry, J. That was insensitive of me.' Manda put a hand on Janie's shoulder. The touch, light and welcome, reminded her of

Jayne McIntyre and Cerys Powell. A sharp contrast to Pete Nelson's painful grip, and it occurred to her she'd not told Manda about that yet. Tonight wasn't the time, though. She was too tired, and her brain was too full.

'No bother. I'm just tired and grumpy. Too much work, not enough bodies to do it. Same as everywhere, I guess.'

'Tell me about it.' Manda leaned forward and slid the pizza box towards her, flipped the lid with practised ease to reveal only a couple of pieces had been eaten. 'Actually, forget that. I'll go warm this up and grab you a glass of wine from the fridge. You look like you need it.'

Manda stood up with a clicking of joints and a groan, closed the lid down on the pizza box and grabbed both it and her wine glass. Janie slumped back into the cushions again, felt the tension ease out of her shoulders as she stared up at the ornately moulded ceiling rose above her. She might have fallen asleep then had her flatmate not given her a toe-stubbing kick in the leg.

'Ow. What's that for?'

'You want pizza and wine?' Manda nodded towards the door. 'First you need to shower and change. I'm not watching Outlander with Auld Reekie for company.'

41

January 10th 1983 – Monday

No school today because of what happened at the church. Spoke to a police man who wasn't wearing a uniform. He said he was a defective or something, so maybe that's why. He asked me lots of questions and said it was OK when I didn't know the answers. I must always keep God's secret or I will go straight to hell. That's what Father O'C tells me when I try to sleep at night. He's with me all the time now. In my head. He makes me touch myself in God's special way, even when I do not want to. I wish he would go away.

42

A light drizzle smeared the windscreen as McLean drove silently across town in Emma's electric Renault. He'd been about to leave for the station when Harrison's text had come in, meaning a bit more of a fight with traffic as he navigated less familiar roads to Corstorphine. Sat Nav took him straight to the address, but he parked a couple of streets away. He'd brought his coat, and even remembered a hat this time, so the rain wasn't much of a bother as he approached the security cordon.

'Heard you were back, sir. Good to see you again.' Police Sergeant Kenneth Stephen greeted him at the blue and white tape, lifting it up so McLean could stoop underneath. Further down the street, a lone fire engine would have blocked the traffic had any been allowed in.

'Strictly consulting. I'm not sure I want to go back to the grind again.'

'Aye, right.' The sergeant grinned his disbelief. 'You'll still need to see the Crime Scene Manager before you go poking around in the ashes.'

McLean thanked him and set off towards the fire engine. As he approached, he could see the damage caused by the fire more closely. A bungalow, set back from the pavement by a small concrete garden, it had been completely gutted by a fire that must have been well set before anyone had arrived to try and put it out. The roof had collapsed in, leaving grey-harled gable end walls, melted uPVC windows offering a view of only rubble inside.

'Ah, you're here already, sir—Tony.' Detective Inspector Harrison emerged from behind a police van that was parked beyond the fire engine. She wore a set of disposable paper overalls, and judging by the smears of wet black ash on them had already been closer to the ruined building than was perhaps advisable.

'From your text it sounded important. What's the story here?'

'This is – was – Ray McAllister's house. Jay and I searched it briefly after his body turned up in St Michael's church a couple of days ago. We've been a little busy since then, as you know. Had planned on getting forensics in today. Only this happened last night.' Harrison waved at the blackened ruins, and as he looked over them again, McLean saw a few tiny wisps of steam rising from the mess.

'Convenient for someone,' he said.

'Too bloody right. There were cars abandoned at each end of the street to make it difficult for the fire engines to get close. They've been sent off to the pound and we'll see if we can't get anything from them, but they were both stolen, cloned number plates. Chances of finding out who brought them here aren't good.'

'Someone's covering up something, that's clear enough. Any reason you felt the need to call me out to see it?' McLean turned up the collar on his coat and shoved his hands in his pockets as the rain grew heavier. 'Not that it isn't nice to be out and about rather than stuck in a stuffy office.'

'Aye, I know.' Harrison had pulled up the hood on her overalls, but it wouldn't keep her dry for long if the weather continued to deteriorate. 'Thing is, we found some well-dodgy video tapes in there and I'm sure there would have been a lot more besides. McAllister used to be Seagram's main enforcer in his younger days, right? Liked breaking heads and worse.'

'That's what we put him inside for. Only, we never could tie him to Seagram. He wouldn't rat on his old friend then, and it's not as if he's going to, now.' McLean glanced up at the buildings either side of the bungalow, fortunately untouched by the blaze that had devoured it. 'I take it you didn't leave the tapes in there?'

'No, they're back at the station, logged into evidence. I also asked Jay to get a couple of constables assigned to guard this house.'

'Not like him to forget something like that.'

'He didn't. I've spoken to him, and he's got everything recorded. Apparently, there was a squad car outside here until about three hours before the fire must have been lit. I've spoken to some of the neighbours, and they said those two cars were parked up around about eight last night. I got a call about the fire at half nine.'

'Someone called them away? There was an emergency locally?'

Harrison wiped rain from her forehead with the back of her hand, leaving a black smudge in its place. 'That's what I'd like to know. Getting the run-around at the moment, though. I think someone's covering their arse, but I also think someone higher up told them to reassign those officers.'

'And you'd like me to do a little off-the-books digging, I take it.'

Harrison looked back at the police van, as if someone inside might be listening to their conversation. 'Not really sure who to trust right now. And you being both out of the loop and knowing everyone . . .'

'On account of my advanced years?'

'Aye, well . . . I didn't want to say.' Harrison smiled, her shoulders sagging in relief.

'I'll make a few discreet enquiries. Maybe tap the cold case unit for some ideas too. There's not much goes on anywhere in this city Grumpy Bob doesn't know about.'

'Thanks. Probably should have thought to ask them myself.'

McLean shivered as a gust of wind blew rain down the back of his neck despite his collar. It was getting heavier now, and he was all too aware of how far away he'd parked Emma's car. 'You hanging

277

around here for anything else?' he asked. 'Can't imagine there's going to be much for forensics to work with.'

'Aye, you're right. Should probably be getting back to the station.' Harrison checked her watch. 'Need to break the bad news to the detective superintendent. Kirsty too, if she's in.'

McLean nodded, precipitating another cascade of water down his neck. He'd heard enough from Grumpy Bob over the months of his retirement how much time DCI Ritchie was spending with the NCA these days. Only a matter of time before she made the jump, and best of luck to her. It would mean the team was short a DI and a DCI though. Not easy positions to fill.

'I'll see you back there then.' He made to leave, then stopped. 'Oh, and Janie? You might want to wipe your face before you go.'

His first stop was only at the end of the street. Police Sergeant Stephen had retreated to the relative comfort of his squad car, a young constable in the driving seat beside him. McLean bent down and tapped on the window, feeling yet more rain on his neck as it slid slowly down.

'Seen enough, Detective Inspector?'

'Not much to see. And there's going to be even less by the time this rain's blown through. What a disaster, eh?'

'Aye, it is right enough. Heard that was Ray McAllister's place. Strange to think of a hard man like that living in suburban paradise, eh?'

'Everyone's got to lay their head down somewhere.' McLean suppressed a shiver that was entirely physical. 'You hear anything about the car that was meant to be out here guarding the place yesterday?'

'Aye, I did. Two constables out of Corstorphine nick. I can get you their names if you want, but it's no' their fault. They got called away to an RTA on the Gogar Roundabout. Some lads having a race like they was Colin McRae, and ran a wee minibus into an artic. Lucky nobody was killed, but it took all night to clear. Dragged in half of the uniforms this side of the city.'

'And nobody thought to tell the major investigation team who'd requested the house be watched?'

'They should have been. Standard procedure. I said the same to Janie, but she can't find any record of it. You reckon it's deliberate and not just some cock-up?'

McLean looked back down the street towards the gently smoking remains of Ray McAllister's house. 'What do you reckon? Two cars blocking the road after the police presence has been removed? I'd bet the hoons on Gogar roundabout were all part of the plan too. And someone on the inside to make sure nothing gets back to Specialist Crime until it's too late. It's a cock-up all right, but a deliberate one.'

'You want me to ask around? See if anyone knows anything?'

'Speak to those two constables. Find out who called them away. It'd have to be a specific request, so there'll be a name. Let me know, and I'll take it on from there.'

PC Stephen nodded his understanding, went to close his window. McLean put a hand out to stop the glass from rising. 'And don't talk to anyone else about it, aye.' He looked past the police sergeant to the constable in the driving seat. 'That goes for the both of you.'

The call came in on his personal number as McLean manoeuvred the electric Renault into a space in the station car park reserved for electric vehicles. He'd have happily parked elsewhere, but all the available spaces were taken. Clearly a busy day at work. The screen identified the caller as Kenneth Stephen, so McLean tapped to accept, hopeful that the hands-free setup wouldn't cut him off like it so often did. This time he was lucky.

'Forgot I'd given you this number, Kenny. You find anything for me?'

'Aye. Spoke to the two constables who were meant to be watching the house. They were told to attend the RTA by control, like pretty much every other squad car in the area. They called into Corstorphine nick for confirmation, given they were on a job for you lot at Specialist Crime. Seems they were told to do what control said, even though when they got to the Gogar roundabout there were more than enough uniforms already there. When they called it in again, they were told to stay where they were.'

'You know who told them?' McLean asked.

'Aye. There's no log of the chatter back and forth, which is not good. I spoke to one of the PCs, though. Ruth Christie. She's reliable, doesn't take shit from anyone. Think you'd like her. She says they spoke to the same sergeant both times. Colin Graham. Don't really know him except by sight. You want me to ask him what he's about?'

McLean stared unseeing out through the windscreen for a while as he let the information sort itself in his mind. He knew Sergeant Stephen would do whatever he asked of him, but there were unintended consequences to every action, and having even a respected police sergeant asking those kinds of questions might mark him out.

'No, thanks. You've done more than enough. I'll take it from here.'

By the time he'd finished parking, found the right cables and plugged the car in for some free juice courtesy of Police Scotland, McLean badly needed a coffee. The day had started earlier than he'd become used to in the months of his retirement, and the trip across town to look at the damp remains of a fire-damaged house had interrupted his normal schedule. Up on the third floor, in what had once been his office, there was a half-decent filter machine that might be coaxed back into life, but the chances of there being any ground beans worth filtering were slim. The cluster of uniforms around the entrance to the canteen suggested a long wait to be served there too, so instead he descended once more into the bowels of the station and the Cold Case Unit.

Grumpy Bob had a mug to his mouth as McLean tapped on the open door and walked in. The squared away tidiness of Duguid's desk suggested he was off golfing again. Grace Ramsay glanced up at him briefly from her untidy realm, then went back to reading.

'Don't suppose you've any of that going spare have you, Bob?' McLean asked as the retired detective sergeant placed his mug down beside his laptop.

'Things so bad now, you have to come scrounging coffee down here?' Ramsay asked without looking up. There was no animosity in her voice though. Grumpy Bob swivelled his chair around to reveal a filter machine remarkably similar to the one that had once been in McLean's office on the third floor, poured a measure into a mug with 'World's Best Dad' written on it, added a splash of milk and then held it up.

'Cheers.' McLean sniffed the brew, took a welcome sip. 'I needed that.'

'Heard someone torched Ray McAllister's place last night. You been over there having a wee look?'

'Aye, Janie texted me first thing.' McLean checked his watch, dismayed to find most of the morning already gone. No wonder he'd needed the coffee. 'Actually, I was going to ask you about that, Bob.'

'Oh aye?' The detective sergeant leaned back in his chair, folded his arms over his chest.

'We had a uniform detail guarding the house. Couple of constables out of Corstorphine nick in a squad car.' McLean filled them in on the somewhat suspicious circumstances leading up to the fire. 'I've had a word with Kenneth Stephen, and he reckons it was a Sergeant Graham who ordered them off the job. Colin Graham. You heard of him?'

As he asked it, McLean realised how stupid a question it was.

Grumpy Bob had retired long before even McLean himself, and Detective Chief Superintendent Grace Ramsay had quit the force before it was even Police Scotland. This was a question he should have been directing at the younger officers. Maybe Sandy Gregg would know.

'Only Sergeant Graham I know transferred in about ten years ago, I think it was.' Grumpy Bob rocked forward until he could reach his laptop, hammered at the keys for a moment then fetched his spectacles out of his jacket pocket and perched them on the end of his nose. 'Aye, that's right. Thought so. He came down from Grampian when his wife's work got shifted here. Think he's OK, far as I know. I've no' heard anything bad about him, that's for sure.'

'Aberdeen's Nelson's old patch though, isn't it.' Ramsay had put down her scintillating read. 'Coincidence?'

McLean took another swig of his coffee, enjoyed the bitter taste as he swallowed it down. 'You know, I never was one to believe in them.'

A hum of activity filled the incident room when McLean entered a few minutes later. The coffee had been good, but he really needed to find some lunch as well. Otherwise he knew he'd get an earful from Emma when he went home and raided the fridge.

'Any luck?' Harrison approached from the far side of the room where she'd been adding something to the whiteboard. A black and white photograph of a man's head was all McLean could make out from this distance. He needed to book an appointment with the opticians again.

'The instruction to drop the guard duty outside McAllister's house came from a Sergeant Graham. I've not had a chance to talk to him yet, but he's ex-Grampian Police, if that means anything.'

'Grampian? Like the superintendent?'

'As far as I'm aware there's just the one. Might be nothing, of course. Graham transferred down here ten years ago and by all accounts is a good cop. Our esteemed leader's only just arrived. Chances are they don't even know each other.'

'But the request to stop guarding the house should have been run by us first. I know it was late—'

'It wasn't late, boss.' DC Stringer came to join them, no doubt having overheard the conversation. He gave McLean a short bob of the head by way of acknowledgement. 'Sir.'

'How do you mean?' McLean asked.

'Well, the pile up on Gogar Roundabout happened during the rush hour. About seven in the evening. The squad car was gone from McAllister's house fifteen minutes after that, and the two cars seem to have been abandoned around eight. Or at least that was when one of the local residents first noticed them. The house fire was called in much the same time. First response was on the scene at eight seventeen according to their logs. There's no record of any call to this incident room from Corstorphine station until then. And that was just to inform us about the fire, not ask if the guard duty could be relieved, or even just tell us they'd gone.'

McLean let his focus slide past the detective constable, his mind too occupied with considering the unlikeliness of this being a cock-up. Was it time to get Professional Standards involved? Everyone hated them – uniform and plain clothes – so if they stepped in to investigate, it would minimise the friction between departments; the last thing a seriously understaffed Edinburgh Major Investigation Team needed was belligerent uniform refusing to help out when asked. Professional Standards would take their own sweet time over it though, and possibly cause more collateral damage in the process. Why did it have to be so complicated all the time? This was exactly why he'd not wanted to come back.

'. . . sort it out?'

McLean only heard the last of Harrison's words, his attention

283

elsewhere. With an involuntary shake of the head, he snapped his focus back to her. 'Sorry, what was that?'

The look the acting detective inspector gave him reminded him painfully of his grandmother, lecturing him over the kitchen table about something important as he stared out the window, miles away. 'I said do you want me to speak to this Sergeant Graham? Sort it out?'

'I . . .' McLean started, but the reason his mind had wandered finally filtered through everything else. He squinted at the black and white photograph again. Something about it seemed familiar, but he couldn't see it well enough.

'That picture.' He started to cross the room towards it.

'From the private security camera footage we got at St Michael's church.' Harrison fell into step alongside him. 'Looks like the same fellow might have been at all three murders around the times they were committed. Just need to identify him and we might well have our killer. There's a press conference organised for later this afternoon. We'll let the papers run it and see what comes in.'

McLean barely heard the last of what Harrison said. He'd seen the other two photos of course, but the low resolution and poor angle meant he'd not been able to make anything of them beyond agreeing they could well be the same person. This third picture was different. The face was a little blurred, as always happened with stills from video footage. It was washed out monochrome as it had been filmed at night, he could see that too. Even so, there was no mistaking the person who stared with fearful eyes at a camera he couldn't possibly know was there.

'I know this man,' he said. 'His name's Robert Murphy.'

43

S at in the passenger seat of the unmarked car that had brought him and Harrison over from the far side of town, McLean watched as Robert Murphy was led out of his end terrace house in Shandon and guided into the back of a squad car. In those brief moments between door and car, the middle-aged man looked utterly terrified, eyes wide and darting around the street. He didn't seem to be saying anything though, nor fighting the two burly uniformed officers who held him. Instead, it was as if he feared some invisible watcher, observing and noting his every move.

McLean recalled their first meeting, at the hotel in the St James Quarter. Murphy had been deeply paranoid there, too. They would have to tread very carefully when it came to interviewing him, although deep down McLean still didn't believe charges would be pressed, still couldn't accept Murphy was a killer. It didn't sit right in his gut. There was something else going on here.

'You want to have a look inside?' Harrison approached as the squad car departed, taking Murphy to the station to be processed and put in a cell. McLean clambered out of the car and followed her across the road. Faces were beginning to appear at windows in the neighbouring houses, a few people out on the pavement to see what all the fuss was about. It wouldn't be long before phone camera footage was plastered all over the internet. He'd given up worrying about his face showing up in such things, but it was frustrating all the same.

Stepping past the splintered mess of the front door where the arrest team had used their big red key, McLean found himself in a narrow hallway, made narrower still by a mass of boxes, stacked magazines, newspapers, and many other things generally falling under the description of clutter. The front room, whose bay window would have looked out onto a short patch of dirt before the pavement and street beyond were it not for the drawn curtains, had more of the same detritus filling it. A narrow strip of carpet led from the door to an armchair with an empty plate balanced precariously on one arm, a half-finished mug of tea on the other. Directly opposite, an old-style cathode ray tube television was still showing a children's cartoon. The wall behind it was shelved floor to ceiling and filled with books piled two deep and all higgledy-piggledy.

'Looks like something of a hoarder, Mr Murphy.' Harrison inched carefully into the room, crossed to the television and studied it for a long while before working out how to turn it off. If there was a remote control somewhere, there was no sign of it.

'If this is all his, of course. He's been in and out of care all his life. I'm guessing this was his parents' house and he inherited it. We any idea when they died?'

'His father had a heart attack about twenty years ago, mother worked at the hospital up the road until she retired five years back. She died quite recently. Lung cancer.'

McLean sniffed the air, but detected no residual smell of old cigarettes. The cornice around the ceiling had a pale yellow-brown tinge to it that might have been from tobacco smoke, might simply have been age. Then again, there were other reasons beside smoking to contract lung cancer.

'Doesn't really smell of anything.' He ran a delicate finger across the top of the nearest stack of magazines. The visible cover was a comic of some form, judging by the garish artwork. 'Strange. I'd have thought it'd be musty maybe, or damp. But all this is clean, and it's very dry. What else is there here?'

Harrison led him out of the front room, down the corridor to a decent sized kitchen diner at the rear. This was much like the rest of the house so far: piles of magazines, neatly tied to stop them toppling; cardboard boxes with illegible writing scrawled on them; books everywhere, in stacks that appeared built more for stability than ease of finding anything. Only a small area around the sink and ancient gas cooker was clear, the few pots and pans, kettle, toaster evidence of a very simple life lived within these walls.

Beyond the kitchen, a small laundry room opened up onto a back garden so overgrown it could have been a jungle. McLean thought he might have spotted a shed somewhere deep in the mess of brambles and buddleia, but it was clearly not somewhere Murphy ever ventured.

'Upstairs?' he asked, and Harrison led the way without a word.

There were two bedrooms, a small bathroom and a box room, all as cluttered as the hallway downstairs. Murphy appeared to have kept the smaller of the two rooms for himself, leaving the master bedroom as a place unwanted stuff went to die. Picking through everything was going to be a mammoth task, and yet once more McLean was left with the feeling that the kind of troubled mind that lived this way would not easily be able to lure seasoned villains like Morgan, Creegan and McAllister to late night meetings alone in abandoned churches.

'What about the loft?' He pointed up at the hatch in the ceiling. Some of the other houses in this street had been converted to free up more living space in the roof, but not this one.

'Haven't had a chance to look yet. You think there might be something up there?'

McLean shrugged. The hatch had hinges at one end, a metal hoop at the other. A quick look around the landing revealed a wooden pole with a hook on the end of it, placed carefully on top of a stack of old copies of 2000AD comic tied together with string. He hefted it up, hooked the latch and pulled. The trapdoor swung down easily, revealing a sliding loft ladder that neatly filled a slightly wider space on the floor than was necessary for one obsessive man to get from bedroom to bathroom.

'You want to go first?' he asked.

'Be my guest.' Harrison waved a hand towards the ladders. McLean grabbed the handrail and took a tentative first step, half-expecting the whole thing to collapse. When it didn't, and made no alarming creaks, he hauled himself up until his head was in the loft space. By the light filtering in from below, he could see a switch fixed to the side of a nearby beam. He reached out and flicked it on, bathing the space in bright white.

There were more boxes, more stacks of papers, more rubbish put away generations ago on the off chance it might be useful someday. McLean's gaze barely registered any of that as he climbed to the top of the ladder and stepped into a surprisingly spacious loft. He was fixated by the sight of the gable end wall. The floor there had been cleared, a chair and desk placed up against the old stonework. Above it someone had fixed a massive, triangular cork board that reached all the way to the apex of the roof. And onto that cork board they had pinned photographs, newspaper clippings, pieces of paper with that same indecipherable handwriting as was on all the boxes.

'Oh my.' Harrison emerged through the hatch as McLean trod a careful path to the wall. The top of the desk was covered in more photographs, notes, cuttings, all presumably waiting to take their place on the board. A hard bound A4 notebook had pride of place in the middle. Its cover bore the almost-neatly written name 'Father Eric O'Connell', the careful penmanship rather ruined by having several lines of black biro drawn through it so deeply that had cut through the shiny surface to the paper beneath. He reached out a hand to open it, then stopped himself. Touch nothing for now, only observe. He looked up at the wall, saw the most prominent photographs. All old men, all easy enough to name.

Kenneth Morgan.

William Creegan.

Raymond McAllister.

Archibald Seagram.

It never ceased to amaze him how much paperwork an arrest involved. Add to that the person being arrested having a long and detailed history of mental health problems and the workload could quickly multiply. McLean sat in what had been his office on the third floor, not through any sense of ownership, but because it was somewhere quiet where he was unlikely to be disturbed while he read through what limited history they had been able to pull together so far for one Robert John Murphy.

He'd known Murph's life hadn't been a happy one, but from his brief meeting with the man and their conversation in the hotel in the St James Quarter, he'd not appreciated quite how unhappy that life had been. Murphy's abuse at the hands of the priest, Eric O'Connell, was well enough known from the court case his parents had brought against the church some years after the priest's murder. What was conspicuously absent from the investigation records into O'Connell's death was any mention of the fact Murphy had been in the church when the priest had been attacked, and that he had been the one to call an ambulance. The report was surprisingly vague on who had actually discovered O'Connell lying in a pool of blood by the altar, the first red flag of many about the whole dreadful incident. Worst of all was seeing the name of McLean's old mentor, Bob 'Mac' Duff as Senior Investigating Officer on the case. The Mac he had known would never have been so slipshod. What pressure had been put on him to so monumentally mismanage this investigation?

That was a question for another time, perhaps. More salient to the day's events was the assessment of Murphy's mental health carried out before he was released from psychiatric care to go and live with his mother.

'Thought I might find you in here.'

McLean looked up from his laptop screen, the view of the open doorway blurred by his reading spectacles. He could see well enough that it was DS – no, DI Harrison who had spoken. He slid the glasses off as she entered the room, a tired expression on her face.

'Needed somewhere quiet to read through this.' He waved a hand at the screen. 'If Murphy really is our man, I wouldn't give good odds on him ever standing trial.'

Harrison walked across the room to the conference table and then dragged a chair back to the desk before sitting down. 'How so?' she asked.

McLean swivelled his laptop so that she could see the report he had been reading. 'His diagnosis is dissociative identity disorder. What we used to call multiple personality disorder when I was reading Psychology. Currently controlled with medication and regular therapy sessions. I've put a call in to his therapist, but apparently, she's away at a conference down in London right now, so it might be a while before we get any response.'

Harrison rubbed at her eyes with tired fingers. 'Well, we knew he wasn't working with a full deck. Still need to question him though. I'm just waiting for the duty solicitor to show up.'

'He had a psych evaluation yet?'

'No.' Harrison checked her watch. 'Should be later this afternoon. Then we can see whether he's going to Saughton or Bestingfield Psychiatric Hospital. Not sure which would be the better option, to be honest.'

44

Janie couldn't remember the last time she'd interviewed a suspect so clearly terrified about the whole process. True, she hadn't conducted that many interviews at all, although she'd observed plenty. Robert Murphy was her first murder suspect, and she desperately wished that one of the more senior officers had been available for the job.

He had barely spoken a word since being processed into the station, hardly even acknowledging it when he was read his rights. His history of mental health problems meant that he had to have a solicitor present for the interview whether he wanted one or not. As far as Janie was concerned that was a relief, as Murphy struck her as exactly the kind of person who would waive that right, and exactly the kind of person who needed it most. Now it was just a question of trying to get the man to say anything at all.

'Mr Murphy, as has been explained to you before, the reason for your arrest is that you have been identified as being in the vicinity of three separate crimes within the timeframe of them being committed. Three separate murders and you were close by when each of them was carried out. Do you not think that's a bit too much to be a coincidence?'

Beside her, DC Bryant sat silent, a notepad on her knee. Janie had thought that perhaps having two women do the interview would put Murphy more at ease, but so far it hadn't worked. He didn't even look up at her, had barely acknowledged the presence of either of them since being led into the room, let alone the duty solicitor sitting next to him.

'Mr Murphy, this will go a lot easier if you answer our questions. We know you were close by when Kenneth Morgan, William Creegan and Raymond McAllister were killed. Tell me, do those names mean anything to you?'

Head down, still fascinated by his hands, Murphy didn't so much as twitch as Janie spoke the names. It might have been that he was a brilliant actor, but she suspected it was more that he was too overwhelmed by events to really register what she was saying.

'We've searched your house, Mr Murphy. The loft was particularly interesting. It seems you have been doing some research into Morgan, Creegan and McAllister lately. Also Archibald Seagram. Why would someone like you even know those people? What possible interest could they be to you?'

Again, Murphy said nothing, didn't respond even to Seagram's name. Beside him, Janie could see the duty solicitor getting twitchy. Perhaps he had heard of that unholy quartet, or perhaps he was concerned for his client's mental health. They were pushing their luck questioning Murphy before he'd undergone a full psychiatric evaluation anyway.

'What about Father Eric O'Connell, Mr Murphy? Why are you so interested in him? He died forty years ago.'

Finally, Murphy raised his head. He fixed her with a gaze that wasn't hostile, yet nevertheless sent a chill through her. Janie had seen madness before, but this went beyond it. Through madness and out the other side to a kind of sanity so sharp-focused it could cut you.

'Inspector McLean,' he said.

'What about him?' Janie asked.

'I want to speak to Inspector McLean. No one else.'

Janie began to formulate a response to that, but Murphy's head had dropped forward again, his gaze once more focussed entirely on his hands. They could keep on asking him questions, but she knew that he would give them no answers.

'Interview terminated.' She read off the time and all the other necessary details before tapping the button to stop the tapes. 'We'll arrange a psych evaluation as soon as possible, but for now if you could take Mr Murphy back to the cells?'

She motioned to the waiting uniformed constable to take the man away. Murphy didn't resist, stood when he was bid to do so and allowed himself to be led. He paused only as he passed Janie, looked up at her for the briefest moment, as if he was scared she might guess all his secrets if she could look him in the eye.

'Inspector McLean,' he said, then nothing more.

'That went well, wouldn't you say?'

Still in the interview room, Janie had waited for the duty solicitor to leave before she'd sat back down. DC Bryant leaned against the wall by the door, her notepad still open, the page blank.

'Probably shouldn't be interviewing him at all, boss. Given his background, even if we did find hard evidence to convict him, he'd be in Bestingfield rather than Saughton, if you know what I mean.'

Janie rubbed at gritty eyes with the heels of both hands, hard enough to see weird red spots and little white flashes. 'You'd think that, looking at him. But according to his medical records the drug therapy he's been on is working well. There's nothing to suggest he's stopped taking it, either.'

'You think it's maybe an act? He wants to cop an insanity plea?'

Janie leaned back in her chair, surprised when it almost deposited her on the floor. Some of the interview rooms had all the furniture bolted down, but clearly this wasn't one of them.

'I don't know. I mean, he could be, I suppose. If he's been in and out of care most of his life, then maybe this is his way of getting back in after the place he was in before shut down.'

'Murdering three old men seems a little extreme, doesn't it?'

'Aye, well. You'd think so. But I've heard some tales about folk who go to extremes when they can't cope. Usually self-inflicted injuries mind, not taking it out on someone else. And the dead men, too. Why them? We know they're all connected, but how are they linked to Murphy? And how did he get each of them to go to an abandoned church, alone, at night?'

'He knows something about them we don't?'

'He'd have to, right enough. Maybe we'll turn up something from the search of his house, but it still feels wrong.'

Bryant snapped her notebook shut, stood upright. 'You going to ask the DI to talk to him?'

'I am the DI, Jessica.' Janie heard the anger in her voice, wondered where it came from. 'Sorry, didn't mean to snap at you like that. It's been a tough couple of days. And aye, I'll ask DI McLean if he wants to take over the questioning, but I don't think Murphy realises there'll have to be an audience.'

Janie had almost reached the second floor, on her way to the incident room, when her phone pinged a text. She glanced briefly at the short summons and carried on up to the next floor. DI McLean's door was wide open, but he wasn't there, presumably taken himself down to the incident room. A shame, as she could have done with a chat before facing Nelson. Then again, there hadn't been much room for misinterpretation in the text, so she carried on down the corridor to the detective superintendent's office. Its door was closed, an ominous silence leaking from within until she rapped knuckles against the wooden surface.

'Enter.' Nelson's tone reminded Janie of the headmaster at her secondary school. She'd been terrified of him at the time, but seeing him cuffed and pushed into the back of a squad car halfway through her Highers year had gone a long way towards squashing that fear. It might well have been what put the idea in her head to join the police in the first place, now she thought about it. That and the knowledge that he'd been storing indecent images of children as young as eight on his computer at work.

'Enter!' Nelson's voice again, frustration making him sound even more like old Mr Johnson. Shocked, Janie pulled out her phone as she hastily opened the door.

'Sorry, sir. Text came in just as I knocked.' It was an easy lie, and it seemed to work.

'Heard you brought someone in for the church murders.' Nelson sat back in his office chair, feet up on his desk and crossed at the ankles. If he was trying for an air of casual nonchalance, he didn't manage to pull it off. It could have been that his bollocks still hurt, of course. Maybe that was the only way he could get comfortable.

'Robert Murphy, aye. He's our man from the CCTV and security camera footage. Detective Inspector McLean recognised him.'

The angry scowl at the mention of McLean's name came on so swiftly that Janie had to stop herself from taking a step back. Nelson hauled his legs off the desk to a chorus of squeaks and farts from his chair.

'Throwing his weight around, is he? Typical.'

Janie opened her mouth to protest, her brain processing the ramifications of anything she might say just in time for her to close it again. Nelson disliked McLean, she knew that. Nothing good could come of her trying to defend him. And besides, he was far better at dealing with the likes of the detective superintendent than she was.

'So, what's the story on this man, then? Heard he was a nut job. He had a psych eval yet?'

Of course he hasn't, and you know it. Janie had already hidden her hands behind her back, now she clenched them into fists before relaxing them slowly.

'We're waiting on the psychologist to carry that out, sir. Meantime I have conducted a preliminary interview with Mr Murphy in the presence of the duty solicitor. He is . . . uncooperative would be the word, I think.'

'Sounds like an admission of guilt to me. Reckon he'll cop an insanity plea? Get himself locked up in some nice warm loony bin?'

The similarity to her conversation with DC Bryant on the matter didn't go unnoticed. Janie had her own thoughts about Murphy, but she could see how it would be nice and neat if they could pin the whole thing on someone with longstanding mental health problems. That didn't make it any less lazy detective work, and besides, something didn't sit quite right.

'It's a possibility, sir. Seems he was in an open care situation until about a year back. One of those sheltered units run by the Dee Foundation. Only when that all went . . .' She stopped herself from saying 'tits up', knowing it would either get her a reprimand from Nelson or unnecessarily excite him.

'Brilliant. So all this is McLean's fault anyway? If he'd left well alone, we wouldn't have had our workload doubled picking up all the pieces.'

Janie clenched her fists again, aware as she did so that it was a habit she'd picked up from McLean in the first place. That and counting a silent ten before answering a ranking officer.

'If it helps, Murphy has said he will talk to McLean. They've met before.'

'And you think that's a good idea? Allowing your main suspect to make demands? Set the parameters of the interrogation?'

If it gets him to talk, yes. Janie kept that to herself. Nelson's tone dripped with condescension again, so he was back on that particular approach to dealing with her. Was this what it was like to be gaslighted? It was bloody exhausting trying to second guess the man.

'I was on my way to discuss it with McLean when I got your text, sir.' She put on her best simpering smile. 'I agree it's not good to concede to a suspect's wishes. The clock's ticking on how long we can hold him without charge though. I'd like at least to have made some headway questioning him before making that call.'

'Making that call? You sound like you're in two minds about it. Surely the evidence is right there. Charge him already, get him in front of a Sheriff for god's sake. We've a press conference in two hours. Don't you think that'll go a lot easier if you've charged someone?'

And how much worse will it be when we have to tell those same journalists that we've released them? Janie once more kept her counsel on that. 'Is that a direct order, sir?'

Nelson's face creased into an angry scowl. 'I believe this is your investigation, Acting Detective Inspector. Your call.' He leaned back in his seat to another round of farts and squeaks, crossed his arms and didn't even try to keep the sarcasm out of his voice as he spoke again. 'I will, of course, back up your decision. Whatever it is.'

45

He could tell by the way she banged open the incident room door that Harrison had just been in a meeting with Detective Superintendent Nelson. McLean found the man had much the same effect on him too. She seemed to realise what she had done, pulled herself together with remarkable speed and self-control. Even so, she was muttering gently under her breath when he went over to talk to her.

'Trouble on the third floor?' He meant it as a joke, but had maybe misjudged her mood. The stare she gave him could have turned a man to stone.

'Don't. Please.' She paused for a moment, and he could almost hear the count to ten inside her head. Finally, her shoulders sagged as she let go of the tension. 'Sorry. Can't help thinking things would go much more smoothly without the senior officers getting in the way.'

'Technically you're a senior officer now.'

'Not helping, Tony.' Harrison looked past him to the rest of the room. 'We get anywhere with the stuff from Murphy's loft?'

'It's still coming in. They're cataloguing what they've got at the moment. Not quite sure what to make of it all, if I'm being honest. Most of it seems to be junk like in the rest of the house, although he's got quite an impressive collection of comics.'

'Comics?'

'A lot of rare British titles from the seventies and eighties. Independent label American stuff too. DC Stringer's having the time of his life going through it all down in evidence. They've got more space for it there, and that's where it's going to stay for a while anyway.' McLean gestured towards the tables along one wall of the room, piled with boxes. 'We've got the desk contents in here, but forensics wanted to leave the wall as is for the moment. It'll take time to decipher, if that's even possible. Murph seems to be a rather complicated fellow.'

'Murph? You best buddies or something?'

McLean shook his head slowly. 'Not really. It's just what Dalgliesh called him, when we first met. I get the feeling Mr Murphy doesn't have any friends.'

'Well, he seems to like you. Good as said he won't talk to anyone else, which made our interview earlier a lot of fun.'

'DC Bryant told me, yes. Happy to interview him, but—'

'It's not a good idea to give in to a suspect's demands. Aye, I know that. Not sure how we're going to get him to talk any other way though.'

'Maybe we should go through the items on his desk first. Get an idea as to what's going on in his mind before having another shot at interviewing him.'

'Aye, fair point. Psychologist should be here soon enough.'

They both went to the table, and McLean lifted the lid off the first box. Sat at the top, as if waiting for them to read it, the dog-eared elderly notebook seemed as good a place as any to start. He pulled it out, ran his fingers over the writing on the once-shiny cardboard cover. The scratch lines running through it were deep enough to feel through the tips of his fingers. Angry lines trying to erase the man who had abused him. When had Murphy written the name? The handwriting looked childish, the ink from a felt tip pen faded with time. There was no good reason that he could think of, but somehow the biro lines scored through it felt fresher. More recent.

'You going to open that?' Harrison's voice cut through his wandering thoughts. McLean did as he was told, flipped the cover to the first page. Inside there was more of that childish handwriting. Murphy's name, address and an old Edinburgh phone number from before the code changes had been written in the top corner of the inside, along with a date: Fourth of March 1982.

'That would have been his ninth birthday. Murphy's, that is.' Harrison leaned close for a better look. McLean tried to read the lines of looping script that more or less kept to the faint lines printed on the pages, but he'd left his reading specs in his office one floor up. He could make out the spaces between entries well enough, each new one with a date. Murphy hadn't been regular at keeping his journal, if that was what this was. But then why the name of the priest on the front cover of a diary?

'Here, you read it. I can't make head nor tail of it.' He handed the notebook to Harrison and turned his attention to the rest of the contents of the box. There wasn't much of interest, mostly newspaper and magazine cuttings without any note on them of where they had come from or when they had been written. The theme was easy enough to detect though. It was all references to organised crime in the city, loan sharks, drug dealing, people trafficking, massage parlours and prostitution, here and there a scathing takedown of some local or national politician accused of corruption or general uselessness. Every now and then he'd come across an article written by Jo Dalgliesh, but there were plenty from other journalists he'd encountered over the years.

It was only as he reached the bottom of the box that he realised Harrison had gone very quiet. Glancing across, he saw her slowly flip one page, then another and another. Her jaw had dropped, mouth slightly open as if she'd forgotten it was there. Eyes wide as she scanned the lines, every so often she would give a little shake of the head in denial at what she was reading. Or was it a shudder?

'What is it?' he asked. Then asked it again only slightly louder when she gave no immediate response. Harrison almost jumped as she came back to herself, and her face was pale when she looked at him.

'It's a record of all the times Father O'Connell abused him or the other boys in the choir. Not graphic, I don't think he probably had the words for that when he was nine, but . . .' Harrison held up the notebook, open at a point about halfway through. 'There's so much of it. Month after month. Those poor kids.'

'When was Father O'Connell attacked?' McLean asked.

'No idea.' Harrison flicked through the notebook swiftly until she hit a clean page, then skipped back more slowly to the last entry. 'Could it be twelfth of January, 1983? He's not written anything else in the book since then.'

McLean squinted at the page, wishing he'd not left his reading glasses upstairs. Then he remembered the spare pair he kept in his jacket pocket. A moment to fish them out and put them on, he took the notebook from Harrison and read aloud.

'Mum took me from school early today. She told me Father O'C had passed away from his injuries and we were to go to St Aloysius and light a candle for his soul. Pretended to be sick so I did not have to go. I will not mourn him, will not light a candle for him. He is with me all the time now. I wish he really was dead. In hell. Burning for eternity.'

When McLean looked back up from the page, it was to find that the entire incident room had fallen silent, all eyes upon him. What was that curious expression? An angel passing overhead, that was it. That made as much sense as anything. Finally, Harrison broke the quiet, or the angel reached the horizon.

'Seems like a lot of anger bottled up there. Justified, maybe.'

'Still doesn't explain why he'd start bumping off old gangsters. Or how.' McLean flipped idly through the remaining pages of the notebook, blank after that final, damning entry. Except that they weren't blank. After a gap of about a dozen sheets, the writing started up again. Leaky biro mostly, there were smudges where the ink had run, fingerprints here and there, the stains from carelessly placed mugs. The handwriting was scratchier, more chaotic and less contained by the printed lines. The first new entry began half-way down a page, as if there were some imagined previous entry above it. The date was only eight months ago.

'They have to die. They have to die. They have to die.
They. Have. To. Die. Hell wants them for what they have done.
The devil will not wait. I will not wait. I can send them to him.
If I send them to him will he set me free? Sweet child all grown up
now will you help me send them all to hell the devil wants them
the devil needs them they must pay they must die I . . .'

'What the . . .?' Harrison took the notebook from McLean's unresisting fingers. He watched her as she scanned the entry he had just read out, then the one beneath it, her face growing paler by the line. Finally she very carefully closed the book and put it down on the table.

'This is not looking good for securing a prosecution. I'm surprised his solicitor's not lining him up for an insanity plea already.' Harrison tapped a thoughtful finger on the cover for a moment. 'What do you suppose set him off though?'

'I was thinking much the same thing,' McLean said. 'He stopped putting entries in the journal around about the time this priest died. They were a record of what happened to him at the church, so that makes a certain sense. But that happened forty years ago. Now he's picked it up again. Why?'

'We'll need to go through his medical records, check when exactly he was released, when his mother died, what happened to him eight months ago.'

'Or we could just ask him?'

'You think he'd tell us? You think he even knows?'

McLean had to admit Harrison had a point. The scratchy handwriting, meandering lines, almost stream of consciousness nature of the words had the feel of some kind of psychotic episode. He'd met Murphy, and while he had been paranoid and scared, he'd been more or less lucid. It wouldn't have surprised McLean if the man had no recollection of making these garbled later entries into his old journal. Hadn't he suffered from dissociative identity disorder, after all? Maybe the medication and therapy weren't working quite as well as thought.

'He probably doesn't, but I know someone who would.'

'When I introduced you to Murph it wasn't so you could arrest him for murder, Tony. Poor wee soul wouldn't harm a fly, you know?'

They'd met in a cafe not far from the station, Dalgliesh already on her way across town for the press conference. Although it hadn't taken him long to bring her up to speed, she'd still managed to demolish the large slice of chocolate cake he'd bought for her, and made a start on his own by the time he'd finished. Did she ever actually feed herself? From the look of her, probably not.

'That was my thought too, from our brief meeting. I'm reasonably good at judging character, and I'd have put him on the meek side of the graph.'

'But the meek sometimes snap if you bend them too far, aye.' The reporter spoke through a mouthful of cake, which made the view of the busy road outside the cafe suddenly very interesting. 'Still wouldn't have pegged him for a murderer, mind. And you reckon he's behind these church deaths, too?'

'We have good reason to believe so, yes.'

'Oh, you're a tease, Tony McLean. We're having a press conference in an hour and you're still no' spilling the beans. What've you got on Murph that you're no' telling?'

If it had been his investigation, he'd have been better able to judge what he could and couldn't tell Dalgliesh. As it was, McLean didn't want to second guess Harrison on her first major case. On the other hand, they needed as much information about Murphy as they could get, and as quickly as they could get it. A little quid pro quo was always going to be necessary.

'We've CCTV footage from the nights of all three murders. Not the actual churches, but close by and in the right timeframe. Murphy is in all of them, with no good explanation as to why.'

Dalgliesh said nothing for a while, although that could have been because she was busy eating cake.

'All three murders?' she said eventually. 'So wee Kenny Morgan was done in too?'

'We've no real way of confirming that short of digging him up and letting the pathologist have another look, but aye, we're working on the assumption.'

'So why'd you not pick that up first time around?'

'His head was smashed in when the back wall of the church collapsed on top of him. Made it hard to see any sign of foul play. That and he was an old man who had a heart attack. Apart from who he was, we'd no reason to suspect it was anything too suspicious.'

Dalgliesh forked another large mouthful of cake, chewed absentmindedly. Hadn't quite finished when she spoke again. 'Fair enough. So, you've got Murph in the vicinity on all three occasions. That's quite the coincidence, I'll grant you. But I know you, Tony. There's more to it than that, isn't there?'

McLean gave a slight dip of his head to indicate that there was. 'Only so much I'm allowed to tell you, Jo. I'm not the one in charge of this investigation. Not even a real policeman anymore. Strictly consulting on this one.'

'I did wonder, when you called me. Thought you'd last a full year before going back.'

'Please don't tell me there's a sweepstake.'

'Mebbe.' Dalgliesh slurped down some coffee in a most un-ladylike manner. 'So, who's in charge then? No' Ritchie, surely. She's away with the NCA more often than not these days. Must be your new super from up north, Nelson, aye?'

'Actually, Janie Harrison's SIO. They've promoted her to acting DI, since my replacement decided he'd rather take early retirement.'

The look Dalgliesh gave him was an odd one he couldn't immediately read. Then she broke into a broad smile. 'Seems like it was only a wee while ago you took her under your wing, and here she is now bossing you about. That must be a bit strange, eh?'

McLean shrugged. 'Not really. Kirsty Ritchie came into the team as a DS, and now she's DCI. It's the natural progression of things when you're good at your job. Least it should be. I'm the only one who prefers it in the trenches.'

'Prefers?'

'Figure of speech, Jo. But we're straying off topic. Murphy. I've got to admit I never had him pegged as the killing type, but something happened to him about eight months ago that had a profound effect. You any idea what that might have been?'

'Eight months, you say?' Dalgliesh placed her fork down on the empty plate, dabbed at her lips with a paper napkin, took another noisy slurp of her coffee. 'Aye, I can think of one or two things happened to him. He lost his place at the sheltered housing complex for one. You'd know more about that than me given it was run by your old friend, Jane Louise Dee. Or at least her charitable foundation that collapsed after you showed the world what it was really up to.'

McLean had worked that much out for himself. It didn't seem enough though. 'I heard about it. He moved back into the family home though, didn't he? I've seen the place. It's a bit cluttered but nice enough. Good part of town. And he's financially secure, too. Doesn't need to work. If he can cope, then he's probably better off there than in sheltered housing.'

'Aye, you'd think that. But here's the thing about that house. It's his now, right enough. He inherited it when his mum finally lost her battle wi' the cancer. There was talk about it being sold and the money put into a fund to keep Murph in the home, but that all fell through when it closed down. Way he tells it, that was a rough few months before it all got sorted out. Lots of back and forth between the psychologists as to whether he was fit to live on his own or not. In the end they decided he could, which was a moot point by then as he'd been looking after himself and his mum just fine.'

McLean saw the house in his mind, filled with boxes, bric-a-brac, stacks of newspapers, magazines, comics. The house of a long-term hoarder, but a clean one. The only mess in the place had been the mug and plate in the living room, and that was most likely the meal he'd been eating when the police came calling.

'So his mother was still alive when he moved back in? Wasn't she in a hospice though?'

Dalgliesh gave him a look. 'She was, but it was Dee Foundation too. Closed down about the same time as Murph's sheltered housing. She lasted a couple of months at home before she passed away. So, aye. You could say he had a bit of a traumatic experience eight months ago.'

46

She had attended plenty of press conferences in her time as a detective, but Janie had never before found herself sitting at the top table. No worse than giving a speech at school assembly, she tried to convince herself as the butterflies tumbled and fought in her stomach. Perhaps skipping lunch had been a bad idea, but the thought of the station canteen's famously greasy lasagne had not appealed. A milky coffee and a chocolate bar would have to suffice. Then pizza later, she promised herself.

At least she wasn't the one having to address the assembled journalists. What was the collective noun? An irritation, perhaps? Maybe a scoop? To her mixed relief and annoyance, Detective Superintendent Nelson had announced he was going to be the one doing the talking. No doubt because they'd arrested someone, and so he could bask in the glory of a job well done despite not having lifted a finger towards the actual investigation. DCI Ritchie was here too, and rumour had it that Jayne McIntyre was actually in the building today and might put in an appearance. All of which helped to assuage the growing sense of panic as the large conference room began to fill. She spotted Jo Dalgliesh sneaking in right at the end, so hopefully that meant her meeting with McLean had gone well.

'Thank you all for coming. Let's get this done as quickly as possible, shall we?' Nelson's voice boomed across the room as he leaned too close to the microphone. It shut the audience up, which may have been his intention.

'As you all know, three bodies have been found in disused churches over the course of the past couple of months.' The detective superintendent began going over the details of each of the three deaths. Janie didn't need to listen, so she studied the faces of the journalists instead. A few of them, like Dalgliesh, she recognised. All of them looked bored. Nelson had a lecturing voice that could put hyperactive children to sleep, his delivery monotone and dull. He had mastered that politician's skill of talking with no interruptible pauses, so when the question came from the back it came mid-flow. Nevertheless, it was shouted with enough force that everyone could hear it easily enough.

'Is this the start of some kind of gang war? Are the people of Edinburgh safe?'

An uncomfortable silence filled the packed room at that. Janie risked a glance at Nelson, saw that familiar flush of anger in his cheeks, the bulge of his eyes like a frog in hot water. He was about to say something, and she knew it wouldn't be good, when DCI Ritchie reached across and pulled the microphone towards her.

'We'll have plenty of time for questions at the end, Jeremy. But in answer to that particular one, no, we don't believe these deaths are gang related. Even though the victims are all connected with the criminal underworld.'

'How can you be—?'

'How can we be sure?' Ritchie interrupted the question. The detective chief inspector sat on the other side of Nelson from Janie, so she could see them both in profile. Ritchie was all calm competence, Nelson barely contained rage. He'd be worth avoiding once this was all over, although Janie had a nasty suspicion he'd be seeking her out, however much she hid.

'I think in answer to that question I should hand you over to the SIO on the case, Detective Inspector Harrison. Janie?'

For a moment she froze. It felt like an age but was probably no more than a couple of seconds. Enough time for Janie to take in Ritchie's genuine smile and Nelson's murderous scowl. Then, as if someone else was operating from deep inside her, she reached for the microphone.

'Thank you. Yes. Well. I've seen the speculation, and believe me when I say we've been concerned about possible gang connections since the first body was found. All three victims knew each other, and all three had served time in the past for various gang-related crimes. However, we have managed to place an individual in the vicinity of all three deaths within the right timeframe. This press conference was initially called to share photofit ID of that suspect with a view to identifying him, but we managed to do that on our own in the end. A man was arrested early this morning.'

She slumped back in her seat, ready for a barrage of questions, but before any could come, Nelson had taken up the microphone again.

'Thank you, Detective Ser—Inspector Harrison.' The gap between the mistake and its correction was just long enough to leave Janie in no doubt that it had been intentional. 'We have our prime suspect in custody and are currently conducting an in-depth search of his home. Early findings connect him firmly to the three victims, and it's possible he had designs on at least one other person. You'll understand that I can't go into great detail right now, as I don't want to prejudice any future trial. I would like to say however that thanks to the hard work of our team of detectives a dangerous criminal has been apprehended and a threat to the city curtailed.'

Finished with his prepared speech, Nelson settled back into his seat and gazed out across the collected journalists, the hint of a smug smile on his face that was worse than the angry scowl as far as Janie was concerned. At the far end of the table, Sergeant Dan Hwei, the press liaison officer, stepped down off the podium with a roving microphone, ready for questions. He needn't have bothered, as they came in a series of chaotic shouts.

'Can you tell us the suspect's name?'

'What evidence is there that you've got the right man?'

'Is it true the victims all had a cross burned into their foreheads?'

This last one caught Janie by surprise, and her gaze darted over the assorted faces in search of whoever had asked it. They had released very little detail about the dead men, particularly with regards to how they had died. But then again, both Creegan and McAllister had been first discovered by members of the public. No matter how much you tried to impress on them the importance of telling no one, that sort of salacious detail had a nasty habit of getting out. She hadn't read it in any of the reports so far; the papers hadn't really been paying too much attention until the third body turned up, and that had only been a couple of days ago.

'All three men were discovered in churches. Is this a hate crime? Is it religiously motivated?'

That voice, Janie did recognise. Even from the back of the large room, Jo Dalgliesh had a way of projecting that could be easily heard over the hubbub. She could have been a great stage actress, and a lot less of a pain in the arse.

'One question at a time, please. Or you'll get no answers at all.' DCI Ritchie took control of the situation with her usual calm. 'It's true that there appears to be a religious element to these murders. We've been pursuing that as one of the lines of investigation.'

'Rumour has it your suspect was abused by a priest as a child. Can you confirm that's the case?'

That last question had been one of many cast out at the same time, and yet somehow it rose over the others and stifled them all. A hush fell on the crowd as the implications of it sank in. Janie assumed it was Dalgliesh who had asked it, given that she knew the most about Murphy. But as she scanned the back row and saw the reporter, Dalgliesh shrugged and slowly shook her head. The voice behind the words had been wrong for her, too.

'We are keeping the identity of our suspect under wraps for now,' DCI Ritchie said. 'Should he be charged later today, then his name will be released to the press. Until then, I can neither confirm nor deny that speculation.'

Janie hardly listened to the rest of the questions. It wasn't all that much of a surprise that members of the press knew exactly who they had arrested and his background. Plenty of curtains had twitched in the houses neighbouring Murphy's. They'd even had to move the cordon further down the street for a while, to keep the phone camera toting rubberneckers away. Police officers were notorious gossips, too, and not above taking the occasional bribe for information. It hurt that there should have been a leak in her first major investigation as SIO though, and it didn't bode well for Murphy if his identity was already public knowledge. Seagram would want his pound of flesh and more, even if he was currently in a cell in Saughton Prison.

'Well, ladies and gentlemen. I think that just about wraps things up for now. We will of course update you of any significant future developments.' Nelson leaned into the microphone to amplify his voice again. 'I think you'll all agree that this has been a successful investigation, and I'd like to remind you all that we have our man in custody. The city can sleep safe tonight.'

There was a switch on the side of the microphone to turn it off, but instead he tugged at the cord clipped into its base until Sergeant Hwei hurried over and took it off him. Standing, the detective superintendent tugged down his jacket to smooth out any creases, cast a final glance over the audience, then turned and stalked out of the room.

Janie had hoped to avoid Nelson after the press conference, even hanging about in the conference room until the last of the reporters had gone. Jo Dalgliesh had loitered at the back like a teenager playing hooky, giving Janie the occasional conspiratorial nod and at least one wink, but even she had left eventually. And yet, when Janie had gathered up her papers and stepped through the door at the rear of the room, the detective superintendent had been waiting for her.

'Well, that could have gone better,' he said in a tone that could have been chummy but instead came over as threatening.

'I thought they went quite easy on us, actually, sir, all things considered. And we still don't know why Murphy killed those men, assuming he actually did.'

'What do you mean by that, Harrison? Of course he killed them. He had their pictures up on the wall of his little murder den, for fuck's sake. How much more do you need?'

Janie was about to say 'some actual forensic evidence from the murder scenes' but managed to stop herself. It had taken her a few months, but she was beginning to understand Nelson now. He wasn't a good detective, but then plenty of others had told her that already. What surprised her was how bad he was at reading people, and at reading himself. She was loath to use labels on people, but narcissist fit the bill with the detective superintendent. How he'd managed to rise to DCI in Aberdeen was a mystery, and it was an indication of just how desperate they were here that he'd been picked for the post he now held.

'I want to have another crack at interviewing him, sir. Just to be on the safe side. I'll ask McLean to sit in on it, but I'll be the one asking the questions.'

Nelson's scowl came back. 'Pandering to a suspect is hardly going to get us very far, is it?'

'We have absolutely nothing from him, sir, and I really don't think sweating it out of him's going to work either. He's not some kind of hardened criminal who'll respond to threats. He's mentally unstable, even if the psychologists reckon he's fit to be charged. I'd at least like to have something from him on record before he's hauled in front of a sheriff. Everything we've got on him so far is circumstantial. It won't stand up.'

'Do I need to remind you that the clock's ticking here? We have to charge him or let him go soon. Can you see how well that'll play with that lot in there if we do?' Nelson gestured towards the conference room, even though there were no journalists left inside.

'That's another thing, sir. You heard the questions. At least one person in there knows full well who we've arrested. That means they all do, and so will Seagram and his men. I genuinely think Murphy should be in a secure ward at Bestingfield, but until that can be arranged, he needs to be in protective custody. He won't last half an hour if he's sent to general population at Saughton.'

Nelson let out a sound not unlike the one he'd made when she'd kneed him in the bollocks. 'Have you any idea how long a full psych evaluation will take to get him admitted? How much all that costs?'

'Is it more or less than a man's life, sir? And even if we don't think Murphy's is worth much, our friends in the press will, if he dies on our watch. And believe me, that's Seagram's preferred outcome to all this.'

'And just how do you figure that?'

'Seagram knows why his mates were killed but he's no' telling us. Why? I don't know, but my best bet's it's because whatever it is will implicate him in something that could get him locked up.'

'Newsflash. He's locked up already.'

'Aye, I know that. You really think that'll stop him? Murphy might be box of frogs mad, but if Seagram thinks he's killed his pals and knows some terrible secret about the four of them, then he's not going to let him live, is he?'

There was a battle going on in the detective superintendent's head. Janie could see it written plainly across his face. What she

313

couldn't understand was why he had to make everything so complicated for himself. And by extension for everybody else too. Finally, he seemed to come to some decision, even if it was with obvious reluctance.

'Fine. Do it your way. But I want him charged as soon as possible. Saughton can deal with keeping him safe until the shrinks can decide where he should be; that's their job. Just get him out of this station and off our hands.'

Janie opened her mouth to speak, but Nelson simply turned and strode off down the corridor. As if that wasn't petulant enough, it soon became obvious that he'd gone the wrong way. She stifled a sigh and went back into the conference room to let him retrace his steps without too much embarrassment. Pulling out her phone, she flicked through the contacts until she found McLean's number, sent him a quick text, then went off in search of the custody sergeant. It was going to be a long afternoon.

47

It was a while since he had last been in an interview room. Longer still since he'd been the one with the notebook staring silently at the subject, and not the one asking the questions. McLean studied Murphy as the middle-aged man sat opposite him, head down and inspecting his fingers. He'd not looked particularly healthy when they had first met, in the lobby of the hotel in the St James Quarter. But that was nothing compared to how he was now. His thin hair hung from a sweaty skull in matted lines that revealed far more scalp than they hid. His eyes, on those few occasions when he looked up, were sunken and dark. If it was possible for someone to lose a substantial amount of weight in less than a day, then Murphy had done so. He seemed gaunt and frail, closer to seventy than his actual age of fifty.

'Mr Murphy, do you remember me?'

Slowly, as if the muscles in his neck were atrophied from years of staring at the floor to avoid eye contact, Murphy raised his head and squinted. He'd not been wearing spectacles the last time they had met, but he might have had lenses in that time. So much about this man McLean didn't know, none of them knew. Not even Jo Dalgliesh, although she was probably busy digging deep into his background right now.

'You're McLean.' Murphy's voice wavered slightly as he spoke. 'You were supposed to be on my side.'

'And what exactly is your side, Mr Murphy?' Harrison asked. In theory she was the one conducting this interview and McLean was only there to support her. So far, the middle-aged man had done his best to ignore both her and his lawyer.

'You claim that the priest, Father O'Connell, is still alive and at large in the city. That's right, isn't it?' McLean tried his best to catch Murphy's eye, but it wasn't easy. Even when he answered it was to his hands, cupped together in his lap.

'I saw him. He's alive.'

'That's right, you told me before. You saw him on Ferry Road, not far from St Andrew's Church, and on Gorgie Road a couple of weeks later, close by the street where St Mark's is. What about St Michael's? You were seen walking past there a few nights ago.'

'I like to walk.'

'Aye, I know. It helps you keep the troubled thoughts at bay. What was troubling you that night, Mr Murphy? When you walked past St Michael's at close on midnight?'

'I keep seeing him. Sure, he's following me an' I don't know why.'

'Father O'Connell is following you?' Harrison asked. 'You sure it's him?'

A little colour rose in Murphy's cheeks, tiny mottling of capillaries as if he were a seasoned drinker. Or maybe afflicted with brucellosis in his youth. More likely he just wasn't used to talking to young women, certainly not used to being addressed by them.

'You can talk to Detective Inspector Harrison, Mr Murphy. She's not going to scoff at what you say. We just want to find out what's happened.' McLean tried his best to be conciliatory, all too aware that the slightest thing might push Murphy back into his reticent silence. The man wasn't well, it was patently clear. How could he have been evaluated as fit to be charged?

'Where's Jo? I want to speak to her. She understands. She believes me. Knows I'm telling the truth.'

'I want to believe you, too, Mr Murphy. But you really do need to talk to Detective Inspector Harrison here.'

Murphy stared at him for a long while, almost to the point of it being uncomfortable. McLean willed himself not to look away, kept his features bland, and waited for the man to accept that sooner or later he was going to have to talk to the young woman whose presence he found so troubling. That was his problem, McLean had worked out. Murphy was deeply shy, amongst other things. He could talk to Dalgliesh because she was as old as his mother. He could talk to McLean because he was a policeman, with the emphasis on man. He struggled even to look at Harrison, but finally managed to summon up the courage from somewhere deep inside. With the faintest of nods, aimed at McLean not Harrison, he went back to studying his hands. It was enough.

Janie saw the nod, knew it was about as good as she was going to get from Murphy right now. Beside her, McLean had fallen silent too. Time for her to try again. She took the old notebook from a bag at her side, described it briefly for the recording, and placed it on the table between them. 'Do you recognise this, Mr Murphy?'

No answer, and Murphy didn't even acknowledge that the notebook existed.

'You should do. It has your name written inside it, your address. It's a journal of sorts. The first half of it was written about forty years ago, if the dates by each entry are correct. They detail the systematic abuse you and your fellow altar boys suffered at the hands of Father Eric O'Connell.'

Was that a flicker of movement at the name? The slightest twitch? Janie pushed on to see if she could get more of a response this time.

'Father O'Connell died in 1983, of course. From injuries

sustained when he tried to stop some burglars from stealing the church silver. But you'd know that, because you were the one who found him, called an ambulance. All of this . . .' Janie laid a hand gently on the cover, obscuring the priest's defaced name '. . . and yet you still tried to save him.'

This time Murphy glanced up, locked eyes on her for perhaps two seconds. He looked like he was almost about to say something, but then he let his head drop again.

'You'd have been, what? Nine, then? Ten? And he'd been abusing you and the other boys for over a year. Christ knows how many others before that. And yet you still called it in. Still tried to save his life. That'd been me I'd've left him bleeding out. Pretended I'd never seen nothing.'

'Din't work though, did it.'

The words were so quiet, Janie almost didn't hear them. It took her a moment to parse the noise into some kind of meaning, and even then, it didn't make much sense.

'How no'? You don't feel guilty because he died, do you?'

Slowly, Murphy raised his head again, those puffy eyes fixing her with an alarming intensity. 'Because he's not dead. He's out there, and you've arrested me because of it.'

'Are you trying to tell me that Father Eric O'Connell murdered Kenneth Morgan, William Creegan and Raymond McAllister?' Janie asked. 'Because that's quite an impressive feat for a man who's supposed to be dead and would be close to a hundred years old if he wasn't.'

Again, Murphy made no indication of recognising the names. Nothing like the visible tic when the priest had been mentioned.

'I don't know who those people are,' he said.

'And yet you have photographs of them pinned to the wall in your loft, cuttings from newspapers and magazines mentioning them, notes about where they live and their daily movements. How do you account for that, Mr Murphy?'

Now some expression began to creep across the man's face. But it wasn't the guilt Janie might have expected. Not the dawning realisation that his secret has been uncovered and there's really no point in lying any more. No, Murphy looked genuinely confused. And not a little scared. His voice, when he spoke, was different. He sounded younger, more vulnerable.

'I . . . I don't go into the loft. Mother won't let me. She says it's unsafe. I might fall down the ladder and break my neck.'

'Are you sure of that, Mr Murphy?' Janie tried to get him to look at her, but he was still fixated on his hands. 'Only, we've been up there, and your fingerprints are all over the place. The photographs, the boxes, the light switch. Even this book.'

'I don't go . . .' Murphy's voice dwindled almost to nothing, his head drooping, shoulders hunched as if he was trying to make himself small enough to disappear. Janie pulled the notebook towards herself and opened it, flipped through the pages of childhood entries until she finally reached the new writing.

'And yet that's where we found your notebook. The one you kept as a boy, and then took up again just recently.' Janie turned the book around, so the words were the right way up for Murphy to read, then slid it gently across the table until it was right in front of him. 'This is your handwriting, isn't it?'

A stillness fell over the interview room then, a quiet as if someone had hit a mute button for them all. Even the mechanical whirr of the tape machine seemed to fade to nothing as Murphy reached a tentative hand out towards the open page. For no obvious reason, Janie felt a chill as if the temperature in the room had dropped ten degrees. This time, when Murphy spoke, his voice was changed. Older, stronger, deeper. A voice that made her skin crawl.

'They had to die. They deserved to die. It is His will, my sacred task. Their souls are in hell now, where they belong. Their torment shall be for all eternity.'

Slowly, Murphy raised his head until his gaze met Janie's. Gone was the slack-jawed, slightly jowly middle-aged sag of a man. It was almost as if he was a different person, his posture more certain, his eyes cold and calculating. The hand that had reached so hesitantly for the notebook now clenched into a fist placed firmly on the page.

'The last one will die soon, and then I will be free.'

Before Janie could react, McLean reached forward and tugged the notebook away. It slid from underneath Murphy's fist, the paper beginning to tear from the pressure as it came free. With a deft flick of the wrist, McLean closed it and turned it over, all in one motion, so that the scrawled-out name on the front could no longer be seen. The stare Murphy gave him might have turned lesser men to stone, but at least it took Janie out of the spotlight. Beside him, Murphy's lawyer shifted uneasily in his seat, as if his client had suddenly grown a second head.

And then, as swiftly as it had begun, the moment ended. Murphy's face went slack again, the faintest shudder running through him. His eyes widened in surprise as he saw that he was looking directly at McLean, his gaze dropping swiftly. Only then did he seem to notice one hand balled into a fist on the tabletop, and he withdrew it swiftly.

'Might my client and I have a moment?' The lawyer still wore an expression of alarm, but his professionalism was commendable. Janie reached for the tape recorder, ready to bring the proceedings to an official halt.

'I think that would be a good idea.'

48

None of them really felt like celebrating, McLean could tell. He'd experienced it before, the dull sense that while they had probably got the right guy and justice would be served in the end, this wasn't a very satisfactory conclusion to a particularly unpleasant investigation. It didn't help that Detective Superintendent Nelson seemed intent on taking all the praise, although looking around the crowded pub, McLean couldn't see the man anywhere.

He spotted Harrison over by the windows, nursing a glass of white wine and chatting with a woman he'd not met before. A civilian, by the look of her, not police. Comfortable with the assorted constables and sergeants though, so probably working in some adjacent capacity. She might even have been admin support for all he knew. He'd been out of the loop for a while.

It was a while, too, since he'd last been in this pub, but it hadn't changed much. Still a hangout for officers just off their shift, and a convenient place for a team to celebrate their wins or drown their sorrows after a loss. Having driven to the station, he was sticking to water for a change. Taking his half pint that might conceivably be mistaken for a very flat gin and tonic, he wove a careful route through the crowd. Harrison looked up as he approached, a tired smile to greet him.

'Here he is. The man of the hour.' She waved an open hand at the stool on the other side of the table. McLean sat, having first checked the seat was clean and dry. Before he could ask, the other woman had leaned across the table, hand out for shaking.

'Cerys Powell. I work at the mortuary with Tom MacPhail. Heard a lot about you, Detective Inspector.'

'You have?' McLean took the proffered hand. 'All good, I hope. And it's Tony, please. Bad enough this lot all calling me sir like I'm their teacher.'

'Tony. Fine.' Cerys picked up her glass and took a deep draught of the black Guinness inside it. Harrison played with her wine glass, but didn't drink. It looked like she hadn't touched a drop of it yet.

'Back in a mo.' She stood up, slid out from behind the table and headed off towards the Ladies. McLean watched her go. Something was bothering her, it was obvious, but he couldn't work out what. No doubt she'd tell him if she wanted to. He turned his attention back to the mortuary assistant, Cerys.

'You just work with Tom, or do you help Angus from time to time?' McLean asked as she wiped beige foam from her upper lip.

'Angus is mostly retired these days, but I help out wherever and whenever. He's the biggest source of stories about you. And all the other senior officers, of course. But mostly you.'

'I've known Angus most of my life. He worked with my gran when she was city pathologist. The mortuary won't feel the same when he finally leaves. You enjoy it there? Must be a change from Wales.'

'I don't know. A dead body's a dead body far as I'm concerned. Though I must say it's been an interesting few weeks, what with these old boys turning up with crosses burned into their foreheads. Never saw anything like that in Cardiff.'

'Careful you don't get caught talking shop. They'll force you to buy the next round.'

'Is that the rule? Thanks for letting me know.'

'Usually at these things one of the higher pay grades gets the drinks in.' McLean looked around for anyone above the rank of sergeant. 'Looks like Nelson's a no show.'

'No great loss,' Cerys said. 'Man shouldn't be in charge of a traffic sign, let alone a whole department.'

The vehemence in her tone took McLean by surprise. True, Nelson wasn't overly liked in the station, but it seemed unusual for someone like the mortuary assistant to be so bitter about him. When had they even met?

'That sounds a little . . . personal?'

Cerys had her pint in both hands, but McLean noticed the glance towards Janie's untouched glass of wine. The briefest flick of the eyes that most would probably not see, let alone understand.

'He tried something on?' he asked. 'With Janie?'

'Just out there.' The mortuary assistant threw her head back towards the window and the darkened street beyond. 'Same night he made her up to acting DI after she found that fetish brothel or whatever it was. He was pissed out of his skull, and Janie kneed him in the bollocks for it, but it should never have happened, see? Men like that. They think they can get away with anything. And most of the time they can.'

'You saw this happen? It wasn't just something Janie told you?'

Cerys eyed him suspiciously for a while before answering. Was there something similar in her own past? Maybe that was what had driven her from Wales all the way to Scotland in search of a new life.

'I saw it. Most of it. The important part at least. Where he grabbed her, tried to drag her back into that little alley and she gave him what he deserved. Told her I'm happy to back her up if she wants to make a formal record of it, but she doesn't want to rock the boat. Only, that's how they get away with it, isn't it?'

The anger in Cerys's voice couldn't be denied. There had to be a reckoning with what Nelson had done, but McLean was all too aware of how tricky that could be.

'In an ideal world he'd be sacked for that. Clear evidence from the assaulted and a reliable witness. At the very least it'd be disciplinary proceedings. Professional Standards would get involved.'

'Professional Standards?'

'The police who police the police, if you like. Used to be called The Complaints. They're more often concerned with bent coppers taking bungs, or nicking stuff from evidence and flogging it. But sexual assault is definitely in their remit.'

'So why's he still superintendent then? Why's he still in a job at all?'

McLean opened his mouth to answer, but was interrupted by the subject of their conversation returning from the Ladies.

'You two look right pally.' Harrison slid into her seat beside Cerys, picked up her wine glass, looked at the contents and then put it back down again. McLean glanced at the mortuary assistant to see if she was going to say anything, but she only shook her head slightly and nudged her companion.

'Still serving it warm, are they? I'll go get you some ice cubes if you want.'

'Nah, it's OK.' Harrison pushed the glass carefully to the centre of the table. 'Think I might give it a miss. Promised myself a pizza tonight, and I think I've earned it right enough.'

'Pizza, eh? Girl knows how to celebrate.' Cerys knocked back her pint and reached for her coat. 'Let's the two of us get away from all these coppers, right?'

'Should probably get a round in first. Since this is my investigation we're all celebrating.' Harrison reached for her bag, but McLean held up his hand to stop her.

'Hope you don't mind, but I stuck some money behind the bar for the team already. Figured your Detective Inspector's salary probably hasn't kicked in yet.'

'Who knows? Maybe it never will.' Harrison managed a weak smile. 'But thank you all the same, sir . . . Tony, sorry.'

'No bother.' McLean eyed his glass of water without enthusiasm. 'Think I'll maybe head home too. Let this lot blow off some steam. There's still plenty to do tomorrow.'

Mrs McCutcheon's cat greeted him with a look of utter disdain as he let himself into the kitchen. McLean was used to it, although the similarity between the cat's expression and that of Detective Superintendent Nelson was remarkable. For a while now, he'd wondered why Nelson hated him so much, but his conversation with the new mortuary assistant, Cerys, went a long way towards explaining the tension.

The noise of water splashing into the kettle hid his weary sigh. It was bad enough that half of the station had thought he and Harrison were carrying out some kind of ill-advised affair despite his every effort to give the lie to such rumours. That Nelson had at first thought Janie fair game because of it, then held her refusal of him against McLean seemed doubly unfair. It explained a great deal, though, and was going to be a tricky minefield to negotiate without at least someone losing a limb. Of the three of them, he knew who he would prefer to be sacrificed, but Nelson was also the most senior.

'Thought I heard the door.'

McLean turned to see Emma. She was leaning on the table for support, but had come into the kitchen on her feet rather than using her wheelchair. The sight of her like that made his stomach flip. So strong, so determined to fight all that the world had thrown at her.

'Sorry about being late. The team all went for a drink to celebrate.'

'Aye, I know. You texted me, remember?' Emma stood up straight, shuffled around the table to where he stood. She kept one hand knuckle down to the surface for balance. 'And it's not that late, really. Can't have been much of a celebration if you're home already.'

McLean shrugged. 'A man's been arrested and charged, but, well, it's complicated. Doesn't quite feel like the win it should be.'

'And you can't tell me any details, I know.' Emma reached out with her free hand and rubbed his back. Her touch felt warm, even through his jacket. A welcome soothing relief from a day of frustrations.

'Tea?' he asked.

'Best make a pot. Rose is in the library, and you know how she goes through the stuff.'

McLean did as he was told, hopeful that there might be some cake or at the very least biscuits to go with the tea. He'd not picked up a takeaway on the way home, and lunch was but a distant memory. How easy it was to slip back into old habits.

Through in the library, the medium stood peering at the books, face so close to their spines she might have poked them with her nose. When she saw him enter, bearing a fresh pot of tea and a mug for himself, she beamed a great smile.

'Tony. How wonderful. Em reckoned you'd not be home for hours yet.'

'Not as heavy a celebration as I was expecting. Plus, I had the car, so couldn't really drink anyway.' The McLean of old would have left the car at the station and got a taxi, of course. Who was this imposter in his home? Then again, the McLean of old lived in a tenement flat not more than a quarter mile from the pub where they'd all been drinking. The McLean of old would have ended up with half of the detective constables sleeping off their drunken stupor on his living room floor. Times changed.

'Is that more tea?' Rose asked. She had one slim book in her hand which she carefully returned to the shelf before crossing the room to where a low table sat in front of the sofa. A tray already lay there, and she busied herself tidying it up and making room for the replacement. Emma walked slowly in as McLean was pouring, but he had learned well enough to let her do her own thing until she asked for help. Sure enough, she made it to one of the high-backed armchairs before falling into it with a creak of old springs and a quiet sigh.

'More therapy, or was this just a social visit?' McLean asked as he handed Rose a cup.

'Can it not be a bit of both?' The medium gave him a wink. 'Now, what have you been up to that warranted a celebration?'

McLean took his own cup of tea, along with a couple of chocolate Hobnobs, and settled into a chair before answering. 'We identified a suspect, arrested them and then charged them. Can't really say much more about it than that, since I'm only working the case as a consultant.'

'I quite understand.' The medium took a delicate sip from her cup, pinky finger pointing out in a deeply exaggerated manner. 'And how does it feel to be back at work, Tony? Even if it is only in a consultative role.'

'Strange, really. Everyone treats me as if nothing's changed. Apart from the new boss, who'd be happy to see the back of me. Anyway, the arrest we made was the case I was called in to consult on, so chances are that's me done for now.'

'So soon?' It was Emma who spoke, and she hastily added 'that didn't come out how I meant it to, sorry' before falling silent again.

'No offence taken. I'll be back there again tomorrow anyway, helping out where I can. Probably end up in the Cold Case Unit with Bob and Dagwood. And Ramsay, too.' Saying the retired detective chief superintendent's name reminded him of their last conversation, and it occurred to McLean that there was another good source of information from the city's murky past sitting on the sofa just opposite him.

'Rose, did you ever hear of a fellow called Eric O'Connell? Catholic priest over Craiglockhart way. Died in 1983, I think it was.'

The medium gave him one of those knowing stares of hers, head cocked ever so slightly to one side. Of course she knew about the priest. She knew about everything. The only question was why had it taken him so long to ask her?

'Eric O'Connell.' Rose put her cup back in its saucer and placed both carefully down on the table. 'Now there's a name I've not heard in a very long time.'

'But you have heard it, I assume.'

'Oh yes indeed. Eric and I locked horns many a time. He was quite the firebrand when he was younger. One of the country's top exorcists, you know.'

'He . . . What?'

'Oh, I know. Most Catholic priests can perform an exorcism if asked. But there are those who specialise in it, go searching for the demons and root them out. Eric was one of a group who travelled all over Europe plying his grim trade.'

'So, what happened to him then? How did he end up at St Aloysius?'

'Well now, that's quite the tale.' Rose fell silent for a moment, settling into her seat. McLean gave her the time she needed. He knew how much she liked to put on a show.

'When I first met Eric, he was very devout. Bright, too. As sharp as a tack, but with that central certainty I've seen in a lot of his kind where God is concerned. He came from an Irish family, but they'd settled in Edinburgh before he was born. He studied for the priesthood here, and developed a keen interest in demonology. That's how our paths crossed, naturally enough.'

'Naturally.' Emma's voice rose from the depths of her chair, reminding McLean that she was there, and listening. And sceptical, if you could read so much into the stress of a single word.

'I have long been fascinated with the workings of the Catholic

Church, especially when it comes to their dealings with . . . how might I put it? The forces of evil?' Rose paused for a sip of tea. 'I have quite the collection of scholarly works on the subject. Eric bought a few. He didn't have much money though, so sometimes we bartered. Or I'd let him borrow them in exchange for conversation. He always tried to convert me, bless him.'

'And he became an exorcist?' McLean prompted. He recognised the look on Rose's face. That far-off gaze as she slipped into not-so-relevant memories. She fixed him with a stern glare that swiftly melted into a warm smile.

'Indeed he did. So impressed his superiors they invited him to join their specialist team. A Catholic Flying Squad, as it were. He moved away, first to London and then all over the world. But occasionally his work would bring him back to Edinburgh, and we'd always have a cup of tea. Catch up. You know how it is.'

'So, what happened to him then? How did he end up back here and abusing boys?'

'Well now, Tony. That's the nub of it, isn't it. Something happened to him. I'd hazard a guess that an exorcism went wrong, but I know how little truck you hold with such things. Whatever it was, though, it changed him. He fell into bad habits. Not just the child abuse, although that was shocking enough. I didn't know about that until after he died, and even then, the church hushed everything up so well barely anyone knew. He was expelled from his order and sent home, essentially. I think they thought he couldn't do much harm at St Aloysius, that he'd be able to repent his sins and adopt the simpler life of a parish priest. But he was drinking heavily by then, and gambling money he didn't have. When I tried to help him, he shut me out. Called me all manner of rude names.'

'Can't imagine you standing for that,' McLean said.

'I did what I could, but sometimes you have to walk away. Sometimes I wish I'd tried harder, but there were plenty other things to keep me occupied. This city was a wild place in the early eighties. And then I heard he'd died.' Rose fell silent again, her gaze not quite on McLean but focussed on a point behind his left shoulder. Or maybe forty years in the past. Finally she looked straight at him.

'I think I understand why your celebrations this evening were curtailed. The boy who found him half dead beside the altar. Would I be right in assuming he wasn't in the church for his spiritual salvation?'

'Indeed not. Whoever it was attacked O'Connell stopped him from abusing the boy that time, but we've evidence to suggest he'd already been doing it for months, possibly years before that.'

'And yet the wee lamb still called an ambulance? How ingrained the urge to help, to do good, is in some people.' Rose paused a moment, her gaze unfocussed again. McLean had the impression it was all an act, as so much of the medium's behaviour was. Had she been waiting for him to ask his question? Had she known all along?

'That poor wee boy. He'd be all grown up now. Middle-aged. That's if he even made it to adulthood. So many victims of that kind of abuse never do.'

'Oh, he's still alive. Not sure he's had such a happy life though. And now he's convinced O'Connell never died, is still out there, stalking him.'

'Poor sod,' Emma said, her voice so quiet McLean almost didn't hear it. 'No wonder you didn't feel much like celebrating.'

'I never . . .' He started to deny it, then gave up, shrugged. 'What I don't get is why he did what he did. I've seen abuse like that have terrible effects on the victims, but this lashing out seems so focussed, so deliberate. Almost as if . . .'

Rose was staring at him with that half smile on her face again, her head cocked to one side like an inquisitive puppy.

'Christ, but I can be slow on the uptake sometimes. Gambling, you said? Money he didn't have?' McLean shoved his hand in his pocket, looking for his phone so he could call Harrison, or at the very least text her.

'I think it can wait until the morning, can't it?' Rose reached across the table and laid a large hand on his arm, holding it in place for a moment before letting go. 'Let poor Janie have one evening off, won't you? I think she's earned it.'

49

Rain slowed his journey to the station the following morning, and an accident on Melville Drive didn't help. As he slowed to pass the scene, waved on by a bedraggled uniform constable, McLean saw a couple of cars angled-on to the direction of traffic, a third on its side with a nasty-looking dent in its roof, broken glass everywhere. Memories of the night his old Alfa had been written off came unbidden to his mind, although that had been a snowstorm rather than this incessant rain, and despite what everyone thought, he knew he hadn't lost control.

The incident room bustled as he entered, considerably later than he'd have liked, but it didn't have the energy about it associated with an ongoing investigation. Not surprising, given that everyone thought they had their man locked up. Now came the slog of preparing evidence for the Procurator Fiscal, so that Robert Murphy could be put on trial. Unless further psychiatric evaluation deemed him unfit, and he was instead sent to the Bestingfield secure hospital in the borders. On balance, McLean favoured the latter option. Murphy's had not been a happy life, and McLean doubted it would be a long one should he end up in jail.

'Morning, sir—Tony.' Harrison smiled at her mistake as she greeted him. 'I'll get used to that eventually, sure I will.'

'Some things are drummed into you from an early age, I know. You get your pizza last night OK?'

It was meant to be a light-hearted comment, but the acting detective inspector's reaction was not what he'd expected. She looked momentarily flummoxed, for want of a better word.

'Aye, we did,' she managed eventually. 'Not sure about the rest of this lot though. A few sore heads this morning.'

McLean looked around the room, seeing detective constables, admin staff and a few uniformed officers all looking fairly much the same as any day.

'Well, I'm not sure if it's important, but I had a word with Rose last night. About Father O'Connell.'

For a moment Harrison looked flummoxed again, so maybe that was what she was doing this morning. Then realisation dawned. 'Oh, right. The priest who abused Murphy. What did Rose have to say about him?'

'Well, apparently, he was part of an order that specialised in exorcism. Quite the high-flyer until something went wrong. Left him a changed man, according to Rose. And not just abusing boys. Seems he developed a fondness for drink and gambling.'

'I thought priests were meant to be, I don't know, godly? You'd think someone higher up would've been keeping an eye on him, wouldn't you?'

'The Catholic Church has a history of covering these things up, Janie. They're better at admitting it now, but O'Connell died forty years ago, remember.'

'Aye, I guess. So, what's the priest got to do with this anyway?'

'Well, I'd have thought it would have been obvious, wouldn't it? Although I say that now, but I only saw it last night after speaking to Rose. The people who killed O'Connell were never found, and I use the plural advisedly. Murphy didn't see them, and wasn't even sure it was more than one person involved, but what if it was a gang of them? O'Connell was gambling, had debts he couldn't pay. Who's he going to owe money if his god's not looking out for him when the horses cross the finish line?'

Harrison's face scrunched into a frown. 'You think Seagram and his pals went round the church to collect? Things got a little out of hand, and O'Connell ended up with his head smashed in against the altar. Then they panicked, nicked the silver and ran off, leaving him to die.'

'It's a theory,' McLean said. 'Fits the timescale, too. That would be when Seagram was beginning to build his empire, still doing his own dirty work. And those three – Morgan, Creegan and McAllister – were all part of his crew then.'

Harrison went for a different expression this time, not so much flummoxed as unconvinced. 'I don't get it. Even if it's true and Seagram and his pals were the ones who killed the priest, why would Murphy track them down and murder them? Surely he'd be wanting to thank them all. I don't know, buy them a drink or something. They saved him from his abuser. And why go after them now? All these years later?'

McLean leaned against the nearest desk, crossed his arms. 'As to your second question, I suspect that has a lot to do with his being kicked out of sheltered accommodation, moving back into the family home and then looking after his mother until she died of cancer a couple of months later. You saw the entries in his note-book. They start up again around the time she died. Maybe he found it when he was looking through all his parents' stuff and it sparked a memory. Tipped him over the edge.'

Harrison gave a half-hearted nod to accept the plausibility of the theory without embracing it enthusiastically. 'Still don't get why he'd kill them all, though.'

'The mind's a curious thing, especially when it's broken. Murphy sees O'Connell as an important figure in his life. Yes, for bad reasons, but still important. He identifies with him, in many ways becomes him. Avenging his death is something of a quest, an obsession even.'

Harrison's face told eloquently of the doubt in her mind. 'It's quite a stretch, though. And even if it is the reason. Even if Murphy really is our killer. How did he do it?'

'How bothers me too. How did he persuade them each to go alone to a church? Why would they do that and not take some of those young lads with them for backup? And you've seen Murphy. He's a weed. OK, they've all got twenty years on him, but any one of his victims could have broken him in half. Ray McAllister would've turned him into a bloody pulp.'

'Well, none of them are going to be able to tell us, and I doubt Murphy's going to let on. Seems like there's only one person we can ask,' Harrison said. 'Think we need to go and have a word with Archie Seagram, don't you?'

McLean had gone ahead to the car park to unplug Emma's Renault while Harrison phoned the prison and made the necessary arrangements to interview a prisoner on remand. He was just about to climb into the car when the back door to the station swung open with force and the acting detective inspector stormed out with a fury that would have done a Hollywood actress proud.

'What's up?' he asked as she reached the car.

'Can you believe they let Seagram out on bail last night and nobody bothered to tell me? I'm only the bloody SIO on this case.'

McLean didn't have the heart to point out that Seagram's arrest had been a Vice operation and Jo Dexter was senior investigating officer. All the same, it would have been polite at the very least.

'They say why? I mean, he was determined to go to prison when he was interviewed.'

'I didn't even know you could apply again so soon after telling

335

the sheriff you didn't want it, but this is Seagram we're talking about, and he's represented by Fraser MacFarlane.' Harrison played with her hands while she spoke, a sure sign that she was angry.

'Probably heard that we'd charged Murphy with murdering his friends. No point him being locked up if the boogeyman is behind bars.'

'Cynical, but right. Apparently, he's been fitted with an ankle tracker and has to report in to his local nick every day. He'll still stand trial, but Christ only knows how long that'll take to come round. And the whole case relies heavily on witnesses who were trafficked here. That means they're illegal immigrants, technically. Who knows what the system will do to them before they can testify? How well can we protect them from Seagram's men?'

'Both questions for DCI Dexter's team, and I'm sure Jo will be right on top of it all. It's a setback, I agree, but don't sweat it, Janie. I'd worry more about poor Robert Murphy.'

'He's meant to be segregated from general population. I specifically asked he be placed under protection. He should be OK.' Harrison's voice wavered as she finished the sentence, more so when she added, 'Shouldn't he?'

'Remember this is Archie Seagram we're talking about. He's been one step ahead of us his entire career. Getting at a prisoner wouldn't be difficult for him. Even one in protective custody.'

'Shit.' Harrison set off towards the station door again. McLean paused to lock the car, catching up with her as she reached the bottom of the stairs. She'd covered quite the distance in her anger-fuelled haste.

'Hold up a moment, Janie. Some of us aren't as young as we used to be. And it's not as if Murphy's going anywhere in a hurry.'

'We need to get him out of there and into somewhere safe. Not entirely sure where just yet, but—'

'Ah, you're there, boss. Hoped I'd catch you.'

They both looked up to see Detective Constable Bryant at the second-floor landing. Her normally cheerful face was as much a picture of worry as Harrison's.

'What's up, Jessica?'

'It's the prison. There's a problem. Robert Murphy.'

'He's been attacked already?' McLean asked. Perhaps it was unsurprising that Seagram would move so quickly. There were plenty in the prison who'd happily do his bidding, safe in the knowledge that they would be well rewarded. The question still remained as to who had told him about Murphy in the first place, but that was something to worry about later.

Bryant's worry turned to confusion. 'Aye, but . . . How did you know? I've just had the call through now.'

'Call it intuition. Was it bad? Is he alive?' McLean reached the top of the stairs a little behind Harrison and considerably shorter of breath. Bryant had her phone clutched in one hand as if she'd not had time to put it away in the rush to bring them the bad news.

'Far as I know he's still alive, aye sir. But they've taken him to the Western General so it must be bad.'

McLean looked out over the railings and down the two flights of stairs to the ground floor. A shame Bryant hadn't found them a couple of minutes earlier.

'OK. Get in touch with the prison and let them know we'll be over soon. Might as well talk to them directly first. Give the doctors time to deal with poor old Murph.'

50

His Majesty's Prison, Edinburgh. Saughton to all those who knew and loved it, sitting in the shadow of Corstorphine Hill to the west of the city centre. McLean had visited it plenty of times in his career, and every time felt like one too many. No pool car available, he'd taken Emma's little Renault Zoe across town, Harrison silently fuming in the passenger seat most of the way. He didn't try to wheedle a conversation out of her, knew all too well the stress when a neatly ordered investigation suddenly collapsed before your eyes.

DC Bryant's phone call and acting DI Harrison's warrant card got them through to the staff car park and on into the body of the prison itself. There was always a tension about the place, but the air felt particularly charged in the aftermath of a violent attack, half the wings locked down and prison officers bustling around in groups. McLean had the distinct impression the last thing they wanted was to have to deal with a couple of detectives as well. No one was actually rude to them, but they were ushered into a waiting room, left with assurances that the deputy governor would be with them soon, but without any offer of coffee.

After a few minutes of silent waiting, a middle-aged woman appeared at the door opposite the one they had entered. She directed her words towards McLean. 'Detective Inspector Harrison?'

'That'd be me.' Harrison stood up, crossed the room. 'This is my colleague, Detective Inspector McLean.'

'Two DIs? This must be important.'

'I'm technically retired,' McLean said. 'Just consulting on this case.'

'Retired?' The woman's tone was sceptical, and she stared at him for a moment before remembering herself. 'Rosalind Wyse. I'm the deputy governor. I take it this is about the prisoner assault?'

'Robert Murphy, aye,' Harrison said. 'Can you fill us in on the details?'

Wyse sighed, her shoulders slumping as she gestured for the two of them to follow her. Through the door, a short corridor led past a few empty offices. At the end, a larger room housed a couple of desks and a number of video screens mounted above a console. The deputy governor waved them in the direction of a couple of seats on the wrong side of one of the desks, sliding in around behind it to sit down herself.

'Murphy is . . . was . . . on the secure ward. Just like you requested. We'd probably have put him there, anyway, given who he's alleged to have murdered. Even if there wasn't a price on his head, there's plenty people in here would shiv someone like that. Easy way to curry favour with Archibald Seagram, offing the man who killed his best mates, right?'

'So, what happened?' Harrison asked. 'We only heard he'd been attacked.'

'Sorry. I thought you'd been briefed.' Wyse shifted uncomfortably in her seat. 'Aye, he was. Early this morning. Still no' sure how it happened, but someone got into his cell when it should have been locked down. Beat him unconscious.'

'Do you know who did it?' McLean asked. The deputy governor didn't need to speak to give him his answer. He could see it clearly in her expression, the slump of her shoulders.

'That's the nightmare of it, no. We didn't even find him until one of the officers unlocked his cell this morning. Found him smashed up on the floor, lying in a pool of his own blood. We thought he was dead.'

'What about CCTV?' Harrison hooked a thumb over her shoulder to the console and screens.

'I've been going over that since we found him. There's no camera in his cell, but the corridor outside is well enough covered. And it's not as if you can wander around the building after lights out anyway.'

McLean decided it best not to point out that you could if you were a prison officer on duty. So far Wyse was being helpful. Harrison must have read his thoughts and kept her criticism to herself too.

'I take it that's not proved much help,' she said instead.

'There's nothing to see at all, which is troubling in itself. Officers should be walking that corridor regularly during the night shift and that should show up on the camera. There's going to be a few embarrassed faces and quite a lot of disciplinary action, mark my words.'

'So, what time did he get taken to hospital, then?' Harrison asked, again taking the diplomatic line.

'He was discovered around half-six. On-site medical team did their best, but it was obvious he needed more than we could give him here. Ambulance took him off at a quarter-past seven.'

McLean didn't need to look at his watch to know that it had then taken the prison the best part of five hours to inform them at the station. 'Why did it take so long to tell us? DI Harrison is SIO on the team that sent Murphy here. Shouldn't she have been informed straight away?'

Wyse rubbed at her temples again, but not for so long. Her gaze flicked from Harrison to McLean and back again, but her expression was one of confusion rather than guilt.

'I don't understand. You're saying you're the Senior Investigating Officer? Not Detective Superintendent Nelson?'

'Nelson's Edinburgh Region Chief for Specialist Crime Division. He oversees all of the investigations in its remit. He's not in charge of them though.'

Wyse shrugged. 'Well, he's the one I was put through to when I called this morning. I'm sorry he never passed the message on.'

The journey to the Western General took longer than it should have done, bad traffic and worse weather combining to slow everything to a walking pace. Neither Harrison or McLean said much, each of them digesting the implications of what the deputy governor had told them, both about Robert Murphy and Detective Superintendent Nelson. In the end it was McLean who broke the silence, as they parked the car.

'Your friend, Cerys, told me about what happened, the night the Vice team celebrated their win.'

Harrison said nothing as they walked to the front door, only nodded that she understood. Inside, the hospital was its usual frenetic self. McLean found himself reaching for a warrant card he no longer carried as the two of them approached reception. He needn't have bothered.

'Detective Inspector McLean. It's been a while, has it not?' The nurse behind the desk smiled at him with genuine warmth. 'It'll be about the poor fellow brought in from the prison, will it?'

'Robert Murphy, aye.' Harrison had pulled out her warrant card, but the nurse waved it away.

'He's in one of the private rooms at the back of the west wing. You can't miss it, there's a constable on the door. Touch and go for a while there, but I think he'll pull through.'

'Touch and go?' Harrison echoed the nurse. 'How badly was he injured?'

'Och, you'd have to speak to the doctor about that, but I know he went into cardiac arrest a couple of times. They even got a priest in to say last rites. Can you imagine?'

McLean could, although mention of a priest gave him an uncomfortable chill in the pit of his stomach for some reason. He thanked the nurse, assured her that he knew the way well enough.

'What's the rush?' Harrison asked as she trotted to keep up with him down the shiny linoleum-floored corridors.

'I've got a bad feeling about this,' was all he could say. That was all it was: a bad feeling. But he'd had them plenty of times before, hadn't he? And there was usually a reason.

As the nurse on reception had said, a uniform constable sat outside a closed door to a private room. He was doing something with his phone, probably playing a game or chatting on social media, but he noticed the two of them coming and hurried to his feet.

'Sir, Janie—sorry. Ma'am. Nobody said . . .'

'At ease, Barry,' Harrison said. 'How's the patient?'

'Unconscious when they wheeled him in there. All hooked up to machines and stuff. Whoever had at him gave him a proper going over. Don't think I've ever seen anything like it, an' I've worked traffic.'

'Is anyone in there with him now?' McLean asked. Some of the private rooms had windows onto the corridor, so you could see what was going on inside. This wasn't one of them.

'Aye, no. Last one out was the priest. Nobody else been in since then.'

'The priest's gone?' McLean asked.

'Aye. About half an hour ago. Full blown Catholic black robes and stuff. Think they got him to do last rites or something? Y'know, in case he didnae make it?'

McLean went to open the door, but the constable stopped him and produced a clipboard and pen. 'You'll have to sign in first, sir. Sorry.'

'Never apologise for being right, Barry.' McLean looked at the sheet of paper, a list of doctors and nurses, and then one final name scribbled at the bottom. The priest, presumably. He signed himself in, handed the clipboard to Harrison. It was only as he was reaching for the door handle that what he had seen sank in.

'The priest. What did he look like?' he asked.

The constable shrugged. 'About your height. Thin face. Dark hair a wee bit on the long side and greasy, you know? Creepy eyes, an' all. Like he was looking into my heid an' judging me, ken? Mind all priests give me the heebie-jeebies anyway.'

'He say anything to you?'

'No' really. He kind've grunted when I gave him the clipboard tae sign.'

'You saw him go in?' McLean asked.

'No. Figure he was already in there wi' the doctors when I got here. Nobody else in after that. Is it important? I got him tae sign oot proper, like.' The constable nodded at the clipboard.

'Give me that a minute, Janie.' McLean peered closely at the last name. Difficult to read, as the handwriting was scratchy. He'd seen that script before somewhere recently, and it took a while to work out where. At the same time as it clicked, he also deciphered the name. He showed the sheet to Harrison again.

'Tell me that says Eric O'Connell. And it's the same handwriting we saw in Murphy's notebook.'

As Harrison stared at the page, McLean pushed open the door. He knew what he was going to see, even as his brain failed to parse any logic in the situation. One step into the room and he stood at the end of the bed, staring at the white sheets, the drip bottles and tubes. Everything needed to keep a very seriously injured man alive.

Except that the bed was empty.

Murphy wasn't there.

51

'Get onto control. We need to find out where Seagram is and warn him there's a threat to his life.'

McLean cursed the lack of pool car that had left him driving Emma's electric Renault across town. The unmarked police cars all came with flashing lights hidden in the grille, and sirens that could be used to force a way through traffic. The Zoe had nothing so useful, and while he might toot the horn, he doubted anyone would pay him much heed.

Beside him, Harrison had her phone out and was already making calls. She hung up as they reached a set of traffic lights and once again ground to a halt.

'Already done. We'd be better heading straight out to his place though, don't you think? That's where he'll be.'

'Good point. You know where he lives?'

Harrison took up her phone again, made another call. By the time she had the answer, they'd moved perhaps a couple of hundred metres down the road and were stuck at another set of lights. She let out a little yelp of surprise as McLean took the briefest of opportunities to execute an illegal U-turn.

'How the hell does someone who's meant to be at death's door get up and walk out of a guarded room in a hospital, and then just disappear?' she asked once they were moving a little faster in the opposite direction.

'I haven't got the faintest idea,' McLean said, although he had a nasty suspicion Madame Rose would have some theories on the matter. 'We can worry about the how of it once we've found him. Meantime, our best bet is he's going after Seagram. We wanted to talk to him anyway, so I guess this is two birds with one stone.'

Traffic slowed again as they reached the start of the Queensferry Road. McLean eyed the range indicator nervously, although the car still had plenty of charge in it. More than enough to get to Broxburn and the address where Seagram lived. It was lucky they were making this journey at midday, rather than trying to do it come rush hour.

'The name on the check-in sheet. Eric O'Connell. That's not a coincidence, is it.' Harrison voiced her words as a statement, not a question.

'You know me, Janie. I don't believe in coincidences. That's far too on the nose to be anything but deliberate though.'

'But why?' Harrison shook her head.

'The constable on guard duty. You know him, right?'

'Barry? Aye. Not well, but we used to bump into each other on football duty sometimes.'

'He's reliable?'

'Never heard otherwise. Seemed competent enough when we worked together. Knows the job and takes it seriously.'

From Harrison that was high praise indeed. 'So, what he told us about the priest . . . He's not making that up to cover his arse?'

'Why would he?'

'That's what I thought. Just trying to get my head around what's happening. Nothing seems to make sense though. I mean, even if Murphy made a sudden miraculous recovery, he couldn't have walked out of that room without being seen. And your pal Barry says the only person to leave who wasn't a doctor or a nurse was the priest who claims to be O'Connell.'

'Who it can't be,' Harrison said. 'Because he's dead. And even if he wasn't, he'd be pushing a hundred. That doesn't match the man Barry saw at all.'

'You ever see a photograph of O'Connell from the time when he died?' McLean asked as he accelerated onto the dual carriageway north of Cramond Bridge. 'Because the description matches him from back then pretty closely.'

'But that . . .' Harrison didn't finish the sentence.

'Makes no sense, I know.'

Neither of them had anything to add to that, settling into their own silent thoughts as they covered the miles to Broxburn. Harrison's phone pinged the arrival of a string of texts at measured intervals, but whatever they said she didn't feel the need to share. McLean followed the instructions on the sat-nav, through the centre of Broxburn itself and then out past the massive earth bings left behind by the shale mines. Along a narrow country lane flanked by well-tended hedges, they arrived finally at a wide entrance to a substantial property set far back from the road.

Through an open set of heavy iron gates of a kind McLean would more associate with an industrial premises than someone's home, an arrow straight tarmac drive led them to an ugly lump of a modern building. The term McMansion sprung to mind as he took in the odd angles, strangely placed dormer windows, unnecessary crenellations and general lack of cohesion about the design.

'I guess what they say is true,' Harrison said as they came to a halt in a wide turning area in front of an open porch, its twin doric columns quite out of place compared to the rest of the building. 'You can't buy style.'

A man built like a night club bouncer approached the car as McLean stepped out. He wore a dark suit that struggled to contain his steroid-pumped musculature. His buzzcut hair and absurdly broad chest conspired to make his head look a size too small, but the face was familiar. Seagram's driver might have been expected to greet them with suspicion or even aggression, but instead his expression was one of deep concern.

'What's up?' McLean asked, because something always was. He had a horrible suspicion he knew what, too.

'It's Mr Seagram,' the man said. 'He's gone missing.'

The nightclub bouncer's name was Stefan, and he introduced himself as head of Seagram's security rather than the old man's chauffeur. McLean suspected there was probably more to his job than that, but now wasn't the time to push the point.

'When was the last time you saw your boss?' he asked as they sat in a large room off the main house that had been turned into some kind of office.

'Just after ten this morning. We had a security briefing, same as every day. Mr Seagram had no plans and no meetings scheduled. Here or in town. Days like that, he often just sits in the library and reads.'

McLean found that hard to imagine. 'Any unexpected visitors since then? Phone calls?'

Stefan's brow furrowed, the wrinkles carrying on up his scalp to the top of his shaved head. He looked like he was trying to make a difficult decision for a moment, then he reached into his pocket and pulled out a mobile phone. 'No visitors, but I did hear Mr Seagram on his phone earlier. He left it on the hall table.'

'Is that normal? For him to go off without his phone?' Harrison asked.

'He often leaves it there when he's at home.' Stefan tapped the screen, inputting the code to unlock it. Well, he was the old man's head of security, McLean supposed.

'Can I see the call list?' he asked, not really expecting to be handed the phone so pleasantly surprised when Stefan did so. It

---

took a moment to work out how to access the call log, a list of numbers, the time and the duration of each conversation. The most recent call was from a withheld number which had come in at seventeen minutes past eleven, and lasted for three minutes. There had been nothing since, but a string of calls to and from another number preceded it. Someone had been talking back and forth with Seagram all morning.

'What about the garden? Grounds?' Harrison asked.

The bouncer shook his head. 'I've checked close by. Sent a couple of my . . . men out to look further away, but Mr Seagram doesn't walk so well these days, and he rarely visits the farm. He'd have said if was going to. Would have asked me to drive him.'

McLean recalled the stiff movements of the old man as he climbed out of his Range Rover. The cane he used for support. He'd be unlikely to leg it anywhere.

'Do you have security cameras?'

'Aye, there's cameras all over the place. Never know who might try and break in.'

McLean doubted any burglar stupid enough to try it would get very far.

'What about in the hall, where the phone was?' Harrison prompted. It took Stefan a surprisingly long time to get the point.

'Oh, right. Aye. Let me see.' He sat down in front of a computer screen, pulled the keyboard close to him and started to stab at the keys with one finger of each hand. While he was distracted, McLean took out his own mobile and snapped a photograph of the call log screen. There was something bothering him about the number Seagram had called and which had called him back, although he couldn't immediately place it. Something to follow up once they'd found the old man.

'Here we go.' Stefan slid his chair to one side so that McLean and Harrison could see the image on the screen. Wide-angled lens distorted the entrance hall, but it was clear enough to see as

Seagram shuffled out of one door, leaning heavily on his cane. He stopped close by an antique sideboard, propped his cane against the wall beside it and then pulled out his phone. There was no sound on the recording, but the old man's annoyance was evident in his every move as he tapped at the screen and held the handset up to his ear. Had he thought it was the mysterious number calling back again? Was that why he'd not bothered checking the screen to see who it was?

Whatever the reason, and whoever had called, the effect was almost instant. Seagram's shoulders slouched, his whole body sagging as if he'd been delivered the worst possible news. He put the phone down on the sideboard and walked stiffly off camera. Only once he had gone did McLean notice that his cane was still propped against the wall.

'Where is that he went?' he asked, although from their brief route from front door to this office, it looked like the old man had come this way.

'Looks like he came through here,' Stefan said.

'And nobody saw him?'

'I was out the back.' The bouncer looked a little shifty. McLean hadn't caught a scent of tobacco smoke off him, so his vice of choice was something else.

'What about his car?' Harrison asked.

'Mr Seagram has several vehicles.' Stefan gestured to the rear window, where the Range Rover could be seen parked in a court-yard formed by this wing of the house and a couple of garage blocks, three doors to each. At the far end of the office, a second door presumably led to them without having to step outside.

'Have you checked the other cars then, if he has more than one?' McLean asked.

Beyond the office door there was a narrow corridor with a couple of small rooms off it, and then another door that opened onto a garage. Of the three bays, two were occupied by an ancient

Land Rover and a Lamborghini that McLean doubted Seagram would be able to get into. Certainly wouldn't be able to get back out of.

'What about this bay?' He pointed to the nearest space as Stefan stepped into it.

'Range Rover gets parked in here.' He walked past the other two cars to where another door took them through to the next garage. Following the bouncer, McLean almost collided with him as he stopped abruptly in the doorway, like people always seemed to do at the supermarket.

'The Mercedes is gone,' Stefan said as McLean pushed past him. Like the other garage, this one had three bays, two occupied. Furthest away, one of those off-road side-by-side buggies sat amongst a load of boxes. In the middle bay, a couple of quad bikes. The nearest bay was empty, the snake-like coil of an electric charge cable looped neatly around the same charge port as McLean had installed at home.

'So, where might your boss have driven himself on a day like today?'

Stefan shrugged. 'Mr Seagram doesn't drive anywhere. It's always me or one of the lads who does the driving.'

'OK then. Where might he ask you or one of the lads to drive him?'

'I think I might know.'

They both turned to face Harrison. He'd been so intent on finding out what had happened to Seagram, McLean had completely forgotten that technically she was the ranking officer here. If she was at all put out at his taking over, she hid it well.

'Where?'

'Well think about it. We've lost Murphy and at the same time Seagram goes off on his own without telling anyone. Doesn't that fit a pattern we've seen already?'

'You think he's going to meet him?' McLean asked. 'But why? He must know it's a trap.'

'Creegan should have known that. So should McAllister. They went anyway. Don't ask me why. I don't even know how Murphy's even walking. But you saw how Seagram reacted to that call. Almost like he'd given up.'

'But how . . .' McLean began to ask, then stopped himself. 'Not important, I know. But where would he go?'

'Back to where it all began,' Harrison said.

'Where . . .?' McLean's brain was working too slowly, the end result of so many months away from the front line. Then the penny dropped. 'St Aloysius?'

52

'I'm sorry. I rather took over back there. Force of habit, I guess.'

Speeding towards the city, McLean was beginning to find the limitations of the small Renault. In town it nipped along quite happily, but a heavy right foot resulted in the remaining range meter dropping at an alarming rate.

'To be honest, I didn't really notice. Just seemed like how we always used to work.' Beside him, Harrison had finished calling in to get searches begun on both Seagram's car and ankle bracelet and now played idly with her phone.

'You'd think a few months away would be enough to unlearn bad habits. Clearly not.'

'It's fine. Useful, really. Maybe I'm not ready to be in charge just yet. Not of a whole investigation, at least. Seems whatever decision I make it's the wrong one.'

'It can be a bit overwhelming, promotion. I remember when I first made DI. Got lumbered with something that should have been a cold case, except we didn't have the CCU then. We did have a handful of other DIs and a couple of DCIs, just in the one station. Lots of experience to tap into, which you lot don't have.'

'Jo Dexter's helpful, and I can always talk to Grumpy Bob. Kirsty helps when she's actually around. But aye, we could do with a bit more depth to the team.'

McLean had no answer to that. He knew that his departure had left a hole, but he'd thought it would have been filled months ago. Instead, the constables and sergeants were being stretched ever thinner. It was a miracle nothing had broken yet. Was it the restructuring around the formation of Police Scotland that had been the start of it? Maybe Specialist Crime, with its focus on individual skills over deep knowledge of a region was to blame. Or it might simply be down to too much work and too little money.

'That's St Aloysius up ahead, isn't it?' Harrison leaned forward, neck craned to see past the trees that lined one side of the road. A spire reached into a sky fast turning black with threatened rain. McLean looked around for a parking space, and spotted a car that had been not so much parked as abandoned at the entrance to the churchyard. The same sleek black Mercedes that had given him a lift across town the best part of a month ago.

'Well, I think we know where he's gone.' He pulled over and parked on a double yellow line. Harrison was out of the passenger door before he'd even undone his seatbelt. Phone held to one ear, she was busy calling in the find, and requesting backup as McLean tried the door of the Mercedes.

'Unlocked,' he said as it popped open. A shiny key fob lay in a little cubby hole in the centre console. 'Good thing this isn't a rough neighbourhood.'

He reached in and picked up the fob, locked the car and then turned to look at the church. Built from sandstone in hues ranging from palest pink through to dried blood red, it sat back from the road, surrounded by a small graveyard. A low wall encircled the whole plot, separating it from the prosperous houses to either side. The path from pavement to front entrance was made of uneven stone slabs, the occasional missing piece filled in with smoothed off tarmac.

'How do you want to play this, boss?' McLean asked Harrison.

The look she gave him would have boiled water, but she suppressed the obvious retort, rolled her neck slightly.

'If the car's here, then chances are he's in there.' She nodded at the church. 'I guess we go and look.'

As they set off up the path, a distant rumble echoed across the city. At first McLean thought it was an airplane headed for Turnhouse, or maybe some nearby building site. Then, raindrops the size of marbles began to spatter against the path, the grass, his head. Without a word, the two of them hurried up the path and under the shelter of an open porch at the entrance to the church.

'Just about missed the worst of that,' Harrison said as another rumble of thunder rolled across the city. The rain boiled off the path, and the road beyond the churchyard had turned into something that looked more like a river.

McLean ran his hand through his damp hair and wished he'd worn a coat. Stone steps led down to a pair of ancient wooden doors, closed against the elements. He reached for the handle, turned and pushed gently. Something blocked the way.

'Locked?' Harrison asked.

'It would appear so. Maybe he's not here after all.'

Even as he said it, McLean didn't believe the words. Seagram's Mercedes was abandoned at the other end of the path, for one thing. As he looked back at it, the downpour suddenly fizzled away to nothing, a still quiet falling upon them. And in that moment before the city's roar reasserted itself, he thought he heard something. The softest murmur of chanting, like monks at prayer.

'Did you hear that?' he asked, but the look on Harrison's face was answer enough.

'Someone's inside. Must be another door.'

McLean looked out the side of the porch to the dark clouds overhead. Another distant explosion of thunder dulled the sounds of the city, but he'd seen no lightning. No idea how close the centre of the storm might be. When the next deluge might fall.

'Round the other side,' he said. 'You wait here for backup. I'll go check it out.'

Harrison opened her mouth to object, as he knew she would. As he knew she was right to, although he'd never admit it out loud. He waved away her protest, pulled up the collar of his jacket and hurried out into the weather.

By the time he reached the rear door, McLean's hair was plastered to his scalp, his shoulders soaked. Damp seeped through the heavy tweed of his jacket, giving off a slight whiff of wet dog. Well, he'd only himself to blame.

A heavy wrought iron handle poked from the age-blackened oak. Beneath it, scratch marks around the large keyhole showed where generations of priests had been less than careful coming and going. If the front entrance to the church was locked and yet someone was inside, then this had to be the way they had come. McLean gripped the handle, feeling unexpected warmth in it, turned the latch and gently pushed.

The door swung open on oiled hinges. No BBC sound effects department screech here. Pausing for a moment, he strained to hear anything over the roar of the rain. Was that chanting from within, or his imagination playing tricks on him? It came and went like fluctuations in the atmosphere, which was quite possible given the rumbling thunder still circulating overhead.

The door opened onto a small room lined with dark wooden panelling. Cassocks hung from a row of pegs along the far wall, a battered cupboard presumably the place where a nine-year-old Robert Murphy had been hidden away all those years ago. As he closed the door quietly, cutting off the noise from outside, so McLean could hear clearly now a quiet, rhythmic chant. It came from a door at the other end of the room, cracked slightly open to reveal the chancel beyond.

His shoes squelched on the stone tiles as he crept to the door and inched it open. Beyond, he had a good view of the altar, the life size wooden Christ on his cross, staring down at the back of a dark figure who stood as if addressing his congregation. From the side, and in the gloom of the unlit church, McLean couldn't make out his features, obscured by the hood of his cowl; more the garb of a monk than a priest. Beyond him, kneeling at the rail and head bowed in supplication, was Archie Seagram.

More chanting echoed in the empty cavern of the nave. Not like the Gregorian chants that had been all the rage on the radio a few years back, these sounds were discordant, hard to listen to. They conjured up images of suffering and torment, the wailing of souls condemned. A choir of the damned, the noise came from nowhere, from everywhere. McLean fought the urge to close the door and flee that grew in him as the ululation rose to a crescendo. The black-clad figure raised hands towards the ceiling, or maybe the heavens, clutched in one of them a silver cross much the same size and shape as the marks branded into the foreheads of William Creegan, Ray McAllister and probably Kenneth Morgan. Despite the gloom that failed to penetrate the stained-glass windows, it seemed like a shaft of crimson light struck the cross and it blazed with flame. As if compelled by some invisible hand, Seagram lifted his head up at that moment, a look of utter terror in his eyes.

With a roar more animal than human, the dark figure brought the cross down and pressed it hard to the old man's forehead. Transfixed, he couldn't even scream, although a strange gurgling sound bubbled from his mouth, flecks of spittle arcing to the floor. McLean caught the stench of burning flesh, saw the smoke as Seagram's skin caught fire, thin hair frizzing away to nothing.

Without thinking, he pulled open the door, crossed the short distance at a run. In the instant before impact, he saw Seagram's wide eyes flick in his direction. The figure reacted too slowly, and McLean collided with them all. He felt the searing heat of the cross even as he ducked and pushed Seagram away from its horrific touch. The old man finally managed to scream as he toppled to his side and lay still.

'You dare to interfere with God's work!'

The shout was a warning. McLean twisted to one side, felt again that impossible heat as the priest swung his fiery cross as a weapon. Trying to keep his balance, he caught his foot on Seagram's outstretched leg, heard a grunt that might have been the old man or might have been himself. And then pain flared in his hip where he'd broken it years before. His leg gave out under him, but before he could crash to the ground a hand grabbed him round the throat. He was pulled upright and off his feet by impossible strength, his neck squeezed so hard he couldn't breathe. Brought closer and closer towards the face of madness.

Vision fading, he struggled to make anything out within the shadows of that hood. And yet at the same time McLean could see all too clearly some bestial nightmare demon crawled from the pits of hell, with eyes of flame, skin that bulged and writhed as if a legion of insects crawled beneath it.

'You dare defy me!'

The voice was so loud it drowned out everything else, echoed inside McLean's skull as he struggled to free himself. Bringing up his hands felt like dragging them through thick oil, and when he tried to grasp the arm that held him, he had no strength. All he could see was those twin points of deep red fire, his vision tunnelling down to nothing as his brain was slowly starved of oxygen.

'Then you will join them all in hell.' The other hand came up, still clutching that flaming cross. Its heat seared worse than the midsummer sun and brought with it a stench of sulphur, of hot rocks banged together. Closer it came, McLean unable to focus on anything else now. His fate sealed.

'You will join the—'

The words ended abruptly, cut off by a crump like distant thunder. In an instant, the flame was gone, the cross dissolved to nothing. The grip on McLean's neck released and he dropped to his knees, gasping for air, barely registering as his assailant first swayed and then crumpled sideways to the floor. Looking up, he saw what he thought for a moment was an angel, her head haloed by the sun now streaming through the stained-glass window. Then, as he started to get his breath back, the angel morphed into the form of Acting Detective Inspector Janie Harrison. She clutched the largest bible he had ever seen, needing both hands to wield it.

'Thought you were going to wait for backup,' she said.

Still uncertain whether he'd be able to stand, McLean half crawled over to where Seagram lay, sprawled across the low steps that led up from the nave to the chancel. The old man's face was horribly, deathly pale, save for the livid mark of the cross burned into his forehead.

'Is he alive?' Harrison asked as McLean felt for a pulse. It was there, but ragged and weak.

'Just about.' He croaked out the words, then coughed and wished he hadn't as his throat screamed in agony. In seconds Harrison was by his side.

'You OK?'

McLean began to say, 'will be,' but settled for a nod instead. With Harrison's help he struggled to his feet, hip still stiff but nothing like the sharp pain that had come over him at the start of the fight. Flexing his leg gingerly, he hobbled over to the communion rail, looked down at the prone figure stretched out in front of the altar.

'Hope I didn't hit him too hard,' Harrison said. 'Could only find that book, and it must weigh the same as a concrete block.'

Sprawled on his side, his black hood still covering his face, the figure looked smaller than the giant who had lifted McLean off his feet with one massive hand while holding a flaming cross in the other.

'Help me.' McLean winced at the words as he stepped over the rail and crouched awkwardly beside the robed figure. Close now, it looked all wrong. Nothing like his muddled memories told him things should be. Those hands were too small to have inflicted the damage he felt to his throat, surely. And where was the cross? Leaning forward, he tugged the hood gently aside to reveal not the face of some hideous demon of vengeance come for the men who had killed a priest in this very church. Not even that priest himself, somehow still alive and not aged a day in forty years.

'I . . .' Harrison began, then fell silent. McLean couldn't blame her. This made no sense at all. He reached a tentative finger, felt for a pulse, found none. The man wearing priestly robes and lying dead before the altar was Robert Murphy.

53

Water had never tasted so sweet. McLean stood beside Seagram's abandoned Mercedes and sipped from an ice-cold bottle one of the uniform constables had miraculously found for him. Well, they were outside a church.

A commotion at the front entrance was the paramedics as they wheeled out Archie Seagram on a stretcher. The old man hadn't regained consciousness in the half hour it had taken for the ambulance to arrive, but neither had he died. McLean found himself glad of that, even hoped Seagram would make a full recovery. He needed to stand trial for what he'd done; dying would have let him off too easy. Even so, the collapse of his criminal empire was going to leave a vacuum for all the wannabe gangsters to try and fill. Interesting times.

Moments after Seagram, a second gurney followed carrying a zipped-up bodybag. As it wheeled past, McLean reached out and stopped the paramedics. He fumbled with the zip for a moment before opening the bag up to reveal the dead face of Robert Murphy. He might have looked at peace were it not for the obvious signs of the punishment beating that had been meted out to him in his prison cell.

'I . . .' Harrison's voice beside him was a wavering thing. 'I didn't think I hit him that hard.'

McLean pulled the zip closed again, turned to face her as the paramedic wheeled the gurney away. 'You didn't. Robert Murphy was dead long before either of us got anywhere near him.'

'But that doesn't make sense. I saw him. He was trying to kill you.'

McLean swallowed, winced at the pain, gently felt the bruises on his neck. 'Someone was trying to kill me, and Murphy's going to get the blame of it all. But it wasn't him. Not really. Don't think he's been him in forty years.'

Harrison fixed him with a stare that was equal parts disbelief and worry. McLean could see the thoughts chasing each other around her brain, knew a little of what she must be going through. And of the troubling interviews and debriefs that were in both of their immediate futures. He reached out and laid a hand on her forearm.

'You didn't kill him, Janie. He succumbed to his injuries after attacking Seagram and me. OK?'

A long pause before Harrison gave a slow, single nod.

'Good.' McLean reached up and gently touched the skin of his neck again. The bruises were tender, and he knew he'd get an earful from Emma when she saw the marks. Someone had grabbed him by the throat and near choked the life out of him. Someone had been strong enough to lift him with just one arm, while they brought the other to bear down on him with a fiery cross, hadn't they? Except that search as long as they might, they'd not been able to find anything to match the mark on Seagram's forehead. Croaky voice and bruises aside, McLean was beginning to have doubts about the whole thing.

'Going to be a bugger to write up, mind,' Harrison said.

'Aye. Don't envy you that job. Guess we'd better get back to the station and make a start.'

'We?'

'Well, you can do the report writing, but there's someone I need to have a wee word with too. Not sure it's going to make me any friends though.'

For all that they'd caught a killer and saved one of the city's most notorious gang lords from a sticky end, there was little in the way of excitement when McLean arrived back at the station. No one greeted him and Harrison with excited congratulations, or even much notice at all. At least the pain in his throat had begun to ease, which was just as well as he had a lot of talking to do.

'You want me to come with you?' Harrison asked as they climbed the stairs.

'Probably best if I do this alone. If you're not there, you can't be blamed. Not saying you won't get dragged in later, but for now best if you keep out of sight.'

Harrison nodded her understanding, and they parted company on the second-floor landing. McLean felt the niggling ache in his hip as he hauled himself up the next flight, a twinge in his arm reminding him of other recently broken bones. He really should try to be more careful out there.

Chief Superintendent McIntyre's secretary sat at her desk in the small reception area outside the main office. She raised an eyebrow as McLean approached, and it occurred to him that maybe he should have checked himself in a mirror before coming here. Harrison was too polite to mention it, but chances were that he wasn't looking his best.

'She's in a meeting with the detective superintendent. Judging by the shouting, I reckon she'd appreciate a distraction right now.'

'Thanks, Mandie. How do I look?'

'Like you've been in a fight and maybe didn't come first?' The secretary smiled. 'Go right in. She's expecting you.'

McLean heard the raised voice as he knocked on the door and pushed it open. Detective Superintendent Nelson's nasal whine was annoying at the best of times, but never more so than when he was complaining.

'. . . no respect for procedure. Swanning off whenever she likes.'

'Well, you're the one put her forward for the job, Pete. Oh, hello, Tony.'

He'd known what to expect, but all the same, McLean was surprised at just how red in the face Nelson was. He stood on the naughty schoolboy side of the chief superintendent's desk, fists clenched by his side, posture all pent-up macho aggression. In comparison, Jayne McIntyre looked relaxed as she leaned back in her chair. Like she'd seen it all before and wasn't particularly impressed this time.

'What the fuck are you doing here, McLean? This is a private meeting. You can't just barge in unannounced like—'

'Calm yourself, Peter. Tony would never interrupt if it wasn't important.' McIntyre swivelled in her chair to face him. 'You wouldn't do that, would you?'

'Were you aware that Robert Murphy was attacked in his cell last night, almost killed?'

'Peter was just telling me. They took him to hospital. Is he going to be OK?'

'He's dead, actually.' McLean studied Nelson as he said the words, unsurprised by the relieved slump of his shoulders. 'But not before he very nearly killed Seagram in a church in Craiglockhart.'

At the mention of Seagram's name, Nelson's shoulders stiffened again, and all the blood drained from his face. He kept his mouth tight shut though.

'Almost killed me, too.' McLean ran a hand through his unkempt hair and then gently touched the skin on his neck above his shirt collar. 'Hence my slightly dishevelled appearance and more husky than usual voice. Thought it important I come and talk to you both first before going off to get changed.'

'Are you OK, Tony? You want to sit down?' McIntyre was on her feet in a moment, but he waved a hand for her to sit.

'I'll be fine, thanks, Jayne. The thing is, though, the prison called in with the news about Murphy as soon as they sent him off to hospital, but the message didn't reach the major investigation team for several hours after that. Funnily enough, nobody told us Seagram had been let out on bail late last night either.'

The colour had been leeching back into Nelson's face as McLean spoke, and now the detective superintendent finally managed to find his voice.

'What's all this got to do with me, McLean? More to the point, what the fuck has it got to do with you? This is Harrison's investigation, isn't it? You're just a consultant.'

'Oh, I know that. Janie's preparing her report right now. Seagram's been taken to hospital. He's unconscious, and he's old, so who knows how that will go? Murphy's gone to the mortuary, I presume. Poor sod. That's all under control though. It's something else I wanted to talk to you both about.'

McIntyre eyed him suspiciously. 'Go on.'

'Well, it was when we went to Seagram's house. Ugly new build out past the Broxburn bings. I'll not bore you with the details of how, but I managed to get hold of the call list on his mobile. He'd left it behind, you see. When he went off to the church. There were quite a few calls last night and this morning, back and forth, all the same number.'

McLean took out his mobile, thumbed it awake and flicked through to the contact page he'd created on his walk up to the third floor. 'Shall we see whose phone it was?' He hit dial, and a few seconds later a shrill ring tone exploded from Detective Superintendent Nelson's pocket. After a couple of rings, McLean killed the call and the pocket fell silent.

'How long have you been on Seagram's payroll, Pete?'

'I . . . This is preposterous.'

McLean thumbed redial and Nelson's pocket sprang into life again.

'All right, all right. So, he called me. That doesn't mean anything.'

'Twice in the course of one morning. The first call lasted two minutes, the second five and a half. I wonder what the two of you might have been discussing.' McLean killed the call again. That ring tone really was very annoying.

'He wanted to know about your man Murphy, if you must know. No idea how he got my number.'

'Here's the thing though.' McLean flicked the screen until he found another contact entry, hit call again. This time it took a little longer to connect. When it did, the ring tone was completely different, and came from Nelson's other pocket. 'That's your work phone. The other number's not listed on the police directory at all. My guess is it's a burner, and you've been using it to feed Seagram information all along. Yesterday evening, for instance. Was that you letting him know which cell Murphy was in so one of his goons could go put the boot in?'

'I'm not going to stand here and listen to these baseless allegations.' Nelson's face was red again, beads of sweat on his forehead as he jabbed a finger in McLean's direction. 'And you? You're out of here. Access privileges revoked. If you're still in this station in five minutes, I'll have you arrested.'

'Detective Superintendent Nelson.' McIntyre's voice would have done a parade ground sergeant proud. It cut through the man's bluster, and he came almost to attention as she stood up.

'Ma'am?'

'These are very serious allegations, backed up by evidence. And it's not the first time I've heard about your conduct since you arrived here. As such I have no option but to suspend you from duty until such time as Professional Standards have had an opportunity to look into the matter. Your warrant card, please. And while you're at it, I'll have that phone, too.'

McLean watched a deflated and soon to be ex-Detective Superintendent Nelson walk out of the office, his shoulders slumped, tread as slow as an octogenarian waiting for a hip operation. He went to follow, knowing full well that McIntyre wouldn't let him off that easily.

'Not done with you yet, Tony. Close the door, will you?'

He did as he was told, thought about taking up Nelson's spot in front of the chief superintendent's desk, then realised how that would look. Instead, he pulled a chair over from the conference table and sat down.

'I know it's bad form to shoot the messenger, but could you no' have picked a better time to collapse the entire Edinburgh Major Investigation Team in on itself?' The chief superintendent had the good grace to smile as she complained.

'It's not my fault Nelson's a prick. Why d'you think Aberdeen let him go in the first place?'

McIntyre rubbed at her forehead with one hand, trying to smooth away the wrinkles. Her hair had more grey in it these days, McLean noticed. Perhaps that was why she kept it cropped so short.

'It's your fault we've had to cast far and wide for senior officers though, isn't it? By rights you should be superintendent by now, but you keep on getting yourself demoted. Or quitting altogether.'

'Honestly, Jayne. Can you see me in strategy meetings? Playing nice with the politicians? I'm not an administrator. Never will be. You should give the job to Kirsty. She'd be much better at it, and it might stop her jumping ship to the NCA.'

'Aye, well. It might come to that. Still, that'd leave us needing a new DCI and at least two DIs. Probably time some of the constables stepped up to sergeant too.'

'Someone given you a new budget?' McLean asked.

'I think the message has started to sink in higher up. A few folk seem to have noticed how much we were relying on the charity sector after your old pal Jane Louise Dee took all her money away. We're no' exactly flush with cash, but things are looking better.'

'Glad to hear it, and it's about time the team was expanded. You're going to make Harrison's promotion permanent then?'

'It's a tricky one. There's plenty will say she was only given the acting post because she shagged her boss. Even though we both know that's not true. She's not actually passed her inspector's exams yet either, hence only acting DI at the moment. She's young still, but I've been impressed with how she's coped with this investigation. And she stood up to Nelson when he tried it on. But . . .' McIntyre didn't finish.

'Kneeing a senior officer in the bollocks so hard he couldn't walk straight for a day is likely to be a black mark against her, I know. And the rumours about how she's made her way up the greasy pole don't help either, even if they're all nonsense.'

'Both fair points, but I was thinking more it's not been all that long since she made detective sergeant. Sandy Gregg has far more experience.'

'You said you needed at least two DIs, so promote them both, if they can pass the exams. I'm fairly sure Stringer and Blane are both ready for sergeant. Bring in some new constables for them to break in, and we're done.'

'Almost done,' McIntyre said. She reached for the drawer at the side of her desk, pulled it open and fetched out a single sheet of paper. Even upside down, McLean recognised it.

'Gail had a lot of faults, I think we can both agree on that. She made some poor decisions on her way to the top and they've rather come back to bite her.'

McLean kept his mouth shut, said nothing. He knew where this was going. Had done right from the start, if he was being honest with himself.

'One thing she did right though. She never filed this. Not officially.' McIntyre slid the letter across the desktop towards him. He recognised the signature at the bottom of the page beneath a couple of short, typed paragraphs. His signature.

'Technically you've been on extended medical leave, Tony. Recovering from injuries received in the line of duty.' McIntyre went back to the drawer and took out something else. When she put it on the desk beside the letter, McLean recognised his warrant card. Had he known they were both there? Deep down he suspected he had.

'So how about it, Detective Chief Inspector? You fancy coming back to work now?'

54

Spring had finally arrived as she stood at the gates to Mount Vernon Cemetery and watched the hearse slide quietly past. Robert Murphy had no family left, but his parents had been buried here, and now he would join them in eternal rest. Janie felt, on balance, that he had probably earned it.

No family meant few mourners and a mercifully brief service at the nearby Catholic church. Once the funeral director's team had done their bit, only four people clustered around the empty grave, Janie herself, soon-to-be Detective Chief Inspector McLean, the priest and Jo Dalgliesh. Janie had been surprised to see the reporter there, although it could always be that she was still chasing the story and not actually showing the slightest signs of an emerging conscience.

Nobody said anything as the priest went through the motions, each of them alone with their thoughts. It was pleasant enough in the sun, the lightest of breezes tugging at her hair. In truth, Janie wasn't entirely sure why she'd even come at all, although she didn't particularly regret it. There was no Detective Superintendent Nelson waiting in the station to make life miserable for her anymore. Currently suspended while Professional Standards looked into his misconduct, it was most likely he'd be given early retirement, the whole sorry affair quietly covered up.

Professional Standards had talked to her too, of course. The coffin six feet down in front of her was reminder enough of that. Nobody had suggested she'd done anything wrong, but the only suspect in the murder investigation she had been in charge of had died after she'd whacked him across the head with a very large bible and before he could do anything helpful like confess. McLean had defended her, and the damage to his neck from Murphy's attack – had it been Murphy? – had been severe enough to give credence to their story of what had happened in St Aloysius church. Tom MacPhail's post mortem examination had strongly suggested Murphy's death was entirely down to the beating he'd received in the prison. No forensic evidence, but the pathologist had helpfully speculated that Murphy must have taken some powerful stimulant drugs to aid his escape from the hospital, and whatever they were, they had done for him in the end. Janie owed MacPhail many drinks for that.

The sum of it was that nobody was blaming her for Murphy's death. Except her, of course. She knew it wasn't straightforward, but she still had that horrible feeling it had, in the end, been her fault. Perhaps that was why she'd come here to see him laid to rest. It was certainly why she'd let Jayne McIntyre know that she wasn't quite ready to take on the mantle of detective inspector yet. The chief superintendent had been understanding about that, even as Janie could see the held back sigh. They'd need to find someone else from another region, and who knew what that would bring?

Movement in the corner of her eye caught Janie's attention. She turned a little too swiftly; a click of pain in her neck that made her wince, dulled her vision for a moment. And all for nothing, it seemed. There was nobody nearby save for McLean and Dalgliesh, the priest retreating in the opposite direction, hearse and funeral director long gone. Not far off, the neatly tended part of the cemetery gave way to rougher ground, graves slowly being swallowed up by vegetation and neglect. A thin, whippy elder bush sprouted from the end of what might have been a grave, its white flowers giving off a delightful scent. As she stared at it Janie remembered the last time she'd been here, stood in almost exactly this spot.

Leaving the other two, she picked a careful path through the overgrowth until she stood at what was indeed the end of a grave. The headstone had cracked in two, and she could still see the engraved date on the lower half, the year 1983.

Some long-ingrained sense of propriety stopped her from stepping on the grave itself, but she edged her way through the weeds until she was close enough to crouch beneath the elder. The rest of the headstone lay behind the piece still standing, cracked into a half dozen or so chunks of stone as if someone had swung a heavy mallet at it many years before. Or maybe it had been struck by lightning, the hammer of a vengeful god. Shaking away the thought, Janie leaned in and pushed aside thin branches until the light hit the stones. Much of the inscription was missing, but it was easy enough to read the name.

Eric Michael Pius O'Connell.

The nods and smiles from nurses took him back over a decade as McLean walked the familiar corridors of the Western General Hospital. True, he'd been here many times since, some might say far too many. But this was the route he had trod, if not quite every day, then most days for the better part of eighteen months after he'd found his grandmother collapsed unconscious in the library. She had never woken from that stroke, slowly slipping away while those same smiling nurses tended her.

And now he was back, once more visiting the coma ward where his grandmother had finally died, and Emma had managed to make it out alive. Or at least he was peering through the small window in the door, unwilling to commit himself to the actual room. Only this time the figure lying in a bed, hooked up to monitors and drips, was a man.

A month on from his fateful trip to St Aloysius church, Archibald Seagram had still not awoken. It was uncertain whether he ever would. He'd taken on that pallor McLean associated with sickness and death, his face slack as gravity pulled at his jowls. His thinning white hair had been trimmed to allow the medical staff best access to the wound on his forehead, the cross a livid mark that still oozed thin yellow fluid after all this time. Should he ever awake, Seagram would spend the rest of his life a branded man. Some small justice for all the evil he had done, but never enough.

'No change, I'm afraid, Tony.'

He looked around to see senior nurse Jeannie Robertson approaching. She had tended his grandmother and Emma both, and here she was still. A rock unmoving in the current of lives that came and went from this place.

'I'm beginning to think he doesn't want to wake up. Hardly surprising given what's waiting for him if he ever does.'

Nurse Robertson inclined her head a fraction in understanding. The collapse of Seagram's criminal empire had been in the news almost every day since he'd been attacked, with more and more revelations emerging from Billy Creegan's laptop and Ray McAllister's collection of snuff videos. Identifying the victims had not been fun, but it had opened the lid on an organisation more far-reaching than even the NCA had suspected. The only place the old man would be going to from hospital would be a prison cell, and perhaps somewhere deep in his sleeping mind he knew that.

Or he was already in hell with his friends, and his body just hadn't caught up with him yet?

'How's Emma doing? We've not seen her in a while.' Nurse Robertson's question filled a silence McLean only heard once it was gone. He turned from the small observation window in the coma ward door. Back to the living, and the smiling, caring faces of the nursing staff. Archie Seagram could go rot, as far as he was concerned.

'Much better, thank you,' he said, and together the two of them walked away.

Acknowledgements

It might be my name on the cover and my words in between, but a great many other people have contributed to the book you've either just read or are flipping through in the bookshop and wondering whether it's worth buying (hint: it is). Thanking them here is fraught with the danger of missing someone out, but I'm going to try anyway.

I would not be where I am today without the help of my agent, the tireless Juliet Mushens and the rest of the team at Mushens Entertainment. Thank you Liza, Kiya, Rachel and Catriona. Oh, and Den too!

I'm lucky to have an excellent team at Wildfire working to make these books as good as they can be. Thank you Alex, Jack and all the others whose toil is largely unrecognised but without whom this book would be an unholy mess.

Thanks, too, to Russel D McLean (no relation), whose eagle eye caught all my typos and continuity mistakes. If you spot errors, they are mine. The fact there are fewer than there might have been is down to Russel.

A huge thank you to Barbara, my better half, who keeps things on an even keel while I'm away with the fairies (and demons, djinn, ghosts, cannibals, spirits, werewolves, vampires...)

Let us not forget the legions of booksellers out there doing the good work. I am humbled by your dedication and enthusiasm. Not just stacking the shelves and manning the tills, but running pop-up bookshops, author signings and other events. Thank you all.

And last, but by no means least, the biggest thanks of all goes to you, my readers, whether this is the first of my books you've picked up or you've read them all. I'd probably still write stories without you lot, but it wouldn't be half as much fun.

About the Author

James Oswald is the author of the *Sunday Times* bestselling Inspector McLean series of detective mysteries and the epic fantasy series *The Ballad of Sir Benfro*, as well as the new DC Constance Fairchild series. James's first two books, *Natural Causes* and *The Book of Souls*, were both shortlisted for the prestigious CWA Debut Dagger Award and he was shortlisted for the National Book Awards New Writer of the Year in 2013. *For Our Sins* is the thirteenth book in the Inspector McLean series.

James lives in North East Fife, where he farms Highland cows by day and writes disturbing fiction by night.